#1 *NEW YORK TIMES* BESTSELLING AUTHOR

KRESLEY COLE

◆ ◆ ◆

KISS OF A DEMON KING

"Perennial favorite Cole continues to round out her Immortals After Dark world with kick-butt action and scorching passion!"

—*Romantic Times*

"Kresley Cole knows what paranormal romance readers crave and superbly delivers on every page. . . ."

—Single Titles

"Full of magic, mayhem, sorcery and sensuality. Readers will not want to miss one word of this memorable and enchanting tale. The closer to the end I got the slower I read because I knew once the story ended I would be left craving more of this brilliant and emotionally gripping saga. . . . It is truly one of the most amazing tales Kresley Cole has ever released."

—Wild On Books

"Cole deftly blends danger and desire into a brilliantly original contemporary paranormal romance. She neatly tempers the scorchingly sexy romance between Sabine and Rydstrom with a generous measure of sharp humor, and the combination of a cleverly constructed plot and an inventive cast of characters in *Kiss of a Demon King* is simply irresistible."

—ReaderToReader.com

Pleasure of a Dark Prince
is also available as an eBook

DARK DESIRES AFTER DUSK

"The snappy dialogue and sensual tormenting make this the best in the Immortals After Dark series so far!"

—*Romantic Times*

"Kresley Cole is a gifted author with a knack for witty dialogue, smart heroines, fantastic alpha males and yes, it has to be said, some of the hottest love scenes you'll read in mainstream romance.... You're in for a treat if you've never read a Kresley Cole book."

—RomanceNovel.tv

"A wonderfully romantic tale of two people from the opposite sides of their immortal world.... I'm sure I will re-read *Dark Desires After Dusk*, the love story of Cadeon the rage demon and Holly the halfling Valkyrie many, many times as it was everything I had hoped it to be and so much more!"

—Queue My Review

DARK NEEDS AT NIGHT'S EDGE

"Poignant and daring. You can trust Cole to always deliver sizzling sexy interludes within a darkly passionate romance."

—*Romantic Times*

"The evolution of this romance is among the most believable and engrossing I've ever read. Cole's Immortals After Dark series continues stronger than ever with this latest installment."

—Louisa White, Fresh Fiction

BOOKS BY KRESLEY COLE

The Sutherland Series
The Captain of All Pleasures
The Price of Pleasure

The MacCarrick Brothers Series
If You Dare
If You Desire
If You Deceive

The Immortals After Dark Series
A Hunger Like No Other
No Rest for the Wicked
Wicked Deeds on a Winter's Night
Dark Needs at Night's Edge
Dark Desires After Dusk
Kiss of a Demon King

Anthologies
Playing Easy to Get
Deep Kiss of Winter

KRESLEY COLE

PLEASURE OF A DARK PRINCE

POCKET BOOKS

New York   London   Toronto   Sydney

Pocket Books
A Division of Simon & Schuster, Inc.
1230 Avenue of the Americas
New York, NY 10020

This book is a work of fiction. Names, characters, places, and incidents either are products of the author's imagination or are used fictitiously. Any resemblance to actual events or locales or persons, living or dead, is entirely coincidental.

First Pocket Books paperback edition March 2010

POCKET and colophon are registered trademarks of Simon & Schuster, Inc.

For information about special discounts for bulk purchases, please contact Simon & Schuster Special Sales at 1-866-506-1949 or business@simonandschuster.com.

The Simon & Schuster Speakers Bureau can bring authors to your live event. For more information or to book an event contact the Simon & Schuster Speakers Bureau at 1-866-248-3049 or visit our website at www.simonspeakers.com.

Cover design by Lisa Litwack
Cover illustration by Craig White
Designed by Julie Schroeder

Manufactured in the United States of America

10 9 8 7 6 5 4 3 2 1

ISBN 978-1-4165-8095-9
ISBN 978-1-4165-8355-4 (ebook)

Dedicated to the Immortals After Dark *readers,
for sharing a love of the Lore with me
and for spreading the IAD word.
Thank you all!*

Glossary of Terms
from

THE LIVING BOOK OF LORE

THE LORE
"*. . . and those sentient creatures that are not human shall be united in one stratum, coexisting with, yet secret from, man's.*"

- Most are immortal and can regenerate from injuries. The stronger breeds can only be killed by mystical fire or beheading.
- Their eyes change to a breed-specific color with intense emotion.
- Also known as Loreans.

THE VALKYRIE
"*When a maiden warrior screams for courage as she dies in battle, Wóden and Freya heed her call. The two gods give up lightning to strike her, rescuing her to their hall and preserving her courage forever in the form of the maiden's immortal Valkyrie daughter.*"

- They take sustenance from the electrical energy of the earth, sharing it in one collective power, and give it back with their emotions in the form of lightning.
- They possess preternatural strength, speed, and senses.

- Without training, most can be mesmerized by shining objects and jewels.
- Also known as shield maidens.

THE LYKAE CLAN

"A proud, strapping warrior of the Keltoi People (or Hidden People, later known as Celts) was taken in his prime by a maddened wolf. The warrior rose from the dead, now an immortal, with the spirit of the beast latent within him. He displayed the wolf's traits: the need for touch, an intense loyalty to its kind, an animal craving for the delights of the flesh. Sometimes the beast rises . . ."

- Also called werewolves, war-wolds.
- Each possesses the *Instinct*, an inner guiding force, like a voice whispering in one's mind.
- Enemies of the Vampire Horde.

THE VAMPIRES

- Two warring factions, the Horde and the Forbearer Army.
- Each vampire seeks his *Bride*, his eternal wife, and walks as the living dead until he finds her.
- A Bride will render his body fully alive, giving him breath and making his heart beat, a process known as *blooding*.
- *Tracing* is teleporting, the vampires' means of travel. A vampire can only trace to destinations he's previously been or to those he can see.
- *The Fallen* are vampires who have killed by drinking a victim to death. Distinguished by their red eyes.

THE HORDE

"In the first chaos of the Lore, a brotherhood of vampires dominated by relying on their cold nature, worship of logic, and absence of mercy. They sprang from the harsh steppes of Dacia and migrated to Russia, though some say a secret enclave, the Daci, live in Dacia still."

- The Fallen comprise their ranks.

THE FORBEARERS

". . . his crown stolen, Kristoff, the rightful Horde king, stalked the battlefields of antiquity seeking the strongest, most valiant human warriors as they died, earning him the name of Gravewalker. He offered eternal life in exchange for eternal fealty to him and his growing army."

- An army of vampires consisting of turned humans who do not drink blood directly from the flesh.
- Kristoff was raised as a human and then lived among them. He and his army know little of the Lore.

THE HOUSE OF WITCHES

". . . immortal possessors of magical talents, practitioners of good and evil."

- Mystical mercenaries who sell their spells.
- Separated into five castes: warrior, healer, enchantress, conjurer, and seeress.
- Led by Mariketa the Awaited.

THE WRAITHS

". . . their origin unknown, their presence chilling."

- Spectral, howling beings. Undefeatable and, for the most part, uncontrollable.
- Also called the Ancient Scourge.

THE TURNING
"Only through death can one become an 'other.' "
- Some beings, such as the Lykae, vampires, and demons, can turn a human or even other Lore creatures into their kind through differing means, but the catalyst for change is always death, and success is not guaranteed.

THE ACCESSION
"And a time shall come to pass when all immortal beings in the Lore, from the Valkyrie, vampire, Lykae, and demon factions to the phantoms, shifters, fey, and sirens . . . must fight and destroy each other."
- A kind of mystical checks-and-balances system for an ever-growing population of immortals.
- Occurs every five hundred years. Or right now . . .

◆ ◆ ◆

Some secrets can never be known. They go to the grave with you like children never born.

—LUCIA THE HUNTRESS,
Valkyrie of mysterious origin,
world's most skilled archeress

If I have to scour the entire earth, I'll hunt her down. I will no' falter. One day I will bring my female back to my home—back to my bed. . . . She was born to be found by me.

—GARRETH MACRIEVE,
king of all Lykae

PROLOGUE

Thrymheim Hold, the Northlands
Home of Skathi, goddess of the hunt
In ages long past . . .

Lucia the Maiden cracked open her eyes and found herself atop an altar, staring up at a furious goddess. Somehow her younger sister, Regin the Radiant, had found Skathi's temple and had brought Lucia here.

From one altar to the next, she thought deliriously as her fever raged. Pain roiled inside her broken body. Her fractured limbs . . . never had she imagined such agony.

"You deliver this into my sacred place," Skathi the Huntress of the Great North said to Regin, "and desecrate my altar? You court my wrath, young Valkyrie."

Regin—all of twelve years old, with Lucia's blood covering her glowing skin—said, "What can you do? Torture my sister? Murder her? She has already survived the first and is about to succumb to the second without your aid."

"I could murder *both* of you."

In answer, Regin pursed her lips, looking as if she were sizing up Skathi's shins for a good kicking.

Lucia struggled for consciousness, labored to speak. "Don't hurt her, please . . . my fault, my fault . . ." But her words were drowned out by a rumbling boom. This hold was carved into the heights of Godsbellow Mountain, shaken continually by thunder.

Skathi asked Regin, "Why bring her here?"

"Because you're both neighbor and nemesis to the one who did this."

Had interest flickered in the goddess's eyes? "The Broken Bloody One?"

"Aye."

Canting her head at Regin in an appraising way, Skathi said, "You're not even old enough to be a true immortal yet. For one so powerless and insignificant, you dare much, Valkyrie."

"For Lucia, I dare this and more," Regin answered proudly. "Best be forewarned."

"Regin!" Lucia gasped. The girl had lost her mind.

"What?" She stomped her foot. "What'd I say?"

Instead of smiting Regin, the goddess impatiently gestured for her guards, the legendary Skathians. They were renowned archers, all females who underwent grueling training rituals to serve the goddess. "Take the glowing one down the mountain. Make sure she does not remember the way back."

When Regin charged toward her, Lucia cried, "Nay, Regin . . . leave me!"

The Skathians snagged Regin around the waist, forcing her out as she flailed and shrieked, biting them.

Lucia heard one of them say, *"Ow! You little ratling!"* And then they were gone.

Skathi regarded Lucia's battered face impassively. "You worry for her? When she has been spared? You, however, will not last the hour."

"I know," Lucia whispered. "Unless you help me." She caught Skathi's gaze as she pleaded—a mistake to look directly upon the great and terrible goddess. Meeting her fathomless eyes brought on the sorrow and fear of all her prey over the ages. It sank over Lucia like a bitter frost. *"Please. . . ."* When Lucia held up her crimson-stained hand in supplication, the wound across her torso she'd been holding welled with blood, flowing over her sides. A fountain of sticky warmth coated the altar beneath her, surrounding her battered body, but it quickly cooled on the chill stone.

Each drop lost left her shuddering harder, even more desperate. The pain of her injuries maddened her.

"You made your decision, Valkyrie," the goddess said in answer. "And reaped what you sowed when you disobeyed those you were born to obey. Why should I help you?"

Because I've only lived sixteen years, Lucia thought, but she knew that wouldn't sway Skathi, a timeless being who could scarcely comprehend death—or youth.

"Because I'll do . . . whatever you ask of me," Lucia said at last. The shuddering was getting worse; the altar beneath her was so cold. "P-pay any price."

"If I saved you, I would impart my essence to you. A being like you would bear my mark of favor and be tied to the bow forever," Skathi said, strolling to an opening overlooking her mountain, guarded by miles of deadly woods that swallowed unwary travelers. Lucia barely remembered traversing the mystical forest as Regin dragged her across portals and dales for days.

"Lucia, I'm taking you to Skathi!"

"She will . . . not help."

"She will! *The Skathians fight him every five hundred years. . . ."*

Thunder boomed once more, the sound seeming to soothe the goddess. "Where my followers have sacrificed to become expert markswomen, you would simply be gifted with my hunting skills. An unequaled archer, better than them all. Why do you think you're worthy of that? When they have trained so hard? When they are pure of heart—and body?"

The Skathians lived by an ascetic code—and despised men. *I understand why now.*

"They are not tainted as you are," Skathi continued. "As you *willingly* offered yourself up to be."

Dim memories arose of her last nine days as prisoner of Crom Cruach—the Broken Bloody One, a monster with the face of an angel. Had that animal bitten her? She refused to look down at her body, but she suspected he'd *gnawed* at her skin once she'd blacked out. And that she'd fought him before she'd mindlessly jumped from his lair—chunks of scaly flesh were still embedded beneath her claws.

Lucia ruthlessly stamped out those visions of her captivity. She would never let herself remember them, especially not that last night.

What happened in the dark. Blood streaming down my thighs.

"I didn't know. . . . I never knew." Regret

washed over her. "I'll s-sacrifice anything, Skathi."

"Gifts from gods always come with a price. Are you ready to pay mine?"

Lucia nodded weakly. "I can become . . . p-pure hearted. And I'll shun men." *She must know I'll never be fooled again.*

"Virgin from this day forward?" After a long moment, Skathi said, "You escaped the Broken Bloody One this time—courage, or cowardice, making you leap— yet Cruach will come for you in the next Accession if he escapes his jail."

Yes, but by that time I'll be truly immortal. I'll run farther, faster.

"He shall merely do this again. Unless . . . you fight him."

"I want to fight him." She never wanted to see his hideous visage again.

"Every five hundred years, he would become your bane and you his jailer."

"Let me live to face him." *Lying to a goddess?* But Lucia was desperate.

Skathi's face took on a thoughtful mien. "Yes, I have decided to heal you and make you an Archer—so long as you remain chaste. Yet any time that you miss a target, you shall experience the pain you are about to suffer. You shall always remember what brought you this low and never repeat this fall from grace. *That* will make you a Skathian."

Dizziness overwhelmed Lucia. She was so confused. "*About* to suffer?" This torment could not be *worse*?

"Yes, pain to hone your mind. Agony to sharpen

your resolve like a blade stone." As she placed her milk-white hands over Lucia's torso, Skathi murmured, "Ah, young Lucia, in the end, I believe you shall wish I'd let you perish." The goddess's palms began to glow with blue light.

Brighter, brighter . . .

Suddenly Lucia convulsed, shrieking as her infected wounds pulled taut, purging blood and pus, her fractured bones grinding as they knit together. Her fingers clenched tight, her back arching—like a bow.

"You'll be my weapon," Skathi cried, her face becoming a frenzied mask. "You'll be my instrument!"

On and on, the light burned, until abruptly there was none. Lucia was healed—but changed. A bowstring coiled around her body like a serpent. And in her trembling hands, a black ash bow and a single golden arrow had appeared.

"Welcome back to life—to your new life. You are now an Archer." Skathi met her eyes, and Lucia felt the weight of overweening dread, just as a thousand other souls had before her. "And, Lucia, you shall forever be nothing more."

ONE

---◆◇◆---

Southern Louisiana
Present day

"Munro, you daft git, pass the ball!" Garreth MacRieve yelled at his kinsman over the thunder and howling winds.

Tonight was their yearly skins-versus-demons rugby match—a tradition for Garreth and his clan, meant to take his mind from the anniversary this day marked. Garreth was barefooted, wearing only jeans and no shirt. Rain pounded in strengthening intervals, turning this abandoned grassy airstrip in bayou country into a mire of muck and turf. Sweat mingled with mud—and some blood.

He almost felt . . . not numb. And that in itself was a feat.

Munro flipped him off but did finally sling him the ball. The leather was coated in grit, mixing with the filth covering Garreth's bared chest. He feinted left, then sprinted right around two colossal Ferine demons, shoving his hand in their faces, stiff-arming them.

As he ran, with his heart pounding in his ears, he

could forget. The exertion and the aggression were both so welcome, he wanted to beat his bare chest.

The swift Ferines surrounded him, so he tossed the ball to Uilleam, Munro's twin, who took it in to score. His brothers-in-arms were strong and ruthless contenders, as was he. The beasts inside them loved to fight, to *play*. Rough.

The demons responded to the goal with trash talk and shoving. Like a shot, Garreth was in the middle.

"You're raring to fight for an heirless king," Caliban, the Ferines' leader, sneered. "Nothing new—you Lykae go through kings like I piss demon brew."

Of all the sore subjects to bring up, Garreth's kingship was the one most infuriating. And on this day?

He launched himself at Caliban, but Munro and Uilleam heaved him back. As other demons steered Caliban away from the scuffle, Munro said, "Save it for the game, friend."

Garreth spat blood in Caliban's direction before letting the two lead him away to cool off. While Uilleam and Munro stayed with him, the other Lykae on the team made their way to the sidelines to mingle with the "cheerleaders."

The demons took the opportunity to take a timeout and drink demon brew. The only bad thing about playing with demons—one of the few species in the Lore that could contend with the Lykae in a physical contest—was their continual "brew breaks." Only seemed fair that Garreth and his kinsmen shoot copious amounts of whiskey to mitigate their advantage.

They swilled it straight from the bottle, each one with his own, the Lykae version of Gatorade.

Their cooler was full of fifths.

"You've got to let this go, Garreth," Munro said, taking a deep drink.

Garreth swiped his hand over the back of his neck, getting the feeling that he was being watched. But then, he and all the other players *were*. Nymphs lined the field, oblivious to the rain, touching themselves and sucking on their own fingers as they impatiently waited for this game to turn into an orgy.

He irritably gazed at the females. "Why'd you invite them?" he demanded. "Damn you both, I weary of this. Did you never think that I doona like nymphs?"

"Nay," Uilleam said with a swig. "Any being that sports a penis likes nymphs."

Munro drained his bottle and added, "You canna argue with medical facts."

Garreth knew Uilleam and Munro meant well, but this was getting old. "I doona like them. They're too . . . too . . ."

"Beautiful?"

"Lusty?"

"*Easy*," Garreth said. "They're too easy. For once I'd like to have a female give me a challenge. One that would no' fall into bed with me because I'm supposedly a king." When Munro opened his mouth to speak, Garreth said, "Aye, *supposedly*."

Munro shook his head gravely. "And still you believe Lachlain will return."

The three had been round and round about this for one and a half centuries, since the time his older brother had vanished after setting out to hunt vampires.

Uilleam and Munro told Garreth that he awaited Lachlain unreasonably. Best accept that his brother was gone, especially after so long had passed since his disappearance. One hundred and fifty years—to the day, *this* day. They said Garreth hadn't moved on and accepted his responsibilities as king.

They were right.

"When will you believe he's no' coming back?" Uilleam asked. "Two hundred years from now? Five hundred?"

"Never. No' if I still *feel* he's alive." Though vampires had killed the rest of his immediate family, for some reason, Garreth still sensed Lachlain lived. "No' if I feel it as I do now."

"You're as bad off as Bowen," Uilleam said, finishing his own bottle—and opening another.

Bowen was Garreth's first cousin, a shell of a man since he'd lost his mate. He spent every waking moment in agony, yet he wouldn't accept the loss and end his life as most Lykae males would have in his situation. "No' like Bowen," Garreth said. "He saw his mate gored, saw her death. I dinna see such proof with Lachlain." *No, I searched and searched and found . . . nothing.*

"Game on!" a demon called.

Garreth shook himself from his memories, swigged whiskey, then mustered to the field with his kinsmen.

Caliban bared his fangs at his opponents, a gesture Garreth returned as the teams huddled up.

Quick snap. Ball in play. Passed to Caliban. Garreth saw his chance, charging for him, pumping his arms for speed . . . faster . . . faster . . . He leapt for the demon, tackling him with all his strength.

As they careened to the ground, a length of Caliban's horn snapped off, and he bellowed with rage. "You're going to pay for that, Lykae!"

For miles, Lucia the Huntress had been stalking her night's prey, growing increasingly perplexed when the tracks she followed led her closer to what sounded like a battle, echoing with roars and curses.

Mayhem? Without inviting the Valkyrie? *And in our territory, too?* If beings were going to trespass in order to war, they should at least have the courtesy to invite the host faction to the conflict.

When she came upon the battlefield, Lucia canted her head to the side. *Clash of the Loreans,* she thought as she beheld modern gladiators—not at war, but at play. *Immortal rugby.*

Winds whipped along the mile-long field, and lightning flashed above them, mirroring the intensity of the contest. It was like a ceremony celebrating . . . maleness.

Lucia easily recognized the horned players as demons, and she suspected their shirtless opponents were Lykae. If so, then the rumors were true. The werewolves were in fact encroaching on Valkyrie territory. She was surprised. In the past, they'd kept to themselves, staying at their sprawling compound outside of the city.

Congregating at the sidelines, Nymph spectators

trembled with excitement, likely seeing this as no more than a mud-wrestling match between brawny heart-throbs.

A ruthless hit on the field made Lucia raise a brow. Not at the violence—she was a shield maiden after all—but at the *unthinking* violence. Though these Loreans all trespassed, they were oblivious to an Archer in their midst, one who could inflict serious damage—very swiftly and from a great distance.

Levelheaded Lucia, as she was now known, didn't comprehend *unthinking*. But then she didn't comprehend men. Never had.

Luckily for them, the only violence she'd deliver this eve would be to her targets: two kobolds—vile gnome-like creatures—who'd been seen stalking human young to feed on.

Her sister Nïx, the half-mad Valkyrie soothsayer, had dispatched her to these bayous to dispose of them. Lucia had asked Regin to join her, but she'd declined, preferring to play video games in the comfort of their coven over another "rain-drenched bug hunt."

Lucia had jumped at the chance. After donning a T-shirt and hiking shorts, she'd strapped on her leather thigh quiver, archer's glove, and forearm guard. With her trusty bow in hand, she'd set out at once. . . .

Another brutal hit. She nearly winced at the impact from that one—a piece of horn skipped down the field like a lost helmet—but she wasn't surprised. Lykae and demons were two of the most brutal species on earth.

Worse, one of those bare-chested males had caught Lucia's attention. Completely. No matter how badly she wished otherwise, Lucia still noted attractive men, and as the teams skirmished, she couldn't help but appreciate the power in his towering frame, his speed and agility. Though mud splattered his torso and a shadow of a beard swathed his lean face, she still found him handsome in a rough and tumble way.

His eyes were a burnished gold color with rakish laugh lines fanning out from them. At one time, he'd been happy; he clearly wasn't now. Tension radiated from his body, anger blazing off him.

When those golden irises flickered a bright ice blue, she confirmed what he was. A Lykae. A werewolf.

An *animal*. His handsome face masked a beast, literally.

"You call that a hit, you bluidy ponce!" he yelled at one of the demons, the muscles in his neck and chest standing out in strain as he bowed up and bared his fangs. His accent was Scottish, but then most of the Lykae were Highlanders—or they used to be, before homesteading southern Louisiana. *"Aye, Caliban! Go fook yerself!"*

Others were drawing him back from a particularly large demon, seeming exasperated, as if the male had been picking fights all night. Probably had. The Lykae were considered a menace in the Lore, with little control over their ferocity. In fact, they seemed to revel in it.

One hundred percent unadulterated male, alpha to the core. And still he was making her . . . lust. As the game continued, Lucia waited for revulsion to drown out her attraction. And waited.

Yet with each pitiless blow the male gave—and

took—and with each of his growled threats and taunts, it burned hotter. Her breaths shallowed and her small claws went from straight to curling, aching to clutch a warm body to her own.

But when she remembered the last time she'd felt like this, a chill swept over her. She dragged her gaze from his antics and surveyed the nymphs frolicking on the sidelines. Lucia had once been like them—hedonistic, serving no higher purpose.

Am I still *to be like them?* No, she was disciplined now; she had a code. *I'm a Skathian—by right of pain and the blood I've spilled.*

With a hard shake of her head, she forced herself to focus on her mission—dispatching the kobolds. To the naked eye, they appeared cherubic, but they were actually ground dwellers with reptilian features. And when their populations went unchecked they tended to snatch human young, which jeopardized all of Lorekind.

The pair had split up, one of them fleeing deeper into the swamps, while the other hid behind the wall of nymph spectators, assuming itself safe in this crowd.

Lucia absently fingered the flights of the barbed arrows strapped to her thigh and savored the comforting weight of her bow over her shoulder.

Her prey assumed wrong. The Archer never missed.

TWO

Garreth swiftly broke away from the pack of demons at his heels, gaining more and more ground toward the goal. Rain pelted him as his speed increased.

This would be an easy score, taking him nearly the entire length of the field. Finally the demons pursuing him gave up, slowing one by one, hailing curses.

Yet then, in the most bewildering moment of his life, Garreth's lids grew heavy and his dark claws bit into the ball he carried, puncturing it. As he inhaled deeply, he isolated a new, exquisite scent from a thousand threads of them—the coppery smell of lightning, cut blades of grass, the swampy bayous all around them. Sensations overwhelmed him, racking his muscles as he slowed.

Her. My mate. She's near. . . . She was downwind but close enough that he detected her. He didn't know what she looked like, what her name was, or even her species. Yet he'd been waiting a millennium—his entire existence—for her. His head swung around in the direction of the scent.

A small female stood alone off to the side of the field.

At his first sight of her, his breath was lost, his Lykae Instinct roaring to life within him.

—Yours. Take her.—

She was half a mile or so away, but he saw her clearly through the rain, could make out every detail. She had pouting pink lips and flashing amber eyes. A black bow was strapped over her petite body, and she'd tied a leather quiver full of arrows to her thigh. Wee pointed ears poked out through her mane of long, wet hair. *Yes, mine.*

Gods, she was as exquisite as her scent—

Wham! The demons tackled him with the force of a freight train, flattening him on the field, piling on top of him. His left shoulder popped from its joint. A knee to his jaw wrenched three back teeth loose. He growled, not with pain but with frustration, punching the still-hitting demons with his one good arm. As he battled to free himself, he sucked his teeth into his windpipe.

The twins ran to help him, finally peeling the demons off him. Garreth struggled to his knees, futilely coughing, hacking as he watched the strange female.

Suddenly, in a laserlike movement, she readied her bow, nocked *three* arrows from her quiver, and drew the bowstring to her cheek. *What the hell? Everything happening so fast . . .* Aiming for the nymphs? *No, not them.* A kobold cowering among them. *Never hit it from so far away.*

She was poised, motionless, for a shot. Though rain and wind whipped her hair over her cheek, she never blinked, never took her eye from her target even after she released that bowstring.

The arrows flew between two nymphs and sliced through the kobold's neck, severing its head from its miniature body. A fantastical shot. Yet she appeared bored with the result.

Heaving, choking, Garreth saw her casually wend her way through the stunned nymphs. Once she reached the two pieces of kobold, the archeress chucked them into the nearby swamp.

She replaced the bow over her body, then strolled back in the direction she'd come from. When she realized all attention was on her, she slowed. "Oh." She gave them a Queen Elizabeth wave and said, "Play on."

As he wheezed and his cousins whaled hits on his back like anvil blows, she met Garreth's gaze. He reached a muddy hand toward her, but she frowned with disdain, then disappeared into the brush. Finally Uilleam kicked Garreth in the back, and his back teeth flew from his windpipe like Chiclets.

"What in the hell's the matter with you?" Munro demanded.

Between labored breaths, Garreth clambered to his feet. He'd been told what to expect when finding his mate, but never had he imagined the strength of his reaction. "It's . . . happened."

They knew immediately what he spoke of. Munro looked incredulous; Uilleam, jealous. How long had they both been waiting?

"The archer?" Uilleam asked. "Never seen anyone shoot like that. But she looked like she might be . . . a *Valkyrie*."

Munro swore under his breath, "Bluidy bad luck."

"Just force my shoulder back in place! Be quick, man!"
Naturally, the first time Garreth encountered his mate—

the one he'd awaited so long—she'd seen him calling his competitors pussies and playing by dirty rules. He was shirtless, well on his way to being drunk, and filthy with blood and mud. He wasn't even wearing shoes.

And it probably appeared as if he'd been about to take part in an orgy.

"You tell no one of this," Garreth grated.

"Why the hell no'?" Munro gave a hard yank on Garreth's arm.

"Whatever she may be, she's *other*," he said. "And she's to be the Lykae queen? *No one* knows, not until she's marked and mated. Vow it!"

"Aye, then, we vow it," Uilleam said.

The second they popped his shoulder back in, he took off at a sprint. —*Track her. Claim.*— With his Instinct louder and sharper than it'd ever been, he ran headlong through the rain.

He'd just been despairing over another year without his older brother, another year of royal responsibilities that he'd never thought would fall to him. On this day, the fates still refused to surrender Lachlain. But they'd given Garreth his mate in that ethereal creature.

As he charged forward, excitement welled within him, followed by overwhelming relief. With the way the rain had been pouring earlier, he could've missed her scent. Now he was on her trail.

Yet at the line of moss-curtained cypresses—the entrance to the most remote section of the swamp—he slowed. Somehow her scent was emanating from four different directions. He decided on one to follow, then raced through the brush, hurdling streams and bogs.

When he reached the source of the scent and there was no sign of her, he turned in place. Then gazed up to find one of her arrows lodged in a tree, so deep only the flights showed. And to those, she'd tied little bits of her T-shirt. *Clever girl.* She'd used her arrows to obscure her trail.

But he would follow each to the end, tracking her for as long as it took. She'd been born for him. *And I was born to find her. . . .*

Terrain passed beneath his feet for half an hour before he located her true trail. With the innate stealth of his kind, he prowled closer, hunting this huntress in the now drizzling rain.

The swamp made it easy for him to approach her undetected. There were a thousand shadows to conceal him, with animals constantly creeping about to distract her.

Once he spied her again, he just stopped himself from sucking in a breath. Up close, she was even lovelier than he'd thought her. She had to be a Valkyrie, one among a species of women both notoriously beautiful . . . and notoriously fierce.

Her features were stunning—high, bold cheekbones, plump lips, and a slim, pixie nose—but her coloring made her beyond compare. Her skin was golden and smooth, her eyes the color of Scots whiskey.

She was of middling height and curvy, wearing a wet white T-shirt that hugged *generous* breasts. Khaki shorts fitted tightly over her pert arse and displayed shapely legs. Her hair was long—a dark mane, heavy with rain.

On her right hand, she wore a leather shooting glove. A long leather forearm guard stretched from her left wrist to her elbow. *Who knew archery gear could be so sexy?*

His female would wear her leathers when he took her curvy wee body tonight. At the thought, his shaft hardened in his damp jeans, and he almost growled.

Instead, he silently followed her, watching as she closed in on the prey he'd already scented in the burrows beneath them.

If she was in fact a Valkyrie, she'd possess superhuman senses like his own—keen hearing and the ability to see in the dark or over long distances. Yet her sense of smell wouldn't be nearly as developed as his own. She'd need to track the creature by sight and sound—and she was doing so expertly.

But all the while she would freeze, jerking her head back in his direction, her pointed ears twitching.

Without warning, she leapt up into a waterlogged oak, crouching there as she resumed her shooting stance, nocking another arrow. From a distance, her short bow was unassuming, a recurve bow with the ends arching away from her and a thickened grip in the middle. Typical, if old fashioned. But as he neared he could see there were etched gold markings in the polished black wood.

Her weapon was as fine and proud as its owner obviously was. . . .

She went motionless, aiming directly for the spot where he'd scented her prey. Did she plan to hit it through the earth?

Aye, because in a reaper's voice, she whispered, *"Underground won't save you."*

THREE

❖

I can hear its breath, muffled now. Lucia knew the kobold had gone underground, scurrying for its life. She'd trailed it here, easily reading the signs that all prey left behind.

From this angle in the tree, she could shoot into the ground, piercing her arrow straight into the tunnel beneath. Her *special* arrow—it'd go in sleek and aerodynamic until contact, then it would release three razor-sharp barbs.

Soon she'd report two confirmed kills back to Nucking Futs Nïx. Just as Lucia always did. And then what? *Then I'll repeat days like this, over and over, until the Accession.*

When the nightmares came.

For now, kill the kobold, go home.

Yet for some reason, instead of focusing on her target, she recalled broad shoulders and lean cheeks, remembering how the Lykae had looked at her just before he'd been tackled. He'd stared, heaving breaths with that barrel chest, sweat trickling down his muscled torso. Until he'd gotten flattened by some of the biggest demons she'd ever seen.

His interest had disconcerted her. In fact, all eyes

had been on her—something that didn't often happen since Lucia usually had the brazen, showstopping Regin the Radiant to distract notice from her.

But if anyone, including that male—who surely hadn't been reaching for *her* with that grubby paw—had gotten curious and actually followed her, she'd taken care to cover her tracks.

Lucia shook her head hard, refocusing, inhaling a breath. Once she exhaled, she held herself motionless, sighting down the arrow's length. The ancient inscriptions on her bow seemed to glow. . . .

She released the string. With a *thunk*, the arrow punctured the ground, boring deep, all the way to the kobold burrowed below. A muffled shriek sounded.

Target hit. Even underground, she'd nailed it. Not surprising—she hadn't missed a shot in centuries. Skathi's essence literally worked like a charm.

Lucia swung her bow back across her body, then leapt down to finish off her immortal prey with a swift beheading. *It's hard being this good*, she thought as she sauntered to the spot of contact. *It's harder to act modest.* She sighed. *My cross to bear.*

Three tenets comprised the Skathian code: honesty, chastity, and humility. She managed honesty—mostly—and chastity totally. But she couldn't grasp the reasoning behind humility.

When she neared, the creature scurried in the tunnel beneath her feet, making the arrow shaft dart frenziedly in the mucky ground, which amused her.

This was her greatest pleasure—the hunt. When she

was out like this, she felt less like an imposter, filled with shameful secrets. In these moments, she didn't feel as if her sins were stamped upon her like a scarlet letter for all to see.

And she could briefly forget what would soon befall her in the approaching Accession.

Shaking away that thought, she crouched to dig free her prey, hauling it out by the ankle in a rush of mud and roots. Still in cherubic form, the kobold squirmed frenetically, her arrow jutting from its throat.

She dropped it to the ground and plucked free her arrow, taking half its neck with those barbs. The creature transformed, growing reptilian, with snakelike eyes and scaly skin. When it snapped its now elongated fangs at her, she turned the arrow lengthwise, pressing the shaft down over what was left of its neck.

As blood sprayed up her arms, she grinned, relishing her job as enforcer of laws.

Lucia had just beheaded the thing when her ears twitched with awareness yet again. *Something's watching me.* She leapt back to her feet, eyes darting. Something *close.*

The male. She sensed it was him—but how had he gotten the drop on her?

She peered into the shadows and almost gasped when golden eyes glowed back. "Why are you following me?" she demanded. On occasion, she acted as a negotiator between factions because she was so patient and levelheaded—or so everyone thought. Perhaps he sought her help to solve some grievance.

The male stalked closer to her, ignoring the natural path, heading directly for her. A Lykae had made her the object of its interest. Never a good development.

"How could I no' follow a lass as bonny as you?" he asked in a raspy brogue. The mud had washed clean, revealing the perfection of his still-bare chest and torso and all the strong planes of his face. His chin was stubborn with a hint of a cleft, his skin tan, with those faint laugh lines etched beside golden eyes. Rain spiked his lashes.

His thick hair was wet and dark, whipping across his lean cheeks. She'd bet it'd be a rich brown when dry.

His gaze met hers for long moments before he leisurely took in every feature of her face. The way he looked at her was consuming, savoring—as if she were the most beautiful creature on earth and he'd been starved for the sight of her.

She frowned as a sense of awareness seemed to tingle through her every nerve.

When his gaze dipped to her body, he raised a shaking hand to run over his mouth, clearly liking what he saw.

What's not to like— No! Act reasonable and serious. Above all things be rational. "Who are you?"

"I'm Garreth MacRieve of the Lykae clan." He drew nearer and she sidled back. They began circling each other. "Never seen anyone shoot like you."

That truly never got old. "Because no one can," she answered matter-of-factly.

Had the corner of his lips briefly curled? "What devil did you make a deal with to shoot like that?"

She almost sighed. Devil? *I did something entirely different with him.* She stifled the memories that had begun to surface more and more often.

"Mayhap your bow's enchanted?"

"My bow's not enchanted—merely unequaled." For over a thousand years, it'd held fast, as perfectly honed today as it'd been the night of Lucia's transformation. The black ash wood was polished to a sheen and carved with elaborate inscriptions. In a long-dead language, it was written that Lucia was a servant to the goddess Skathi. Forever. "You don't think mine could be a natural"—*goddess-given*—"talent?"

"Aye. But to marry talent *and* beauty such as yours as well? Hardly sporting to other lasses."

She'd often thought so herself. Luckily for them, she had no interest in garnering a man's attention.

"And you could no' be bonnier."

In fact, she could be. Her hair was drenched. Her clothes were boring—a serviceable pair of shorts and a plain T-shirt. She wore no makeup or jewelry, but then, she never did. Not since she'd started wearing the bow.

"Are you fey or Valkyrie?"

I'm an Archer. A celibate in plain clothes. A shadow in the background. "Guess." At least he got points for not mistaking her for a nymph. Unfortunately, the two species resembled each other with their elven features. That was where all similarities ended.

"With the bow and the pointed ears, I'd normally say fey. But you've wee fangs and claws, so I fear it will no' be so easy as that."

"Easy? What are you talking about?"

He opened his mouth, then closed it, slanting his head at her in an appraising way. She sensed that whatever he'd been about to tell her, he decided against it, instead saying: "Seduction. Valkyrie are notoriously difficult to seduce."

He wanted to seduce her? No talk of a date, of courting, just sex. *Men!* "Difficult, you say? If you've made a go at one of us in your current state—unshaven, bloody, half-dressed, and covered in mud—I just can't imagine why. Not to mention that you smell of mash and distillery. Be still my heart."

He scrubbed a palm over his face, seeming surprised to find stubble there. "Today is no' a good day for me."

"Then you should go back and enjoy your groupies. I've always heard that nothing brightens one's outlook like an orgy with nymphs." Why this sharp tone? As if she were jealous. A spark of disquiet arose in her.

"Doona want them." He drew closer. "Even before I saw you." He gazed deeply into her eyes, as if he could see through her chaste, ascetic shell and recognize how wild she truly was. As if he knew her façade was a shaky house of cards that could be felled with a touch.

You have a darkness in you, Lucia, Skathi had warned her eons ago. *You must constantly be vigilant against it.*

Yes, vigilant. Lucia needed to get home, away from this rumbling-voiced werewolf. A face like his had been her undoing once, a handsome face that had concealed a monster.

Just as this one's did.

"The attraction isn't mutual," she said crisply. "So be on your way." With that, she turned to dispose of her kill, intending to throw the pieces into the water for the animals there to feed on. When she bent for the kobold's head, the Lykae picked up the body, as if he were being gentlemanly, retrieving a dropped handkerchief. *So surreal.* They lobbed the pieces into the murky water.

Her task done, she brushed off her hands and turned for home.

He followed.

She stopped, glaring briefly at the sky before telling him, "Werewolf, save yourself both time and effort. Whatever is the opposite of a *sure thing*, that's me."

"Because I'm a Lykae?"

Because you're a man. "You were right earlier—I *am* a Valkyrie. And my kind considers yours little better than animals." They *did.* Though Lykae weren't formal enemies like the vampires, older Valkyrie had battled them in the past, during bygone Accessions—factionwide wars in the Lore. They'd said it was rare to see one fully turned unless you threatened their mate or offspring, but that even a hint of the beast that resided inside them was harrowing. . . .

So where was the conviction in Lucia's tone?

"Aye, mayhap they do, but what do you consider me?" He narrowed his eyes. "Surely you doona agree with them or you would no' want me to mate you now."

Her lips parted. "*Mate* me? I've met arrogant males in my day, but you are the king of them."

A shadow passed over his face. "The king, then?

What a way of putting it." But he quickly recovered. "Then give me a boon for taking the prize. Tell me your name."

She exhaled, then grudgingly said, "I'm called Lucia the Huntress."

"Lousha," he repeated.

Everyone she'd ever known had pronounced her name *Loo-see-ah*. With his thick Scottish accent, the werewolf pronounced it *Lousha*. She just stopped herself from shivering.

"Well, then, Lousha the Huntress"—a roguish grin curled his lips—"you've snared me."

Tingles danced over her body, but just as swiftly foreboding filled her. She had no business responding to him. He'd just left the nymphs and a guaranteed orgy. He would expect sex from a female this night.

Which she could never give—even if she wanted to—without disaster.

So why was her gaze descending along his damp chest? Her eyes followed the trail of hair from his navel down to the low-slung waist of his worn jeans, then lower . . . she almost gasped to see the bulge there.

She realized he must have been doing the same perusal of her—because the bulge *grew*. She quickly glanced up, found the Lykae's gaze was riveted to her breasts. Her nipples were straining against the wet material of her shirt, and he was staring hard at them as if he wanted to remove her top—with his mind.

When their eyes met once more, his flickered blue again, reminding her anew of why interacting with him was unwise. "Run along, wolf. Or I'll make you wish you had."

"That will no' be happening, Valkyrie."

"Why?" At his determined look, a suspicion arose in her, one so ridiculous it hardly warranted another thought. But she couldn't shake it. "I'm not . . . your mate, or anything, right?" She couldn't be.

"Nay. Though I might wish it otherwise."

Thank the gods for that. "Then—leave."

When he instead drew nearer, she yanked free her bow and nocked an arrow, drawing the string without thought. She aimed straight for his heart, which wouldn't kill an immortal like him but would put him down for a good while. "Stop right where you are, or I'll shoot."

He didn't stop right where he was. "You would no'. When I mean you no harm?"

"This isn't an idle threat," she said in a steely tone. His expression turned impatient, as if he couldn't understand where her caution was coming from. "I *will* shoot you if you come closer."

He came closer. So she shot him in the heart. Or four inches to the right, having decided at the last second to vary her aim by a degree.

The arrow landed in his solid chest, drilling through his muscles until only the flights were visible. "Bluidy hell, woman!" he bellowed, scowling down at his chest.

In a placid tone, she reminded him, "I told you not to come closer."

He fisted the flights, trying to draw the arrow free, but those barbs made it impossible. Reaching around awkwardly, he grated, "Help me get this thing loose!"

She blinked up at him. "I put the arrows *in*. I don't take them out."

His chin jutted. "You do with me."

The corners of her lips quirked, surprising her. *What a wild, mad Lykae.* She schooled her features. "Why would I ever?"

"Because, Valkyrie"—he started for her again, apparently planning to ignore the arrow in his chest—"by the close of this night we'll be sharing a bed, and you'll feel foolish to have shot up your bedmate."

With a sigh, she let sail another arrow. "Oh, dear, how *foolish* of me. You were saying?"

He continued closer. "When I set to kissing those pouting lips of yours—"

Another arrow sunk into his chest.

Now three wounds marred his gorgeous body, three trails of blood tracking over the rises and falls of rock-hard muscle. Gritting his teeth, he said, "This hurts like hell, lass, but it's heartening."

"How do you figure?"

"At fifty times the distance, you dispatched that kobold with three arrows to the neck. I've earned a trio to the chest. Seems you slapped him while you're tickling me. You doona want to kill me, which is a good sign. Maybe this is your way of flirting?"

She sobered once more, reality washing over her. "I'm not flirting—trust me, you'd know." *Because disaster would be imminent.* Damn it, he kept coming for her.

"If you're truly a hunter, you will no' leave a wolf to suffer. I'll bet you usually shoot to kill—no' merely to torment."

He had a point. It wasn't in her nature to torture a being. Unless they had it coming. "Oh, very well. If I help you remove them, will you leave me alone?"

"Leave you alone? I'd rather bluidy wear them, Valkyrie."

With that, he slammed his fist against the end of the first arrow, sending the shaft jutting farther out his back. He reached behind him, now able to just snag the tip. Clenching his jaw, he threaded the arrow through his chest, the flights disappearing beneath the surface of his skin as he pulled it out from his back.

While she gaped at his resilience, he cast the bloody arrow aside, then started on the next, repeating the process. With each one, the muscles in his body went tense; once the arrow was freed, he groaned and relaxed—somewhat. Almost as if he'd taken sexual release but wasn't sated.

A part of her was flattered that he'd rather go through this than receive her help. She could've snapped the ends, allowing him to pull them forward, but instead he withstood this pain—because he didn't want to leave her alone?

His strength amazed her, his fortitude imposing. That awareness returned, and her skin pricked in the clammy night air.

When he began removing the last arrow, he advanced on her once more, tearing it free as he stalked closer, barely giving a wince, that determined mien never faltering.

She took a step back, debated using her one remaining arrow to put him down. She couldn't kill him, but she could slow him with a shot between the eyes.

"I believe I've earned the right to stay—as well as a kiss from you."

She made a sound of frustration. "As if you'd be happy with a kiss? You expect to have sex with me and it simply will not happen—"

"But you want it to, do you no'?"

To have him take her here, hot and sweaty in the swamp? She swallowed. He was a Lykae—he'd want her on her hands and knees . . . Her heart sped up at the thought, but she shook her head stubbornly. "Of course not! Understand me, MacRieve, I'm a Valkyrie. I'm not bound by your . . . animalistic needs."

His voice a low rasp, he said, "After one night with me, Lousha, *you will be.*"

FOUR

‹◆›

Adrenaline and need coursed through Garreth, muting the pain of his wounds, until all he could feel was the growing pressure in his shaft and an overwhelming lust for the creature before him.

A Valkyrie. Again, he marveled that Fate had given him a shield maiden for his mate. Now he didn't know whether to laugh or howl. He'd likely have been damned happy about the fact if she'd stop resisting the fierce attraction between them.

Just earlier he'd wished for a more challenging female. Now he wondered *why* she was fighting this. She was aroused; the scent of his mate's desire was mouthwatering, making him want to go to his knees in thanks—and to taste her. Her nipples were so hard they had to be throbbing.

So why wouldn't she surrender to him? Aye, he regretted his wish. He dimly wondered whether she would fall into bed with him if he told her he was a king.

Then he frowned as a thought surfaced. "Does another male . . . have a claim on you?" He might be needing to make a kill this very night.

"A male's claim? On me? No one!"

Her heart had not been given. *So it's mine to win.* He found his lips curling.

"Nor will they ever," she vowed.

"Uh-huh. That so?"

His amused tone must have flustered her. "A-again, not interested. You couldn't find a more uninterested female."

"You forget I'm a Lykae. I can scent your *interest.*" Gods, her scent was like a drug to him, her arousal so sweet.

Her face flushed, a light pink along high cheekbones. "Maybe I was *interested* in one of the other males on the field."

Jealousy seared him inside. Never had he felt its equal. He was upon her before she could raise her bow again, his callused palm wrapping around her delicate nape. "Take it back, female." He'd been able to rein in his aggression from the game. With more difficulty, he controlled the adrenaline pumping through his veins after finding her at last. But this jealousy was overwhelming.

"Or what?"

"Or I'll kiss you till you canna remember another." He would seduce her, using everything he'd ever learned about women to coax his way inside her. "Kiss you deeply, thoroughly. Till you're panting for more."

Lightning struck nearby, though she seemed not to notice. He could tell she wanted him to kiss her, was unconsciously rocking her hips to him, driving him wild. Why couldn't she let go?

She stared at his lips as if she were trying to imagine

it just then. But then she muttered, almost scornfully, "You win the timing award, Lykae. That's for certain."

"Doona understand you, Valkyrie," MacRieve rasped. "When is it ever bad timing for a kiss?"

What would his be like? As if she had anything to compare with it. *Playing a dangerous game here, Lucia.*

He leaned in to nuzzle her hair, his breath hot against the pointed tip of her ear.

Not the ears! She was so sensitive there, and he grazed his lips right over the tip. *That feels so good. . . .*

"Ah, my lass likes that?" he asked, nuzzling again. When she sagged into him, he took the opportunity to back her into an old oak.

He rested his hands against the tree on each side of her head, reminding her of his incredible strength. The Lykae were the most physically powerful beings in the Lore, could lift trains. He could have broken her like a doll, yet he'd been so gentle with her, even after the brutal contest earlier.

Even after I shot him.

He eased even closer, until their bodies were touching. When his gaze dipped to where her breasts met his battered chest, she felt his penis pulse harder in a rush, and a last ounce of sanity told her, *Stop this!*

She needed to get away from this werewolf, but she couldn't outrun him all the way back to Val Hall. Besides, fleeing from an enemy was something Valkyrie tended never to do.

Have to shoot him between the eyes if I must. From close range. Otherwise, with his speed he could dodge the shot. And put her in agony. "MacRieve, I'm giving you one last—"

He silenced her with a sizzling kiss to her neck, his tongue flicking against her chilled skin. Shivering with pleasure and surprise, she gazed up at the tree limbs above her, biting her lip.

Yet when he pressed his erection against her, she cried, "Let me go *now*!"

He didn't, so she gouged her thumb into one of his wounds. His dark claws dug into the tree, but he didn't release her. "Woman, that bluidy hurts."

"Then stop kissing me!"

"Nothing hurts *that* bad." His mouth descended to her neck once more. He seemed to be not only kissing her but tasting her . . . *gentling* her.

"I can make it hurt that bad," she said inanely, striving to keep her eyes open as his tongue darted.

"I feel only one ache in my body." He drew back, and the corner of his lips curled. "And you're soon to ease it."

So earthy and sexy. Lucia couldn't remember the last time she'd felt this much excitement with a male. . . . Her thoughts trailed off.

No, I can *remember the last time.* Vividly. Lucia was still paying for it. She attempted to pull away, but he clutched her to him. And Freya help her, she wanted him to. *No!* No more pretending that she was a normal woman about to have a clandestine affair with the most sexually attractive male she'd ever seen. "Never, MacRieve."

She could be as vicious as any of her sisters. Just because a Valkyrie's innate ferocity wasn't her first impulse in a conflict didn't mean she couldn't draw on it when she needed to. "Kiss me again, Lykae, and I'll make you regret it."

He kissed her again. So she kicked him between his legs, ducking from him. As he dropped to his knees, she hastened away. But she heard him grunt, *"Still doona regret it."*

FIVE

——◆——

Stalking her through the bayou once more, he tracked her heady scent—with his bollocks aching from her kick and his chest wounds on fire.

"I can scent you, know you're near." Yes, she was close. He circled in place, his eyes narrowed. "Doona run from me! You will no' get away." *And we crave the chase. Ah, gods, we crave it.* "You've only got one arrow left."

"But I'm going to make this one count," she whispered above him.

Before he could swing his head up at the sound, she'd tackled him into a bed of moss, knees into his shoulders, her arrow pressed into his forehead.

In a slow, awed tone, he rasped, *"I—like—you, lass!"* So lovely, so wild. An avenging angel, with her bizarre bow seeming to glow above him.

When blood welled on his forehead and trickled down his temple, he said, "You canna release your arrow, Valkyrie. You feel something for me, too." She looked stunned, as if her hesitation baffled her. "I'll bet when you set a course of action, you doona falter."

At that, she gritted her teeth, like she was redoubling her resolve.

"But you canna do it." The instant she relaxed the tension on her bowstring, he tossed her on her back, covering her body with his. He groaned to feel all her lush curves pressed against him. Both of them were out of breath, her breasts rising and falling so temptingly.

She was a wee beauty, with her smooth golden skin and plump lips. Her hair had begun drying into a deep caramel color. It felt like silk and smelled like heaven. *Like home.* "You ken this feels right between us."

Ah, gods, it does. As if they'd done this before. As if she recognized his touch and remembered the breathless way she felt at this moment.

What was happening to her? He was right—when she set a course of action, she'd never once faltered. Yet she couldn't shoot him!

His mouth descended on hers. Just as she was about to shove him away, he groaned, as though the mere contact of their lips brought him so much pleasure he couldn't contain it. He deepened the kiss, pressing his firm lips harder, coaxing her with his tongue to respond.

The shock of being kissed after so long. The heat of his body over hers in the cold rain.

Lightning struck above them, and she knew it came from her. Her bow hand unclenched, her other palm clasping the back of his neck. When she parted her lips on a gasp, he stroked her mouth with his delicious tongue while she remained still, merely taking his attentions.

Breaking away, he stared down at her, giving her a

look—a purely masculine expression of intent—that promised he was about to do wicked things to her. *Oh, that look.* Robbing her of thought . . .

"Your eyes are goin' silvery," he said, his accent growing thicker. "You want me, too." Before setting in again, he commanded, "Now kiss me back."

Over her long lifetime, many men had tried to seduce her, but she'd easily disregarded them. What was so different about this Lykae? It was as if he knew exactly how to tap into her need, into the wildness inside her.

That dark part of her she feared took over and *ruled* her. *This won't be more than a kiss. I'd never let it be more than that. . . .*

In a rush, her body flooded with desire, her breasts growing heavy. *The wildness within me. Can't fight it . . .*

She was starved for this. And a bounty lay before her. Pleasure building . . . losing control . . . losing . . .

Lost. This felt so . . . *right.* With a moan, she surrendered.

The Instinct was screaming inside him. —*She needs you. Aches for her male.*—

At last, she offered her lips up to his, freely, letting him in. He delved with his tongue, tasting her, drinking her in. When she kissed him back with a tentative lick, he groaned against her, squeezing her tighter to him.

She's yielding to me. Garreth wanted to growl with pleasure. *I'm bringing home my woman this night.*

Into my bed, into my life. Finally, after so long waiting for her.

For . . . *Lucia.*

With each shy lap of her tongue, she stoked his need. When their tongues began tangling in earnest, when they began sharing breaths, she gave a surprised moan into his mouth.

Then it was as if a dam had burst, as if she, like him, had been waiting centuries for this night. She seemed to share his unimaginable need—or even suffer from it more keenly.

He kissed her deeply, squeezing the flare of her hip and raising his other hand for one of her breasts. He hesitated just above her chest. But like a dream, she arched to his palm with a plaintive whimper, pressing her breast into his hand. Against her lips, he said, "Gods, you madden me, Lousha." He cupped her generous, soft breasts, one, then the other, learning them.

She trembled from his touch, crying out as he circled one of those stiff nipples with his thumb. When he bent down to close his mouth over one of her tight buds, she said, "What are you—"

He suckled her through her shirt, and her words died in her throat, replaced by a moan. When she completely relinquished her bow and clutched the back of his head to hold him to her breast, the world seemed to fade away until all he knew was his mate—her scent, the sight of only her, the feel of her sensuous body. As he sucked her, he reached down, unfastening her leather quiver, tossing it away.

Her arms laced around his neck, her moans growing more frantic, mingling with his groans as he explored her.

But then she whispered, "Not more than this. Mac-Rieve, only this . . ."

"Aye, only this." *For now.*

His assurance seemed to embolden her, melting any lingering resistance to him. She rolled over atop him, rocking her sex against his. He yearned to claim her, to mark her tender flesh so badly, but he'd never imagined a female in need of release like this. When she ground against his shaft, nearly robbing him of his seed, he hastily tucked her beneath him.

Aggression ruled them both—each trying to get the upper hand, rolling over again and again.

He was all for her riding him like a horse if she wanted—later. Right now he needed her hands pinned above her head, her thighs spread to cradle him, her eyes gazing up at his. So he shoved her beneath him, wedging his hips solidly between her legs.

At last, she surrendered to him, but not before those little claws scored down his back. He threw back his head, roaring with satisfaction. She made him wild, frenzied for her. With each of her cries, he fell deeper under her spell. *How'd I ever live without this?*

But then came a trickle of unease. Never had he been so crazed for a female. He comprehended his life would never be the same if he continued tonight. A daunting thought for any male. Yet when he gazed down at her, Garreth knew he had to have her no matter what.

With that in mind, he reached down, using his foreclaw to slice the crotch of her shorts. As he shoved the material to her waist, he clumsily fumbled his jeans to his knees.

Her panties were black and sleek—sexy as hell. He hooked his fingers into the material, about to tear them off her, but she grabbed his wrist. "Don't!"

"Canna wait, waited so long . . ." *My cock's about to go off.* He wanted it to—*inside her.* Needed to pump his semen deep into her womb as he marked her as his own forever.

She shook her head, her expression growing panicked. "I can't! They . . . they stay on."

Confusion. —*Seduce her.*—

So he bent down between her legs and kissed her through the damp silk of her panties. She gasped, but her gasp turned to a moan when he licked, nipped, and nuzzled in bliss. Once she was helplessly undulating her hips to his mouth for more, he again tried to rid her of her panties.

"Wait!" she cried.

With a growl, he covered her body with his own, wrapping her hair around his fist. "Lousha, I have to have you. I'll bring you pleasure, make you come till you scream." He punctuated his words with a rock of his hips.

When his cock rubbed over her silk-covered sex, her eyes went wide. "Oh . . . *oh!*"

"You're about tae, are you no'?"

She nodded up at him. "I think. . . . I don't know—"

You'll know. He'd make her. He bucked against her.

"Ah! Don't stop *that! Please. . . .*"

"This?"

"Yes, there! Ah, yes!" Her head thrashed on the ground. "Just don't stop!"

"Will no'. I may come atop you—but I will no' stop." He ground against her, struggling to hold his seed. He was on the verge, spasms already beginning in his swollen shaft, the head moist.

Lightning struck a tree directly beside them—she didn't notice and he forgot when he saw her lost expression, her silver eyes. . . . *Ah, gods, she's coming.* "Yes, Lousha!" Bucking furiously, pants at his knees, he grew desperate to shove into her, to feel her clenching around him. "Come hard for me. . . ."

She screamed, her knees falling open as she pressed those big breasts into his chest. As his hips pumped over her, she dug her claws into his back, holding him tight to her.

Mine! Now you're mine. . . . He leaned down to her ear. "You've maddened me for you, have changed everything." Reaching between them, clutching her panties, he rasped, "So I'm going to fuck you long and hard, beauty, because if I'm to be enslaved by you—I want to be your master as well."

He yanked free her silk, and the head of his cock slipped against the slick folds, soaked from her orgasm. His eyes rolled back in his head just as she screamed, "No!"

She shoved against his chest. "No, don't!" It was as if he'd doused her with ice water, her passion evaporating in a rush. "I can't do this!"

"The hell you say!"

She continued scrambling from him. "Let me go!"

—She knows fear.— Though his cock was about to explode, throbbing so hard it felt like it'd been slammed in a door, he finally let her up. His bollocks were heavy, aching with seed.

"I don't want this . . . didn't want it."

He'd been a thrust away from claiming his mate . . . "You dinna want it?" He shot to his feet, dragging on his jeans. When he tried to zip them over his swollen shaft, lust turned to anger and frustration such as he'd never known. "Then why were you riding my crotch like a wanton as you sucked my tongue?"

She gasped, trying to put her clothes to rights, darting for her bow and quiver. Once she'd collected her weapons, both of their gazes fell on the black panties he'd ripped free. She reached forward, but he snatched them from her, stuffing them in his pocket.

She blinked in confusion, backing away.

"Doona walk away," he growled. "You think I will no' follow?"

"You don't understand!"

Her eyes are . . . haunted? "Then make me understand! Is it because of what I am?"

"If you try to follow me, I-I'll hate you forever."

Damn it! What was happening here? She looked like she was about to flee for her life.

Suddenly thoughts of his cousin Bowen's tragic history arose in his mind. Deadened Bowen was a cautionary tale to all Lykae males of what happened when a mate—who was *other*—ran.

Bowen's female had perished as she'd fled from him, dying gruesomely.

Cold fear suffused Garreth at the thought of Lucia hurt. He inhaled sharply, wrestling for control, even as he watched what he coveted most in the world slipping from his grasp.

SIX

What just happened? How?

Lucia had almost been . . . unchaste, about to lose her purity—and therefore her abilities—right before the Accession!

One misstep had nearly cost Lucia her powers. Because Skathi hadn't *gifted* her with anything. Lucia's archery skills were on loan—and conditional.

How close she'd been. How close . . .

Yet even now her body was still thrumming for his touch—for more.

Lucia made it really simple for herself. The Accession meant Cruach. Succumbing to this Lykae meant no archery. She'd be defenseless if the Broken Bloody One escaped his prison and returned for her. *Returned to make me pay . . .*

Whatever MacRieve saw in her expression had him backing away with his palms raised. "There, lass. Doona be afraid. You've nothing to fear from me."

She knew her eyes were wild, her heart racing with dread. "I-I'm not afraid of you!" *I'm afraid of* him— *afraid of being trapped back in his corpse-ridden lair.* She put the back of her hand against her mouth as she retched.

Lucia, I gave you meat and wine. . . .

"Now, Valkyrie, just wait. I dinna mean to upset you." MacRieve absently swiped a hand over his still-engorged shaft, as if it pained him—even now her body responded to the sight.

"If you're bent on leaving, then meet me here this weekend," he said tightly, as if this was a great concession. "Saturday at noon, we'll return. That'll give us both time to cool off, to think about this."

His offer did surprise her. "I . . . I don't know." He'd told her that she wasn't his mate, but she thought he'd lied since his reaction had been so fierce. Now she began to believe again, because otherwise he'd have been thumping his chest and snarling, "Mine!" as he slung her over his shoulder. "All right. I agree to it," she lied, feeling something she hadn't in a long time with a male. Five hundred years to be exact.

Terror.

There was no rain in the bayou Saturday night. Only quiet.

Garreth had been waiting here since quarter past ten this morning. He'd risen at dawn, too anxious to remain abed, and begun to get ready. He'd intended to take care with his dress, to present himself as a male of worth, like the leader that he was. Not like the hard-drinking, foul-mouthed brawler Lucia likely thought him.

Then he'd realized he owned nothing but hole-ridden jeans, broken-in boots, and pullover shirts.

Hardly a fitting match for a lass with her delicate beauty. Hell, it hadn't mattered anyway. *She's no' com-*

ing. What he didn't know was *why*. Yes, the Valkyrie hated the Lykae, considered them animals. But she'd responded to him.

Gods, how she'd responded. She'd taken her release and left him stranded and aching for his. He'd witnessed Lucia in the grip of passion, and she'd been like no female he'd ever imagined.

At the memory of her lust, his cock swelled in his worn jeans, and he rubbed the heel of his palm down his raging erection. All week, he'd been like this, randy as a lad in his first brothel, no matter how many times he took release. He'd hoped to be inside her this day, imagining it in a thousand different ways.

But she's no' meeting me. He checked the clock on his sat-phone. Ten at night. Clearly, he needed to call this. Lucia, it seemed, was in no way *easy*. He'd gotten his wish, and wished he hadn't.

As soon as she'd left him here that night, Garreth had dragged Munro and Uilleam out of the still-going game and told them, "We need to find out everything we can on our new neighbors, the Valkyrie. All of them." He'd been amazed at how little the Lykae knew about that faction of the Lore. And again he'd sworn his friends to secrecy. "Say nothing about this to *anyone*." If word got back to the clan elders that they were about to have a Valkyrie for a queen . . .

He and the twins had agreed that no one could know about Lucia until she was bearing Garreth's bite mark upon her neck. The beast inside any Lykae would recognize the claim as Garreth's, would know she was forever under his protection.

Then the three of them had combed the streets of New Orleans, a city they hadn't visited often, and all the while, Garreth impatiently counted down the hours till this day.

Finding information had proved difficult. Big Easy Loreans were suspicious of the Lykae newcomers to their city and on guard with the Accession approaching. Garreth had come up empty in his search, but the twins had charmed a voodoo shopkeeper who'd told them much.

Now as Garreth waited in the swamp, he thought back over all they'd learned about Lucia. . . .

"She's legendary for her archery skills," Munro had said. "Nothing else unique about her."

That was all she was known for? "There must be more. What does she like to do? What are her interests?"

"No one knows," Uilleam had answered. "She's just the Archer." As if nothing more needed to be said about her. It was how she was identified.

Munro had added, "But it's rumored that she feels agonizing pain whenever she misses a target."

Luckily, Garreth couldn't see that happening too often with her skill. But then his chest had grown heavy.

Was that how she'd gotten to be so good?

Above all, they'd learned the Valkyrie were peculiar creatures. Their origin alone fascinated him. Each Valkyrie had *three* parents. Whenever a maiden faced death with uncommon bravery, the Norse gods Freya and Wóden struck her with lightning, rescuing her to Valhalla. The maiden would wake there—healed, safe, and pregnant with a Valkyrie daughter.

The birth mothers hailed from all Lorekind—furies, witches, shifters, even humans. So the daughters would each possess the unique coloring and characteristics of the mother, but they all inherited Freya's fey features and her notorious acquisitiveness—in fact, they could be mesmerized by shining jewels, diamonds especially.

The Valkyrie were rumored to have glass-shattering shrieks, preternatural speed, and no need to eat or drink. Instead they consumed electrical energy from the earth and produced lightning when they experienced sharp emotions.

That had been a legend about Valkyrie he'd never quite believed until he'd been in the throes with one. Lightning had speared the night, and not only from the storm.

Garreth had learned about various individual Valkyrie as well. Nïx was their soothsayer, rumored to be three thousand years old and mad as a hatter. Regin was the last of the Radiant Ones and had skin that glowed. Annika was the dauntless leader of the New Orleans coven, a master strategist who lived to war with vampires.

No one knew who Lucia's birth mother was—or *what* she'd been—but the shopkeeper had said this Accession would be Lucia's third. Which meant that she was over a millennium old—near his own age.

In the end, Garreth had more questions about her than answers. . . .

She's no' coming. Damn it, why? He'd shown her passion—and patience. But she'd been skittish toward the end. Wild-eyed and spooked. Perhaps she feared the intensity of her own reaction? Or of *his*?

He recalled what Bowen had once told him. "We doona understand our own ferocity." His cousin's deadened eyes had been filled with loss. "What's normal to us is no' to others." Bowen's own mate had loved him, until she'd seen him turned. Then she'd fled.

Lucia too had fled—yet she hadn't even seen a glimpse of the beast.

The Lykae called their transformation *letting the beast out of its cage*. Garreth would grow taller, his muscles extending, his fangs and black claws lengthening. The brutal and menacing shadow of his beast would flicker over him.

No, Lucia dinna see me like that. He scowled at the waxing moon. *But she soon will.*

She would run far, if he wasn't careful. Another glance at the moon, and he knew what he would have to do on that night. "Ah, Lousha, my lass. It's going to hurt. But there's no getting around it."

For now, she wasn't coming to him, so again he'd go to her. He stood and turned for the Valkyrie's home of Val Hall. Since he'd met her, he'd staked out the bizarre place. Lightning bombarded the property, flashing constantly above the antebellum manor. All over the grounds, lightning rods jutted up. Smoking moss dangled from burned oaks. From within, Valkyrie shrieks sounded.

None of that mattered but for the fact that Lucia would be within. He strides took him closer and closer to her.

SEVEN

"Lykae in our backyards. Horde vampires seeking out Valkyries all over the world. Happy Accession!" Regin cried from her "command center," also known as the dining room table, which now stood covered with maps and papers—all lit by her glowing face.

The more excited Regin became, the more she glowed. Yet that wasn't the only reason she was called the Radiant One. . . .

Lucia made a noncommittal sound, only half listening. She'd thought she'd spotted something outside the manor. She was curled up in a window seat, bow in her lap, peering out at the night. The gaslights flickered outside Val Hall, like tentative steps into the blackness.

On this day, she was supposed to have met the werewolf. All week she'd been in a daze, knowing she couldn't meet him, yet tempted to so badly. She wanted to know if she'd imagined the addictive taste of his lips. She wanted to discover why she hadn't been able to shoot him between the eyes. Why had everything in her rebelled against the idea?

And why had he taken her underwear?

That had confused her as much as anything from that night. Unlike her sisters, who were all obsessed with lingerie, Lucia wore athletic underwear—seamless, utilitarian. She didn't buy sexy silks like Agent Provocateur, instead favoring brands like Under Armour—the kind sold in a pack. She'd never expected anyone to see them, yet he'd stolen them. Why?

She sighed. Surely MacRieve would leave her alone now that he'd been stood up. Even as she thought this, she half expected to see him advancing on the manor, pissed off, his gorgeous face creased in a scowl.

But nothing was out there now. She relaxed a touch.

Ultimately, the choice of whether to meet MacRieve or not had been taken out of Lucia's hands. Her day planner had gotten filled to the gills when their coven had learned that Horde vampires were hunting for a particular Valkyrie, though they didn't know who.

Vampires were the Valkyrie's most hated enemies. They could *trace*—or teleport—from one location to another, disappearing and reappearing at will, making them difficult to slay. When the Valkyrie's mighty queen Furie had gone to face the Horde leader Demestriu, she'd never returned. . . .

Worse, Ivo the Cruel, second in command to Demestriu, and his men were searching *here*. Rumor held that Ivo was up to something even more nefarious than usual—and that he'd teamed up with the vampire Lothaire, the Enemy of Old, an ancient foe of theirs as well.

"If I had to guess," Regin said, "I'd bet the leeches are looking for me. Because I glow and I'm wicked smart. They probably want to breed with me."

Lucia sighed, hoping Regin was kidding. "Doubtless."

"And what the hell is Lothaire doing here? He was always creepy. It boggles the mind that some women think he's hot." She shook her head, sending blond locks bouncing over her glowing shoulders.

Another secret from Regin. Lucia was one of those women. She'd always found the powerful vampire—with his blond hair and light red irises—*compelling*, attractive in an is-he-going-to-kill-me-or-kiss-me type of way. And Lucia was far from alone.

"You think Annika's really going to find any leeches in NOLA?" Regin asked.

"Dunno." In the wake of this news, Annika, their fierce coven leader, and other Valkyrie had set out to find them in the city. "They've always stayed away from the States before." Which was why the Valkyrie coven had moved here. Lucia had heard that was the reason many Lykae had come here from Scotland as well.

"I hope they're in town. I want to face them!" Regin stood and brandished one of the two swords that she usually wore in sheaths crisscrossed over her back—in addition to the dagger sheath she customarily wore on her forearm. "I'll lunch on their balls!"

That was Regin's new threat: to lunch on enemies' balls. "Reege, when you threaten males with that, I don't think it has the result you intend. They think less *Lunchables*, more *tea bag*."

"Huh? Whatever!"

Before Annika had left, she'd ordered Regin and Lucia to contact traveling coven members and get them home at once. But above all else, they were to make sure

Emma, Annika's halfling foster daughter, returned to Val Hall from Paris.

Unfortunately, once they'd gotten in touch with Emma at last, the normally meek half vampire/half Valkyrie had *declined* to return. There was talk of a man she'd met—a *hot* man.

Annika was going to go berserk. Regin secretly called their coven leader Annika the Aneurismal for good reason.

"Dude, you've been antsy all day," Regin said, sheathing her sword. "What's wrong with you?"

I stood up a Lykae with delicious lips and intense golden eyes who, for a time, looked at me like I was the best thing in the entire world.

"Is it because of the new neighbors you saw?" Regin asked.

Lucia had reported back to the coven that Lykae were encroaching on Valkyrie territory.

"Ah-oooooo, werewolves in NOLA." Regin gave a snort. "If they're going to be sneaking out of the kennel, then I guess 'out of sight, out of mind' no longer applies, huh?" Regin had nicknamed their compound the *kennel*. To her delight, it'd caught on.

"Sneaking?" Lucia said. "They acted as if they owned this place."

"Well, maybe we need to Cesar Millan their asses and show them who's boss. Tsst, tsst!"

"I'm sure that'd do it," she answered, relieved when Regin's attention fell back to her papers. Sometimes her sister could be a handful even for Lucia, especially if Regin wasn't engaging in regular, fatiguing battles—

Lucia tensed, again thinking she'd spied movement in the bushes outside. Was it MacRieve?

Since the night they'd met, she'd learned much about him. When his older brother Lachlain had disappeared, Garreth MacRieve had become the *king* of the Lykae clan—though he'd never thought he'd be their leader. Before assuming the throne, he'd been wild, a ladies' man and a brawler, so bad he'd been nicknamed the Dark Prince.

He was the best kisser she'd ever imagined.

And what would Lucia say if MacRieve showed? *It seems you want to have an affair with me. But I can't have sex. Though I want to in the worst way.* Duty, chastity. Lucia was sick of them. Yet she'd had her shot to find a good man. Her shot at a normal life.

And I blew both targets by miles.

She squinted, identifying what had moved. A nefarious tomcat. As she exhaled a pent-up breath, she realized she'd been clutching her bow hard. This morning, she'd checked her abilities, and her skills remained intact. They must truly be penetration-based.

Still, all day she'd held on to her bow, absently running her fingers over the raised inscriptions. Skathi had hesitated to let Lucia leave Thrymheim with that bow, because of her "darkness."

To other Valkyrie, Lucia and Regin were relatively young, but Lucia had lived a long time and seen many things. Never had she encountered a male who brought out her darkness like MacRieve.

He might be her worst weakness. If so, he couldn't have come at a more inconvenient time. With a glare,

Lucia glanced over at their command center. Her duty was coming online soon. She and Regin would do as they did every five hundred years and prevent Cruach from rising.

But this time, instead of using Skathi's golden arrow to weaken him until the next Accession, Lucia wanted to discover a way to kill him *for good*.

One problem: the Broken Bloody One was a . . . deity. The ancient horned god of human sacrifices and cannibalism.

So now Lucia and Regin sought the only thing that could obliterate him, a *dieumort*—a god killer. Extremely rare, the dieumorts were created by the Banemen, a league of immortals from all factions. They'd discovered a means to destroy gods, who in turn sentenced all the Banemen to death. The league had disbanded and fled, hiding their power in talismans, weapons—even in beings—all over the world and adjoining planes.

Any vessel of the power was considered a dieumort. And there were whisperings of an *arrow*.

Lucia and Regin had hundreds of leads, everything from riddles to ancient journals to mapped clues. They were nearing the time for action, gearing up for their worldwide search, and Regin liked to spread out their calculations, tips, Post-its, and atlases for clarity when they knew no one was home.

Tonight Nucking Futs Nïx was the only one upstairs, but she didn't count—since she truly was mad. She could see the future so clearly that the present and past gave her fits. If Nïx did stroll by the command center, she'd probably forget or would look at the maps and think to herself, *Greeting cards. Must be December.*

Lucia and Regin had repeatedly requested her help in their quest. The first time they'd asked, she'd answered, "What's a dieumort?" Once they'd explained, she told them that she'd look into it. When they'd followed up, Nïx had said, "Now what's a dieumort . . . ?"

No one in their coven knew that Lucia and Regin spent a good deal of time researching the god killer, because they'd never told another soul what had happened with Cruach. Their sisters knew that Lucia felt pain when she missed a shot, but they didn't know *why*. Nor did they know Lucia was a Skathian. There simply was no reason to tell anyone. Lucia had cleaned up her mess last Accession, and the one before that, and she would again—

Her ears twitched just as Regin said, "Someone's coming!"

"Hide everything!"

"Hey, let's *don't*," Regin said. "I'm sick of sneaking around, being all furtive and guilty like we stole Freya's car and wrecked the alignment. Let's hang a lantern on this. Get everyone involved this time."

At the idea, Lucia grew nauseated. "You swore, Regin!"

"For once, I'd like the coven to know I'm a mastermind." At Lucia's unbending expression, Regin added, "No. Really. Do you know how bad their heads would

explode if they knew we are masterminds? Instead of
video-game flunkies?"

"Regin!"

Lucia must have looked as aghast as she felt, because she muttered, "Fine. We can act like we're fuck-
ups idling about. As per our usual. But if we cap a god,
I'm telling *everyone* I know! Two words: Press. Confer-
ence."

As they hastily hid their materials, Lucia said, "It's
probably Annika." Who would *not* welcome the news
Lucia and Regin would have to deliver. *Your foster
daughter met a man and told us she'd be home . . . basically whenever her happy ass felt like it.*

Finished stowing their papers, she and Regin sped
to the couch. By the time Annika burst through the
door, they were sitting in the great room, painting each
other's toenails while watching a TiVoed episode of
Survivor.

With no hint that the two were conspiring—to exterminate a god forever.

Gasping for breath, Annika asked them, "Is Myst
back? Or Daniela?" She weakly hung on the thick door,
peering out into the darkness. "Have they returned?"

Regin said, "We thought they were with you."

"Nïx?"

"Hibernating in her room."

"Nïx!" Annika yelled over her shoulder. "Get down
here!"

Lucia wanted to tell her, *Good luck with corralling
Nïx.* The soothsayer worked only on Nïx Standard
Time.

Annika slammed shut the front door and bolted it. "Is Emma on her way back yet?" She put her hands to her knees, still catching her breath.

Lucia and Regin shared a guilty look. "She's, uh, she's not coming back right now."

"*What*?" Annika shrieked. Aneurism in five, four, three, two . . .

Regin offered, "She met some hottie over there—"

Annika held up her hand. "Got to get out of here."

Where was the cataclysmic freakout over Emma? Lucia frowned. "I don't understand 'got to.' Sounds like you want us to leave?" *Or even to flee?* Valkyrie simply didn't flee—from anything. *Monsters flee from us.* Just as it'd always been.

You ran from that Lykae.

Shut up.

"There's a plane about to crash, isn't there?" Regin sighed. "That is *so* gonna hurt."

Lucia agreed. "I might run from a crashing plane—"

"Go . . . something's coming," Annika said. "*Now* . . ."

"We're safest here," Regin said, wriggling her toes and turning her attention back to her painting. "The inscription will keep anyone out."

The Valkyrie had bought protection from the House of Witches—their allies. The spell kept most nuisances out of Val Hall.

Regin quickly glanced up. "But, I, uh, I might not have renewed the inscription spell with the witches."

Lucia said, "I thought we were on auto-renewal. They charge our credit—"

"By Freya," Annika yelled, "*I—mean—now!*"

At that, Regin shot to her feet, lunging for her sword. Lucia was right behind her, scrambling for her bow. She'd just strapped on her quiver when the front door burst in.

EIGHT

◆━◆━◆

As Garreth ran for Val Hall, he began to grow uneasy, his hackles rising. Though Lykae loved to run—they'd traded tearing across the Highland hills and crags for tearing through the swamps and bayous—he took no comfort from the exertion.

He sensed something wasn't right but couldn't pinpoint his disquiet. He frowned when his sat-phone rang in his jeans pocket, then slowed to answer. "What?"

Munro said, "Can you come back to the compound? There's some news . . . possibly."

"Have you told anyone about Lousha?"

"No, I have no'! Where are you?"

"On my way to Val Hall. Concerned about my mate."

"Aye, Garreth, you need to know. Vampires are here, crawling all over the city."

Bluidy hell. "Which faction? Horde or Forbearer?" While the Horde was the Lykae's oldest and most hated enemy, the Forbearers were relatively new players in the Accession game. They were rumored to *forbear* from taking the flesh, refusing to drink blood directly from others.

Some in the Lore considered them noble vampires— as much an oxymoron for Garreth as *cuddly snakes*.

"It's the Horde," Munro said. "Ivo and Lothaire, specifically."

Ivo was cowardly—Garreth had never considered him a threat. Lothaire, the Enemy of Old, was a different story altogether. "What the fuck are they doing here?"

"The Horde might be . . . hunting Valkyrie."

Lucia. This was what he'd sensed. Just as Garreth was about to hang up, Munro said, "Wait! There's something else—"

"No' now!" Garreth yelled as he sprinted, slamming the phone closed so hard, it lay crushed in his palm.

Hunting Valkyrie. Lucia was in danger from the Horde, a filthy species responsible for the deaths of Garreth's entire family. If he lost his mate to them as well . . .

Never. Already turning.

Only a dozen miles away. Letting the beast out of the cage. *Never wanted her to see me like this . . .*

An immense *horned* vampire filled the doorway of Val Hall, peering keenly at Regin and Lucia with eyes the color of blood.

"What is *that*, Annika?" Regin drew one of her swords. "A vampire turned *demon*?"

"Not possible," Lucia said. "That's supposed to be a true myth." Whatever it was, it had made Annika run like hell, and she was a notorious vampire killer.

"Has to be." Annika panted. "Never seen one so powerful."

"Is he one of Ivo's minions?"

"Yes. Saw him giving orders to this one. They're still searching for someone."

Lucia nocked her arrows just as two more vampires traced behind the demon.

"Just go," Annika hissed to them. "Both of you—"

Ivo the Cruel materialized then, appearing directly in their living room, his red eyes surveying the scene.

"Hello, Ivo," Annika said gravely.

"Valkyrie," he responded with a bored sigh.

When he sank onto their couch and carelessly kicked his boots up on their coffee table, Annika said, "You still have all the arrogance of a king. Though you aren't one." She shook her head. "Can *never* be one."

"Just a wittle wapdog," Regin said with a snort. "Demestriu's wittle bitch man—"

Annika rapped the back of Regin's head.

"*What?*" Regin stomped her foot. "What'd I say?"

"Enjoy your taunts, Valkyries—they'll be your last." Ivo turned to the demon vampire. "She isn't here."

"Who?" Annika demanded.

"The one I seek," he answered cryptically. Which Valkyrie had he been searching for all over the world?

Suddenly, Lucia spotted the faint outline of a figure wavering behind Ivo. *Lothaire?* He'd traced into the room, lurking in the shadows, as sinister as she remembered, with his red-tinged irises and menacing face.

When Annika caught sight of him as well, the vampire put his finger to his lips. *Why would he be hiding from Ivo, his cohort?*

Ivo rubbed the back of his neck, clearly sensing a presence behind him. But when he whipped his head around, he saw nothing; Lothaire had already disappeared. Why wasn't the Enemy of Old standing shoulder to shoulder with Ivo, poised for a fight? Or shoulder to head—Lothaire was as big as the demon, and both towered over Ivo.

Seeming to dismiss his apprehension, Ivo ordered his minion, "Kill these three."

At once, the demon vampire teleported behind Annika with mind-boggling speed. The other two vampires traced for Regin and Lucia before Lucia could get a shot off. Regin traded sword strikes with one, while Lucia kicked the other in the chest, sending him back so she could take a shot. But he traced forward too quickly. Lightning flashed with increasing furor.

Out of the corner of her eye, Lucia spied Annika getting in some good hits on the demon vampire. As he yelled, spraying blood, Annika kicked him between his legs so hard he crashed into the ceiling.

But when he landed, he grabbed her neck and hurled her across the entire great room into the fireplace forty feet away. Annika hit headfirst, with so much force that the first layer of bricks turned to dust from the impact.

"Ah, gods! Annika!"

Just as another layer of bricks dropped onto her limp body, Regin scrambled from the vampire she'd been fighting to guard their fallen sister. Lucia dashed to Regin's side, finally garnering enough room for a shot.

"Lucia, the big one," Regin said between breaths. "As many arrows as you can. I'll pry his head off."

She added two arrows to the pair she'd already nocked, pulling the bowstring so tight, intending a kill shot. She released her volley . . .

The demon's muscles went rigid. He brushed three arrows aside like they were gnats. He *caught* the fourth.

Incomprehension. She'd . . . missed? *No! How?* Ivo's laughter echoed as the pain assailed her. She dropped to the floor from the sudden onslaught.

Too much! The remembered agony. Bones grinding . . . skin so tight.

Her body twisted and her fingers clenched as a shriek was ripped from her chest, then another and another. Every window and light in the manor shattered all around them, raining daggers of glass, leaving them in darkness.

Over the pain, she dimly heard a Lykae's beastly roar answering in the distance. . . .

Annika unconscious. Regin fighting off two. Want to tell her to run. Ivo and the demon watching. Can't move . . .

Another roar, even closer. MacRieve? He'd heard her. Was he coming for her? Would he help her sisters?

Through the chaos, she caught sight of movement across the murky room. White fangs and pale blue eyes stood out against the blackness, but she could barely see him through the dust and haze of her tears.

Then lightning illuminated him, and she recoiled, her pain redoubling. *Can't be him . . . can't be.*

He was massive, even more towering than before, his fangs and dark claws longer and sharper. A shadow of a ferocious beast flickered over his body.

MacRieve. A monster from legend.

As he crept over to where she shook on the floor, she gritted her teeth but couldn't move, crippled by the pain.

Crouching over her, he reached for her face with his huge hands. When his claws glinted like onyx, she flinched. What would he do . . . ?

He's trying . . . to pat my tears? "Shh, female." He scooped her into his arms while she stared up with dread. "Do no' fear me." His voice was guttural, his ice-blue eyes burning with possession.

In an instant, she comprehended two things: why immortals feared the Lykae.

And that she was this one's mate.

"Protect you."

Yes, he could never hurt her, would believe he'd been born to safeguard her life. "And my sisters," she weakly bit out.

He gazed at the door, clearly wanting to remove her from the threat—

"Please, Lykae . . . fight these vampires."

Finally, a jerk of his chin. He carried her out of the way, gently tucking her behind a table. In that beastly voice, he grated, *"I'll give you . . . their throats."* He gazed at her with such longing, but she was horrified to see him completely turned. He knew it, could see—she was in too much pain to hide her disgust.

He twisted from her and reared up with an awing fury against the vampires. After recovering from her surprise, Regin teamed up with the Lykae, each facing off against a vampire. The demon vampire held back, guarding an enthralled-looking Ivo.

There was no contest against MacRieve. With dizzying speed, he lunged forward before the vampire could trace a retreat, snapping his jaws closed on his opponent's neck. Bones cracked and arteries spurted as he ripped the vampire's throat out.

In a gruesome spray of gore, MacRieve spit it into the male's shocked face. Then his Lykae claws sliced through the rest of the vampire's neck cleanly. Head and body dropped to the crimson floor.

MacRieve turned to Regin's vampire next. She'd stabbed it several times, but it was tracing around her like crazy, materializing and vanishing, delivering blows. She couldn't land a killing strike.

Seeming to predict where the male would appear next, MacRieve sprang for the vampire. He tackled him between traces, pinning him to the floor. The Lykae's head descended, and he savaged that one's neck as well.

In mere moments, the two enemies were decapitated.

Confronted by a fully-turned, battle-maddened Lykae, Ivo and the horned one traced away, *fleeing*.

As soon as the threat was gone, MacRieve sped to Lucia's side, crouching with blood dripping from his fangs. She stared up with revulsion. *"No, no."* Just like before, a handsome face concealed a monster.

Delirious, shuddering, suddenly she was back in Cruach's lair. The Broken Bloody One was above her, blood pouring from his gritted fangs, splashing into her eyes. Crimson pools and grisly leavings all around them. *I give you meat and wine, my love. . . .*

"Lousha," MacRieve grated, rousing her back to the

present. "You're . . . safe." He tenderly skimmed the backs of his wet claws along her cheek.

"No, get away . . . get away from me."

Brows drawn as if in pain, he rose and loped out into the night.

The deadly shadow that was Garreth MacRieve disappeared.

But she knew he'd be back.

NINE

He *hadn't* been back.

But unfortunately for MacRieve, for most nights over the last week, he hadn't strayed far from Lucia.

"Celts' pelts! Celts' pelts!" Nïx cried happily, summing up the reason there was a hunting party of over two dozen Valkyrie gathered in a remote swamp on this desolate eve.

Lucia, Regin, Annika, Nïx, and several others were stationed in a carefully selected clearing, while even more Valkyrie were positioned throughout the misty bayou to call in sightings from distant vistas or trees.

All this effort was to trap . . . *Garreth*. And Lucia was the bait.

"Helloooo." Regin snapped her fingers. "Lore to Lucia!"

"Huh? Yeah."

"You're spacing again." Regin's look of irritation immediately shifted to one of concern. "It's too soon. I told Annika it was too soon."

Though Lucia had just missed a shot so recently, the coven had asked her to shank one more, predicting that if Garreth had come running the first time, he would again. "No, I'm good," Lucia said. She'd had to delay them a few days to build her strength—and nerve—back. She paid for each miss, had nearly forgotten how much, it'd been so long since the last time.

"You sure? Let's call this off." Regin alone comprehended how punishing this would be.

"I can handle it," she insisted, even as she nervously plucked her bowstring.

"All right. They wouldn't have asked, but. . . ."

But aggression against any of the Valkyrie was always met with a show of force—swift, vicious force. And a Lykae had seriously aggressed them.

Garreth's older brother, Lachlain MacRieve, had returned as if from the dead to reclaim his crown. But his very first order of business? Nabbing little Emmaline the Timid, Annika's foster daughter.

King Lachlain had been the "hottie" Emma had mistakenly trusted in Paris. And now he had her trapped at the Lykae castle in Scotland.

After Annika had gone aneurismal, shrieking until car alarms blared in three parishes, she'd hatched this plan: trap Lachlain's only living immediate family and use him as leverage to get Emma back.

Garreth MacRieve. With his firm lips and maddening touch . . .

Regin said, "If not the pain, then what gives with you? You're not thinking about MacRieve, are you?" She tossed up her dagger, catching the tip in her foreclaw. "Since you're his mate and all. And for the record, *ewww.*"

Lucia drilled her knuckle into Regin's upper arm. "Take it back."

"Yow!"

"How many times do I have to tell you? I'm not his mate! Full moon—no MacRieve. Case closed." To her everlasting confusion, he hadn't come for her the night it'd been full. Legend held that nothing could stop a male Lykae from reaching his mate on that night.

Lucia had been so sure she was his. Now she didn't know what to think.

Of course, she'd been pleased to confirm that she wasn't. Who would want a hulking male like that, one with a face that fell away, revealing a beast?

Yet, strangely, seeing him at his worst during the vampire attack hadn't been as bad as she'd imagined it. He'd been brutal and unsettling, but the terror she'd felt that night had ebbed—because once she got past her memories of Cruach, she saw how different MacRieve was from the Broken Bloody One.

That didn't mean she liked MacRieve's beast or anything; it just reminded her that *nothing* could be as bad as Cruach.

"Wait!" Nïx suddenly blurted. "Is anyone else seeing a pattern here?"

They all stared blankly at her.

She tilted her head. "Yeah, me neither." Then she grew enthralled with her palm. *Nïx, crazy as ever.*

Still rubbing her arm, Regin asked, "If you're not MacRieve's mate, then why does he keep following you?"

"I don't know," she lied. MacRieve had clearly ground out the words *protect you.* And she suspected he had been doing just that.

Just last night in the city, as she'd hunted back alleys for kobolds, an animus demon had been hunting *her*. Right when she'd been about to confront the colossal male, she heard a thud behind her. She'd whirled around and had seen the demon on the ground. Or at least his legs. The rest of his body had been concealed behind a building, but only for a split second, before he'd been yanked back out of her sight. . . .

Annika hastened by then, with her blond brows drawn together, checking all the logistics of her trap, as meticulous as ever. Though she could motivate people and was a legendary strategist, she was never supposed to be leader of their coven—the missing Valkyrie queen Furie was.

Once Annika had buzzed past them, Regin said, "Things are getting intense around here, eh, Luce? With the vemon attacks—"

"Dempire," Nïx corrected, glancing up from her palm. "Demon vampire equals *dempire*, not vemon."

Regin shook her head hard. "Which sounds so lame. Say it in a sentence, Nïx. 'I got my ass kicked by a dempire.' Forget it! Vampire demon. *Ve—mon*."

"You're taking this stance just to be contrary," Nïx sniffed.

In truth, things *were* getting intense. The Valkyrie were on red alert. They'd hired the Wraiths, the Ancient Scourge, to protect Val Hall. That measure was drastic, but the vampire demon had shaken them.

Vemons were supposed to be truly mythical. The one they'd faced had been nearly invincible, which made them wonder how a creature like that had come to be—

and how many more of them existed. They'd known Ivo was up to something nefarious.

"And now the long-lost werewolf king is in play as well," Regin said, tossing up her dagger.

Lucia herself had spoken to Lachlain, the werewolf king. That long-distance call had been so surreal, for more than one reason. She'd been standing in a room full of Valkyrie, and neither they, nor Lachlain, had any idea she'd been with his brother mere days ago, occupied with—oh, how had Garreth put it?—*riding his crotch like a wanton as she sucked his tongue.*

As the "reasonable" one in the coven, Lucia had entreated Lachlain to release Emma. He'd refused. She'd asked him to be gentle with her. He hadn't sounded capable of gentle.

At least he hadn't seemed to *want* to hurt Emma—and he had protected her from a vampire search party, killing the three who'd come for her.

Annika's own attempts to further *negotiate* with Lachlain had ended with his roared *"She's mine!"* and Annika's chilling vow to go hunting for "Celts' pelts."

Afterward, everyone in the coven had voiced disgust for the Lykae, calling them dogs, animals, or worse, sub*human.* Making Lucia's guilt mount. Aside from her own personal reasons, she simply had no business being with a Lykae.

Regin leaned in. "Luce, what's really going on with you?"

"I just think this is a bad idea." She plucked her bowstring faster.

"He's an animal. One hunt among many."

But that "animal" had used his unimaginable strength and ferocity to save their lives. Another example of how different he was from Cruach.

Lowering her voice, Regin said, "We keep secrets from everyone else—*not* from each other. I know you're holding back from me. Haven't I proved that I'm a vault where your secrets are concerned?"

Guilt flared. "Yes, always." This was too true, and besides, could anything be as shameful as Cruach? "Look, in a moment of temporary insanity, I might have . . . MacRieve and I"—she paused, then added in a rush— "we might have fooled around a little."

Regin's glowing skin paled. *"What?"*

Remaining away from Lucia had taken everything in Garreth. He needed to ease her pain from the night of the vampire attack, was frenzied to slaughter more of their kind for her.

Never had he seen a being in agony like his mate after she'd missed a shot. When he'd stormed into Val Hall, she'd been curled on the floor, writhing with her fingers knotted.

Gazing up at me in horror. He was desperate to erase that image of himself, to remind her how he normally looked. But the Instinct warned him to take it slowly with her. *—She will run. Be cautious.—*

So he'd been shadowing her, camping in the bayou near Val Hall. As long as Ivo, Lothaire, and that demon vampire remained at large, still looking for a specific Valkyrie, Garreth refused to leave the area, not even to return to the Lykae compound.

Leaving behind his kinsmen hadn't been as disagreeable as he'd thought—especially not those Lykae who'd found their mates within the clan. They had it so easy, were nauseatingly content. *How I envy them.*

But Garreth could still safeguard his own mate. He hadn't been able to spare the rest of his loved ones from the Horde—but he'd be damned before they hurt his woman. Whether Lucia wanted it or not, he'd watched over her every second he could. Except for the night of the full moon.

When he'd made *other* arrangements.

Not that she needed protection within her home. The disquieting manor house at Val Hall had just grown more so. After the vampire attack, the Valkyrie had called upon the Wraiths, the Ancient Scourge, to protect them. Red-robed skeletal females flew in a circle around Val Hall, their guard impenetrable. Each time a Valkyrie exited or entered, she lopped off a lock of her hair, handing it to the Wraiths—as if in payment. The creatures would then cackle with glee over the token.

Tonight, Lucia and at least two others had gone out in the bayou. She'd peered keenly into the darkness as if she sensed him, so he'd been keeping his distance.

But for how much longer could he silently follow . . . ?

TEN

⬥⬥⬥

"Keep your voice down!" Lucia hissed to Regin. "And you didn't tell me this? I mean, it *is* gross, and I will rag you about this for the rest of our immortal lives."

"It's not that bad—"

Regin gave a mock shudder. "Dude must've been picking vampire flesh from his teeth for days. And you kissed him with that mouth? In any case, do you want Skathi to kick your ass? Or repo your powers? Who am I going to hang out with when you're a talentless nobody?"

Lucia glared.

"Wait! It all becomes clear—this is your chance to make up for that grossity, Luce. Bag and tag the Lykae!"

"Has everyone forgotten what he did for us?" Mac-Rieve could have escaped with Lucia but he'd stayed and defended them. He'd done that *for her.* And how was she about to repay him? With deceit.

Annika overheard that and crossed over to where Lucia was setting up her shot. "It seems *you* have forgotten his brother has my foster daughter." She punctuated her words by cocking her tranquilizer gun. "I know you don't feel right about this after what he did for us, but we need him to get my Emma back from that fiend."

"I'm here, aren't I?" Lucia said testily, making everyone stare. Levelheaded Lucia didn't get testy often. "Though I'm the one who's going to pay for this."

"No one wants you to get hurt," Annika said, then added more softly, "But, Lucia, you know Em must be terrified."

Cosseted Emma would in fact be *losing her shit*. Though Lachlain knew she was a half-vampire, and most of his family had been murdered by them, he hadn't sounded like he planned to hurt Emma. Didn't matter. Em would be terrified just by what he was. She didn't come by her name Emma the Timid lightly—she was afraid of her own shadow.

If only she'd been able to trace like other vampires, then she could've escaped Lachlain. They'd tried to teach her, but Emma had always been too weak. . . .

"Yo, Annika. How much tranquilizer do you got in there?" Regin asked. "I don't want to merely piss Mac-Rieve off. You didn't see him fight—because of the being covered in bricks and all—but he's *brutal*."

"I got the mixture from the witches," Annika said. "They swore it'd take down elephants."

Regin shook her head. "Dude's a werewolf, that won't be en—"

"*Fifty* elephants."

"Oh."

"Are you ready?" Annika asked Lucia.

Sure, Annika. I'm ready to go through agonizing pain, so you can catch my would-be lover. Why the hell not?

Though her thoughts were crazed, Lucia evenly said, "I'll do what I have to in order to get Emma back."

"Good," Annika said with a firm nod, moving to stand at her side. "Then let's get this started."

As the others took their places, Lucia readied her bow, nocking an arrow. *Duty to family. Loyalty to them and Emma.* Gritting her teeth, she aimed for a distant cypress, drawing the bowstring. At the last millisecond, just as Lucia's fingers relaxed to release the string, Annika shoved her to the left. The arrow missed the tree.

At once, pain seared her—the agony of bones grinding, poisoned blood wrung from her body. . . .

Lightning exploded, and she dropped to the ground, helpless not to scream.

Lucia's scream pierced the night.

Roaring in answer, Garreth raced in her direction. *Vampires are hunting Valkyrie.* And she'd just screamed. If they hurt his woman. . . .

His fangs sharpened; rage burned hot. *My mate in jeopardy.* Somehow he charged faster. Tree limbs raked his face and body, animals skirting out of his way as he plunged deeper into the swamp.

He was already turning. *Letting the beast out of the cage.* He knew he horrified her like this but he couldn't help it—the need to protect overwhelmed him.

As Garreth ran for her, he scented other Valkyrie. There must be vampires, attacking in number. But as he neared, he smelled none.

He burst into a clearing, spied Lucia on the ground, twisting in pain.

Turning even more fully. He'd slaughter whoever did this.

—What you see is not so.—

He felt a prick on his neck, slapped at it. A dart? *Oh, fuck no!* Still struggling to reach her, he felt his body go boneless, his legs giving way.

Garreth crashed to the ground right beside Lucia, landing on his side. As Lucia gazed at him vacantly through tears, smirking Valkyrie surrounded them. Realization struck. Lucia had done this on purpose. She was the bait.

"You . . . helped them?" His words were slurred, rough.

She nodded. Despite the fact that she'd deceived him, he couldn't stand the sight of her tears. He reached forward to brush her face, but his arm went limp. "Why?" he rasped. "Why, Lousha?"

She whispered, "He took her . . . took Emma."

"Who?"

"You don't know?"

"Know . . . what?" He saw her lips moving but heard nothing as consciousness faded.

ELEVEN

"For the love of all that's unholy, *will he not shut up*?" Regin demanded, pausing her video game.

MacRieve had been roaring in his cage in the basement for hours now, keeping Lucia on the razor's edge—an uncomfortable place to be with her muscles still aching from the night before. Gods, how she paid for those missed shots.

And more unnerving, Nïx was perched on the back of the sofa, absently braiding her long sable hair, studying Lucia's reactions. Nïx, usually so vacant eyed, was watching her keenly. *She knows how I feel about him. . . .*

Or how she'd *felt* about him—*before* Lucia had seen him turned, his face savage, his fangs so sharp.

"Let me the bluidy hell out of here!" sounded up from below.

Regin glared at Lucia, as if this were *her* fault. "He is harshing my buzz, and I am"—Regin turned to yell over her shoulder—"not interested!"

"Open this fucking cage, you glowing bluidy freak!" Gods, he was fierce.

Yet as soon as the thought arose, she recalled how he'd awkwardly patted her tears. And last night, even after realizing what she'd done to him, he'd still reached for her.

"Somebody needs to make Scooby a snack or something, 'cause *this howling is freaking old!*"

They could hear him banging against the bars, but he could never break them. Though the Lykae were the strongest species in all the Lore, the metal was indestructible, made so by spells purchased from the witches.

"You go, Luce," Regin said, eyeing her video game longingly.

"What do you think I can do?"

"He's attracted to you. Skeevy as that is . . . At least go try. Just don't lift tail for him or anything."

"Regin!" Lucia snapped, slanting a telling glance at Nïx.

With a roll of her eyes, Regin said, "Oh, yeah, like the soothsayer doesn't already have your number."

Nïx winked at her.

"Come on, I've never gotten this far in the game."

Lucia rose slowly, stifling a wince when her muscles protested. "Fine, I'll go," she said, acting put out over seeing MacRieve, though she'd wanted to since he'd awakened. She wanted to finally thank him for saving her life—for painstakingly hiding her away, then rising up like wrath embodied against the vampires who'd invaded her family's home.

Apparently, the beast could be tender. Or deadly. No matter what he was, or what was inside him, he deserved her gratitude.

And she wouldn't mind a chance to find out why she

reacted so intensely to him. How could she still be so drawn to him, even after she'd seen what he was inside?

"You owe me one, Reege," Lucia added in an aggrieved tone.

Nïx easily saw through her act and winked again, growing happy, entertained by Lucia's behavior. But when the soothsayer followed her to the basement door, Lucia turned and said, "No, I want to talk to him alone."

"Even when I already know everything you're about to say? Just as I already knew about the saliva swap at the swamp you two attended weeks ago." Then, more gently, Nïx added, "You like him?"

Lucia sighed, leaning her shoulder against the wall. "I don't understand it. He's like my kryptonite. Just his brogue . . ."

"Makes your claws curl?"

"Big-time. When I was with him, it was like I had no defense. He got this look in his eyes, and my mind went blank," she admitted. "Have you ever fought an opponent you had no defense against? Like a fire breather or an acid spitter?"

"Once I faced a female with diamond skin," Nïx said breathlessly. "I was transfixed—even as she was choking the life out of me."

"Really?"

"No, I saw that character on *X-Men*. I just wanted to commiserate. Alas, I have no weaknesses."

"Except your insanity," Lucia pointed out.

Sigh. "Well played, Archer. Then carry on. . . ."

With a deep breath, Lucia opened the door. When she descended the steps, MacRieve's gaze locked on her, his eyes ice blue, his dark brown hair disheveled. He wore another pair of worn jeans and a long-sleeve black sweater. Simple clothing. Though she might yearn for more elaborate garments for herself, she liked simple for men. *Another grudging check in MacRieve's plus column.*

He immediately clamped his hands on the bars, straining to break them, his arm and shoulder muscles rippling.

"You can't budge them, MacRieve. They've been reinforced by the witches."

He released them at once, with his lip curled in disgust. She'd always heard the Lykae had an aversion to witches. Evidently, that rumor was true.

"Why've you done this to me? You help them trap me after I saved your life from those vampires? You're bluidy welcome!"

And there went her plan to express gratitude to him. She averted her gaze, letting her hair fall over her face.

"In thanks you cage me in this shite hole."

She glanced around. Inside the cage were facilities and a nice cot. "It isn't that bad down here," she said, inwardly conceding that it might be a bit dank—the half-basement had been built before people realized cellars didn't really work in soggy southern Louisiana. "It's got a window," she muttered defensively.

"Lousha, you can free me."

"Bring that up again, and I'll leave."

"Then tell me what I'm doing here!"

"Would you believe me if I told you that Lachlain

lived? And that he kidnapped my niece Emmaline, claiming she was his mate?"

He froze. "Nay, I would no'. You've made a mistake."

"There's no mistake." She frowned. "How is it that you wouldn't know this?"

"Have no' been back to the compound in a while. And now, conveniently, I *canna* to verify your tale. How long will I be down here?"

"Until we get Emma back," she answered.

"And you'd do this after I saved you—and your sisters?"

"I don't owe you an explanation. We're enemies."

"No, we're no'! We're . . ."

"We're *what*?"

"Compatible," he answered so smoothly.

"Why did you come to Val Hall that night, anyway?"

He hiked those broad shoulders. "I was in the neighborhood."

"And you were last night as well? You've obviously been following me. You told me I wasn't your mate. Did you lie?"

"You're going to accuse *me* of dishonesty when you've just used yourself as bait to trap me, and then lied to my face?" When she was clearly unconvinced, he said, "Think about it—if you'd been my mate, then how would I have stayed away the night of the full moon?"

"A cage like this."

"Lykae do *no'* ally with witches." He seemed to stifle a shudder at the thought.

So I'm not his. "MacRieve, your brother *is* alive."

"You're saying he's come back from the dead after

one hundred and fifty years, and his queen, this Emma, is a Valkyrie?"

"Not exactly." *She's a halfling vampire.* How would Garreth react to the fact that his brother's mate—though bashful and kind—was a blood drinker?

"Tell me *what*, exactly," Garreth demanded.

"Just forget it."

"Then I'll have to see Lachlain's return to believe it," he said, even as hope welled inside him. Though it was a fantastical tale, Garreth himself had never accepted Lachlain's death. For decades, he had searched to find the mystically hidden Horde capital. After the first thirty years of wondering and investigating, he'd admitted to himself that it might be better if Lachlain had been killed.

Demestriu was known to torture in unimaginable ways.

Now, if Garreth allowed himself to truly believe his brother had returned and then learned it was a mistake . . . he didn't think he could lose Lachlain twice.

"You weary my patience with this, Lousha." She did, and would have even more if his "capture" hadn't been somewhat voluntary—he'd woken briefly as they'd transported him here. Checking his bindings, about to rip free of them, he'd asked, "Where are you taking me?"

She'd been wan, her eyes glassy with lingering pain. "To Val Hall."

Garreth had stopped struggling. After all, he was a Lykae—no cage could hold him and she was taking him into her home. He'd thought this would prove to be a fortuitous turn. He'd be closer to her, better able to protect her. Now he was trapped. *Bluidy witches!*

Taking a seat on the floor, he leaned back against the wall, drawing a knee up. "Sit," he commanded, adding in a softer tone, "It's the least you can do."

With a glare, she drew a chair in front of the cage and gingerly sat. *She's hurting still.* He hardened himself against the concern he felt. "Why were you in agony the night of the vampire attack? I scented no blood on you, saw no injury."

"It's not your concern."

"So you *do* feel pain when you miss a shot?"

She looked startled, distinctly on edge, letting her hair fall over her face again. She was wearing thick braids over her pointed ears, but the rest of her shining mane flowed freely, locks tumbling over her forehead. "What could you possibly know about me?"

"More than you think. Made you my subject of study. Dinna find out all I'd aimed to, though. Most folks just know you're *the Archer.*"

Seeming relieved, she said, "That's me. All there is to know."

"What about your family, your birth mother? Who were her people?"

She glanced over her shoulder at the stairs before facing him again. "I don't know who she was. I don't even know *what* she was."

"She could've been a Lykae?"

Lucia shrugged her slim shoulders. "For all I know."

"Ah, so that's why you're more reasonable with other

factions. You could be related to them," he observed. "In any case, if your intent was to be mysterious, you've succeeded."

"Oh, *I'm* mysterious? You showed up out of nowhere to decapitate two vampires in my living room."

"Ask me anything, and I'll answer."

She raised her brows in challenge. "Really, Dark Prince?"

"Aye. That's what I was called." Garreth had never thought he'd be king, not with an immortal older brother, and he'd behaved accordingly, saying and doing things Lachlain never could have. Garreth had been a wild one, dubbed the Dark Prince before he'd reached twenty. *And yes, the association with Lucifer was on purpose.* Responsible Lachlain used to bail him out of scrape after scrape. "You've been digging for background on me?"

"Digging? Your background's pretty notorious."

"Maybe. I've doubtless made mistakes." *Big ones.* If he'd been more involved with the clan, and less involved with himself, perhaps his brother wouldn't have set off alone that fateful night. "But at least *I* own my actions when I bollix things up." *Unlike you, little mate.*

Ignoring his pointed comment, she asked, "Why have you brought your people here? To Louisiana?"

"After my brother went missing, many of the Lykae wanted to be as far away from the Horde as possible. This was no' the first place we picked, believe me." Once he'd inherited the crown, he'd cleaned his act up, then begun scouring the earth for a new home for them, wanting to do at least that for his people. "But in the end, it made sense."

After another glance over her shoulder, she said, "It made sense to trespass in Valkyrie territory?"

Aye, or I might no' ever have found you. "We're no' so bad as neighbors, lass. And the Valkyrie and Lykae are no' enemies."

"Except at the Accession. When we're all forced to fight."

Every five hundred years, pivotal events in the Lore began to take place, each one forcing conflicts between factions. Some said this concentration of incidents was a mystical mechanism to cull an ever-growing population of immortals.

There was no grand war to decide it all—at least there hadn't been in the past—but the battles and confrontations made for a war of attrition. Once the Accession had swept through, the faction with the most players still alive won. "The Lykae will no' be fighting any Valkyrie this Accession."

"You know what's driving all this. You won't have any control over it," she said with another glance over her shoulder.

"Would your sisters frown on the fact that you're attracted to me?"

She faced him at once. "I'm not!"

"Lie to yourself, Lousha. No' to me. I was there with you that night, remember? You might be trying no' to recall it, but it's seared into my head."

"No, actually I want to recall it—I like to remember my mistakes. So I don't repeat them."

"A mistake then? Is that what Valkyrie call scream-wrenching orgasms?"

Between gritted teeth, she said, "I asked you not to do certain things, and you just ignored me."

"Like what?"

"Like not taking off my underwear. You ripped them from me, then *stole* them! Why would you ever?"

He cast her a shameless grin. "To do unseemly things with them."

She held up her hand. "I don't want to hear more. Again, MacRieve, why did you come to Val Hall that night?"

"Because you were screaming like a banshee? I saw scattered arrows on the floor. No' a one bloodied. Did you pay for missing? Maybe you did make a deal with the devil to shoot like that."

Her eyes flashed silver. "You know nothing!" She shot to her feet and ran, climbing the stairs without looking back.

"Come back here, Lousha!" The charade was over; he wanted out of the cage. Clenching his jaw, he tried to bend the bars—nothing. "Damn you, Valkyrie."

Once he got loose . . . all the witches in the world couldn't protect her.

TWELVE

◄━◆━►

Lucia had told MacRieve that she wasn't bound by his animalistic needs. And in that deep rasp, he'd replied, "After one night with me, Lousha, *you will be*."

He'd been right. She couldn't stop thinking about him, recalling how he'd touched her.

Now in the dead of night, she lay in her bed—a *single* bed because she was never supposed to be sharing it— puzzling over the male trapped downstairs. Desperate to determine his power over her, she stared up at the ceiling fan, as if it would have all the answers to the conundrum that was Garreth MacRieve.

Granted, the Lykae had obvious attributes: his golden eyes, his muscular body, his broad shoulders that seemed made for her to hold on to.

His firm lips. Not a minute passed without her remembering how they'd felt on hers. She didn't know how she'd gone so long without kissing. Or how she could ever go back.

Lucia even appreciated the ferocity she'd witnessed when he'd bitten that vampire's throat out. But something more was at work, some connection to him. Even during their exchange earlier tonight, he'd affected her. But he hadn't given her *that* look—the one that said he was about to do wicked things to her body—which was probably the only reason her mind hadn't gone blank.

She feared he was the type of man women got reckless over, made stupid decisions for. He made her think, *Vows of chastity? What vows?*

That night in the swamp—when she'd been so close to letting him take her—had been the first time she'd had an orgasm with a man. No wonder she was continually thinking about him—he'd made her climax. *Of course.* Naturally she'd want to experience it again.

Just recalling how his eyes had been filled with lust made her heart race all over again. She'd witnessed him almost completely naked, with only his jeans at his knees, and had seen tantalizing glimpses of his thick erection. If she'd had any hesitation about being with a male, or fears from her past, he'd quelled them with his toe-curling kisses against her panties.

Now her nipples budded against her camisole, her breaths quickening. She was wet for him, aching for more. She turned onto her front—which was worse, so she flipped back over. Glaring at the ceiling, she realized there was no fighting it.

Her hand eased into her panties.

Something woke Garreth, putting him on edge. It was an uncanny feeling, as if the air were crackling with electricity. Shouldn't be surprising—lightning struck constantly in this bizarre place, like ongoing mini-explosions.

Some bolts hit so close, the entire manor quaked, dust raining from the ceiling—ominous signs in a structure built so long ago. And between the lightning strikes, he heard Valkyrie shrieks, the drone of the TV, and jaunty video game music that was like nails on slate.

Adding to his misery, Garreth could scent Lucia at every hour, could hear her voice, hear her whispers to the glowing freak:

"I sense he's getting more powerful than ever before," Lucia had said this afternoon. *Who?*

"Then I'm glad we have a back-up plan," Regin had replied. *Back-up to what?*

"Everything depends on finding it. If I have to go inside for this round, then I want to be able to get back out." *Find what? Where the bluidy hell is she going?*

"How much time do we have?"

"Maybe a year. Before they come . . ."

Before who—or what—came? What had Lucia meant?

It maddened him, and she wouldn't return no matter how much he bellowed. The most mysterious female he'd ever imagined, and all day and night, the mystery deepened—

Suddenly, he caught the scent . . . of her desire? He felt the current in the air, sensed it came from her.

Realization hit. *No, it canna be. She would no' be. . . .*

Lucia's eyes slid shut as her fingers dipped into her panties, seeking—and finding—wet flesh.

With a sigh, she gave a stroke against her swollen clitoris, fantasizing about MacRieve's body. The already continual lightning built. Another stroke as she envisioned his poor battered chest, packed with muscle. She rubbed faster . . . faster . . .

His torso tapering to his narrow hips. She moaned. *That trail of dusky hair leading down to his shaft—*

"Lousha!" he bellowed.

She shot up in bed, yanking her hand away. He couldn't know . . . surely not.

"Come to me!"

He did know! *Oh, gods, what do I do now?* Her sisters were already suspicious, intimating that maybe the interest went both ways. *What to do?* Her eyes darted around the room.

When he yelled her name again, she leapt from the bed and snatched a robe from her closet. Hastening from her room, she stole down to the basement.

Once she entered, he quieted. Like the trapped beast that he was, he eyed her every move.

"What's the matter with you?" she demanded as she neared the cage. "Why do you keep roaring for me? I'm the one with *no* power to free you."

"You can unlock this."

"I won't. Save your breath."

Studying her expression for weakness, and apparently finding none, he changed tactics.

"Then come to me." His irises wavered from blue back to gold.

"Why?"

"So I can finish for you what you started in your bed."

She felt her cheeks flame. "I don't . . . wh-what are you talking about?"

"Come here, Lousha." His voice was as mesmerizing as his eyes.

"If you think to seduce me to free you, it won't happen."

"Seducing you is its own end, love."

She hesitated, glancing over her shoulder.

"Remember how good it was that night in the bayou? How I made you feel?"

A night of sweat and need and lightning. She shivered at the memory. "That was a mistake—I shouldn't have encouraged you."

"Come to me." He had *that* look in his eyes again.

"And do what?" *Mind going blank.* Damn him, what hold did he have over her?

"Let me kiss you."

Her lips parted and lightning struck just outside. "Through the bars?" That aspect actually appealed to her. The bars were about six inches apart, so it'd be possible for them to kiss—but unlikely to get out of hand.

I could control the situation better than before.

"Aye. Just need to kiss you. Touch you."

"No, I can't," she whispered, even as she found herself easing closer to him, as if drawn by a magnet. "Why do you keep pursuing me—when you say I'm not your mate?"

"Because, Valkyrie, you're the most desirable female I've ever known."

And you're the most desirable male I've ever imagined. Yes, through the bars. She could satisfy her curiosity— determine his appeal. *So I can better fight it.*

Her legs felt weak. *I could control it; we'd just bring*

each other pleasure. When she reached forward to steady herself, putting her fists on the bars, he snatched her hand. He sucked the tip of her finger—the one she'd masturbated with—between his lips, growling, "Ah, gods, woman, *your taste . . .*"

Lightning built to a furor, and she melted for him.

THIRTEEN

※◆◆◆►

Garreth sucked, shuddering in bliss. Licking her honey from her own finger. When he'd scented her desire earlier, every muscle in his body had clenched with want. Lykae males yearned to pleasure their mates, and he was crazed to satisfy Lucia.

The cage, her deceit, the unsettling news she'd delivered earlier—all became secondary to the need to make her come, as she obviously yearned to.

Slowly, he withdrew her finger from his mouth. Cupping the back of her neck, he brought her face close to the bars for a kiss, slanting his lips over hers. With each stroke of his tongue, she began to relax. She grasped his shoulders, her wee claws digging into them.

He broke the kiss to say, "If you start this, Lousha, you finish it."

Her eyes were half-lidded. "What does that mean?"

"It means that unless you're going to make me come this time, you'll be icing down my aching bollocks, just as I did that last night."

She frowned, "Why didn't you, you know . . . ?"

"I *did*," he rasped. "Again and again with those sleek panties of yours wrapped around my shaft. I could still taste you on my lips. It maddened me."

Her breath hitched at that, her eyes growing silvery.

"Do you want to start this, then?"

She looked dazed. "I . . . we . . ." With a hard shake of her head, she said, "We can't have sex." Her eyes darted. "Because of the bars."

"They're half a foot apart—I should be able to squeeze my shaft between them."

"MacRieve, I'm serious!"

"The bars would no' stop me. I could take you from behind, just spread you in front—"

"N-no sex."

Garreth narrowed his eyes. Could she be . . . *virgin*? At a thousand years old? Maybe *that* was why she'd stopped them the other night. "Verra well, no sex," he lied. *Until I seduce you into it.*

"Then . . . then what do you want from me?"

"I want to stroke you until you come and have you do the same for me."

She swallowed. "Would you turn again?"

"Nay, lass," he said absently, struck anew by how lovely she was. Her long hair curled around her elven face, the tresses as shiny as the modest silk robe she wore. Her whiskey-colored eyes were sultry, her cheeks flushed.

But he wanted to see her body, naked to his gaze. "Let me take this off you." He reached forward to tug free the sash on her robe, then skimmed the material over her shoulders. When it pooled at her feet, she was left in skimpy panties and a filmy camisole top. Her nipples were hard, her lips parted and moist, so sensual. . . .

My mate's incomparable.

At this point, he wanted to chew through the bars to get to her.

Even more so once he worked her top off, baring plump, perfect breasts that taunted his grasping palms. The peaks were dusky rose and begged for his lips around them.

In a moment of insight, he realized he could forgive much in the face of those exquisite breasts. He'd best never let her know that.

"Look at your nipples pouting to be sucked." He reached forward, pinching one to hold it in place as he lowered his head. She seemed to stop breathing.

He brought his mouth close, tickling her with his breaths as his free hand skimmed down her flat stomach, but she tensed.

"Uh, wait. What about you?" Her hands went from clutching his shoulders to exploring his body. "You said we'd *both* touch each other."

Her words made his shaft go so hard, he thought he'd bust through his zipper. When she brushed her fingers near his cock, he shot upright. "Take it out for me, then."

As he shook with anticipation, Lucia drew down his zipper. Tentatively she reached into his pants for his shaft, gasping when it sprang forth. He thought she whispered, *"Oh my."* She also seemed to be about to lose her nerve.

"Ease me, Lousha."

Though she nodded up at him, she acted as if she'd never done this before. Sensing her hesitation, he took her hand, placing his cock in her warm palm. Just preventing himself from running his shaft over it, he grated, "Make a fist."

She couldn't close her fingers around it. "I can't," she murmured, then glared at him when he had to bite back a chuckle.

"Then just stroke it like that." With her first tentative glide up and down, his breath whistled out. "You doona know how good that feels tae me."

As she began slowly stroking, she gazed up at him, her dark eyes studying his reaction. His little mate was learning what pleased him. The idea of that gratified him beyond measure.

"There's my good lass. *More.*" When she did it harder and faster, he groaned, "I've got tae touch you now. Take off your panties."

She shook her head.

He growled with frustration. "Woman! When I finally do get your panties off, I'm going tae be wedged so deep inside your body, you will no' know where you end and I begin."

"They stay *on.*"

"Then I'll be going *in.*" As he eased his fingers into her panties, he felt her body trembling—with nervousness? Eagerness? He kissed her again, twining his tongue with hers, as he dipped lower through soft curls.

When he found slick flesh that wept at his touch, he groaned against her mouth. She gasped against his. Between kisses, he grated, "Gods, you feel so damned good . . . hot and wet for me."

But when he delved near her opening, she tensed. *So*

that's the way of it? She *was* a virgin. She began to draw back from the kiss.

"Shhh, Lousha, I will no' do that again. Only this." His forefinger covered her swollen little clitoris and slowly rubbed.

With a moan, she tightened her grip on him, panting as she stared up into his eyes.

Building her pleasure, he lazily stroked her while thrusting into her fist. His hip bones banged against the bars, but he didn't care. Once she was ready to receive him, was wetting his fingers with need, it was everything he could do not to turn her around and take her. He could force her back to him, capturing her wrists behind her, then be inside her slick heat in a heartbeat's time.

—*She'd never trust you again.*—

Yet it was so close. *A thousand years I've waited for this. . . .*

Just as he'd taken her right to the edge, MacRieve slowed his touch to keep her in agony, murmuring "*Do you ache here?*"

Her toes curled—she realized she loved it when he talked to her like this, with his accent growing so thick. In fact, she was learning much from this time with him.

She'd been amazed to discover how such a small touch, a mere caress on his shaft, affected him so strongly. But if that caress had affected him, this hard, steady milking made him *crazed*. As she neared her peak, the head of his penis grew moist, and he bucked his hips madly.

"Just hold me tight. I'll do the rest." At her ear, he grated, "Now do you feel we're *enemies*, Lousha? When I'm about tae come in your hand and you on mine?"

The *last* thing she considered him at that moment was an enemy.

"Has another male made you feel this?"

"No, no!"

"Then tell me I'm the only one." When she didn't, he slowed his fingers and she whimpered in distress. "Tell me, Lousha." He kissed her hard, seeming to brand her.

Against his lips, she moaned, *"You're the only one."*

In reward, he cupped her flesh completely, pressing the heel of his palm against her clitoris. As he worked it against the swollen bud, she went boneless, her eyes sliding shut. In a harsh rasp, he commanded her, "Look at me when you come!"

Her lids fluttered open. Their eyes met. *Lightning, heat, tension building, building. Then release.*

He covered her mouth with his own, drowning out her scream, as the pleasure went on and on. . . .

But when she could take no more, he wouldn't let her stop. "Again!" His fingers rubbed her clitoris so fast it was like he'd put a vibrator against her.

"MacRieve, oh, gods!" And she climaxed so easily for him. He kissed her once more as she cried out against his lips.

He finally broke away to say, "Watch me coming for you. I want you tae see it." His shaft was throbbing under her fingers . . . he seemed in torment, his expression agonized as she worked his engorged flesh.

Then with a brutal yell, he began to ejaculate. "You madden me, Lousha. *Madden me!*" As his semen spurted before her dazed eyes, he buried his face in her hair, groaning deeply, grinding his shaft into her fist as arc after arc of seed poured from him. . . .

When he was spent at last, he drew her hand away. As they fought to catch their breath, he leaned his forehead down to hers. "*That* was why I keep pressuring you. I knew it would be this way with you. You pleasured me well, lass. Tell me I did for you."

She murmured, "You know you did."

He grinned. "Oh, aye, just wanted to hear you say it. And it will only get better between us."

She drew back, shaking her head. "We can never do this again—it was a mistake."

"Because I'm a Lykae? We're no' so bad, Lousha."

"This won't end well between our factions. The Valkyrie are ready to go to war." Already, Annika planned to storm Kinevane castle to retrieve Emma. They were to leave at dawn.

He gave a harsh laugh. "Again, the Lykae will no' war with Valkyrie, no' while I'm king."

"That's just it, MacRieve—you're not."

She spied a flare of hope in his eyes before he schooled his features. Earlier, she'd wondered how Garreth would feel about Lachlain's return. Would he be gladdened to have his brother back? Or angered that he'd be demoted to a prince?

She should have known Garreth MacRieve loved his

brother. As much as the Lykae were known for their ferocity, they were also known for their loyalty.

"If I'm king or my brother is, there will be no war."

"MacRieve, the Valkyrie will get Emma back, and if Lachlain comes after her . . . he'll lose his life. Just when he's gotten it back."

FOURTEEN

Yesterday, a band of Valkyrie had gone to Kinevane Castle in Scotland to retrieve Emma, but had returned empty-handed.

Today, Emma had escaped by herself. She'd found her own way home, teleporting back to Val Hall, having somehow finally learned to trace.

Now, she lay in her little princess bed . . . dying. Something had attacked her, something with *claws.*

Lucia sat at the edge of her bed, gazing down through her tears at Emma—the niece she'd held as an infant and watched grow to womanhood. Emma's skin was ghostly pale, her body frail and bruised. All along her side ran long gashes, as if she'd been gored by an animal. The serrated flesh around them was angry with infection.

Though Emma was an immortal, she showed no signs of regeneration. Unable to keep blood down, she was wasting away from thirst. She muttered delirious ramblings about random things: their missing queen, an obscure rebel vampire king, wars she'd never been in.

At times, Emma had screamed that she was being put into a fire.

Lucia could do nothing but watch—and remember. Like Emma, Lucia had been a young immortal on the verge of death. . . .

Emma's lids fluttered open, revealing frightened blue eyes. "Aunt Luce, am I dying?" *The fear in her gaze. Lucia knew exactly what she was feeling.*

"Of course not, sweet," Lucia said, choking back a sob.

Who could have hurt Em like this? When they'd asked her, she'd answered unintelligibly. Annika was beside herself with worry, inconsolable and casting the blame at Lachlain, but Lucia knew it was not him. Gentle Emma had faced something far more horrifying than even a crazed Lykae.

Em raised a hand to Lucia. *"Please . . ."*

Just like Lucia had pleaded a thousand years ago. *But I have no power to save her.*

The pain, the fear . . . *I feel it as if it were yesterday.* Tears tracked down her cheeks. *Just don't let her suffer.*

Damn that bluidy dart. Garreth slapped his neck, too late.

Outside his cell, Regin cackled. "Watch big werewolf go boom!"

As his body dropped to the floor, his last thought was: *I'm going to kill that glowing bitch. . . .*

When he came to, his hands were shackled behind him, and Regin was shoving him up and out of the cell, while Lucia quietly admonished her for being unnecessarily rough.

He must be getting inured to the tranquilizer—he

was shaking off its effects much faster than before. He could have escaped, was longing to block Regin's next hit and toss her on her arse, but he knew where they were taking him, had heard their whispers. The Valkyrie, at least, believed Lachlain was alive.

And they believed some dying vampire female named Emma was his mate. Regin and Lucia were taking Garreth to her.

Lachlain's mate a vampire? The idea was laughable. No one had despised leeches like Lachlain.

Once they entered a bedroom upstairs, Garreth saw Annika, standing beside a bed. A female lay atop it, shivering as she fitfully slept, though she was covered to her chin with piled blankets. Her face was pale, her cheekbones jutting. She hardly looked like a proud werewolf's queen.

Seeming to shake with rage, Annika pointed at her. "Is this who Lachlain should take his vengeance out on?"

As if Lachlain would harm an insignificant female like this. If he even lived.

"We've all suffered at the vampires' hands," Annika continued, "yet that dog thinks to punish our Emma, who is nothing but innocent and kind." She snatched the blankets from Emma, uncovering her leg. "Look at these gashes! They won't heal! What has he done to her? You will tell me or—"

"Christ," he murmured. Annika had also uncovered the vampire's neck. Was that a Lykae's mark? *Is it my brother's mark?* "That's his . . . no, it canna be." He strode forward, but Regin yanked on his bonds. "Let me closer," he growled over his shoulder. "Closer, or you'll get no help from me."

When Garreth closed in on Emma, he lost a breath. *My brother's claimed her.* As well as Garreth could recognize his brother's signature, the beast within him recognized the mark as Lachlain's.

He truly was alive.

This should be a time of jubilation, but the relief he felt was replaced by dread. Lachlain's pale-haired little mate would not last the week.

If she succumbed, Lachlain would be lost all over again. Garreth's voice grew deadly. *"Get her well."*

"We've tried everything!"

"Why will she no' drink? Aye, Valkyrie, I hear your whispers. I know what she is. What I doona know is how she is my brother's mate." A vampire, a blood drinker. He gazed at Lucia. Her expression was inscrutable.

Annika answered, "Emma will never be a 'mate' to one of you!"

But 'twas done. A male marked his woman to keep other males away, to brand her as his. Yet since the bite was done in the throes of taking her for the first time, it could also be an indication of how much he wanted his female. Any doubt that Lachlain wanted Emma for his own vanished with one look at her neck.

Lachlain had marked *the ever-living hell* out of her. Vampire or not, he desired this female desperately.

Any thoughts of escaping vanished as well. Garreth knew he had to remain here. This was where Lachlain would be. Just a matter of time. "It has been done," he grated. "I assure you."

Annika struck him.

He gave her a killing look. "He's marked her," Garreth bit out. "He'll be coming for her. I'm just surprised he's no' here already."

Annika raised her hand again, but Emma had awakened and murmured, "Annika, don't. . . ."

"Force blood down her throat," Garreth said.

"You think we have not tried that? She can't keep it down."

"Try other blood, then." Though being bitten by a vampire was considered deeply shameful by Lykae, Garreth said, "Take *mine!*"

"Why do you care?"

"Because that's my queen, and I'll die for her."

"Now do you believe me?" Lucia asked in a deadened tone. Hours after MacRieve's confrontation with Annika, she was sitting outside his cage once more, watching him pacing within. "Your brother abducted her in France."

"Aye, but he would no' harm the female like that!"

"We know Emma was with him for weeks, and now she returns to us delirious, talking about fires and war and blood. She mumbles about Furie, our missing Valkyrie queen, and about Kristoff, the rebel vampire king. Lachlain captured Emma, and now she lies *dying*."

MacRieve shook his head hard. "It was no' Lachlain."

"How do you know what he's capable of?" Lucia asked. "You don't know where he's been for nearly two centuries. He could've been trapped somewhere, tortured. He likely was—there are rumors that Demestriu has Furie chained to the bottom of the ocean, dooming her to die and regenerate back to life over and over. Maybe he did the same or worse to your brother." She shuddered. "Lachlain was famous for his hatred of vampires, and Emma is one. You can't speak for him."

"You'll never convince me of this. I *know* my brother."

"Annika will exact retribution for this."

"And what will you try to do to him?" Garreth demanded. "Kill him?"

"MacRieve, you can't just abduct one of our own and not suffer repercussions. Your clan would do the exact same thing."

She was right. "Lachlain *will* be coming for her."

Lucia met his gaze, her face hard, another facet of her revealed. "We're counting on it."

FIFTEEN

That night, Garreth shot upright on his cot. He sensed Lykae all around Val Hall. Were they planning to war with the Valkyrie to free him and retrieve their queen?

Please, gods, let his brother be one among their number. . . .

"I'm taking Emma from this place tonight," Lachlain called from outside the manor.

His brother's voice. Garreth's eyes slid shut, and he sagged with relief. *Just doona war with them, doona hurt Lousha.*

Annika called back, "Never would I give my daughter to a dog."

Good luck with that one, Lachlain.

"Then trade me for my brother."

Wait, bargaining himself for Garreth? Oh, bluidy hell no. Brotherly irritation—so welcome to Garreth—flared. In Gaelic, he bellowed, "Goddamnit, Lachlain, I just got *into* this house!"

"Or take both of us," Lachlain amended. "Just let me talk to her."

More whispers from within. They'd be fools to turn down his offer—and the Valkyrie were no fools. Moments later, Garreth heard louder footsteps upstairs and scented his brother inside. They were bringing him to the basement. *So I can see him for myself.*

Once they led Lachlain down the stairs and into the cell, Garreth stared at him as though seeing a ghost. Lachlain didn't resist, even when the door clanged shut behind him.

Since the last time Garreth had seen Lachlain, his brother's appearance had been altered—his build was rangier, his countenance more haggard. But it *was* Lachlain before him. Running a hand over his face, Garreth muttered, "My eyes doona betray me?"

"No, it's me."

Garreth rushed to him, grin in place, and whaled slaps on his back. Now everything would come together. Lachlain would explain what really happened to the vampire, and they'd figure out how to heal her. Lucia would see that the Lykae weren't that bad. *Aye, all will be better with Lachlain's return.* "Well, brother, what have you gotten us into now?"

He raised his brows. "It's good to see you as well."

"I thought you were . . ." Garreth trailed off. *Gods almighty, my brother is just here before me.* Shaking himself, he said, "When they said you'd taken Emma, I thought they were mad. Until I saw her, saw you'd marked her." He frowned. "Marked her hard, no?" He shook his head. "Ach, anyway, it's good to have you back. Under any circumstances. I've so many questions."

Where have you been that I could no' find you? Why did you leave against our warnings?

Are the rumors of Demestriu's tortures . . . true?

Yet Lachlain looked so tormented with worry over his mate, Garreth said, "But that can wait. You need news about her?"

At his nod, Garreth said, "She's injured, Lachlain. She has gashes down her side, and she could no' drink though she was . . . she was about to die in just the first couple of hours."

Now the scent of blood arose. Garreth glanced down, saw Lachlain's claws stabbing into his palms. His voice a rasp, he said, "What saved her?"

"An IV."

When Lachlain's brows knit in confusion, as if he'd never heard the term, a jolt of dread ran through Garreth. Where had his brother been? Lucia had said, *He could've been trapped somewhere, tortured.*

Garreth explained, "They gave her blood through a tube that fed it straight to her veins. They think she's stabilized, but the gashes will no' heal. I suspect whatever got her had poisoned claws. Maybe a ghoul, but I doona know."

"I do." Lachlain ran his hand through his hair. "Demestriu did this to her. I saw it all."

Demestriu. Garreth gnashed his teeth. For millennia that evil fiend had been a scourge on their family. What else had he done—what else *could* he do? *This time* I *will find him, destroy him—*

Lucia entered then. His plans for revenge immediately shifted to concern for his mate. He could see that she'd been crying, and even after all she'd done to him, and to Lachlain, Garreth's chest ached at the sight.

• • •

As Lucia descended the stairs, Garreth shot to his feet beside his brother, both standing so tall and proud. She was struck by how similar they were in looks, with the same rich brown hair, the same intense golden eyes.

Absently, she wondered if Lachlain had told Garreth about the Valkyrie's incursion yesterday at Kinevane—specifically Lucia's own actions. And she might have felt a twinge of guilt that the brothers' reunion had to be as prisoners in her basement.

"Lucia?" Garreth said, a question in his gaze.

Not wanting the Lykae to see she'd been crying, she tilted her head so her hair covered her face.

"She's no' better?" he asked.

Lucia shook her head. *"Aunt Luce, am I dying?" Keep it together, Lucia!*

Lachlain clenched the bars, looking to be in agony over Emma. "She heals whenever she drinks from me."

Garreth appeared stunned. "*You* let her . . . ?" When Lachlain nodded, Garreth said to Lucia, "Then Lachlain must go to her."

"Annika forbids it. He's not to go near her. Emma sees things that aren't there, mumbles nonsense as though she's gone mad. Annika puts the blame squarely on his shoulders."

Garreth asked, "What does she see?"

"Emma says that Demestriu was her father, and he put her in the fire, so she killed him."

Lachlain answered, "She—did."

Both of them swung their heads toward him.

"She did. She killed Demestriu."

Lucia shook her head. "Sweet Emma? Kill the most powerful and deadly vampire ever to live?"

"Aye. He hurt her. Do none of you believe her?"

Garreth gave him an incredulous expression. "Demestriu's finally dead? Because of that wee thing? I've seen her—she's as fragile as an eggshell."

Lucia added, "Lachlain, when she finds a moth inside and tries to free it—well, if she accidentally dusts its wings, she's distraught for an entire night. I just don't see her killing this fiend on his home ground when our fiercest Valkyrie have failed to do so on a field of battle. And Furie, the strongest of us? If Demestriu could be killed by a Valkyrie, then surely she'd have done it."

"You doona know Emma as I do. No' anymore—"

"Then what does she mean when she says Furie is alive but shouldn't be?" Lucia demanded, afraid to hope. . . .

"She's been imprisoned by the Horde. Demestriu never expected her to live this long."

Lucia swayed. *Imprisoned? Perhaps trapped at the bottom of the ocean?* In a smaller voice, she asked, "And when she says King Kristoff has her blood?"

"They're first cousins."

Her lips parted in surprise. *"Furie lives."*

"If you doona believe me, there's a video of the entire fight. I left it with Bowen, a member of our clan."

Garreth stopped gaping at Lachlain and turned to Lucia. "Go get it. For Annika to see."

She raised her eyebrows. "You want me to go to the clan?" *To the compound? The kennel?*

Garreth said, "Tell them I sent you, and they will no' hurt you. I vow it."

Please. "I know they won't *succeed* in hurting me. But you're sending *me*, who'll be carrying a *bow*, among your people. They will not thank you for it."

"I would do it myself," Garreth snapped. "But I canna since I've been put in a cage after coming to *your* rescue."

What if all he said was true? Then Emma desperately needed to drink from Lachlain. But Annika would never allow it without proof. "I'll retrieve and review it," Lucia said, "then give it to Annika, if it's as you say."

Lachlain growled low in his throat, straining against the bars. "Damn it, that will take too long. Can you no' just take my blood for her to drink?"

"Annika forbids it. I'm . . . sorry." She turned for the stairs.

Regin met her as she was hurrying toward the front door, about to haul ass to the kennel. "Where are you going?"

"Apparently I'm traveling to the Lykae compound. Lachlain swears there's a film that shows little *Emma* killing *Demestriu*. Stay here and call me if *anything* happens."

Once she was gone, Garreth continued to stare at the door, telling Lachlain, "Lousha will be quick about it."

"How long have you known she's yours?"

That obvious? Garreth faced his brother. "A while now."

"I wondered why you were so eager to remain,"

Lachlain said, examining the cell for weaknesses. "You've no' told her?"

"Lousha's tricky. And I suspect she's a runner. Tell her something she does no' want to hear and she'll disappear. And she feels no love for me. She's the reason I'm here in the first place," he admitted. "She's an unmatched archer, but suffers agonizing pain when she misses her target— that's why she's so bluidy good. Annika set a trap, baited it with Lousha missing and screaming in pain, and I ran headlong. I should have known there was no way she'd miss again. You've never seen a creature shoot as she—"

"I have a good idea." Lachlain drew his shirt aside, exposing a wound on his shoulder.

I'll bluidy kill her. She went to Scotland and shot my brother!

"I harbor no anger toward her." Lachlain fisted two bars, struggling to stretch them apart. "They've reinforced these?"

"Aye." Garreth joined him, grasping the same bars Lachlain contended with. "These creatures ally with the witches. Annika told me nothing *physical* can bend these."

When they both failed to make a dent, Lachlain began pacing, only stopping to punch one of the cement walls.

"I canna believe she shot you." Garreth had known she'd been gone for an entire day before Emma had returned but hadn't thought she'd been to Scotland and back. "When we get out of here, I'll—"

"No, I doona care. Especially since you seem to accept that my mate's a vampire."

Not bothering to hide his exasperation, Garreth

grated, "I would no' give a damn if she was a Fury, as long as you are content with her. And it's clear you are."

"Aye, but I have to get to her." Lachlain knelt down, clawing at the floor.

"At least we're no' chained. When they open this door, we can attack."

"I'd prefer to be only chained," Lachlain said, his eyes wild. "I'd take off my hands before I let Emma suffer any longer."

Garreth studied his brother's expression. Any Lykae would do the same for his mate. But Lachlain had made that statement as if he spoke . . . from experience. *What has happened to you out there, brother?*

"Trust me, Garreth, it is no' so bad as this feeling—"

When a whimper sounded from Emma's room, Lachlain growled in answer, pounding at the bars. Then he deliberately raised his gaze to the ceiling. "I can dig through."

"Lachlain, I doona think that's wise. This house is centuries old and gets battered as you would no' believe."

"Doona care."

"You might care that all three stories are tongue-and-groove construction. One piece falls, it'll be like a domino effect. War, hurricanes, and constant lightning have made it unsound. I doona think Val Hall can take a Lykae biting through the first floor."

"Support it while I'm gone."

"Hold the floor? If I canna, you could be hurting both our mates. This place could come crashing down."

Lachlain slapped him on the shoulder. "Be sure that you doona drop it."

SIXTEEN

Princess freaking Lucia.

Her trip to the Lykae compound had been like a bucket of ice water tossed in her face. Because the denizens there had welcomed her—as Garreth's "mate." She'd heard the whispers, the truth out loud: *"That's Princess Lucia, the Archer."*

He lied! I am his mate. He'd deceived her to get what he wanted. *Typical male.*

Now as she hastened out the door with the tape, she called Regin. "I'm walking out right now with the video—it's all true. Get Annika to let Emma drink from Lachlain! Right now, Regin! Demestriu was the one who hurt Emma, and she did truly kill him."

"You're a little late. Take your time."

Lucia froze, dread seeming to stop her heart. "Emma . . . ?"

"Oh, no, she's bingo! Just like you said, she drank from Lachlain and healed right up."

Lucia sagged with relief, sinking onto the front steps of the kennel. *Emma's going to live!* Then Lucia frowned. "Annika allowed this?"

"Hell no. The wolves escaped. And then Emma the Timid bitchslapped me when I went after Lachlain!" she added happily. "I mean really hard, and didn't telegraph the move—*at all*. Finally, all those years training her paid off."

"What are you talking about? Where's Garreth?"

"Holding up, like, the entire floor of Val Hall while we get repairs done. Lachlain tore and *bit* through the ceiling over the cage to get to Emma, and now our whole house is sagging, about to fall down. Just goes to show you, Lykae are *outside pets*," Regin said with a snort. "And Em loves Lachlain, and they're getting married, I shite you not. Annika is freaking. I myself am torn. I mean, if Emma's going to be their queen, her first decree could be that all Lykae are the Valkyrie's bitches. She's resistant to the idea, but I'll wear her down."

Emma was safe—healthy. And in love. "How are the others reacting?"

"They're kind of feeling that if Emma wanted the wolf bad enough to go tag Demestriu, then felicitations to them both. And Lachlain did just save her life. Also, no Valkyrie were injured in the making of their recent escape. Still, doesn't mean we want to hang out or anything."

Emma would wed Lachlain and be his queen. Now everything between the Valkyrie and Lykae would be different.

Didn't matter. Garreth was a liar—and she wanted nothing to do with him. Most of the time. Except when he was touching her.

"So what's the kennel like?" Regin asked.

Lucia turned toward the building with narrowed eyes. *Before or after I get through with it?*

"Do they have food bowls and chew toys all around?"

"The 'compound' looks like a Scottish hunting lodge." The whole vibe was so . . . normal. It'd rattled her all the more because she *could* see herself hanging out there. Yes, there were some claw marks on the walls, but hell, Val Hall had its own "love stripes."

"And?" Regin asked.

"What?"

"What else happened?" Regin said. "I can hear something in your voice."

"I'm definitely . . . his mate."

Regin made a wincing sound. "Dude. Sorry."

"I've known, but I've been in denial. *He* even denied it." Which proved that he was a cool customer, able to control himself instead of bellowing *mine* as he demanded her eternity. "But to hear the reality said out loud, and to see his clan treating me like one of their own, like their *princess* . . . it was just too much."

Before, as long as it hadn't been acknowledged, she could pretend it wasn't so.

Now, the truth sunk in, her suspicions were confirmed, his lie revealed.

"He won't leave you alone. Especially not until he's claimed you," Regin said.

"I know." Lykae simply didn't give up. They were the living embodiment of obsession. Just like Lachlain with Emma, Garreth would never rest until he'd possessed Lucia completely.

"And you can't have sex. So what're we going to do?"

Since I also can't seem to deny him . . . "I'm going to get out of town."

"Where're we headed?" Regin asked. When Lucia didn't answer, she said, "Like I'm letting you go out into the world by yourself to let life kick you in the ass. We're *both* getting our asses kicked or not at all! We're a team, Bonnie and Bonnie, together forever."

Lucia's lips quirked. No one could have a better friend than Regin. "We start the hunt for a dieumort." She stood and turned back inside the compound, striding for Garreth's quarters. "Pack a bag for me—I'll be back in an hour. For now, I'm going to act out, demonstrate that some Valkyrie aren't house-trained either."

"Ooh, break something for me!"

Inside his rooms, Lucia kicked an expensive-looking lamp, sending it crashing to the floor. "Any other requests?"

"Yeah, since matehood means you own fifty percent of all his swag, then bring me home any vinyl LPs you may come across, some weapons, and of course, anything shiny."

"On it."

"MacRieve'll follow us."

Yes, but Lucia would protect herself, do whatever she had to do. She had no choice. "Then let the games begin."

Lachlain MacRieve and his brother stood outside on the grounds of Val Hall, drinking a couple of rounds of longnecks before Garreth's imminent departure.

"You sure you canna stay?" Lachlain was loath to see his brother go. He'd been so panicked about Emma that he'd barely registered the time he'd spent jailed with Garreth.

"I need to follow Lousha."

Unfortunately, Lucia the Huntress had disappeared. Lachlain had heard she'd "gone on vacay" with her "partner in crime" Regin. The new lingo of this time still stumped him, but he'd gleaned enough to know that Garreth had been right about his mate: Lucia was indeed a runner.

"Aye, o' course you must go after her. But maybe you could leave after my wedding?" Lachlain was to marry Emma tomorrow. Though the Lykae considered mate-hood eternal—marriage was a bit superfluous—the Valkyrie insisted on some kind of binding ceremony. Or as Annika had choked out, "Something a little more respectable—than a *bite*."

More important, my lass is excited about it. In less than twenty-four hours, he'd take his sweet Emma as his wife. Those hours couldn't pass soon enough for him.

"I canna." Garreth took a swig. "No' unless you need me. To help you . . . acclimate." His expression darkened.

Though Garreth had been utterly accepting of Emma's vampiric nature—even the fact that Lachlain himself fed her and relished doing so—he hadn't taken the news of Lachlain's decades-long imprisonment and torture well. And Lachlain had downplayed the worst of it.

"No, I can manage," he said. "Especially now with the vampire threat lessened." His wee Emma had somehow slain Demestriu, and Lachlain himself had killed Ivo the Cruel.

Garreth said, "Lessened but no' gone."

Lothaire still lived. There was something about that vampire, something that tugged at Lachlain's subconscious. A threat even greater than it appeared on the surface . . . "When you return, we'll strategize what to do about the Enemy of Old."

"Aye," Garreth agreed. "For now, you need to concentrate on your queen. And hup two with the bairns, old man. Tired of being your heir."

Lachlain drank deeply. "Doona hold your breath. You saw how delicate she is—will no' relish the idea of getting a babe on her."

"Delicate?" Garreth raised his brows. "The rest of the Lore, and especially the Lykae, see her as a fierce warrior queen who slew the Horde king. And you still see her as delicate."

Lachlain scowled. "First impressions are lasting. In any case, doona be concerning yourself with this—you've enough on your plate. Do you know what spooked your female in the first place?"

"Oh, aye. She found out she was my mate, though I'd lied about it."

Lachlain rubbed the back of his neck. He'd done just the same with Emma. Mates that were *other* didn't often find the news welcome. "How'd she find out?"

"I'd made the twins vow no' to tell anyone about her. But when they thought they were about to war with the Valkyrie to retrieve me and cover your incursion, they gave an order that Lousha could no' be hurt. Upon pain of death, she was to be spared. I appreciated the fore-sight, but the clan quickly figured it out."

"Where do you think she is?"

Garreth said, "I have some leads."

"Nïx?"

"Aye."

Nucking Futs Nïx. Lachlain owed everything to that soothsayer. She was the one who'd coaxed Emma to go to Paris in the first place. If Emma hadn't been there, then Lachlain never would've had the strength to escape the vampires—who'd imprisoned and tortured him for over a century. . . .

Tamping down those memories, Lachlain said, "Before you go, I wanted to pass on some advice. Emma told me that to win your mate, you have to accept Regin. The two are thick as thieves. Always have been. Since they were children."

"So calling Regin a glowing bluidy freak dinna help my cause? On top of the lie? Christ, I've bollixed this up."

"But you said she's no' immune to you. You can win her."

With a firm nod, Garreth said, "Aye, then, I will. I'm off." He hugged Lachlain, clapping him on the back. "It's good to have you back, brother."

When they finally broke apart, Lachlain was choked up, clearing his throat. "Right, then."

Garreth stared down at his beer, muttering, "Got something in my eye." Turning to go, he said, "Take care of our queen."

"You just be careful." The two brothers had always been protective of each other, so Lachlain was uneasy that Garreth had no one to watch his back. "And stay out of trouble." Garreth was a hell of a fighter, but on occasion, he needed a wingman.

Over his shoulder, Garreth said, "Doona worry. Mark my words, I'll have her back in two weeks."

SEVENTEEN

❖

One year later, the Northlands
Possibly the mountains of Thrymheim Hold,
but probably not

"Is this a bad time?" Nïx asked cheerily.

"You are fully aware that this is a damned bad time," Lucia said. "Currently I'm suspended from a mountain ledge, four thousand feet in the air." She hung on to a rock cleft with the tips of her fingers—of one hand. The other she'd used to click on her sat-phone earpiece.

Sometimes Lucia wished satellite phones *didn't* work everywhere on earth.

"You sound awful," Nïx observed. "Have you been taking your Flintstones?"

Lucia's muscles burned. She hadn't slept in days. *The games*, it seemed, would not *end*. And Lucia was in a grueling fourth-quarter situation—with a team mate lost. "Nïx, did you call for a reason?"

"Are you any closer to finding Thrymheim?"

Lucia had relinquished her lofty goal of locating a dieumort and killing Cruach—now she'd be satisfied if she could merely keep him jailed for another five hundred years.

She needed Skathi, or more accurately, she needed one of Skathi's arrows, but Lucia couldn't even locate the goddess. "If it's not at the top of this peak, then this range is a bust."

Lucia had been so sure this was Godsbellow Mountain. Now she grew increasingly doubtful. She vaguely remembered an ever-ascending path to the peak. She could find no path. So she was climbing. "Don't suppose you'll finally tell me where the temple is?"

"I thought if a Skathian was pure of heart, she could always find her way back to the goddess."

Pure of heart? *Not in the least.* Though Lucia and MacRieve had never shared more than those two nights together, she couldn't stop thinking about him, lusting for him. Whenever she touched herself, it was his body she fantasized about. "I'll find my way back, Nïx. One way or another." *Push on, Lucia!* What choice did she have? She leapt for another handhold.

"Well, actually, that's why I'm calling. Now, I know your to-do list is varied and important. Finding Skathi, preparing for your five-hundred-yearly confrontation with the revolting Cruach, the epitome of pure evil, et cetera."

Speak of the devil—literally. Though the Broken Bloody One was a hideous abomination, he could disguise himself with a face so beautiful ... *it made me weep.*

The modern idea of Satan originated from him.

He was the being she would be forced to confront. And soon. She always knew when. . . . That night so long ago when she'd been about to depart Thrymheim as a new Skathian, Lucia had asked the goddess, "What do you want me to do?"

"Just before he rises, you'll go to his lair, and shoot him in the heart with the arrow I've given you. Every five hundred years, I'll provide you with another."

Return to his lair? Never. "How will I know when Cruach will rise?" *So I'll know when to run.*

Skathi's face had been impassive. "When the nightmares begin."

The first time Cruach had risen under Lucia's watch, she'd been plagued by nightly visions so harrowing, she'd been driven to face her worst fear.

Now, just as before, her nightmares were becoming more frequent, more punishing, which meant time was running out. . . .

"Yeah, Nïx, I'm a little swamped right now."

"And on top of everything you have to evade your Lykae."

"I'm not evading him." *I'm totally evading him.* "And he's not *my* Lykae." Had those two passionate interludes been enough to blind Lucia to the sanctuary at Thrymheim? No, no way—she still had her abilities.

"After all you've done to MacRieve, I'd be running, too."

And all I continue doing to him. His pursuit had been relentless, so she'd protected herself—and her chastity—often in ruthless ways.

But she'd never shot *him*, not since their initial meeting. She knew he wouldn't even try to dodge the arrow for fear of what it'd do to her.

Nïx said, "Regin bragged to the entire coven that you two had him trapped in a river canyon in logging country with an eighteen-wheeler full of trees parked on the rise above him. You shot the fastenings with arrows and a pile of logs rolled over him." Nïx chuckled. "If that wasn't enough, you and Regin then threw the eighteen-wheeler on top of him!"

It was all true. He'd been nipping at their heels for days. "Just tell me how Reege's doing." Since Lucia had been forced to leave her behind—after only their first four weeks on the lam.

"Badly. She's acting out, getting high, picking fights with beings bigger than she is. She's furious that you 'abandoned' her 'like last year's wardrobe.' Especially when she was sleeping off an intoxispell hangover."

Lucia had the text messages from screen name *Reg-Rad* to prove all of the above. Months of emotional rollercoaster-y texts.

Nïx continued, "She teamed up briefly with Kaderin the Coldhearted for the Talisman's Hie, but Kad booted her. I've been assigning her busy work, inviting old nemeses to New Orleans to try to kill her and such. But nothing keeps her down. She *has* been taking her Flintstones, incidentally. We all eagerly await the time when you can *finally* return to deal with her."

Lucia climbed higher, leaping for a taunting overhang. *Got it.* "You know why I've been forced to travel all over the world." For months, Lucia had dreamed of a dieumort arrow, envisioning a gold and flawless one like Skathi's—but imbued with the Banemen's power, the one-time power to kill a nightmare incarnate. She'd failed to locate it.

And now that she'd decided to settle for one of Skathi's arrows, had planned to return and grovel to the goddess, Lucia couldn't locate her either.

She was running out of time, and every step of the way MacRieve had hunted her, no matter how far-flung her destinations had become. She also suspected he'd been protecting her. Even now. Even after all she'd done to him.

She'd seen him in a village in the Northlands just two nights ago. What would he do to her if he caught her? She wondered this *constantly*.

"Nïx, is this why you called? About Regin?" Lucia asked. "I can try to talk to her."

"Actually, I called because there's this pesky little apocalypse brewing. I need your help."

Sweat dripped into Lucia's eyes. She irritably wiped it away, gazing up at the peak above her with yearning. *Deep down, you know it isn't Thrymheim, Lucia.* "Why me?" There were dozens of other Valkyrie as strong as or stronger than Lucia. "Why not Cara or Annika?"

Nïx answered, "You're the Valkyrie's greatest hunter."

"Yes, I *know* this," Lucia said, immodest as ever. "But what's the mission?"

"What's *what* mission?" Nïx said softly, then with growing enthusiasm, "Am I to go on a mission?"

"Nïx, the apocalypse! Come on, snap out of it!"

Silence for a long moment. "Oh, I remember," she sniffed huffily, as if Lucia had broken her sunshine. "Yes, I have all your deets right here—where you need to be and what you need to do. All the specifics already foreseen. Basically you have to be on a particular boat in the Amazon jungle by three sharp tomorrow afternoon."

"The Amazon? That's thousands of miles from where I am. Besides, I'm a hunter—not an explorer. *Find someone else*," she grated as she maneuvered another dozen feet higher. Her fingertips were on fire.

"Ah, but would anyone be as qualified as you? You see, the source of this apocalypse is . . . Cruach."

Lucia felt like her stomach dropped the four thousand feet to the ground.

"Yes, I thought you'd want to take care of this one," Nïx said in a thoughtful tone. "*Since he's your husband.*"

EIGHTEEN

◄━━◈◈◈━━►

Iquitos, Amazonia
Fifteen hours later . . .

Lucia sprinted from the heli pad through the remote river-port town, her senses bombarded by scents and sounds: the smell of hot peppers and green bananas in the market stands; the incessant horns from motorcycle rickshaws; street vendors hawking their wares, unaffected by the on-and-off drizzle of rain.

Though already exhausted from the last few weeks and wiped out from the constant travel over the last day, Lucia adjusted her backpack and travel bowcase to run even faster.

The time was a quarter after three.

Breakneck flights had gotten her out of the Northlands, then even more connections had followed to get to South America and into Iquitos.

She'd logged seven thousand miles in the last day.

Weary to her bones, she again cursed the instigator of this disaster—Nucking Futs Nïx.

She couldn't have seen a freaking *apocalypse* sooner? To give Lucia time to buy a damned mosquito net, and maybe an Amazon river guidebook!

Lucia was almost to the water—not difficult, since Iquitos was encircled by the Amazon and two other tributaries. The sun peeked through lowering clouds, spawning a vibrant rainbow that seemed to end on the far banks of the Amazon.

Soon, a red clay shore came into view. Just at the water's edge, a neighborhood of thatch-roofed houses floated on balsa platforms. A few large riverboats were lined up beside them, beached on the muddy banks.

As she ran headlong, she recalled the rest of that fateful conversation with the soothsayer:

"Nïx, how can Cruach bring about an apocalypse?"

"Apparently, he's no longer your personal domestic problem. It's foretold that he'll start a plague of human sacrifices."

Cruach's other name was To Him We Sacrifice. He had the power to infect beings, engendering a mad need to kill whomever the victim loved most. *"A plague?"*

"Before, he could only afflict one with his madness by direct contact and only once he escaped his lair. But soon his influence could potentially be spread like a disease, passed from one person to another."

"How? Black magic, the help of another god—"

"The countdown has begun. Ticktock, ticktock."

"What do you want me to do?"

"Go to the docks. I've got you booked on a ship called the Contessa. *For weeks, you'll travel into the jungle, to the deepest, darkest part of the Amazon where no other boats dare to go. Find the Rio Labyrinto—a mystically hidden tributary. Have you heard of it?"*

Lucia had exhaled a stunned breath. *"Yeah. No one*

comes back when they go looking for it. Not even immortals."

"Are ya feelin' lucky, punk?"

"What's there to help me fight Cruach? A weapon? An ally? Don't suppose I'll find a dieumort there."

"Now what's a dieumort?"

"Never mind! Nïx, what's down there?"

"Call me when you arrive on time—otherwise all this could be moot—then I'll reveal the rest to you. Unless, of course, I forget." Which was entirely likely.

Lucia had known Nïx wouldn't divulge more logistics. She divvied information like a miser parting with gold coins. Lucia had learned, like all other Valkyrie, to go on a little faith—and forbearance—with Nïx. "At least tell me what the stakes are," Lucia had demanded impatiently. "What happens if I fail?"

"The end of life as we know it."

"Nothing else you'd like to impart?"

"Everything you'll need will be aboard the Contessa." A blare of static-like noise crackled. "Oh, and beware of the *barão da borracha and the* guardião."

Lucia knew some Portuguese. "Beware of the rubber baron and the guardian?"

More static sounds. "Can't hear . . . call back . . . good luck . . ."

"Nïx, I know you're faking the static." She could picture her sister blowing into her fist directly at the receiver. The static abruptly stopped. "Why?"

"It seemed less rude than the alternative."

"What's that?"

Click.

Lucia slowed, her eyes widening when she spied a wave of riverboats leaving. Was she too late?

She asked fishermen returning from the day's runs to direct her to the *Contessa*. They all laughed in answer. Once she finally happened upon it, beached on a section of trash-ridden shore, she realized why.

The *Contessa*—such a bold and noble name—was a relic. With its three stories and latticed railings, it looked like an old river cruiser from the rubber-boom days. But it was in no way preserved—rotting holes dappled the wood just above the waterline, and the windshield in the pilothouse was fractured from one edge to the other. Any visible metal was corroded, oozing rust down the faded hull like runnels of blood.

The roof on the third-story observation deck was . . . thatched.

She scrunched her face. Departure at three sharp? Nothing concerning this vessel could be classified as sharp. *Nïx, you little rotter.* Why would her sister have booked her on this ship?

No, Lucia didn't have to accept this—she could get another ride. She stepped back to survey the only other boats still beached. Any that remained looked to have been abandoned in haste. The closest one still had tablecloths and utensils on its soaked outdoor tables.

Aboard the *Contessa*, voices sounded dimly from indoors, and one—maybe two—males stomped around on deck.

At least it had people on it.

Beggars can't be choosers. She checked the braids she'd plaited to cover her ears, then called, "Is anyone up there? I need to board this"—*tub, wreck, joke of a*—"boat."

A crusty boot slammed on the gunwale, and a big, bleary-eyed man leaned over it to peer down. "Ship, lady. This here's a *ship*," he said defensively, as if she'd told him, "Your penis: I find it minuscule." The man's accent was American Southern, his voice raspy.

With blood-shot gray eyes, he gave her a once-over, then drawled, "Dr. MacRieve, I presume?"

Dr. *MacRieve?* Nïx had just gotten elevated from ass-kicking to certain death.

When dealing with humans, Lucia had always used Archer as her last name. Since she would never own up to her real one.

"From LSU?" he asked, snagging a hip flask from his jeans pocket for a generous gulp.

Wondering what else Nïx would have told this man, she answered, "Yes, that's me. And you're the . . . captain?"

"That I am. Captain Wyatt Travis." He wore a white button-down, mostly unbuttoned, and when the wind blew off the river, the material billowed, displaying a surprisingly rock-solid torso.

Lucia supposed he wasn't *un*fortunate looking, with his carelessly ruffled blond hair and stubble, but he was noticeably inebriated—even if she couldn't have smelled liquor wafting from his pores. She conjectured what Travis would blow on a BAC meter, wagering a healthy two-point-oh.

Why would Nïx book her on a rotted tub with a drunken captain? She could just see Nïx clapping merrily and crying *"For fun!"* "And my *assistant* booked a room, right?"

"We've held a cabin for you. Last one left."

"Air conditioner?"

"One. And it ain't in your room, darling." His accent wasn't just Southern. She realized the captain was a Texan.

"Wait, the *last* cabin?" She scanned the decks. The ship looked to have at least half a dozen of them, spaced equally on the first two floors.

He shoved down a rickety gangplank. "You don't have to sound so shocked that we're booked up." *Ruffled feathers.* The only thing worse than a perpetual drunk was a sensitive one. "There're three docs like you aboard and my cook and deckhand as well."

Including the captain that would make six humans. This wouldn't do. Unlike some Valkyrie, Lucia shunned mortals whenever possible. To reveal secrets of the Lore to one of them would draw punishment from the gods, and Lucia was already in a tenuous position with one. *Or two.* "How much for the entire boat?"

"You ain't the brightest bulb in the marquee, are you? I already got these passengers aboard—they're unpacking their scientifical crap in the lab as we speak. We've just been waiting on you."

Weeks on board with mortals? And clearly, she would have to hijack the boat to get to the deepest Amazon, where nobody dared to go. The humans would have to be dealt with then.

Perhaps Lucia could find a Lorean to captain another ship. A river city like Iquitos would be home to countless immortals.

But as she debated her options, that awareness returned, the sense of being watched. She rubbed the back of her neck and glanced over her shoulder, thought she saw a tall male, a *too-tall* male. Was MacRieve closing in on her even now? She knew he couldn't be far behind—because he hadn't been for the entire year.

Or maybe she was overreacting. Exhaustion weighed on her until she felt like falling down, and in the past, she'd imagined him in shadows, over a rise, or on a balcony overhead peering down at her.

For as many times as she'd seen golden eyes glowing with hunger from some nearby shadow, she'd imagined she had.

Her ears twitched. *Awareness.* No, he was near. "I'll take the cabin!" *I can dump the mortals later.* She chucked her pack over the railing, holding her graphite bowcase under her arm as she acted like a human female, teetering up the gangplank.

He frowned. "Uh, don't you have equipment you need to have loaded?"

"Nope. We're all good."

"Orientation and meet-and-greet is required."

"Yes, of course." She could play along, be sociable, or act like she was. "But we need to leave immediately."

"We're on river time here." He offered her a hand she didn't need as she stepped aboard. "Now, you're in the seventh cabin, first level, all the way fore in the bow. Here's the key—"

She snatched it from him. "I'll double—*triple*—your fare if we leave this instant."

He narrowed those gray eyes. "Quadruple it, and you'll see a big-ass boat go fast."

"Agreed." This heartened her. Mortals who were motivated by money were controllable.

As the captain hastened to the pilothouse, calling out for someone named Chuck to "kick her in the guts!" Lucia climbed to the observation deck. She shaded her eyes with her hand, scanning for MacRieve. Iquitos was the most populous city in the world that couldn't be reached by road. Only boat and air traffic in or out, difficult to get to in the best of circumstances. Maybe she'd lost him.

The ship's diesel engines fired up, coughing black smoke as they sputtered, but they stayed running. Travis began reversing from the shore, narrowly missing a floating gas station, then he increased the speed. The ship surged backward, water swamping the back platform that stretched the width of the boat.

The entire hull groaned, the motion sending Lucia tilting toward the railing. As she balanced herself, she craned her head around, eyes wary.

Nothing. After several heartbeats, Travis shifted gears, and the *Contessa* ground forward. Finally, Lucia breathed a sigh of relief. They were under way. She was on a boat heading out on the Amazon after flying all the way from across the world, in record time.

Really, how could the Lykae have headed her off here? There was no way he could catch her.

And her trail would grow colder in the days to

come. She climbed down to the first level for her bag, then headed for cabin seven to stow her stuff. Just as she got to the door, her sat-phone chimed with a new text message. She peered at the screen, saw it was from Regin. Gods, she missed her sister and best friend like an ache—

RegRad: We're not BFFs anymore, Luce. So SUCK IT!

Lucia sighed. At times she understood why others could only take Regin in short doses.

Suddenly, her ears twitched again, which meant someone aboard was possibly about to attack her or that MacRieve was near. She hoped it was the former as she plunked her case down on the deck. Dropping to her knees beside it, she unfastened the titanium latches and yanked free her bow and quiver from their foam padding.

After stringing the bow, she stood once more. She spied something out of the corner of her eye, something glinting in the sun. She glanced up, over toward the shore.

MacRieve. Just there on the rise. To elude him for this long only to be snared now?

His *timing.* For the love of gods, his timing!

Could he still make the boat? One more dock lay ahead for the *Contessa* to pass, coming up swiftly, but fifty or sixty feet of water separated it from the boat.

Apparently MacRieve thought he could make the distance—he slung his duffle bag over his body and got that intent look she'd become familiar with. *Wait . . .* Did he have *blood* splattered over one side of his face?

No time to contemplate that; she dashed to the

back platform. In a flash, she had her bow up and arrow loaded. His expression turned murderous, and he shook his head slowly, as if vowing retribution.

Damn him! She couldn't shoot, because she knew he wouldn't even *try* to dodge her arrows. He would still do anything to keep her from harm—even as each time she saw him he continued to appear darker, *angrier.*

And gods help her, sexier.

With a sound of frustration, she lowered her bow. MacRieve had already begun sprinting, gaining superhuman velocity, his massive body moving with the speed and smoothness of an animal.

She swallowed. He was nearing the end of the dock but hadn't slowed—was pumping his arms for more speed. *No. No way he can make this distance, werewolf or not.*

Heart in her throat, she watched him spring from the edge in an explosive leap. A second passed . . . still in the air . . . momentum hurling him toward her spot—

Just short! He landed chest-first against the side of the platform, his black claws digging into the teakwood.

After wincing at the sound of his ribs cracking, she remembered herself and reared back her leg for a swinging punt to his head. But he snatched her ankle with one hand, tossing her to her ass. In a single fluid movement, he sprang to the deck to cover her, pinning her arms—and bow—over her head.

A seething, soaked Lykae was stretched over her, his body a cage of damp, rippling muscles. She grappled to get free, a laughable effort against a being with his strength, but only managed to get as soaked as he was.

What would he do to her? What *didn't* she deserve?

"Now, that's no' nice, Valkyrie." His deep voice raked over her as his eyes scanned her face, taking in every feature as if relearning them. "And no way to greet your male."

"You're not *my* male!" He *did* have blood on his face—now it mingled with the water and sweat trickling down his cheek. "Let me up!"

He kept her pinned. "Missed you these months," he said. "Again and again." The double meaning was clear when his eyes flickered ice blue. "But no longer. The game's changed now, beauty."

Snared. Somehow the huntress had been hunted to the ground and trapped.

No! She was on a mission to save the world. She'd lose the Lykae and get on with it. She *had* to.

Or every being on earth would pay for what she'd done—and for what she would never do again . . .

At that thought, she renewed her struggles beneath him. Oh, gods, MacRieve was getting hard!

In a hushed, threatening tone, he said, "We've unfinished business to take care of."

"I want you off this boat, MacRieve!" Lucia snapped.

Garreth was growing erect, stiffening for her with a swift heat, and she had to feel it. "Do you, then?" His tone was disbelieving—because even now his Lucia was responding to him so sweetly. A blush tinged her high cheekbones, and her pupils were dilated with interest. Her lips parted as she stared at his own.

Then her dazed expression seemed to clear. "Get off me, you brute! If you won't leave, then I will!"

"You think I've searched—and fought and protected you from afar—for this long just to let you go now?" Not from *too* afar. Moments ago, he'd slaughtered two demon assassins who'd been lying in wait in an alley—for her. They'd had their swords raised, intending to take her head. He'd collected theirs instead.

But now Garreth had her safe in his arms. The urge to squeeze her into his chest grew nigh overwhelming. To have her truly under his watch ... after so many months when she'd been in constant danger.

Satisfaction soared within him, and he eased his face down to her mane of glossy hair, taking her scent into him once more.

Gods, nothing smelled as fine as Lucia.

"Are you ... smelling my hair?" She sounded aghast. Or titillated. Who could tell with Lucia, the Mistress of Mixed Signals?

His voice was rough when he admitted, "Aye, just one of the things I missed about you." Just as satisfaction mounted, so did lust. The smell of her hair was almost his undoing. And her body was so soft and warm beneath him.

She squirmed harder, but he wouldn't budge. "Mac-Rieve, I'm here on important business! Business that doesn't concern you. If you're trying to win me over—"

"I'm no'. Gave up on that in the first month."

She flushed guiltily, which heartened him. Maybe his female wasn't as cold and unemotional as her vicious sisters, though she'd certainly convinced him otherwise over the last year. "No, my only aim these days is to keep you alive." They were in the midst of an Accession, and in this treacherous time, she'd come here, to his least favorite place on earth.

And one of the most perilous, even for immortals.

She struggled to free her arms and her bow, brushing her hip against his erection. A pleasured breath escaped him. "I remember the last time we were in this position." Of their own volition, his hips curled, making her gasp. At her ear, he grated, "I rocked against your sex till you came for me. You feared I'd stop before you could."

She glanced away, her blush deepening, her squirming intensifying.

"Little to the left, sweet. *And harder.*"

She cast him a withering glare as she thrashed her arms. "I'll shoot you so full of arrows—"

He held her tight. "Eventually, you will run out of those."

"I make my own," she said between gritted teeth.

"O' course you do. But I consider your archery our foreplay. So—fire—away."

"You've stalked me, hunted me to the ground. I'm sick of it! I should have shot you when you leapt."

"Oh, so I'm to be the bad man? Have you forgotten what you've done to me? To my family?" And the worst of it hadn't even occurred until *after* she'd fled New Orleans. Then the fun had really begun—hijinks and traps all over the world for the last year. "And you should no' have run from me with no explanation."

She met his gaze with a mulish look. "I wasn't running from you. I've been doing my own deal. And I didn't owe you an explanation! *Still don't.* Now release me!"

"Maybe you dinna owe me an explanation, but thanking me for saving your life might no' be too much."

Instead, her chin jutted.

So that's how she's to be? Finally, he allowed her to scramble up but shot to his feet beside her, cupping her nape. "Take me to our cabin."

"Have you gone insane?"

"Would you blame me if I had after all you've done to me? All you've *denied* me, denied us—"

"Who the hell is this?" a male demanded from behind them.

Garreth turned, spied a drunken human. Must be the captain. The man eyed Lucia's bow and Garreth's dripping clothes. With the look of a bloke who'd seen it all, he said to Lucia, "Is there a problem, doc?"

Doc? Though the mortal was packing muscle, Lucia had to know that he couldn't do anything to help her.

Her lips thinned. Oh, aye, she knew better. "No, no problem, Travis."

This *Travis* turned to him. "Lemme guess, you're our obligatory stowaway?"

"New passenger." Garreth dug into the pocket of his soaked jacket, then handed the man a soggy wad of cash. "Garreth MacRieve."

Travis glanced from Lucia to Garreth, then to his handful of bills, accepting it with a nod. "We don't have any cabins left—"

"No' a problem. I bunk with this one from now on."

Lucia opened her mouth to protest, but Travis said, "Then welcome the hell aboard." With that, he turned and climbed back up to the wheelhouse.

Lucia jerked from Garreth's grasp. "This isn't over. And if you lay another paw on me, MacRieve, I'll make you regret it."

When she turned from him, he laid another paw on her, giving her arse a possessive squeeze, groaning with pleasure; she whirled around and punched him with shocking force in the Adam's apple, doubling him over as he coughed.

As she hastened away, he grated, "*Still doona regret it.*"

NINETEEN

▬◆▬

On her way back to cabin seven, she swooped up her pack, then unlocked the heavy door, slamming it behind her. The rusted hinges screamed in protest.

At first glance, the wood-paneled room was larger than she'd thought it would be, the bed as well. Probably because both were so old, from a bygone era of luxury.

There was a writing desk and chair, a bedside table and lamp. A mosquito net dangled above the bed. Both a decent-sized bathroom and a cramped balcony adjoined.

After tossing her bag to the floor, she leaned back against the door, propping her bow and quiver against the wall.

What am I going to do? She was traveling on a vessel lousy with humans, dispatched on a mission by a half-mad being, replete with an embarrassing secret identity, an impending apocalyptic deadline, and now a nemesis who could prove her undoing.

A *sexy* nemesis.

Gods, he was still as attractive as ever. His dark charisma—which still seemed to make her mind go blank—was in full force.

Had he really missed her scent? As a Lykae, had he longed to experience it? The idea made her disconcertingly flushed—and irritated with herself. Why was she even contemplating things like that?

Instead, she needed to be worried about how he would retaliate for all she and Regin had done to him. There was no way he'd simply deem the last year water under the bridge. . . .

Nïx had told her, "Call me as soon as you get on board." Oh, she would call all right!

Lucia snatched her sat-phone from her pack, dialing her. But the soothsayer wasn't answering—no shock—so Lucia left a message. In the calmest voice she could manage, she said, "Nïx, it's me. I'm under way. Call me back. Oh, and I think I hate you."

Once she hung up, she saw another text. *RegRad: Didn't mean that last msg. Still BFFs? I should B there w/U. This town=LAME.*

Lucia thought Regin should be with her, too. But at the outset, they'd disagreed on how to deal with MacRieve's hell-bent pursuit. Regin had decided to kill him, which Lucia couldn't abide. Not after he'd saved the lives of Regin, Annika, and herself.

How had Lucia repaid him? With pain.

And now she herself would be paying for that decision—

"Let me in, Lousha," he said from just outside the cabin.

Perhaps I should have let Regin have at the wolf. "Why are you doing this to me?"

"You ask questions that you know the answers to? Now, open up, or—"

"You'll huff and puff?" She glanced around the room, as if to find a way around letting him inside. Before she spied an alternative, he broke the lock, opening the door. "MacRieve!"

He strolled past her with an insolent chuck under her chin, then slammed the door closed.

"You got the cabin in the bow?" he said with a scowl. "Surprised you dinna just go with hammock class."

"If you have a problem with it, feel free to *leave*."

He ignored that, dropping his bulging duffle bag. Then he seemed to scent the area, checking nooks and crannies, rapping a knuckle on the wood-paneled wall, shuffling the faded green floor rug.

She took the opportunity to study him, finding him as insufferably gorgeous as ever. His thick dark hair remained longish and carelessly cut. His customary stubble shaded his lean cheeks and that stubborn cleft chin. Around his eyes, those faint lines fanned out, pale in his tanned skin.

Though he'd lost weight—he clearly hadn't been eating enough—his body was still massive. Nothing could diminish his towering height. Captain Travis was over six feet tall, and he'd had to look up to the Lykae.

Then she frowned. On his left wrist, MacRieve wore a silver cuff that looked as though it'd come from a suit of battered armor. It was what she'd initially seen glinting when she'd first caught sight of him. *How odd.*

"Still as ruggedly handsome," he said without turn-

ing around, "as I was the last time you saw me, Valkyrie."

Her face flushed red. She hadn't forgotten how grav-
elly his voice was, but for so long she'd denied its effect
on her.

He opened up the double doors to the small balcony,
peered out, then turned back to say, "Shame it's in the
bow." Then he crossed to the cabin's sole chair to yank
off his sodden boots.

"Why do you keep saying that?"

"You'll see." Barefooted, he unzipped his waterproof
bag for a pair of faded jeans and a black T-shirt.

Her eyes widened. "You're not changing in here."

Fingers on the fly of his low-slung jeans, he raised his
brows at her. "Oh, I'm no'?" He leisurely tugged down
his zipper. "Leaving on wet clothes in the Amazon? Lesson one—that's no' too bright an idea."

Her first instinct was to whirl around, but then she'd
be turning her back on a disrobing Lykae who lusted for
her. Yet the alternative was just as bad. To see his naked
flesh again?

How many times had she fantasized about his big
shaft, remembering how it'd looked when he'd been
pumping it into her fist between those bars?

Don't look at it. Blushing, she finally whirled around
from him, but then she was forced to listen to the
sounds of his undressing. His smooth, tan skin would
still be damp, as it'd been that rainy night in the bayou.
She swallowed, assailed by memories of touching him,
touching him everywhere. . . .

"So, Valkyrie. Mind telling me what we're doing in

Amazonia, of all places? I'd vowed I'd never return to this hellhole."

Without turning around, she said, "I do mind. And if you vowed never to return, then you—should—leave."

"Here's a thought. In the last year I've been chasing you, did you never consider hiding out at the Ritz?"

"Here's a thought. Stop chasing me!"

Suddenly she felt his breaths—on the back of her neck. She twisted around, craning her head to stare up at mesmerizing golden eyes.

As he gazed down at her, he rested his hand against the wall above her head, fingering a lock of her hair. "Ah, lass, I will. Now that I've caught you."

He had little flecks of black within the gold of his irises. She'd never noticed that before. And she dimly perceived that he had in fact redressed.

Was she disappointed? "Caught me?"

"Oh, aye."

The reality of her situation sunk in. She was the object of a Lykae's unwavering obsession. They just didn't give up. And the Valkyrie's usual remedy for this—a slaying—wasn't an option.

She *was* caught, she couldn't get rid of him, and short of leaving this boat, she was going to have to deal with MacRieve.

She'd have to try to reason with him. The only problem? He made her feel anything but reasonable! Even now, she wanted to rise up on her toes, rubbing against his chest on the way up, to whisper in his ear that she needed to be kissed. "I'll make a deal with you, Mac-Rieve. If you leave me alone for just one year, then we'll meet up. I'll let you court me. But I need you off this boat, now."

"Meet up? Like that time in the swamp?" he said pointedly.

"I'd vow it to the Lore. Just leave here now, and I'll contact you as soon as I return from the Amazon."

"This is no' open for debate. I'm no' *bargaining* with you. That time is past. We do things my way now. I'm in this cabin and in that bed with you. Best come to terms with it."

"You can't be serious!"

"Are you no' tired of running? Settle this with me."

"One more time—I'm not running from you! I have an urgent matter to attend to, and I need to be focused. Which means you need to leave."

"Tell me what you have to 'attend to.' "

For a wild moment, she considered revealing everything about Cruach. She believed that the Broken Bloody One could in fact bring about an apocalypse—if she couldn't cast him back to the bowels of his lair for another five centuries. Nïx had said his power would now spread like wildfire, *like a plague*, if unchecked.

But Lucia knew if she laid it all out there, the Lykae would simply inform her that *he* would take care of Cruach. A male like MacRieve would never accept that she alone had the power to defeat a monster so powerful he could destroy the world.

"Tell me, Lousha. . . ."

She steadied herself. Because she'd trusted one male, she was in this predicament—she wouldn't be blindly trusting another one to get her out of it! So she answered with a question: "How could you possibly get here so quickly? I saw you in the Northlands."

"I have ways. And I'll be as forthcoming as you are with me."

"Damn you, MacRieve, you can't comprehend how important this is."

"Then enlighten me."

She pursed her lips.

"Will no'? Then I doona give a damn about your business. All I care about is having you in my grasp. Maybe I dinna make myself clear. Before I would have been good to you, spoiled you. And I might have bargained with you. No longer. Now I simply want the use of your body and revenge for all you've done to me."

Stunned, she bit out, "Go to hell."

"Been there, Valkyrie. For the last twelve months."

"I'll escape you, MacRieve, just as I have time and again. If you want to play dirty—"

"I'll *always* play dirty with you, because it's the only way to win." His hand shot downward. Would he grab her, stroke her—

But he never touched her. Her jaw dropped. *He snagged my bow!* She lunged for it, but he yanked it back.

With a look of diabolical satisfaction, he said, "Bet this has no' been out of arm's reach in centuries."

"Wh-what are you doing?"

Her look of horror would have told Garreth all he needed to know even if lightning hadn't struck just off the port window. She'd do *anything* to get this back.

"Give it to me!" She made another futile grab.

"Ah-ah, Valkyrie." He half turned from her, examining it, checking the lines. Etched into the wood were bizarre symbols that raised his hackles, made him wary. Esoteric ones that he'd never seen, as mysterious as the woman before him.

Not for the first time, he felt as though he didn't know Lucia at all.

"If you want this back in this century . . . you'll do whatever I say."

Her lips thinned.

"I think we're beginning to understand each other. Now to make you more cooperative." He unstrung the bow, placing it into its case.

"MacRieve, no!"

He tossed the case on the bed. "Calm yourself. I'll give it back when you vow to the Lore that you will no' run."

"I can't believe you would do this to me!"

He cast her an amused look. "Believe it," he said, savoring this victory, knowing he'd finally won a round—and it was decisive. "I'll do this and more. Show you all the mercy you showed me. You'll do whatever I tell you for the duration." He stepped back, his gaze raking over her body. "And right now, I'm telling you to strip for me."

TWENTY

She froze, glaring up at him. "When I get that bow back, MacRieve, I'm going to use it to kill you."

"What's new there?" His gaze dropped to her lips. "For the last year, you've been exploding things at me and trying to end me."

"I've never *tried* to 'end' you before—as evidenced by the fact that you're still alive."

"What about the log truck? And the warehouse fire?"

One single flaming arrow plus a New Year's cache of fireworks equaled a whistling, popping, screeching inferno—that he'd been directly in the middle of.

He hadn't even brought up the Austrian incident: Regin, some shrieks, an avalanche, and a buried, pissed-off werewolf.

"Not to mention what you did to my quarters in Louisiana!"

She might have ordered "her subjects" to relocate the horses from the stable to his rooms. And possibly she'd cut all his more costly belongings in half, removing fifty percent of them. "What about your lies?" Lucia snapped. "Saying that I wasn't your mate!"

He didn't address that. "I've been patient with you, Lousha, forgiven any *slights* against me and my family.

No more patience. I'm a different man now than I was then."

A darker, even more attractive man. Or beast. "Slights? If you wouldn't have *stalked* me—"

"Luckily, I did, so I could repeatedly save your pert arse."

"And yet I survived the previous *millennium* without your assistance!"

"I could have taken you from Val Hall that night of the vampire attack, away from the threat. Instead I stayed to save your sisters' lives. I did this *for you*."

She knew this!

"So I was a shade pissed that I'd made a sacrifice for you and you threw me over at the earliest opportunity. And there are a dozen more incidents when I've had to save you."

"Listen to you, talking about your good deeds!"

"I've got a few of them to speak of where you're concerned. And in the last few weeks, your foes have been increasing in number—"

"I swear it's like you believe your deeds are credits, and if you do enough or remind me enough, then you can buy me."

"No' buy you. *Earn* you. That's the Lykae in me. Could no' turn that off if I tried. Deep down I believe that if I show you I'm a good protector and provider, you'll surrender to me. You'll want me in turn."

"But I *don't* want you. I couldn't have made it clearer over the last year. There's *playing hard to get*, and then there's *take a freaking hint!* When you followed me, you brought all this on yourself." They were toe-to-toe, breathing heavily, and she was uncaring of the consequences.

"Doona want me?" His voice dropped to a low rumble. "Ah, lass, do you really want me to make a liar out of you?"

He was about to kiss her, and gods help her, she feared she wanted him to—

A knock on the door. From just outside the cabin, a male said, "Dr. MacRieve," interrupting her swan dive toward disaster.

The Scot mouthed, *"Dr. MacRieve?"* with a wolfy grin. For the first time his eyes warmed.

She wanted to die!

"That pleases me, Lousha."

"I didn't do it," she hissed. "Nïx did."

"O' course."

At the door, she called, "Um, yes?"

"Charlie here, ma'am. I'm the deck hand." He sounded young, with a light Brazilian accent. "Just wanted to tell you that the meet-and-greet starts now. The other docs are making their way to the salon."

MacRieve murmured, "Tell me this isn't a research vessel."

"What of it?"

With a scheming look, he said, "And you're pretending to be one of them."

More knocking. "Uh, Dr. MacRieve? Can I tell *Capitão* you're coming up?"

Before she could stop him, MacRieve opened the

door. Standing there was "Charlie," a clearly startled young man.

"The wife and I will be up in ten minutes."

"Uh, yes, *apreciável*—"

As she gaped, MacRieve shoved the door closed in his face. "Lousha," he began in a low threatening tone, "no more dallying. Take off your clothes. *Now.*"

"I'm going to kill you, MacRieve!" she said under her breath. "Introducing us as married?"

"It'll happen soon enough." Though matehood was as good as forever for his kind, the Valkyrie preferred some kind of binding ceremony—Annika had backed down from her hostility a grudging inch once Lachlain had agreed to give Emma one.

So Garreth had decided he would marry Lucia, wouldn't rest until she saw their union as eternal. "Mark my words."

"I can't tell you how wrong you are about that," she said in a strange tone.

"Would they no' wonder why we share a last name? Thank your sister Nïx for that."

"You could have told them we were siblings!"

"Like they'd believe that! When you're always seducing me with your eyes."

"I'm not—I never!"

Ignoring her protests, he leaned back on the bed, hands folded under his head. The bow case lay by his side—he all but dared her to try to take it again. "Lousha, you canna go to the meeting sopping wet, now, can you?"

Her eyes darted as she so clearly weighed her options. That she was even considering stripping told him that she did in fact have some serious shite going on down here.

Garreth had figured she was here on some quest—they were common enough in the Lore. Plus, he still remembered her whispering to her sister in Val Hall about locating some mystery item.

Did he need to know what business she had? Absolutely. And the fact that it was here in the Green Hell made him wary. But with Lucia he'd learned to let information unfold—eventually he'd get his way and discover everything. "You want this back"—he smugly patted the case—"then take off your clothes."

Flashing dark eyes promised retribution. "I'll get you back for this."

"You already have, Archer. The shirt's coming off for the logs. You broke my leg that time. Have you ever tried to swim in rapids with a compound fracture? The pants are for shooting a flaming arrow into that fireworks warehouse—*while I was in it*."

"That wasn't my idea, that was Reg—"

"Ah-ah, I'm no' finished. The bra is for shooting no' one but *two* MacRieves."

"What are you talking about?"

"Already forgotten that you shot my brother?"

"While trying to rescue Emma from his castle. And only through his arm, and only because he kidnapped my niece!"

"To make her his queen."

"We had no idea that it could possibly work out between them at the time."

He shrugged. "And the panties are for that first night I almost claimed you. When you left my bollocks so blue, they still have no' been set to rights."

A deep blush stole across her cheekbones. "You're not blameless in this. I wouldn't have continually attacked you if you hadn't *stalked* me. And I'll remind you yet again, you lied to me!"

"I did lie," he said simply. "I dinna want to spook you. But you ran anyway. Why, Lousha? Why run from me?" The question maddened him. At every turn, she appeared attracted to him. He'd scented her interest on more than one occasion. Yet she still fled, still fought, and always swore she wanted nothing to do with him.

"I—didn't—*run*! You know what? Keep the bow!"

"That's no' all I have over you. You will no' tell me what you're doing on this boat, but I ken that it's important to you and that you're posing as a human. If you doona want me to reveal what you are—"

"You wouldn't! You know how you'd be punished."

"You want your bow? Your cover kept?" *Why am I pushing her like this?* Probably because he was still riled over her stunts. Because swimming with a femoral fracture truly was unimaginably painful, and he'd vowed to get revenge.

But mainly because he wanted to behold his mate. He was a male, and a primitive one at heart—he simply wanted to ogle the female Fate had chosen for him. "You're stalling, Valkyrie. We're both adults, and you're in no way modest about anything else."

"Maybe I don't want to get jumped as soon as I strip."

"I vow to give you a reprieve. At least until after your meeting."

"You know what? I'll do it. Just to show you what you'll never have." With a glare, she dug into her pack, snatching out a change of clothes—a pair of plain beige pants, but she'd unerringly chosen a red halter top and red underwear.

"Red," he breathed. The color was an attractant to Lykae males, more so for mated ones. And this lingerie was especially pleasing. There was a ribbon on the back of the panties clearly made for a man's eyes. He imagined fingering it as he put her on her hands and knees. He'd slowly peel the panties down her thighs, just far enough that he could spread her legs and enter her.

She turned to take off her shirt, pulling it over her head. When she removed her bra and reached for the dry one, he caught a glimpse of one of her lush breasts and a dusky rose nipple.

How many times had he ejaculated in his hand, imagining those big breasts? How many times had he come with his teeth gritted with frustration because he was squeezing his cock instead of kneading those mounds of creamy flesh . . . ?

Though his Lucia wasn't shy, she acted discomfited sometimes, behaving in ways contrary to what he'd expect. Not modest in any way yet still shy. She was like that now. Acting as if this were killing her. When in fact, he could tell she was becoming aroused. Her breaths had grown shallow. Her eyes flickered silver. He wondered if she knew that.

She removed her underwear, revealing her taut, work-of-art arse, and all thought fled his brain for long moments. "*Gods almighty,*" he finally breathed, making her shoulders stiffen. "Never seen your arse before. And never seen the likes of it in a thousand years."

He clenched his fists, reminding himself of his ill-advised vow not to jump her. But damn, he needed to cup her there, spank her, nip her. Any way he could touch those generous curves.

She tugged on the lingerie far too fast for his liking, then donned her pants and shirt. Facing him, she said, "There. Are you happy?"

His voice rough, he said, "If happy means hard as stone and heavy in the bollocks, then *aye*."

With a glare, she started for the door. He shot to his feet, stomping into his boots, then slinging her bow case over his shoulder to follow her.

"You can't go!" Her expression was aghast.

"I go where you go."

"But your eyes are turning when you look at me!"

He shrugged. "You affect me." Understatement. He wanted to shove his face into her satiny hair and breathe in deep. He wanted to lick her nipples and know her taste—

"The mortals will see! You have to stay here. Our deal was that you wouldn't blow my cover!"

He snagged sunglasses from his pack. "No' a problem."

"And what about . . . *that*?" She delicately pointed to his erection.

He made a big show of tucking his shaft straight up behind the waist of his jeans. She looked stunned to have seen the head of his cock before he pulled his shirt down. "Ah, lass, you've seen it before. Had your hands all over it."

She was still gaping when he possessively clasped her nape and escorted her from the cabin. He followed the scent of humans to the meeting room.

By the time they reached it, she was still steaming mad. But he had leverage over her now, and he wouldn't be shy about using it. She didn't want to be discovered; he'd threatened to expose her. He'd be ruthless to have her. As ruthless as she'd proved to be to him.

At the door, she hissed, "This isn't finished."

"Been telling myself that for a year." He turned her, capturing her in his arms. She beat his chest with considerable strength, but he didn't budge. "You know when you've been nicest to me? Whenever I was *taking* kisses from you, demanding them as my due. Then you melted for me." He cupped her face, brought her to him, slanting his lips over hers.

After moments of hesitation, she melted, just as he'd remembered. He savored fleeting strokes of their tongues before he somehow broke away. "A taste of what's to come tonight. Because I *will* have you." *Let her get used to the idea.*

He opened the door, entering before her to sweep

a cautious glance around the room. Inside stood two middle-aged men, clearly scientists.

Meet-and-greet with tight-arsed geeks? The things he did for his female.

TWENTY-ONE

＊＊＊

Still flustered, with her lips bruised from MacRieve's kiss, Lucia entered the room; the two mortal males inside gazed at her with open appreciation. She checked the braids over her ears, uncomfortable with their scrutiny.

The pair—a tall middle-aged man with a genial smile and pallid skin and a younger one sporting a cowlick and thick glasses—looked like they wanted to introduce themselves, but MacRieve's aggressive demeanor and dark sunglasses probably put them off.

After unswervingly steering her to this room as if he knew the layout of the ship, he'd demonstrated conclusively that she had no willpower with him. She'd been right to run for the last twelve months, right to strike against him. She would again, but first she had to get her bow back. Before she did something stupid. . . .

The spacious salon had faded maps posted all along the walls and crates of scientific equipment that hadn't yet been unpacked into the adjoining lab. Some chairs were lined up in a U shape with a stool up front and center. A wheezing window-unit air conditioner chugged out cool drafts and the aroma of mold.

The two broad windows were fogged with condensation and draped with embroidered curtains. The bright and cheery material matched the tablecloth at the coffeepot station.

Once she took a seat, MacRieve dropped the long length of his body into one beside it. Determined to ignore him, she gazed around, her attention settling on a sheet posted above the coffeepot. Under a lovingly hand-drawn collage of jungle animals there was a list in calligraphy script:

Fast Facts About the Amazon!

The Amazon River holds 20% of the world's freshwater. At no point is it crossed by a bridge. The river is wider at the mouth than the entire length of the Thames River. The Amazon Basin is 2.6 million square miles, almost as large as the United States.

The water depth fluctuates 40 feet between the December-to-May high-water season and the June-to-November low-water season. The entire geography of the basin is altered every six months. Tributaries appear and disappear each year.

A 30–40% loss of rain forest will create a reduction in rainfall, starting a globe-killing cycle that can never be reversed. 16% of the Amazon is already gone forever. . . .

Tributaries appear and disappear? They were just going into the rainy season. Even in the unlikely case that she found a map to the legendary Rio Labyrinto, how accurate would it be if the waterways were ever changing?

Just as she finished reading, a tall stranger entered. With his inky black hair, jade green eyes, and bronze skin, the man was model handsome, looking plucked from the pages of Latin *GQ*. "Is this seat taken, *querida*?" he said, sweeping an admiring glance over her.

MacRieve growled low in his throat. Sensing the Lykae was about to attack the new male, she furtively pinched his arm, until she was certain blood welled under his skin.

He was undeterred. With a killing look, MacRieve crossed his arms, leaning back and kicking a dirty boot up atop the chair in question. "It's taken now."

The man narrowed his eyes as if he might protest, but eventually he chose another chair on the other side of the room.

Shortly after, Captain Travis swaggered inside, with a fuming mug of "coffee" in his hand and a pretty young woman behind him. Without preamble, he began, "As you know, I'm Wyatt Travis, your captain."

Our drunken, money-grubbing captain. Who'd refused to help a damsel in obvious distress. Not that he could've done anything.

He negligently sat on the stool up front. He might not be as tall as MacRieve—few were—but he was big, like a former NFL player. The love of liquor must have been a recent development, since he was still built like a seasoned athlete. "And the *Contessa*'s my ship. One hundred and eight feet long, she's a light draft, draws only five feet. Lets us get deep into the jungle." He pointed toward the back of the room at a wall-sized map of the river and all its known tributaries. They resembled veins—a rain forest circulatory system. "I'll keep that map updated with our whereabouts." Pushpins had left holes throughout, until the paper was missing in places. The *Contessa*, it seemed, had been just about everywhere in the basin, and she'd been there many times over.

Travis paused for a deep drink from his mug, so she took the opportunity to glance at MacRieve from under a lock of her hair.

He looked suspicious and aggressive, so different from the man she'd first known. He was harder now, darker. *Because of me.* Her lips were still tender from his harsh, demanding kiss—a constant reminder of what he planned to do with her this evening.

He's going to try to have sex with me. Realization fully hit her. *This very night.*

How was she supposed to sit through this meeting, knowing what would befall her when they returned? She was on edge and knew he could sense her tension— because she could sense his as well.

And what would *she* do when he tried to? Earlier, as she'd removed her clothes, the look in his eyes had been delighted, as if he were unwrapping the best gift he could possibly conceive of.

Surprisingly, she'd responded, finding it . . . *erotic* to strip at his command. Maybe she was a closet submissive—who'd needed to dominate every opponent over a thousand years. All except for MacRieve? *Am I delirious?*

"We're heading south toward the very end of the Amazon proper," Travis continued, "then turning off on the San Miguel tributary to some of the most remote parts of the basin. We'll motor all night until the river gets tight." Another swig for the thirsty captain. "Since we're going deeper into virgin territory, this trip lent itself to several different disciplines. Everybody here's in different fields, so there's no direct competition."

He made a negligent hand motion toward the young woman beside him. "This is my cook."

Of middling height, with soulful hazel eyes, the female looked to be all of nineteen. "Hi, I'm Izabel Carlotta Ambos," she said with a confident wave. Izabel was comely, though she wore a shapeless shirt and baggy cargo pants, cinched tight with a belt. "I'll be preparing your meals. My *bife a cavalo* is *deliciosa*, and if you keep the kitchen stocked with fish, I'll keep fresh feasts on the table."

MacRieve perked up at that.

"Some of you have met my twin, Charlie. He's the deckhand." Same Brazilian accent as her brother, same hazel eyes.

Izabel smiled at her, and Lucia gave a pained smile in return. Oh, no, not the *we're the only two females on a ship of males* bonding bit. She had no need for additional "pals." Especially not short-term *human* ones.

Besides, there was something off about her that Lucia couldn't put her finger on. Perhaps Izabel had Lorean in her, somewhere far back in her family line. Or maybe she was completely human, but with a curse hanging over her. *Something* was amiss.

"Yeah, that's right," the captain said. "Chuck is my right-hand man. You'll meet him later." Another draw from his mug. "Chuck and Izabel are new to the *Contessa*—so this trip is the last one of a long trial period. Drop me a dime if they screw up." The captain seemed to have a cosmic inability to call Charlie anything but Chuck. "Now, some of you are already acquainted, but it's customary on this ship to do a round of intros. Tell us who you are, what you study, and why you're here."

The pale man said, "I guess I'll start"—his accent was east coast, upper crust—"I'm Benjamin Rossiter, an M.D. and professor of chemoecology at Cornell. I'll be looking for uncataloged plants in the hope of discovering pharmaceutical uses." Though his manner was relaxed, he had dark circles under his blue eyes and sweat had beaded above his upper lip. "We've only identified one percent of the medicinal plants in the basin, yet that one percent accounts for *twenty-five* percent of all our pharmaceuticals. The potential is nearly inconceivable." He held up a palm, casting them a half grin. "And I'll stop myself there, so I don't make your eyes glaze over." *The guy looks moneyed. So what's he doing on a tub like this?*

The darkly handsome man spoke next. "I'm Marcos Damião, head of the department of social anthropology at the University of São Paulo."

If Lucia had suspected Izabel had some connection to the Lore, she was certain Damião did.

"My specialization is indigenous shamanism, and I'm here to search for uncontacted tribes."

MacRieve still had his arms crossed over his chest.

"If they're uncontacted, do they no' want to stay that way?"

Lucia jabbed her elbow at him, and he grunted.

Damião gave a tight smile that didn't reach his vivid green eyes. "Several large oil companies are bidding on these remote territories, falsely claiming they're unoccupied, so any tribes there will certainly be contacted regardless. My aim for this expedition is to get photos of them from a distance and prove their existence, which would halt all oil exploration on their lands." He waved to the cowlick guy beside him. "Dr. Schecter?"

"Right, right, I'm Dr. Clarence Schecter, a zoologist from UC San Diego." He removed his glasses, polishing them with his shirttail. "My area of study is unculled species of reptiles."

Rossiter raised a brow. "Unculled?"

"Yes, when men hunt, they pick off the largest of the species. Over time, the pool becomes smaller. So the deeper into the jungle we get, the more chance there is of spotting larger-than-normal river specimens."

With all their talk of *going deep* into the jungle, Lucia might not have to dump them as early as she'd thought.

MacRieve scoffed. "What do you mean 'larger than normal?' Normal out here is no' exactly small." MacRieve had said he'd hoped never to come back here. How long had he been in the basin before? And why?

The captain agreed. "I see giant animals every day. Tarantulas with meaty bodies the size of dinner plates. Foot-long scorpions. Twenty-foot-long gators. Giant otters and even catfish'll stretch nine feet."

"And by *gator*," Dr. Schecter said in a patronizing tone, "I assume you mean the South American crocodilian species called the *caiman*?"

At Travis's shrug, Schecter said, "That's the thing. In other areas, we have fossil records of caimans reaching *forty* feet long. But they've been overhunted. Now, once we gain enough distance from civilization, and with the sonic baiting techniques I'll utilize, I'll be able to document primordial specimens."

MacRieve coughed the word, *"Sonic"* just as Rossiter made a sound of realization.

"Megafauna," the man said. "You're searching for megs! If you're a cryptozoologist, just admit it and take your ribbing."

Cryptozoology—the study of creatures from "myth." *They're in a room with at least two cryptids. And they don't even know it.*

"Me? I'm not a cryptozoologist!" Schecter flushed red. "Otherwise I'd be aboard the *Barão da Borracha*."

As Rossiter groaned, Travis's expression turned chilling, while Izabel studied her captain's sudden change in demeanor.

"Wait—what was that?" Lucia asked. Nïx had said, *Beware of the barão da borracha.* The Rubber Baron wasn't a person but a ship? "Why do you say that?"

Schecter answered, "The *Barão* is filled to the bevels with cryzos. You know, cryptozoologists. Captain Malaquí takes them hunting in the jungle for 'demons' and 'shape-shifters' in backwater tributaries." He added, "I've heard passengers go out with Malaquí. But sometimes . . . they don't come back."

Lucia waited for Travis to naysay that, to call it a baseless rumor. Instead he drank deep.

She asked the captain, "Is that ship close by?"

"Headed north in the opposite direction," Travis said tightly. He added in a mumble, "As I like it."

Izabel canted her head at Travis, and her thick black braid swept off her shoulder. The young woman clearly carried a torch for the much older, and remarkably less sober, captain. *Good luck with the male specimen you've got there, Izabel. P.S.: This ship has been over-culled.*

"Where're they searching for demons?" MacRieve asked. "Which tributary?"

Schecter answered, "My guide in Iquitos told me Rio Labyrinto, or some such."

At that mention, Lucia tensed and of course Mac-Rieve noticed. He put his callused hand on her back. It was warm against her, even through her shirt.

"That's nothing but a hokey legend," the captain muttered into his cup. And for a second, Lucia thought he was lying.

Schecter said, "Well, likely so. But I'd taken all that information with a grain of salt since the guide also told me that they were loading a coffin onto the ship!"

Now both Lucia and MacRieve tensed. *A vampire?* What would a leech possibly be doing out here? For some reason she thought of Lothaire. He'd been making power plays throughout the Lore for the last year—

"Your turn, Dr. . . ." Schecter asked her, trailing off.

"What? Me? I'm Dr. *MacRieve*." She grated out the last word, and the werewolf's lip curled. "From LSU."

Damn it, what would Nïx have said was her field? She glanced at Travis. "And I'm a . . ."

He frowned. "Paleopathologist?"

Paleo what? Damn you, Nïx!

Now Dr. Rossiter frowned. "Paleo? How will you find a fossil record in a live river basin?"

"I would love to tell you, but it's a trade secret," she said with a forced smile.

"At least tell us what diseases you are studying as a pathologist," Damiãno said.

"If Dr. Rossiter feared he'd make your eyes glaze over, I could put you to sleep."

Schecter turned to MacRieve. "And what is your field, Dr . . . ?"

Despite the fact that he was a prince, he answered, "*Mr.* MacRieve. I'm here in a security capacity for my wife. She's the beauty and brains—I'm the brawn."

She stiffened again at his calling her his wife. Mac-Rieve had no idea how much that word bothered her.

Schecter asked, "Why exactly would anyone need security?"

"Are you jesting?" MacRieve asked. "You doona know?" He flashed an aggravated look at Travis, then said simply, "Because we're in the bluidy Amazon."

TWENTY-TWO

T he sun had begun to set, filling Lucia with more anxiety. She couldn't remember the last time she'd dreaded nightfall more. And she'd warred with vampires!

She repeatedly debated her options. One idea she'd ruled out? Telling MacRieve the truth. If she revealed to him precisely why they couldn't have sex ever, much less *tonight*, he would no doubt tell her she could live without the archery—because *he* would protect her.

And if he used that reasoning with her, she thought she could hate him.

Once the meeting was over, Izabel brought in a tub of iced-down *Iquiteña* beer for "the doctors." When she set the tub down, her blouse gaped, and Travis's eyes were on her like a hawk. Then he scowled at the glimpse of her exposed bra. A scowl? Most men would be delighted.

With an inward shrug—who could understand the minds of *mortals*?—Lucia crossed to the salon entrance. As she reached for the knob, she noticed that the door was thick, with a security barricade that could be slammed in place. A rain forest panic room? *Interesting . . .*

Once she walked outside, she stopped at the closest rail, nearly gasping at the oppressive heat after being in the air-conditioned room.

MacRieve snagged a bottle of beer, then followed her out, standing next to her at the railing. He held the bottle with his forefinger curled around the neck. Which was so . . . *male.* "Where do you think you're going?" he asked, stowing his sunglasses in a pocket.

"Back to *my* cabin."

"Happy to escort you there." He took a swig, placing his free hand on her lower back.

Dead man walking? Try dead Valkyrie walking. Every step closer was grueling. She was breathless, filled with trepidation. *Why* hadn't she been able to deny him in the past? Part of her whispered, *It's not him you can't deny—it's yourself.*

She was going to have to strike against him yet again. But how? How to get her bow? *And then get him off the boat?*

Silence reigned between MacRieve and her, while all around them the rain forest was awakening. Frogs croaked, building to a deafening crescendo before dwindling to silence, then building once more. Insects whirred and chirped, howler monkeys screeching.

MacRieve took another swig of beer. "Never met so many scientists who needed to get laid."

Unable to help herself, she asked, "What are you talking about?"

He stopped, leaning in, forcing her back to the wall. He rested his free hand against it over her head. "Looks like we're going deep. Gotta get *deep* up the river. Really penetrate the virgin bush, over and over again, till we achieve our mutual aims."

When he grinned, she stared at his lips. Then at his eyes, at those laugh lines. As ever, she was captivated by this big, brawny male and curious about his past. Just from looking at him, she could tell he'd been in the sun laughing in the days before he'd been frozen forever into his immortality.

Another swig. Was he waiting to finish his beer before bringing her to the cabin, or just enjoying the sunset? "Those docs got more bollocks than sense. They have no idea how dicey it is out here."

"How do you know so much about the Amazon?"

"Unfortunately, I'm verra familiar with the Green Hell." He appeared to have mellowed somewhat, though he still seemed preoccupied. "When the clan wanted to leave Scotland, the Amazon basin was one of the proposed settlement options. Lots of room to run, and no humans for thousands of miles in some areas. It sounded perfect."

"But it wasn't?"

"I got down here and learned that the Amazon can even kill immortals. She does no' care which lives she takes and is strong enough to pluck any she chooses." He met her gaze. "It can be lethal—even for us." His brows drew together, as if at some memory.

Had he lost a loved one? Or a lover? A flare of jealousy startled her. Had he kissed another under this very sky? Her gaze fell to his lips.

"You're doing it again, Lousha."

"What?"

"Looking like you want me to kiss you."

She flushed. Was she *that* transparent? "Dream on, werewolf."

"I do, constantly."

Hastily returning to the subject, she asked, "Did you lose someone in your party down here?"

"Nay, I came alone." At her questioning glance, he said, "A type of penance, I guess. It's a moot point now. . . ." He trailed off, his gaze leaving her face to scan the river. His body tensed around hers, his face hardened, and his irises flickered pale blue.

He stared out with pure malevolence, as if he'd not only kill something for threatening her—he'd make it hurt. Not for the first time, she thought, *Gods help any being that means me harm.*

He asked, "You get the feeling we're being watched?"

She did. She'd thought it would fade now that Mac-Rieve was on board with her, but she was definitely sensing an oppressive presence nearby.

He turned back to her, studied her face, and said, "Aye, me too. You know of anyone who'd be trailing you?"

Cruach had followers in his Cult of Death who would do anything to stop her, but they were usually human and easy enough to lose. "Actually, yes," she answered softly, and MacRieve leaned in with interest. "This jackass Lykae who can't take no for an answer is stalking me."

He drew back with narrowed eyes. "Maybe if he ever truly heard a 'no' coming from the female he was stalking, he'd give her up."

With that, he began leading her back toward the

cabin. "So you want to tell me why you tensed when the Rio Labyrinto was mentioned? And unless I missed my mark, the mention of the *Barão da Borracha* and Captain Malaquí dinna coax a smile from you either."

She shrugged. "You can suppose things all you like."

At the door, he said, "At least tell me this—did you get a read on Damiãno?"

She answered quietly, "He's a Lorean."

"Aye, but I doona know what manner of being he is. Intend to find out. Stay here, Lousha. And be prepared to answer some questions when I return. If you ever want to see your bow again." He patted the case.

All that nervousness about being alone with him, until she was nearly sick with it, and now he was just taking off? *With my bow?* "You're . . . leaving?" Had she sounded disappointed?

He grinned, leaning his tall body against the door frame. "I'll be back in fifteen minutes to see to you, beauty. Can you wait that long for it?"

"I don't . . . I never . . ." Inhaling for calm, she said, "Leave my bow, then."

"No' a chance," he said over his shoulder.

Once he'd gone, she paced the stifling cabin, her emotions roiling. Though she could see in the dark, she flipped on the bedside lamp, casting subtle light over the interior. Without the benefit of the sun pouring in, the room seemed smaller—almost cozy.

And he expects to share it with me.

She picked up her phone to call Nïx again and saw another text had arrived from Regin. *RegRad: Gettng tranqued 2nite with the witches. Bet U wish U were here! LOSER!*

Lucia did wish she was there—away from MacRieve, away from the temptation he presented. He was the key to her destruction, the closest she'd gotten to ruin in centuries.

But he wouldn't force her to have sex. She knew that about him. So if she could resist . . . The thought gave her a feeling of some control. *Yes, I can control this.*

Wanting information from Nïx, and needing to vent, Lucia dialed the soothsayer. Surprisingly, Nïx answered.

Lucia wasted no time. "How could you book me as Lucia *MacRieve*?"

In a pedantic tone, Nïx said, "When dealing with humans, you have to provide a last name. I thought you would prefer MacRieve to your real name. Lucia av Cruach."

Lucia of Cruach. That had been her identity—as his possession, an extension of him. "How long have you known?" She'd told no one but had always suspected Nïx knew. Still, it'd been a shock to hear her call him Lucia's *husband.*

"Since the night you jumped to escape him."

So long ago . . . "Nïx, my alias with mortals has always been Lucia Archer. It's on my credit cards, my driver's license."

Sounding confused, Nïx said, "But . . . but MacRieve is *funnier.*"

"And a paleopathologist? What do I know about pathology, much less the paleo kind?"

"You've killed as many beings as some diseases," Nïx pointed out in a chipper tone. "Shots to the heart, and you're to blame."

"I'm going to shoot *you*."

"That doesn't sound patient and levelheaded, Lucia."

"And what about MacRieve? You could have warned me he'd be here."

"Oh, is he? Would you have missed him if you'd been on time, I wonder? Or maybe you *need* him."

"More than my archery? And right before I'm to face Cruach?"

"You'll have to show some restraint."

"That's rich, Nïx. One of the most unrestrained Valkyrie preaching this to me. Just tell me what I'm looking for, so—oh, I don't know—I might know it when I find it!"

For effect, Nïx went quiet for several moments before finally saying, "Have you ever heard the term . . . *dieumort*?"

"Is that a joke?"

"Good guess, yet actually, I believe it's a god killer."

Lucia rolled her eyes. "I am fully aware of what it is!"

"Thunder stolen." Sigh. "I already told you, didn't I?"

"Regin and I have been looking for a dieumort for years! I've been breaking my neck over the last twelve months to unearth one." Then Lucia sucked in a breath. "It's down here," she murmured, excitement drumming inside her.

"Uh-huh. They're rare—like Amphitrite's-tears rare—but a dieumort is in Rio Labyrinto."

A god killer exists, and Nïx knows where it is! "Is it an arrow?"

"Dunno what form it's in," Nïx said. "But I figured we could off Cruach with it."

"*Off* Cruach? Like exterminate, forever?" Lucia gripped the phone hard.

"Forever and ever. Alas, the gods, or at least the ones I'm in contact with, are against this plan. They don't want any knowledge or weapons—or *other*—brought forth. They think they'd rather deal with Cruach. This is a mistake," Nïx said simply. "In any case, more than the Cult of Death will be coming to stop you. Immortal assassins and mercenaries have likely already been dispatched. And this time, they'll be emissaries of the gods."

So to kill one would be punishable by divine power. "How would those gods 'deal with Cruach'?" *In case I fail.*

"They expect you to return to your hubby and appease him for a time, to stall while they come up with a way to destroy him."

Lucia nearly retched. *Appease him?* She'd die first. *The blood spilling through his teeth, the maggots and carnage . . .*

Nïx continued, "The apocalypse has already begun, you see. Just a *smidgen* of Armageddon so far. Still fixable, but not for long. Ticktock."

"How could it have started? He's not free." If Cruach were already free, then it was already over. He could only be harmed—or killed—within his jail, his lair. Only there did he take corporeal form. "I'd know if he were about to escape." *I always know.* Her nightmares had proved uncannily accurate harbingers.

"He's not free yet, but he's been receiving help from his followers."

The notorious Cult of Death worshipped him as their deity, the members calling themselves Cromites. They were robed swordsmen, tattooed with Cruach's mark—a symbol in the shape of his twisting, gnarled horns.

"The cult has grown," Nïx said, "and they're performing continual sacrifices in his name to make him stronger so he can rise."

Cold fear suffused Lucia. Gods derived strength from the amount of worship they received over any given day—Lucia could deal with the cult coming after her, but she couldn't stop their grisly rituals. "What else, Nïx?"

"Honestly, all I know is that a dieumort is in Rio Labyrinto."

"How do I find the river?"

"Everything you need will be on that boat."

"Nïx, you have to tell me more!" Lucia cried. "Why do you always parcel out information?"

"I'm an oracle. It's what we do," she answered. "Now, do I really need to fake the static again?" *Click.*

Lucia paced the small cabin once more, stunned by all she'd learned—and *hadn't* learned. Was this a wild goose chase? Was Nïx even lucid? The soothsayer had been improving mentally over the past few months but still had hellacious lapses. Like the month she spoke in nothing but ancient Babylonian or the weeks when she would only answer if addressed as *P!nk*.

As Lucia gaped at the sat-phone, another text arrived from *RegRad: Jst kdding. Ur not loser. I shld B there w/ U. Kinda miss U.*

Lucia's brows knit. *I kinda miss you, too.*

Pacing, pacing . . . A bead of sweat trickled down her forehead. She wiped it away, but another appeared. She felt grimy, and her legs were still sticky from her earlier contact with river water.

Making a snap decision, she grabbed her toiletries from her backpack, then hurried into the bathroom. Hastily stripping, she hopped into the small shower stall. The water pressure was nil, the temperature less than lukewarm, but it was enough for her to rinse off her body and wash her hair.

After she redressed, she sat on the edge of the bed, but just as quickly shot to her feet to pace some more, glancing at her phone clock. MacRieve should've been back by now. What was he doing?

She crossed to the little balcony and stared out at the river. The *Contessa* was chugging along at a steady clip and apparently would motor all night.

The water was muddy, like the Mississippi, the air as sultry as summers in New Orleans. Though she'd just taken a cool shower, her skin was already heated. She wound her hair up and rubbed her nape.

What was taking MacRieve so long? Since Lucia was hyperaware of the Scot's nearness, she was also keenly feeling his absence.

He'd told her he had questions for her. She had some for him as well. *How'd it feel to lose your crown?* She'd known he loved his older brother and was overjoyed at his return, but to go from king of all Lykae back to the Dark Prince had to have affected him.

How'd you keep from attacking me when the moon was full? She'd feared he'd had other females brought to him on those nights to work off the overwhelming lust he'd had to suffer. So what would keep him from attacking now? In ten days, the moon would be full.

But mainly she wanted to ask, *Over the last year, did you ever consider giving up on me?*

Lucia stared down, nearly hypnotized by the swirling eddies. *Staring at the water . . . memories arising.* All the talk with Nïx about Cruach forced Lucia to remember. How naïve she'd been, how bright her future.

At sixteen she'd had no idea how good she'd had it in the immortal plane of Valhalla. She'd spent much of her time at the exit portal of the plane, longing to leave. She'd found Valhalla *dull*.

Now she knew it'd been a land covered in mists, full of beauty and endless peace.

But the outside world had been so clear, so sharp, so exciting. Lucia had wanted to lie on her back and stare up at the bright stars that she could only scarcely see from her perch. She'd longed for adventure but mainly for *romance*. She'd wanted her own hearth and family—a husband and eventually a dozen children.

Let her half sisters deal with the Valkyrie's duties— choosing the slain and fighting battles. She'd had no interest in death.

Lucia had wanted *love. . . .*

One night, a stranger had appeared at the other side

of the portal. A man—just there, like a dream, as if she'd conjured him. He'd had curling bright hair and blue eyes the color of the cloudless daytime skies she'd glimpsed, but always at a distance. Never had she encountered anything as compelling as the man's angelic looks.

"What's your name, fair Valkyrie?" he asked.

"I'm Lucia the Maiden. What is yours?"

"I'm called Crom. I'm the man you're soon to marry."

She laughed, delighted. "Are you, sir?"

"I will make you mistress of my castle. And shower you with gifts and adoration."

"I do like gifts."

They flirted until she heard Regin calling her for dinner. As young Valkyrie, they still had the need to eat, still were mortal until they were fully grown and had frozen into their immortality. After casting a quick glance over her shoulder, Lucia told him, "I have to go, but will you return to see me once more?"

"I'll be here tomorrow night, eagerly awaiting you," he said. "And the night after and after again. Until you agree to wed me . . ."

That'd been the only promise he'd ever kept.

The cabin door opened.

TWENTY-THREE

Garreth found her on the balcony. At once, her slim shoulders stiffened.

As he crossed to her, he marveled again that she was in his keeping at last. He'd pursued her for so long, he had a hard time believing it.

Tonight, he hadn't wanted to let her out of his sight, but his Instinct had been screaming that his mate was in danger.

He'd just confirmed how much.

Joining her outside, he leaned his forearms on the rail, gazing out at the nighttime scene. With the dense forest closing in all around them, they might as well be in a canyon—a green-walled canyon. Low storm clouds were back building, only adding to that claustrophobic sense.

How he remembered this place. How he'd hoped to forget it.

Finally she turned to him, with her lovely face wan, her expression strained.

"When was the last time you slept?" he asked. After the previous punishing year, he felt like arse. He couldn't imagine how she felt or how she pushed herself like this.

"A week ago, I think." Immortals could easily go a couple of days without sleep, but a week was rough. He knew this well—he'd been up for nearly a dozen days.

She'd showered and washed her hair. Now it smelled faintly sweet, like jasmine. "Showering without me, Valkyrie? Last night *that* will be happening." And she'd dressed fully again. "Do you think a few extra garments will keep me from my aim?"

"I think I'm not going to be awaiting you in my skimpy lingerie."

"Maybe no' *yet*." Before she could protest, he said, "You need to tell me about whatever little mission you're on. Because you're being followed. Seems quite a few Loreans doona want you to reach whatever you need to 'attend to.' So now it's time for you to answer my questions."

"Forget it, MacRieve."

"You'll blindly ignore that you're in danger?"

"Because *you* say so? Oh wait, how did you put it in the meeting? We're in danger because we're in the Amazon. Wow, that specific? Really, I better protect myself from . . . *the rascally Amazon*."

"Lousha, I slew two demon assassins just today in Iquitos—they had their swords raised in an alley you were about to sprint by." He'd nigh missed this boat because of all the beheading he'd had to do in town.

"Then all the better that I'm on the river."

He gave a harsh laugh. "No' quite. You see, I'll be forcibly removing you from the vessel at the earliest opportunity."

"*What?*" Visibly making an effort to calm herself, she said, "MacRieve, let's be reasonable about this. What threat on board has you acting like this?"

"For one, there's Dr. Clarence Ogilvie Schecter—"

She raised a hand to stop him. "And how would you know his middle name?"

When he hiked his shoulders, her face lit with an expression of dawning realization. "You've got to be kidding me. You snooped through their things?"

He'd do that and more to keep her safe. "Aye, while they were upstairs drinking beers." Turning to the bed inside, he dropped his body and the case atop it. "I dinna want you to feel that you were being singled out for my invasions of privacy." At her glare, he added, "I'm a Lykae—if I get curious, I investigate. It's what we do. So anyway, ole Schecter told us he's no' studying megafauna?"

"He is?"

"Oh, aye. He's hunting a goddamned megacaiman."

"What is that, and what does it have to do with me?"

"Schecter plans to *trap* a four-ton caiman with this rickety old bark—no' merely to document one. He's got that 'sonic lure'—patent bluidy pending—and enough tranquilizer to make even your glowing sister happy."

"Now, that *is* good to know," she said, tapping her chin. "But it's still not enough to worry me."

"Ah, but what about Rossiter? He says he's hunting for cures, but he's only interested in one—for Fatal Insomnia Syndrome."

"What is that?"

"From what I could tell from his papers, it's an

extremely rare genetic disorder. Basically, you lose the ability to sleep. You stay awake until you eventually die."

"What does this have to do with me?"

"Doc Rossiter's studying it—because he's dying from it. So he's out here with nothing to lose. He's completely rogue, searching for some rare orchid he believes will hold the cure for the disease."

"First of all, isn't it always an orchid? And second of all—so?"

"So what do you think he'd do if he discovered immortality existed? If he determined that we can potentially live forever—or that I could possibly *make* him immortal?" Not that Garreth ever would. Of all the species in the Lore, the Lykae turned others the least—because of the devastating side-effects.

"And what about Damião?"

"He's got doctored medical records. Definitely no' human."

"Then what is he?"

"Maybe a shifter or warlock? Or a demon? If he's into shamanism, he could be a bluidy witch doctor for all we know."

"Do you think he lied about what he's here for?"

"Doona know what his real aim is—but if it's truly to stop the oil companies, then we're already being followed. They've got mercenaries cruising up and down the river, scanning CBs and sat-phones. A basin-wide intelligence net. Any uncontacted tribe would cost them *billions*. No one will be reporting a sighting," he said. "Lousha, those three all know this is dodgy. It's why they're on a shite boat like this, hiring a drunk captain who's ruled by the dollar. So unless you give me a damn good reason to allow you to stay aboard—"

"*Allow* me?"

"Aye. Second lesson about the Amazon? Might makes right out here."

"I have to be on *this* ship. This one in particular." At his unbending look, she said, "This isn't about me and you. This is much, much bigger. End of the world big."

"Then tell me," MacRieve said, "and I'll help you."

Seeing no way around it, she decided to reveal *some*. "Fine, let's make a deal. You keep my cover, and no more ordering me to strip—"

"Which you loved and were aroused by."

"Do you want to know or not?"

He held up his palms. "Agreed and agreed."

"And we won't be having sex."

"*Dis*agreed. You're acting like you have some bargaining power—I can force you from this ship."

"Don't put my back up against the wall, MacRieve. I might strive to be reasonable, but you have no idea what I'm capable of when cornered."

"Ah, but what are you capable of without drawing human attention? Tomorrow morning, we're gone."

"Very well! I'll tell you," she said, beginning to pace yet again. "You've met Nïx, I'm sure."

"Oh, when I was locked in the Valkyrie dungeon? After you trapped me?"

She pursed her lips.

"Go on, then."

"She contacted me just a day ago, told me the world was on the verge of apocalypse. I was to find Rio Laby-rinto. The river would hold the answer to our salvation. And before you ask, I don't know much more. Nïx won't divvy the details. You don't know what she's like."

"I doona? She would no' tell me why I had to be in Iquitos at precisely three. All she'd say is 'Do you want to see your mate or no', werewolf?' "

"That's how you got here so fast!" *Rotter!* "No, she wouldn't."

"We both know she would and did."

Nïx had *planned* for Lucia and MacRieve to meet. The soothsayer had done him a favor. Why? Nïx might be mad, but she could also be calculating.

A niggling suspicion had been building in Lucia over the last few months. The three-thousand-year-old soothsayer had begun telling people she would soon be a goddess. And that wasn't just an insane musing—it was actually a possibility.

Nïx had been born of gods, and she'd attained the requisite age—ancient. But most importantly, she was collecting lifelong loyalties, which doubled as worship.

If gods derived strength from the number of wor-shippers they acquired, then Nïx was growing more and more powerful. Here was Garreth MacRieve, an-other being who owed Nïx a favor, who'd be thanking her daily for the rest of his immortal life for her help. Like a prayer. Humans might thank God—MacRieve would thank Nïx.

Nucking Futs Nïx a goddess? Lucia wondered if she'd be a benevolent one.

"Doona be angry with the soothsayer," he said. "If she had no' helped me, I would've eventually caught you anyway."

"You sound confident. Makes me wonder why you hadn't before."

"I had an ace in my pocket that I had no' yet played." Before she could question him about his *ace*, he asked, "So did Nïx happen to give you any directions to Rio Labyrinto?"

Lucia shook her head. "She said I'd have everything I needed aboard this ship."

"That so?" he replied thoughtfully. "Then she must've meant that you'd need me."

"Why on earth?"

" 'Cause I've been there, lass."

TWENTY-FOUR

"**B**ut no one comes out of Rio Labyrinto alive," Lucia said.

Garreth lifted his chin. "No one—but me."

Her eyes went wide. "Then tell me about the river! Where is it?"

"First, you tell me what else you know about the apocalypse. You ken you will no' get a word from me otherwise." That wasn't true. If she ever used her wiles on him, he'd likely be putty in her hands.

She paced, worrying her plump bottom lip—the one he wanted to take between his own teeth to nibble on. After exhaling a breath, she asked, "Have you heard of the god . . . *Crom Cruach*?"

He had. But the way she'd uttered, or *barely* uttered, the god's name with a flash of sorrow in her eyes made his hackles rise. "Maybe some scattered tales," he lied. "Canna remember."

She cast him an expression that said she didn't know whether to believe him.

"Gods are no' really my area of interest. Rugby? Now *that* I pay attention to."

After a hesitation, she said, "He's evil to the bone.

His primary power is to make people feel a mad need to sacrifice whoever they love. Only now, that need will be contagious—the lust to slaughter in Cruach's name— passing from person to person. In the past, he's been jailed in a lair, but with each Accession, he grows powerful enough to break from his prison. Every five hundred years someone has to send him back there. Nïx dispatched me to do this."

After Lucia's explanation, he sensed that she knew far more than what she was telling him.

And that she might be about to snap. *Let the information unfold.* "With all the creatures in the Lore that owe the soothsayer, she chose you for this?" He was impressed, and didn't bother hiding it.

"Yes, me." She tucked her still damp hair behind her pointed ear. "Nïx told me there might be a way to kill him. To finally end the cycle."

"A *way*?"

"A weapon. Called a dieumort. It's a—"

"God killer. I've heard of them. And she thinks one's on Rio Labyrinto?"

Lucia nodded. "That's what she said. Now, I've told you my part—tell me about the river. How did you find it?"

"Purely by accident. I'd been chasing game along the riverside, and I saw it disappear right before my eyes. But I could still *scent* it. I followed my nose straight through the portal."

"And? Tell me more!"

"Also known as the River of Doom and the River of

Doors, it's a watery maze of channels and cutouts." He paused for effect. "And it's rumored to be the gateway to El Dorado."

"El Dorado?" Lucia's eyes went wide. "The Lost City of Gold?" Maybe the dieumort *was* the golden arrow of her dreams? "Where? Where is it?" Lucia had already been reeling from the fact that MacRieve knew where Rio Labyrinto was—*everything you need will be on that boat*—and now this?

El-freaking-Dorado.

"As though I'd reveal the location to you?" MacRieve scoffed. "I think no'. I like you dependent on me and my good will."

Apparently she *wouldn't* be taking her bow back from MacRieve and ditching him. "I told you the nature of the apocalypse."

In answer, he gave her a look as if he knew she was holding back.

"Don't you understand? It's critical for me to find a way to destroy Cruach!"

"So if I allow you to stay on the boat, you're at risk from a thousand different perils, and if I take you from here, you're still in danger from an apocalypse?"

"Pretty much."

He exhaled wearily. "Verra well, we'll stay. But we're going to establish some guidelines for our time aboard this ship."

"In other words, you intend to give me rules *to obey*? MacRieve, just tell me where it is—I can do this on my own."

"Never."

"The full moon's coming! Have you thought about that, werewolf? It's only ten days away!"

"You know the dates as well as I do, then?"

"You won't be able to control yourself. You'll attack me. I know what your kind does."

"I'd never put you in harm's way. As long as I'm wearing this"—he pointed to the silver cuff on his arm—"I will no' lose control of myself."

"What does that do?" She eyed it suspiciously. "Where'd you get it?"

"The . . . witches." He seemed to have just stifled a shudder. "The inscription on the cuff makes it so that I will no' change involuntarily."

"I thought you told me you'd never ally with the witches."

"My cousin has since married one, and I approached them about this. I did it *for you*."

Against her will, she felt herself softening. She knew what that must have cost him. "How long have you had it?"

"About ten months. Why?"

"How'd you stay away from me during the first two full moons?"

"I figured out a way," he said with a shrug.

"Did you . . . hurt yourself?"

"Would you care?"

"I'm not unfeeling, MacRieve."

"I figured it out. That's all you need to know."

By using other women? Lucia could just imagine his clan bringing females to satisfy him. She didn't even want to contemplate why the thought burned her, like acid seething on tender skin. "Are you sure that cuff will keep you from going all . . . wolfy?"

He raised a brow. "It's worked for the better part of a year." When she still looked doubtful, he added, "They put a House of Witches guarantee on it."

Then it *would* work.

"*Wolfy*, is it? And what do you know about my turning?"

"I asked around when I figured out I was your . . . mate."

He stood, crossing to her. "Well, let's hear it."

"Basically, you'll lose your mind, turning animalistic, hunting me down until you claim me repeatedly, biting my neck and marking me as your possession. Nothing will stop you—no cage can hold you. Did I miss anything?"

"Aye, Lousha." His gaze raked over her and his voice deepened. "The fact that you're going to like it."

Merely talking about marking her flesh made Garreth grow hard as steel. It was a burning need within him. "Do you want to know the rules or no'?" At her glare, he said, "Now, I'm sure you want your bow back. And every indication from you says you want my . . . knowledge. So you're going to let me have my way with you each night we're aboard. And also whenever there's a storm with lightning to disguise yours—"

"It won't happen! Does what I need or want count for nothing in your mixed-up idea of a relationship?"

"Aye, if you'll admit what you *truly* need and want.

My Instinct's screaming that you need *me,* that you *ache.* I sense it in you—hell, I'm sensing it right now. I canna rest until I ease you."

"I didn't ask for this! For you—"

"You ask for it every goddamned time you're near me, beauty." He closed in on her, until their bodies were only inches apart. "Doona ever doubt that."

She gazed up at him, lips parted, her breaths shallowing.

"Do you know what it's been like to scent your desire for me? I'm lured by it, wanting it so badly, and then you lash out at me. Can you imagine the frustration, Lousha? I've got a year of it pent up inside me." He leaned down, and against her neck, he murmured, "Or what it was like to find my female after so many centuries and then to be a heartbeat away from being inside her?" At her ear, he said, "I canna count how many times I re-imagined that night, fantasizing I'd sunk into your trembling body. In my mind, I've claimed you a thousand times. And from your expression, lass, I am no' the only one who's imagined us together."

"No!" she cried, even as she stared at his lips and moistened her own. Her hips had begun subtly rocking toward him. Her hardened nipples were jutting points against her red shirt. "Let me go!"

"Damn you, Lousha!" He twisted away, launching his fist at the exterior wall, punching a hole straight through. "What do you want from me? Tell me why your words never match your actions! Why you respond so sweetly, then grow afraid?" He exhaled, regretting his show of temper. "It's making me crazed."

She backed away. "I can't. Because you wouldn't understand."

—Soothe her. Be gentle. She knows fear.—

Lucia looked woebegone and fragile. And as much as Garreth talked a big game, the Instinct was driving him not only to claim her, but also to please her.

When she dropped her head into her hands, his brows drew together. "Come now, doona fret like this." He curled his forefinger under her chin, lifting her face. "Vow to the Lore that you never want to see me again. And I'll go," he said. "That's all you have to do to end this running." What a gamble.

What a lie . . .

TWENTY-FIVE

S*ay it!* Lucia's lips parted to answer, to tell MacRieve that she wanted him gone from her life, never to return. To tell him she didn't desire him and never would.

But everything he accused her of was true. He touched her and judgment was lost, discipline gone so easily she knew she never had a chance of denying them anyway.

Damn it, tell him you hate him! No words came out. When she glanced away, he said softly, "Face it, lass. Respect my will in this. I'll be inside you this night."

"I'll fight you."

"Ah, we both know you'll melt for me. One kiss and you're mine."

He leaned down to kiss her ear. *Not the ears . . .* Her nipples budded even harder. Even as she wanted to arch her back to rub them against his chest, she murmured, "Impossible."

Before she could protest, he'd lifted her in his arms.

"MacRieve, no!"

After kicking the balcony doors closed, he carried her to the bed.

"I can't do this! I won't do this."

Once he set her down, she scrambled to the head of

the bed, curling her knees to her chest. "I won't let you make love to me."

"Ach, woman!" He raked his fingers through his hair. "You want me as much as I want you."

"Assuming that's true—"

"It's true."

"—I *can't*. Not now."

"It's no' your time of the month. I know that."

"Ew." Valkyrie didn't have periods. "You're the only one here with a monthly cycle, werewolf."

He scowled. "Then what?"

"Have you ever heard of the Skathians?"

He thought for a moment. "Aye. Man haters. Like the Amazons but crueler. And with arrows."

She raised her brows at that. "I happen to worship the great huntress Skathi." *Worship, but sometimes I hate her.*

"You? Nay, you canna. The Skathians were from ages ago."

"I'm over a thousand years old," she said. "Skathi is the one who gave me my bow." *And my abilities. She can take them away as well. She longs to.* "I'm chaste in her name."

Oh, bluidy hell, no. "You canna be serious."

"I am. I made vows, MacRieve. My reasons are my own, but I will never take a man into my body. It's a religion to me."

Suspicions arose. Was she lying? "I never heard this about you."

She glanced away, and her hair fell over the side of her face. "Besides you, only Regin and Nïx know."

"Why would you do this? A life without sex?" His tone was astonished—he could barely comprehend such a lack.

"Again, my reasons are my own. But it *is* done."

"And can easily be *un*done."

"MacRieve!"

"Never take a man into you? You're . . . a *virgin*?" Garreth had suspected so, and didn't know how he felt about that. Once he introduced her to sex, would Lucia be tempted to sow her oats with other males? His claws dug into his palms at the thought.

"I wasn't born into that order," she said, with a shadow of some unrecognizable emotion in her eyes.

Cryptic words? So she wasn't untouched. Now he had to wonder how many lovers she'd had. "When did you join?"

"What does that matter?" she cried.

"There are no ways around this vow of yours?"

"Skathians are chaste. Period. We're expected to be pure."

"Do you believe that rot? That you have to be chaste or virgin to be *pure*?" he demanded. "Or that it's preferred anyway? Does that mean all mothers are impure?"

"Of course not. But I believe in believing in something, a higher purpose. This is mine." When he was still shaking his head, she asked, "MacRieve, what do you hold most sacred in the world?"

You. "My clan."

"Imagine if I forced you to forsake it for eternity. You'd grow to hate me. The same applies here." She met his eyes. "I will hate you forever if I lose this part of me."

This was the reason she'd run? His hackles rose again. The Instinct was sharp. —*She means what she says. Coax what you can't take.*—

But anger surged inside him. He'd never doubted that she wanted him back, and so for months, he'd wrestled with confusion, grasping for answers. The mystery had eaten at him, the bewilderment . . .

In China, she'd gazed at him with longing—right before she'd loosed a flaming arrow to blow him up.

She *had* wanted him, but instead of welcoming him to her bed, she'd honored this *Skathi*. Lucia had denied them to keep her ridiculous, *useless* vow of chastity. Which was nearly sacrilegious in itself to a Lykae— their kind revered all things physical, like *sex*.

A year of his life . . . *wasted*. He shot to his feet and paced. "This was why you ran? Over some purposeless vows to a second-rate goddess?"

She gasped. "I *left* because I have things to do around the Accession."

"What things?"

"*Private* things!"

"So many bluidy secrets. Has anyone ever told you that you're a high-maintenance mate? By the gods you're a complicated woman! The first night I saw you I wished for a female who would give me a challenge. Now I wish I could take it back." After digging his sat-phone from his bag, he stormed for the door, snatching up the bowcase on the way out.

Out on the deck, the rain was a cool mist. Garreth raised his face to it, struggling for calm. Once he'd gotten the worst of his ire under control, he called his brother. "Lachlain, I have her."

"That's excellent! Are you being patient with her?"

Hesitation, then he admitted, "Nay, no' exactly, but I'm trying to be."

"Watch yourself, brother. I will never forgive myself for the things I did to Emma." Lachlain's voice was rough with regret. "Doona make the same mistake. And no' like Bowen either. Learn from our misjudgment."

Their first cousin Bowen had treated his mate, Mariketa the Awaited, even worse than Lachlain had Emma. Before Bowen had accepted that Mariketa was his, he'd almost killed her.

"Is the Valkyrie bristling that you've caught her?"

"Oh, aye," Garreth said, relating all that Lucia had just told him, from the apocalypse to the vows, finishing with, "I want to throttle her."

"You're no' really letting her go with you to stop this apocalypse?"

"Bluidy hell, no. Just letting her think that until I can get more information out of her."

"Good then," Lachlain said. "For now, you can start fresh with the Valkyrie. You have the opportunity to no' fuck up with her. Find the patience."

Patience? Before Garreth could correct him, Lachlain said, "Take the edge off by yourself if you have to." He added in a mutter, "Gods know I did."

Garreth heard Emma sleepily say, "Lachlain, come

back to bed. It's late." Two in the afternoon in Scotland was late for a vampire.

"I'll be there in a second, love."

Garreth felt a moment of envy, then grew shamed. After Lachlain's torture and imprisonment at the hands of the Horde, he above all men deserved the solace his pale-haired bride had been giving him over the last year. "Go to your queen, brother."

"Call me tomorrow," Lachlain said. "We have much more to discuss. Remember—she'll come around if you treat her well and respect her beliefs."

Her beliefs. *Little hypocrite.* Garreth loathed vows like hers, thought them ridiculous. Lykae revered food, touch, sex. She didn't eat, wouldn't have sex, but by the gods, he'd set to touching her. Tonight. Aye, he would—

"Remember, Garreth, you only get one female. *Ever.*"

After he hung up with Garreth, Lachlain returned to bed, quietly easing in beside Emma.

But she was still awake. "Was that Garreth?"

"Aye." He pulled her into his arms, inhaling her sweet scent. "He's found the Archer."

"How's she taking it?" She briefly peeked up, reading his expression. "That good, huh?"

"It's hard when one's mate is *other*. Think of what we went through. And Bowen and Mariketa?"

Bowen had probably had it hardest of any of them. He'd believed his mate was dead, had mourned her loss for well over a century. Then, just this year, he'd met Mariketa the Awaited, a witch. When he'd begun to fall hopelessly for her, he'd hated himself for his unfaithfulness, hated *her* for tempting him, accusing her of casting a spell over him. Bowen had found out nearly too late that things . . . weren't always as they seemed with Mariketa.

Emma asked, "Do you think it will work out for Aunt Luce and Garreth?"

"I do know this—my brother is nigh head over heels for your aunt."

He could feel her grinning against his chest. "If he's anything like you, then my aunt is going to be head over heels for your brother."

"Let's hope. Garreth has long needed a good woman in his life. Now, *aingeal*"—he curled his forefinger under her chin, lifting her face—"did you happen to wake thirsty?"

TWENTY-SIX

◆━◆◆◆━◆

Though exhaustion weighed on Lucia, she had no
hope for sleep.

A storm was boiling outside, and as the boat slogged
through the night, the bow collided with log after log,
keeping her on edge. Now she understood why the fore
cabin wasn't preferred.

Long after MacRieve had left, she stared at the door,
imagining what would have happened if she'd made different choices, if she could have enjoyed a night with a
virile male, with no repercussions. The only thing between them was her past, her shameful past.

And her blighted future.

If the Scot was disgusted by her vow of chastity, how
would he react when he knew she'd bedded the devil?

She was lying in the dark, peering at the cabin's new
fist-sized porthole, when MacRieve returned, soaked
through. Without a word, he grabbed a shaving kit out
of his bag, then headed for the shower.

Shaving? And he took my bow with him?

When he exited ten minutes later, he wore nothing
but a towel and his cuff. His face was smooth, now clean
shaven. He set her bow case by the cabin door, then
shook out his hair—wolflike.

Dear gods, the man was fine. His damp skin was tan, his chest muscular perfection, with golden hair on the center. She wanted to rub her face against it.

At the mere sight of him like this, her exhaustion began to fade, her traitorous body readying against her will. She dug her curling claws into her palms and furtively clenched her thighs.

"My path is clear to me," he said, his expression inscrutable.

"You'll leave?"

"Nay, beauty. Was thinking." He sat at the edge of the bed. "You weren't completely *chaste* in the bayou that first night. So I figure we can do whatever we did then."

"Whatever we did?"

"You can still be chaste, just no' have intercourse. That's why you stopped me in the swamp—if I had no' tried to take you, I'll bet you would've let me continue to my own end."

Her lips parted. "No, you can't know that."

"You said you will no' take a male into your body. Does no' mean I canna suckle and stroke you. Does no' mean you canna do the same to me."

"We'll lose control." He could seduce her—she would surrender to that wild recklessness inside her. "You'll try to get me to do more."

"Will no'. I'll wait until you tell me you're ready. You'll have to tell me you want me."

She hesitated. "I might get . . . caught up and say something I'll regret."

"Then you'd have to say it when we are *no'* in bed."

He was getting *that* look in his eyes. Her heart be-

gan racing, drowning out any lingering fatigue. Before
her mind shut down, she needed to extract a vow from
him. "No matter what happened. No matter what I said.
Or did?"

"I'd never do anything you dinna want. Why I got
this cuff from the bluidy witches."

"I mean it! You would vow to the Lore?"

"Aye, I vow it," he said. "Are we agreed?"

"I don't . . ." She trailed off, staring up at his
mesmerizing gaze. What woman could turn away a
male who looked at her like this? At length, she gave
a shaky nod.

He wasted no time reaching for her clothes. "Let's
take this off you." He pulled her halter top over her
head, seeming to go speechless at the sight of her dark
red bra. She hadn't chosen red because she'd known
he'd see it tonight—truthfully, almost all her lingerie
was now scarlet and crimson.

She must've been unconsciously buying them.
For him . . .

He pressed her back on the bed, then removed his
towel. Out of habit, she averted her gaze, but everywhere else on his body was titillating too. She wanted to
sigh at those thick muscular thighs, dusted with more
golden hair.

As he eased his towering, naked frame down beside
her, he began slowly undressing her with grazing kisses.
When he bared her breasts, his lips were only inches
away from one of her nipples. They hardened for him,
budding before his eyes.

He flashed her a wolfy, dangerous look, knowing his

effect on her. "They want to be sucked." He leaned down and wrapped his lips around one, flicking his tongue all over it. She helplessly arched up, gasping with pleasure as it pebbled in his mouth. Her gasp turned to a moan when he suckled her, hard, again and again.

Once he moved to her other nipple, he left the first one achy and damp. Dimly, she was aware that he'd continued stripping her but hadn't acknowledged she was naked in a bed with him until he reared back on his knees.

Raking his gaze over her, his voice a deep rumble, he said, "Look at you. You make my mouth water." His rigid penis pulsed, and a shining drop beaded the broad crown.

He began skimming his hand down her belly, but once he reached her sex, she stiffened. She couldn't help it, even after his suckling had made her body boneless with need.

"Let me pet you. Or take my hand and show me how you want me to touch you."

"Just . . . just do it like you did that night in the cell."

"Was so long ago, I canna quite remember. Show me." He seized her hand, and with his gaze catching hers, he sucked her forefinger between his lips, wetting it. Then he placed it against her throbbing clitoris, murmuring, "This is the finger you prefer, if memory serves."

She was too aroused to be embarrassed, too far gone not to begin stroking herself there.

His lids went heavy, and he growled low in his throat. "That's it, lass." He moved to kneel between her thighs.

Masturbating to his riveted gaze, spreading moisture all around, she undulated her hips to her hand, her other arm falling over her head.

He began massaging her inner thighs, spreading her legs wider and wider, while her eyes fluttered shut.

Yet soon she felt *his* fingers stroking her folds, probing her opening. "MacRieve!"

"Keep goin'." His chest was heaving. "I'm going to put my finger in. Nothing more. Just my—"

"No!" She slammed her knees shut.

He forced them back open. "Then just my tongue." With his callused palms flat on her inner thighs, pinning her legs open, he leaned down and set his mouth directly upon her sex.

She sucked in a shocked breath. Lightning lit the room.

He spread her flesh, licking her up and down. "I've waited my whole life for this," he rasped against her, his accent so thick. "Will never get enough of you." Shuddering with pleasure, he began flicking, teasing, nipping. . . .

She moaned—loudly. Rain and wind pounded the balcony doors open. A fine mist dewed her skin.

Seeming drugged with bliss, he asked, "You've never had this?"

"No!"

"You'll be wantin' it again?"

Another thorough lick had her back arching. "Ah, yes!"

"Good lass." He wrapped those brawny arms around her thighs. "Your taste maddens me, dreamed of it, fantasized about doing this tae you." He circled his tongue over her clitoris. "Have you imagined me kissing you here?"

"Yes," she moaned. She had, but had never dreamed it would be this wicked. . . .

His pace was slow, savoring, but his body was taut, tension in every line of his corded muscles. He seemed as if he were only just keeping himself from setting upon her in a frenzy. His knee was drawn up, and his narrow hips were grinding against the bed. She wanted her hands on his rock-hard ass, wanted to feel him moving so sensuously.

As she grew closer to her climax, he gave a harsh groan against her. His eyes had flickered blue, and she'd seen a glimpse of his beast. Yet for some reason, the thought that he couldn't quite control his reaction didn't frighten her—it *aroused* her even more.

The tremors began, pleasure as she'd never imagined. . . .

Just before he took her clitoris between his lips, he growled, *"Come hard for your male,"* then he suckled her.

"Ah, gods!" Her thighs fell wide open as she wantonly bucked to his mouth. Lightning flashed like bomb bursts outside. "Oh, yes!" She drew a breath, *needing* to scream. But he put his palm over her mouth for her to cry out against.

She did. Over and over . . .

He didn't stop licking her orgasm the first or even the second time she pressed his head away. Just continued feasting, grinding his aching cock into the bed.

Finally, he tore himself away from her with a yell, rising up on his knees. Already he was on the verge of coming—even before he saw her spread out before him like an offering.

Her thighs were still parted, revealing her drenched sex. Her soft folds glistened. Her breasts were rising and falling with her hectic breaths.

Her eyes . . . silvery and filled with lust as she stared at his swollen cock.

"Touch it."

She rose up, reaching for him, giving him a slow stroke along his shaft.

"Cup me." When she put her cool palm against his aching bollocks, hefting them, he choked out, *"Now do both."* As she fondled his sac and stroked, he went nigh dizzy with pleasure. Somehow, he managed to utter the words, "Put your lips on it."

She leaned in, looking like she was considering it but then hesitated.

"Have you ever done this?"

She whispered, "No, never."

"Do you want tae?" When she gave a tentative nod, he said, "I'll show you." *She's going to suckle it?* A dream? Another fantasy to join the thousands over the last year?

Holding the back of her head with one shaking hand and his cock with the other, he guided her closer. "Taste me, lass." He was quaking with anticipation, fearing he'd spontaneously lose his seed.

He inhaled a ragged breath as her tongue darted out. She licked the slit; his eyes rolled back in his head, and he bucked uncontrollably to her tongue. When she drew back, he said, "Nay, Lousha, I'll hold still. Just take me in." Feeding his shaft to her once more, he rasped, "Suck it between your lips."

With his gaze holding hers, he pressed his cockhead into her hot, wet mouth, groaning as her tongue greeted him. "Gods, woman!"

Still gazing up at him, she sucked it deeper, with her little cheeks hollowing—

No, no . . . canna hold my seed! With a desperate groan, he tucked his hips under, somehow pulling out of that hungry heat. "'Bout tae come." He pressed her back on the bed, then took his cock in his fist. "Do you want me tae come atop you?" *If I canna mark you in one way, I will in another.*

She gasped at his words, then nodded eagerly, arching her back.

After a single pump of his fist, he gave a brutal yell, releasing his semen over her. As he ejaculated, her body quivered with each drop of his hot seed. Again and again, he lashed her torso and breasts, her nipples. . . .

Once he'd finally finished spending, he wiped her off with his T-shirt, then drew her tight into his arms. They lay with their hearts thundering.

Between kisses on her neck, her ears, her face, he said, "I'll do this to you till there's something to take the place of your vows—until you see the two of us together as your religion. Mark my words, Lousha, in time, you'll be praying for me inside you."

TWENTY-SEVEN

L ightning struck directly outside, a boom that shook the entire boat. But Garreth was already awake.

It was just after four in the morning—the time he was usually on the trail of Lucia, hoping to get a jump on her. If he'd even bothered to sleep.

Earlier, he'd petted her hair until she'd passed out, then he'd dozed fitfully himself—until he'd awakened with his shaft hard as wood.

After debating whether to wake her with his tongue back between her thighs, he decided not to push her too quickly. So he sat in the cabin's chair, ignoring the ache in his shaft, and gazed at her, his favorite sight.

He'd never seen her like this before—*still*. In sleep, she panted her breaths, her brows drawn.

Another bolt. In the beginning, he'd thought all the lightning coming from her would take some getting used to. He'd thought wrong. He craved seeing it, knew it meant she was near, and it alerted him to her moods.

Lightning had struck every time just before she'd attacked him. He liked to think it was from regret. . . .

Now things were looking up for them. The unbelievable pleasure they'd just shared was only the beginning. He'd seduce her to surrender more.

Wait, had she moaned? Maybe she had the same subject on her mind as he did.

He frowned when she did it again, and louder. No, it was a moan not of pleasure but of fear. A nightmare, getting worse. More lightning blasted down, then came a *whimper*.

"Lousha, rest easy." He climbed back in bed with her, pulling her across his chest to run his fingers through her hair again. Though she never woke, she calmed.

Yet not before he felt tears on his chest. "Ach, love, what's this?" he murmured, but she slumbered on.

He needed to uncover what had befallen his mysterious little mate. Lykae reveled in mysteries. He'd peel away the layers, find out everything he could about her. But with care. For Lucia, he would be patient, would temper his selfishness, his aggression.

Ah, lass, your secrets' days are numbered.

"Still as ruggedly handsome," MacRieve rumbled without opening his eyes, "as you found me last night, Valkyrie."

Lucia jerked back, dragging the sheet with her. Luckily he hadn't seen her hand poised just above his cheek. She'd been an inch away from stroking the backs of her fingers against his stubble.

He finally cracked open his eyes. "But look all you like. Happy to show you the whole package again."

"Funny, Scot." When she'd awakened to a cloudless dawn, her first thought had been that she needed to run—MacRieve would be closing in on her! Then she'd remembered the night before.

She'd already been caught. Yet her worst fears hadn't been realized—because he'd vowed not to take her. Relaxing a shade, she'd quietly turned to watch him at rest, inwardly sighing at the magnificent male she shared a bed with.

"How did you sleep?" He gazed at her, studying her face.

She would give anything to know what he was thinking. "Surprisingly well." Like the dead, actually. Odd for her.

"That so?" Why was he staring at her like that?

She tucked her hair behind her ear. This was so awkward. Was he thinking about last night? Recalling how she'd looked naked? Or what they'd done?

The only time she'd been intimate with a male, besides MacRieve, she'd experienced a wedding, dawning horror, and torture. Now she didn't know how to behave.

MacRieve was looking at her like she was a puzzle he intended to solve.

But when the smell of bacon wafted into the cabin, his lids grew heavy. "Smell that, will you? Wish you ate. I'd feed you like a queen. Or at least like a princess."

She *could* eat, but refraining was an inherent form of birth control for Valkyrie.

Ah, gods, was she *planning* on having sex with him?

"I guess I'll have to eat your meals to hold up my end of the bargain," he said. At her raised brows, he added, "Our deal was that I'd keep your cover if you sated me. For a night like the last, I'll keep your cover *a lot*. Speaking of which, I thought I should inquire—are you ready for me to claim you yet?"

When she glared, he said, "I'll give you a few minutes to think about it."

"MacRieve!"

He stood, not caring a whit about his nudity—or his semihard erection. In fact, he stretched in front of her, his muscles tensing and relaxing, playing all over his body. He cast her a grin over his shoulder. "Oh, and how about *now*?"

Her lips quirked, but she hid it. "No, werewolf!"

"It's just a matter of time, Valkyrie—"

"*Goddamnit, Chuck, what'd I tell you?*" rang out from above decks. It was Travis, somehow sounding even more drunk. "*Ship's fine just the way she is!*"

MacRieve raised a brow. "An intrigue. The Lykae in me needs to investigate that, and the bacon. You get a reprieve."

As soon as he donned his worn jeans and a T-shirt and padded barefoot out of the cabin, she hurried from the bed, intending a quick shower.

The door reopened; she froze, naked. MacRieve's lips curled into that lupine grin. "Forgot this." Absently patting around for the bowcase, he ogled her up and down. When he'd snagged the case, he said, "Doona move till I get back."

Once the door closed again, she heard him mumble outside, "*Woman'll be the death o' me.*"

She released a pent-up breath, hurrying for the bathroom. MacRieve continued to surprise her. Last night, he hadn't done more, hadn't tried to seduce her. He'd kept his part of the vow, and since she would certainly never agree to more—especially out of bed—she thought she could handle this arrangement with him.

Yes, a short journey with the Lykae, and if she could stay in control of herself, she'd have some extra muscle who knew the area to help her.

After a hasty shower, Lucia dressed, some imp making her choose a babydoll T-shirt and some of the shorter shorts she'd packed. Feeling more optimistic than she had in memory, she lightly lined her eyes with kohl and brushed on lip gloss.

She was just about to set out when her gaze fell on his bulging duffel bag. He wasn't the only one with a marked curiosity. She knelt beside it, rooting through his belongings. Aside from clothes, she found a large leather bundle with knotted ties—and two condoms.

For other women? They must have been. Valkyrie couldn't get pregnant unless they took steps to, and they had no need for safe sex. Though Lucia had no right to be jealous—she'd sent MacRieve away again and again—the idea left her unaccountably envious.

No, not *unaccountably*. She'd never denied that the Scot's kisses were like a drug to her. Just listening to his raspy brogue made her want to sigh. From the earliest moments with MacRieve, she'd felt possessiveness toward him. . . .

She thought she heard someone coming and stuffed everything back in his bag.

A second later, he burst through the door. "You showered without me again? You're underutilizing me." Before she could reply, he asked, "You ever see a caiman before?" When she shook her head, he said, "You want to?"

"Uh, sure?"

At that, MacRieve ushered her out of the cabin, with his gaze pinned on her and filled with curiosity. He gave her a grin, looking like a crafty wolf.

And she couldn't help but feel like a henhouse he planned to raid. . . .

TWENTY-EIGHT

❦

W hen Garreth had returned to the cabin, Lucia was wearing a small top that molded to her pert breasts and the shortest shorts he'd ever seen her in.

As if she needed anything else to attract his attention.

Add to that his earlier glimpse of her naked body, and he was going to be randy all day, pacing the decks till tonight, when he could bring her down below again.

Unless a storm blew up. Never had he prayed for rain as he would be today.

Now, on their way to the third-floor observation deck, Garreth was right on her heels as they climbed the rusted iron stairs. "Since I was on my best behavior last night," he murmured at her ear, "I bet part of you is wondering if you ought no' have approached me with this deal earlier."

She glanced over her shoulder with a raised brow. "As if you would've settled for this in the beginning. You had to experience a year of nothing for this to be appetizing."

She was likely right about that.

When they reached the deck, Damião was just heading down. "*Bom dia,*" he said pleasantly.

"And good morning to you," Lucia replied with a smile that made Garreth want to eviscerate Damiãno.

Garreth jerked his chin up, the gesture in no way a greeting. In turn, the man narrowed his eyes before descending the steps.

"Am I going to have to separate you two?" she asked when they were alone on the deck.

"No' if he watches his step," Garreth said in all seriousness.

Once he'd ushered her to the railing, he closed in behind her, making her tense against him. He knew she would consider this crowding, but he couldn't help himself. "See it there?" Over her shoulder, he pointed out a four-foot-long caiman lying atop a water lily. "It's a juvenile." Sporting a bony ridge over ruddy eyes and a black body, the creature lay with its mouth wide open, jagged teeth exposed. "They're like a sharper alligator. Physically. Don't know about mentally. Though they do seem to be wilier."

Deftly slipping to Garreth's side, she asked, "How big do they get?"

"The largest one on record was twenty-five feet. But Schecter's right—there are bigger ones way upriver. *Much* bigger."

"You brought me out to see the caiman, and I'm almost more amazed by the water lily underneath it. It's huge, like a table."

"*Victoria amazonica*. They get larger and grow thicker farther upriver as well."

She gazed around. "How far did we travel over the night?"

"I believe we're on a patch of the river where the map was missing, so who can tell?" They hadn't passed a boat all morning. "But far enough out that we're going to start seeing more and more river creatures. Pink dolphins and giant otters."

"It sounds like make-believe," Lucia said, leaning back against the rail. She'd plaited her caramel-colored hair over her ears, but glossy curls tumbled free across her shoulders and around her elven face. He imagined those curls spread over his pillow as he mounted her lush, wee body, imagined them wrapped around his fist as he took her from behind—

"So what was Travis up in arms about?"

"Huh?" *Inward shake.* "Uh, apparently the captain has a standing order that no improvements are to be made to the ship, which—by the look of this wreck—is rarely countermanded. Charlie can fix things, but he'll get his knuckles rapped if he does more."

"That's strange."

"Oh, aye." There was a lot of strangeness about Travis. But the human responded to cash.

Garreth had already bribed him to head in the direction of Rio Labyrinto.

Yet though Travis was an odd bird, there definitely was something up with Charlie. While his sister Izabel seemed confident and open, he had a quiet, awkward demeanor. Today, he'd looked pale, sickly even. Garreth couldn't put his finger on what was *off*, just knew something was.

"Where are the others?" Lucia asked.

"Rossiter is pacing in his cabin. Izabel just finished

up with a gourmet breakfast. Schecter was slinking around the stern scouting for a place to 'deploy' his 'sonic lure.' I asked him if that's what the kids were calling it these days, but he dinna get it," Garreth said, and her lips quirked. Rubbing the back of his neck, he added, "But we're being watched."

"I know. Can you scent anything?"

He shook his head. "Sensory overload." The last time he was here, the same had happened to him; it took him weeks to familiarize himself with all the new scents. "Guess we'll just need to be ready for anything." He gazed out over the churning water. "I bluidy hate this place."

"Tell me what you know about the river," she said. "Tell me some more *dangers*."

"Dangers, then? In the jungles all around us, there are indigenous tribes. They stay hidden—you'll never see a hint of them on this trip. And they're peaceable unless provoked—such as when some git like Damião goes hunting for them with a Polaroid. Then they'll rise up with a fury. No' to mention the fact that the poisons they concoct make the feys' look mild," he said. "Did Nïx give you any indication what the dieumort would be? Maybe it's a poison."

"No indication. But I suspect it's an arrow. Otherwise, why would she dispatch me, an archer, down into the jungle to retrieve a weapon I don't know how to wield?"

"True."

"Are there natives on the Rio Labyrinto?" she asked, her demeanor so guileless, as if she hadn't just slyly segued to what she *really* wanted to know about—the location of the labyrinth.

"No. But there were long ago. I stumbled upon the ruins of a necropolis."

"A city of the dead?"

"Aye, with temples and crypts surrounding a huge tomb," he said. "Everything you read says there are no ruins directly in the basin. The river fluctuations supposedly made building there impossible because any site would be under forty feet of water half of the year. But this necropolis was constructed in a bowl, with mammoth stonework levees all around it—really advanced stuff."

"If the inhabitants are gone, then why is it rumored that no one returns?"

"Probably because it's infested with giant caimans," MacRieve answered. "That and *matora*."

Lucia frowned. "A bull eater?"

"Aye. Sucuriju Gigante. The giant anaconda. Rio Labyrinto is teeming with them."

She raised a brow. "You're saying they exist outside of J. Lo movies?"

"I saw several of them that stretched more than eighty feet, their bodies as thick as an oil drum. They're everywhere. Well, almost. They liked to sun themselves atop the levee walls but never descended into the city."

"I can't believe they're real. And that Schecter's . . . *right*."

"Aye, primordial sizes. You never get the sight of an

eight-ton mating ball out of your head, that's for certain." He gave a mock shudder. "The snakes can strike with a speed that would boggle your mind. Even an immortal could no' fight one off if it wrapped around the arms."

"So anyone unlucky enough to find Rio Labyrinto—which you said is possibly the gateway to El Dorado—would be eaten by various reptiles?"

Shoulders back, he said, "Except for me." He looked as if he'd just stopped himself from thumping his own chest.

"Did you *see* the lost city of gold?"

"Nay, but in the necropolis, most of the hieroglyphs depicted shining treasure in some manner."

"And?" She waved him on. "More details, please."

"After you, Lousha. I ken you're no' telling me everything you know about the god killer."

Seeing no harm in sharing her theory, Lucia said, "I told you I suspect it's an arrow, but I think it's a golden one. Hence my interest in El Dorado."

"Why gold?"

"The goddess Skathi uses golden arrows. And all through history, they've been wielded by great archers. It seems . . . fitting that an arrow with so much power would be incomparable," she said. "Now tell me more about El Dorado."

"Should I reveal all so you can dump me sooner?" he asked in a scoffing tone.

"You call *me* secretive? Besides, you have my bow."

"So I do."

"Scot, I need it back. I'm uncomfortable without it. And I have no other real defense. I'm hopeless with a sword or blade."

"Vow that you will no' sneak off again."

She gritted her teeth. "I didn't *sneak* off."

He took out her bow from its case. "I'll give this back if you vow to the Lore you will no' leave without telling me. When I'm awake and conscious. And you show me how you shoot like that."

"You want me to *teach* you?"

"Nay, lass, I'm quite handy with a bow myself." To illustrate, he began expertly stringing it. "Want you to *show* me."

She peered around. "The others will see."

"Relax. I already 'bragged' to Travis and Charlie about my wife winning the National Archery Championships. Now, do you vow it?"

"I vow it. Until we find whatever we're here for." At his unbending look, she said, "We're just taking a time-out, until the game begins again."

He shrugged. "Deal. By then, I'll have you to where you canna think of leaving me anyway."

From the bowcase, he retrieved a sleeve of spare arrows. "Why do you no' have a never-emptying quiver? Like the fey?"

"I wish." Many of the fey archers had mystical quivers. If you shot an arrow, you would forever have another exactly like it. Extinguish one, and another replaced it. "They're impossible to get. The fey guard them fiercely." Her closest competition in archery, Tera the Fey, owned one.

"Do they, then?" He handed her the bow. "Show me what you've got. See that tree leaning over the water at the bend? There's a patch of lichen—"

Lucia had already fired and hit it before he could finish the sentence. She could still shoot like a goddess! Even after last night, she hadn't broken her code of chastity. She gave him a "how you like me now?" look.

"You get off on being known as *the* Archer."

She blinked at him. "Yeah. I do. I'm the best in the entire world—who *wouldn't* get off on that?" And who would be crazy enough to jeopardize it?

"You're modest to boot."

"Why do females have to be modest when they're good at their careers? When they should be *duly* proud? That's never made any sense to me."

A breeze blew then, tumbling gray clouds toward them, darkening the day. If it rained, would he truly expect her to go back to the cabin with him? At the thought, she was filled with nervousness, and maybe even a touch of . . . anticipation. She moistened her lips.

At once, his gaze locked on her mouth, then he scrubbed his palm over his own. Was he remembering the night before—how she'd tasted him? "Uh, hit that leaf fluttering ahead of the boat."

With her gaze still meeting his, she did.

He raised a brow. "So back to the subject of sex," he said, though they hadn't been on the subject of sex for some time. "Tell me what's so important about being a Skathian?"

"I owe the great goddess Skathi. She gave me her mark of favor." And gifted Lucia with pain to make her remember. *How well are you remembering, Lucia?* "She gave me an identity. Look, you have your clan and the royal bloodline you belong to. But I don't know who my people were, and Nïx said I never will."

Not until I have a child. Which I can never do, though I'd always wanted them. . . .

"So your people became the Skathians."

"Exactly."

"Hit the lily by the log trap," he said, and she nailed it. "What's it like to miss?"

Carefully choosing her words, she said, "It . . . hurts in . . . unimaginable ways."

"How bad was it in the beginning?"

"What do you mean?"

"Were you no' missing all the time at first?"

Everyone assumed this, figuring the pain had taught her. Only Regin knew that Lucia had been *handed* her abilities, without an hour of practice. "It was long ago. I don't really think about it. All I know is that I've definitely earned the right to call myself a Skathian. I refuse to give it up lightly."

"No' even for sex? If no' with me, then someone must've tempted you over the years."

She glanced at him over her shoulder. "Clearly not enough."

"Calling yourself a Skathian is more important than having a family? Or children?"

"Yes, MacRieve! Accept it." If Lucia could accept not having children, then he damn well would! "It's not just my vows. If I surrender to you, then I have no identity."

He shrugged. "Women do this all the time—give up their jobs for their men."

"You didn't just say that." She couldn't remember the last time someone's attitude had grated so much—

Her phone vibrated then, interrupting her. Another text message from *RegRad: Screw U & the Lykae U rode in on. Nïx told me UR on cruise w/ Mac. WTF??*

Lucia sighed, imagining how Regin would act out over that little nugget from Nïx. The soothsayer could have been saying that to stir up trouble, or because she truly viewed it that way.

MacRieve asked, "Who keeps texting you? Nïx?"

"Nïx rarely texts." Because no one ever responded. But how exactly was one supposed to reply to messages like: *Smurf!* or *I'm charismatic . . .* or *Bad dogs get no burgers?* "It's from Regin."

"Ah, the glowing frea— one. Loved to shove me around when I was tranquilized, though I'd fought side by side with her when I saved you and your sisters from the vampires."

Feeling the urge to whistle with guilt, Lucia studiously unstrung her bow and stowed it back in its travel case.

"Before I left New Orleans last year," he continued, "I learned much about your kind. Nigh everything about your coven. Why are you and Regin such good friends? Most people think she's completely—" At her look of warning, he finished with, "A handful."

"What have you heard?"

"She makes rogue demons eat things, like hubcaps."

A lot of Loreans had that idea about her, probably

because Regin had gone through that whole making-her-enemies-eat-things stage. Beer bottles, soccer balls, garbage can lids. "First of all, that was a *phase*, and she's past that now." Mostly. "And second, those demons never messed with her again."

"You make excuses for her?"

"She was built for war, but she has a highly developed sense of"—*lowbrow*—"humor. Add those together . . ." *And season with guilt.* Though Regin's kisses were like drugs, addictive like heroin, she'd kissed a berserker when she was young. Aidan the Fierce. He had been killed trying to win her over, but for centuries, he'd been reincarnated, seeking her again and again.

"Besides," Lucia added, "Regin and I have a history." In the past, when Lucia had gone to the Broken Bloody One's cliff-side cave, Regin had always been there with her, a sister-at-arms.

But hunting Cruach wasn't like hunting a hibernating bear. She and Regin didn't go inside the cave. Instead they waited for him at the bone-strewn entrance of his lair. Right as he was about to emerge, they attacked.

The first time he'd tried to rise, he'd come forth roaring, stamping like a bull, thinking his hideousness would frighten some young Skathian assassin and foul her aim. Lucia had shot true, though afterward she'd shuddered and wept, and Regin had gone to her knees in horror, vomiting energy.

The second time, Cruach had summoned hundreds of his Cult of Death followers, his Cromites, to guard the exit and assure him safe passage out. But as Regin had battled the swordsmen back, Lucia's arrow had found Cruach's black heart.

This third time, Lucia had no idea what to expect, though she feared she'd be hunting the bear *in* his cave. Could she force herself to enter that lair once more? And all alone?

Lucia knew that MacRieve wrongly believed he was going with her. Even if they worked together to retrieve the dieumort, she could never let him near Cruach. Nor could she risk Regin getting too close.

Cruach could infect them. Lucia—as his wife—was immune. . . .

"What are you thinking of that's got you so pensive?" he asked, his words accompanied by distant thunder.

More steely gray clouds were building all around them. "I was just thinking that you ought to be more charitable to Regin."

"Why's that?" he asked.

"If it weren't for her, you wouldn't have a mate. I was sixteen the first time she saved my life. She has countless times in battles ever since."

After digesting that for a moment, MacRieve said, "Regin has no love lost for me."

"No." Had she just felt a raindrop? "But your brother probably feels the same about me."

"Maybe. Then again, I dinna shoot your sister."

Lucia studied a splinter on the rail, grumbling, "I only winged him." A mere shot through the arm.

"Lousha, look just there!" MacRieve said, taking her shoulders and turning her toward a far bank.

She spied several otters with white dappled throats—but these creatures were *giant*, as long as MacRieve was tall. One ravaged a catfish while others snuggled atop a log, cooing to squeaking pups.

"It's a family of river otters. Also known as *lobos del río.*"

Ignoring the drizzle that had just started, she asked, "River wolves?"

"Aye." When the rain intensified, MacRieve took her shoulders and turned her back to him. "Since you're partial to wolves you should appreciate them." He reached forward to stroke the backs of his fingers across her cheek, and his golden eyes promised wicked things.

"Am I partial to wolves?" she asked, her breaths shallowing.

Just like that first night so long ago, his voice went low and rumbly as he said, "Aye, Lousha, you're about to be."

The rain turned to a pounding deluge, lightning flashing all around them.

There was no choice but to go into a dark, sultry cabin with the most sexually attractive male she'd ever imagined, who'd immediately peel off his clothes and expect her to do the same.

TWENTY-NINE

⬥

"That shoal jumped out o' nowhere, eh, Travis?" Mac-Rieve called up to the pilothouse. To Lucia, he muttered, "Is he *trying* to hit things?"

Travis was hung up on a sandbar again—the third time in as many days.

Lucia sighed. She and MacRieve had been enjoying a rare cloudless, and uneventful, morning together. She'd been sunning on a weathered lounge chair on the back deck while he'd unsuccessfully fished from the platform, spurred on by Izabel's promise of seafood feasts.

Travis yelled down from the wheelhouse, "*You think you could drive better, Scot?*"

"Aye, even as drunk as you are, *Tex*!"

"MacRieve . . ." Lucia warned.

"Well, it's true. He needs to lay off the spirits, or we'll never get to our destination."

She wished Charlie was at the helm, but he was on a sleep shift. The young man drove so much better than Travis, not that Charlie would ever admit that. Izabel's twin seemed to hero worship the irascible Texan as much as she did.

Each foul-up like this set them back even further,

and she was running out of time. The nightmares were getting worse.

"Looks like I'll have to go shove the old girl free," MacRieve said. "Again." He stripped off his shirt, leaving him in his worn and faded jeans and his cuff. Shoes were a thing of the past aboard the *Contessa*.

That cuff stood out against his tanned skin, a constant reminder of what he'd done for her. Whenever he embraced her, she always felt the metal against her skin, cool at first on the outside, before it warmed.

Just like last night . . . "MacRieve, do you *have* to go in?" Though the river had been a source of delight—she'd seen pink dolphins, more otters, and tapirs grazing along the shores—it'd also been one of dismay. Caimans constantly prowled and piranhas broke the surface in feeding frenzies.

Just yesterday morning, they'd seen a baby heron fall out of its nest into the water. As the mother bird had squawked in dismay, a swarm of piranhas had annihilated the chick in seconds, picking it clean with their razor-sharp teeth, right down to the bones.

"Seems you're finally believing me about the dangers?" MacRieve said. "Relax, I'm just going in up to my waist."

"And what about the piranhas?"

"I doubt the fishies'll snack on anything critical." He leaned in to murmur at her ear, "They only go for *small* prey."

"Werewolf!" she cried, still a shade surprised every time he teased her. More and more, he'd been softening toward her, his rancor over her past deeds fading. She'd see hints of the man he'd once been, the one she imagined each time she looked at his laugh lines. And when he wasn't simmering with anger at her, she'd found he liked to play. "I'm serious."

"As am I. Will it make you feel better if I keep my jeans on?" When she gave him a grudging nod, he said, "Doona worry. They truly will no' feed on large prey—no' unless it's dead."

When they saw Damiāno coming to the stern to help free the boat, she whispered, "Don't look too strong in front of the others. And *do not* bow up to him again."

"He did it first," Garreth pointed out in a surly tone. Only three days had passed, and already the ship was too small for the two towering males.

"Good morning, *querida*." Damiāno said to her as he drew off his own shirt, revealing a muscled, brawny body.

"*Bom dia,*" she replied with an absent grin.

As Damiāno strolled to the back platform, he returned her smile, white teeth against bronzed skin, then he dropped into the water. The man was sex on a stick—

MacRieve stepped in front of her, clasping her nape, jealousy ablaze in his expression. "Eyes on the prize, woman. It's a werewolf you'll have, or none at all."

"Is that right?"

"Unless you like your men dead, because Damiāno's already at the top of my list." He tugged her to him for a brief but scalding kiss "You're *mine*, Lousha. Doona ever forget that."

With that, he leapt in as well, leaving her

breathless—and convinced she had a thing for jealous alpha males, like this one who kissed as if each kiss were his last. . . .

While those two were busy, Lucia thought she should take care of some shipboard business on the observation deck. She climbed the stairs, then crossed all the way to the back, to a patch of the thatched roof. Earlier, she'd heard rustling coming from within.

Now she spied a hideaway tucked up under the thatching, with two small bare feet sticking out from the edge. *Izabel.*

"What are you doing?"

Izabel exhaled testily. *"Nada."*

Lucia peeked in and found what looked like a luggage shelf with a couple of feet of clearance. Izabel was lying flat up there. Following her example, Lucia hopped up, shimmying on her belly to the end. And found a hideout perfect for spying. From here, they could see the platform and the back uncovered deck, as well as the side gangways—a good bit of the ship.

"You've been spying on us?"

"Why wouldn't I?" she demanded. "All you people are *louco.*"

"Crazy, are we? Well, aren't you the sassiest little—"

"Latina?" She glared. "The spunky *Portuguesa?*"

Sassiest little *mortal*, Lucia had been thinking. "How are we all crazy?"

Izabel jutted her chin. "I don't think you're a doctor."

Lucia shrugged. "I think you're in love with a drunk."

With narrowed hazel eyes, Izabel said, "I don't think you're even married to Mr. MacRieve."

"Is that all you've got on me?" Lucia asked, relieved. She'd thought Izabel had discovered their true natures.

"If you and Mr. MacRieve are married, then I'll eat Schecter's shorts."

"Now that was just . . . unnecessary. And why would you think that about us?"

"When you're not looking, MacRieve reaches for you and pulls back his hand in a fist, like he's *dying* to touch you." *He does?* "Married people aren't like that!"

"Then I'll be honest with you, Izabel. We're not married, but he's . . . old fashioned. He didn't want my reputation to be hurt when I shacked up with him aboard this ship. Anything else?"

"MacRieve keeps giving Travis cash, and we keep going off the planned route."

This was true. The Scot had told Lucia that he'd been steering Travis, paying the captain to take them directly by Rio Labyrinto. "MacRieve has been here before and knows promising research areas." The ship would arrive in the vicinity in a week or so, probably right after the full moon. She and MacRieve had decided not to *lose* the mortals; instead, they planned to sneak out on the *Contessa*'s auxiliary motorboat. "So he's merely been *directing* Travis. Anything else?"

"That's all I've got on you two. For *now*. But the others are just as strange."

"Tell me."

"Why should I?"

"Travis said to drop him a dime if you screwed up. Do you think he'd fire you for spying on his passengers? Maybe sack your brother as well, after all Charlie's been putting up with?" Every day, the captain barked at the young man, ranting at him for repairing anything on board *too well*. Charlie was a good sport, quietly enduring each outburst. "Now tell me, or kiss your big Texan good-bye."

With another glare, Izabel said, "Fine. Take Damiăno. He's definitely *louco*."

Lucia had to agree that something was off about the man, no matter how physically blessed he was. There was a seething intensity about him, much like Mac-Rieve's. Except that when Damiăno smiled, it never quite reached his eyes—and his eyes followed her *constantly*.

"He speaks Portuguese, right?" Izabel said. "So Charlie and I try to talk to him. But he speaks *old* Portuguese."

"How do you mean?"

"It's Portuguese like the conquistadors spoke." *That is strange.* "And then he'll see we're frowning at him, and he'll smile that *magnificente* smile." She sighed. *"Muito bonito."*

"Damiăno *is* hot," Lucia murmured, then realized she'd spoken aloud. "And by that, I mean, I respect his mind."

Izabel tapped her chin. "And Schecter?"

"Not so much with the hot."

"Well, he—"

"Shh," Lucia hissed. "He's coming."

With an aluminum case in hand, the professor slinked to the gangway—out of sight of the men laboring at the platform. His case was a Halliburton—the kind most often found handcuffed to a wrist, carrying missile codes inside. Lucia rolled her eyes.

After glancing both ways, he took out his "revolutionary" lure, which looked like an airplane's black box attached to a rope. When he turned it on, a blinking red light on the top beeped sonic frequencies. They made her ears twitch until he dipped the device into the water.

Under her breath, Lucia said, "Hey, Iz—now's your chance to eat his shorts."

Izabel's eyes widened, as if she were shocked Lucia was teasing her. Then she whispered, "Hold me back. That cowlick? *Muito machão.*"

Lucia couldn't stop a grin.

When Schecter moved on to other parts of the ship, Izabel said, "That one's keeping snakes, lizards, and all kinds of amphibians in his room. Poisonous ones, even. And that lure thing? I'm not a scientist, but common sense says that when you bait something, you better be able to handle its arrival." *Smart girl.* "I know this ship up and down—it's held together by prayers, duct tape, and Charlie—and it couldn't take the visit of a 'mega' anything. So Schecter's either very foolish or very selfish."

Agreed. "What about Rossiter?"

"Now him, I like," Izabel answered. "But he's sick or something. Never sleeps. And I think he's obsessed with flowers, always drawing them—"

Lucia's phone vibrated then with yet another text message. She twisted around in the cramped space to view the screen. *RegRad: Got 2 level 9/ ice wrld. U always do ice wrlds 4 me.* Just as Lucia sighed—she missed Regin like crazy—another message from her arrived. *Got thru it anywy. SO SUCK IT RAW!*

"Who keeps texting you?" Izabel asked. "A twelve-year-old you met at the skating rink?"

"How do you say 'har-har' in Portuguese?" Lucia asked innocently, then she added, "It's just one of my sisters. She misses me." *And resents my being away this long.*

"How many sisters do you have?"

Hundreds. All over the world. "Enough," Lucia answered.

"I wish I had a sister."

"A twin brother isn't enough?"

"I guess," Izabel answered with a shrug.

Now that Lucia thought about it, she'd never seen the two display affection. Likely because they were so different. Izabel was brazen, confident. Charlie seemed unsure and awkward.

"Hey, do you feel that?" Izabel said. "They got the ship loose."

Lucia glanced down just as MacRieve hauled himself from the water onto the platform, the damp muscles in his back flexing so temptingly. When he stood, shaking his wet hair in that wolfy way, his sodden jeans hung even lower on his sculpted torso.

Lucia's claws curled for him. Just as she was thinking, *Gods, he's fine*, Izabel whispered, "I'd lock that one down while you can. *Esplêndido*."

The Scot *was* splendid. And sexy and funny. He knew how to string a recurve bow. Here was a man who treated her well, who'd proved he was understanding about her . . . limitations.

"Chuck!" the captain suddenly called. "Get your ass up here!"

Izabel jumped, knocking her head on the shelf. "I have to go!" Wide-eyed, she shimmied back.

"Why do *you* have to go?"

"To wake up Charlie."

Travis yelled, "Izabel! Where the hell is Chuck?"

"See?"

Lucia couldn't believe this girl had fallen for that querulous captain. To be stuck on this bucket, with no future, no prospects. She was so young. . . . "Izabel, you know there are other *ships* out there for you to work on. Ships that will treat you much better."

Izabel met her gaze. "I'll never want another *ship* as long as I live." And then she was gone, leaving Lucia to her thoughts. Which almost always centered on MacRieve.

In the last three days, Lucia had begun to fear that she was settling in with him *too* easily. She'd been fooled once before, and even after all these years, she was still deeply ashamed of succumbing to Cruach's trickery. Her sisters would have sensed he was evil.

Regin had. She'd taken one look at the fair-haired

man at the portal and run to tell their godparents.
Who'd made her swear never to see him again. Lucia
had fallen right into Cruach's clutches, trusting in him
so completely that she'd broken those vows.

Am I being too trusting with the Scot? As if to remind her why that'd be unwise, the nightmares were
coming every night. Only now, for the first time in
her life, she was sharing a bed with another, a male
who'd begun questioning her, wanting to know what
she dreamed of—

"Lousha?" he called then, and she too hit her head.
As she crawled from the shelf, Lucia could hear him
stomping along the gangway, then to the cabin below.

Just before she'd reached the steps, he bounded up
them. "Where were you?" he demanded, his eyes flickering blue.

"Right up here. You couldn't scent me?"

He visibly relaxed, the tension easing from his broad
shoulders. "It's difficult to find you aboard a ship like
this." At her nonplussed look, he said, "I scent your
bathing suit top drying on the clothesline by the galley." He twined a lock of her hair around his finger.
"I smell a strand from these curls up by the wheelhouse. All around, I detect your scent. It'd almost be
easier for me to find you from thirty or forty miles
away."

"I told you I wouldn't leave. Don't you trust me?"

"Aye, but I chased you for the better part of a year.
Old habits die hard. It actually feels *odd* no' to be running after you. Welcome, but odd."

She tilted her head at him. "In all that time, did you . . . did you ever think about giving up?"

"Never."

"Not once?"

His voice was so deep as he said, "Lousha, you're my lass." He shrugged, as if he spoke an irrevocable truth.

If I'm not careful, I might just prove him right. . . .

THIRTY

◆❖◆

"**Y**ou doona expect to catch dinner with that setup?"
Imagine that, MacRieve taunting Damiāno, Lucia thought. For the last ten days, the two men had been constantly at odds. They neared a boiling point, unable to pass each other on the narrow gangway without slamming shoulders.

"You think *you* could do better?" Damiāno snapped.

"Oh, aye."

"Wager on it."

Lucia sank down on the weathered lounge chair. Elbows to her knees and her chin in her hands, she settled in for the duration—because neither male had caught a single fish the entire trip. And now she could tell that neither would budge until they did. . . .

For each of these ten days, as the *Contessa* had headed deeper down the San Miguel into a primeval jungle, Garreth had grown more on edge. He paced constantly, palpably restless. He couldn't run, and it weighed on him. Lucia knew the Lykae needed to run. Especially with the full moon tonight.

And then tomorrow they planned to arrive in the vicinity of Rio Labyrinto—another source of unease for him. He'd said to her, "I doona suppose there's any way

I could talk you out of going to the labyrinth?" At her look, he'd added, "Dinna think so."

Yet as much as Garreth hated it here, she'd enjoyed it. She recalled that explorers used to talk about the jungle as if she were a mistress, leading men astray, making them shrug off civility. She finally understood what they'd meant.

And she *liked* it.

Levelheaded Lucia was *losing* it. Her façade of control, her tenuous rationality. Everything about this place was sensual—the colors, the warmth, the evocative scents. She felt more alive than she had in memory.

Or maybe that was owing to the werewolf whose bed she shared? MacRieve was wearing her down every day—and night. As if she needed anything to erode her control. Her house of cards was in the midst of a maelstrom. With one stray touch, all would come tumbling down. . . .

Over these days, life aboard the *Contessa* had taken on a routine. Damiăno always seemed to be around, and though she sensed the male could be a threat, Lucia couldn't muster any real fear. Damiăno might have been of the Lore, but no species could match Garreth in strength.

As for Rossiter, when he wasn't pacing in his cabin, the doctor got Charlie to teach him about the inner workings of the ship, and together, they did everything from refueling the generators to changing engine filters.

Lucia didn't think Rossiter had been asleep for an hour since they'd left. He was growing paler, his tall body rangier, and sometimes she thought she detected a growing glint in his dark blue eyes, like a . . . madness setting in. *How could it not?* Like her, Rossiter was running out of time.

Schecter continually crept about at all hours of the night, dipping his sonic lure into the water, and just as continually, Izabel gave Travis long looks.

When Travis didn't think anyone was around, he'd checked her out a couple of times, then had appeared furious with himself. Yet it seemed Travis hadn't noticed Charlie was giving him long looks as well.

Despite the fact that the Texan wasn't particularly kind to either twin, both of them were falling for him.

Lucia actually liked Izabel. For a mortal. The girl was affable and no-nonsense, and reminded her a little of Regin. Though Lucia could never shake the feeling that something was off, it didn't deter the budding friendship. And Izabel had confided secrets, explaining things about the captain that had puzzled Lucia, like his anger whenever Charlie made improvements to the boat—or his irritation at any reminder that Izabel was an attractive young woman.

It turned out that Travis was a widower of eight years. His wife had apparently been a paragon, running tours with him, helping him restore this boat. She was the one who'd lovingly hung all the maps and quaint lists that remained to this day. The embroidered tablecloths and curtains had all been done by her hand.

In Iquitos, it was rumored that Travis remained true to his dead wife, and the *Contessa* was a de facto shrine to her.

Lucia had asked Izabel, "Why don't you just tell Travis you want him?"

"Two reasons. The ghost of his perfect wife. He hates anything that might tempt him from being faithful to her memory. And then there's Charlie. Doesn't matter. *Capitão* will never want me. Not everyone has it as good as you and Mr. MacRieve."

Lucia had been startled by her statement—because things *were* good with MacRieve. Though he was a rough-and-tumble werewolf, he could be remarkably patient. As they walked the decks, he would teach her Gaelic phrases. He'd chuckled a couple of times at her early attempts at pronunciation. Then he'd stopped laughing when he realized how quickly she was learning.

And he was thoughtful. A few days ago, she'd heard MacRieve arguing with Schecter about taking "scientific credit" for a "previously uncataloged find." Curious, she'd sidled to the corner, peeking around.

In his big paws, the Scot was painstakingly cradling a delicate cocoon. Just emerging from it was a butterfly with silver wings, glittering with opalescence. She'd never seen anything like it.

"Schecter, what in the hell do I want scientific credit for?" MacRieve gave a grunt. "Just want to name it."

"Well, if you don't care about credit, then what would it hurt to allow *me* to claim this species and give it a designation? Honestly, *Mr.* MacRieve—"

"Schecter, go fook your science. I'm naming this after my lady, and if you say another word about it, you'll get this butterfly all messed up with your jugular blood."

The professor gaped, speechless for long moments. Finally he cleared his throat and said, "Uh, well, yes, of course. What will you call it?"

"Lucia Incantata," MacRieve murmured. Her toes had curled when he'd absently added, "*Reminds me of her eyes . . .*" She still sighed whenever she recalled the look on his face.

That night, he'd "surprised" her with the butterfly, setting up a mosquito net in the cabin to keep it in.

The offerings only continued. When she'd mentioned how lovely she found the blooms of those Victoria lilies, the next morning, she'd awakened to find a flawless white lily bloom by her bedside. The vase? A rinsed-out Iquiteña bottle.

On top of everything, he'd given her a never-emptying arrow quiver. She'd gasped when he'd proudly handed it to her. "You just happened to find one of these lying around on board?" It was so elegant, with fine leather ties that could be strapped to her back or thigh.

"Had it with me the whole time."

The item in his bag she'd seen wrapped in leather . . . Which meant he'd brought it for her even when he'd been furious with her. "Did you filch this from the fey?"

With a wolfy grin, he'd said, "Well, they damn sure doona sell them."

"MacRieve!" Yet once she'd gotten over her breathless excitement, she'd felt a tinge of sadness. This was a gift from a would-be lover, something to help her archery. Too bad she couldn't keep the archery *and* the lover. Still, she'd rewarded his thoughtfulness amply. . . .

He didn't *promise* gifts as some men were wont to do—MacRieve merely delivered them, delighting her Valkyrie sensibilities.

Yes, atop decks, life was constant. Belowdecks, she and MacRieve indulged their lusts.

Any time it rained during the day, he'd offer his hand with the grated words, *"Come, Lousha."* Just as he would command later when he wanted her to climax. She'd be shivering with anticipation by the time they got to the cabin.

With his palm over her mouth to cover her screams, MacRieve did wicked things to her. During each encounter, he grew more aggressive with her body, kissing her harder, touching her even more possessively. She knew he considered her *his woman*—and the idea only aroused her more.

The first night on board, he'd told her that she'd pray for him to be inside her. Again, he'd been right. When he spread her thighs wide, then lazily petted her sex, it drove her wild. Especially when he stroked just at her core while rasping in her ear, "One day I'm goin' tae be wedged so deep right in here. You'll be hot and wet and fit me like a glove."

Again and again, she tried to imagine how his shaft would feel plunging into her body. Most women in her situation would fear his size. But after his onslaught of teasing and petting . . .

Yesterday, she'd nearly begged, murmuring how much she needed him inside her.

He'd gnashed his teeth, puncturing the paneled wall

above their bed with his claws. "Gods, woman! No' till you ask me. Out o' bed!"

Every night after they were sated—or as much as they could be with their limitations—he held her in his arms. They watched her butterfly dance in the lamp-light, talking for hours.

They'd speculated as to why Nïx had warned her about the *Barão* and why its captain kept returning to remote tributaries if some of his passengers didn't make it back to port. "Maybe Captain Malaquí's been finding demons out there," Lucia had said. "He could be sacrific-ing unwitting cryzos to them in exchange for power."

"We've heard of crazier things in the Lore. . . ."

And MacRieve told her more about the necropolis. If they could locate Rio Labyrinto, they could find the city of the dead. In that place were depictions of gold, possibly directing them to "the mythical" El Dorado—which, MacRieve had told her, might or might not even be a *place*.

"Everyone thinks it's a location, a lost city," he'd said, "but the phrase is actually based on a legend of a native chieftain. He was so rich that he ridiculed anyone who wore the same jewelry twice. Instead, he had his gold ground into a mist, then painted on his body. At the end of the day, he'd wash it away, and it'd be lost forever. El Dorado means 'the Gilded Man.' "

If El Dorado had merely been a man, then he prob-ably would've been buried in a *necropolis*. Had he been buried with his gold? If he were surrounded by his golden treasures—*like arrows?*—then maybe El Dorado could still be a man *and* a place.

Lucia didn't expect a neon sign pointing to the dieumort, but she and MacRieve had enough clues to . . . get them to the next set of clues. In truth, she'd never been on such an ill-defined mission. But if it were easy to find a dieumort, then it would've been found before.

And Lucia sensed they were getting closer, daydreaming incessantly about that perfect golden arrow, imagining how it would hiss through the air once she shot it.

She pictured the look on Cruach's hideous visage when he realized she'd just dealt a death blow. . . .

At other times, Lucia would read to MacRieve from an Amazon guide book that Izabel had given her. As Lucia discovered more about the perils they'd face in Rio Labyrinto—the anacondas and those creepy caimans—MacRieve carved arrows for her new quiver. With that sly look, he'd said, "If I canna fill your quiver in one way, I will in another."

She'd chuckled. "Good one, werewolf."

He'd grown quiet, seeming startled. "First time I've heard your laugh."

"And?"

"And now I canna rest until I hear it again." He'd leapt atop her, tickling her till she'd squealed with laughter. . . .

She was so tempted to tell him everything. Especially when he held her against his chest, warm in the circle of his muscular arms, murmuring, "Let me in, Lousha. Confide your secrets in me."

She knew he wanted her to reveal what her nightmares were about. But Lucia didn't believe in confiding, had never comprehended why others sought to unburden themselves—thereby *burdening another*. No, she'd never understood the act of transferring misery, but especially not with a secret like this.

A fact-of-life secret, something that simply couldn't be changed.

How would MacRieve react if he knew his mate was married? The rage would have to overwhelm him. And when she explained who her husband was and how she'd come to be wed, nothing would stop MacRieve from confronting Cruach. Which would be tantamount to suicide. Or worse.

Sometimes Cruach didn't kill victims. Sometimes he *kept* them.

So she continued putting MacRieve off. Yet she felt he was only biding his time, as if he had no doubt she'd ultimately open up to him.

Which will never happen. Lucia had decided she would do whatever it took to keep her involvement with Cruach concealed from MacRieve. But on other matters, she was less resolved. . . .

Regin always asked herself, *Is the cake worth the bake?* Invariably, for Regin, it was. Now Lucia had caught herself wondering if having a life with MacRieve might be. When all this was over, if she could truly kill Cruach . . .

No! What the hell am I thinking? Even if she didn't have to stop an apocalypse, she couldn't surrender her archery. It would be like erasing her identity.

You get off on being known as the Archer, he'd said.

Yes. Yes, I do. She'd go from being the Archer to being the Lykae's Mate.

Never, she decided.

Then she went to go catch dinner.

THIRTY-ONE

A three-foot-long fish plopped onto the deck in front of Garreth and Damiāno. Jutting from its head was an arrow with a line attached. Bow fishing.

From behind them, Lucia said, "Please put your penises away, gentlemen. Dinner is procured. By a woman."

Garreth twisted around, found her slinging her bow over her shoulder, brushing off her unsullied hands. As she sauntered away, the lass said over her shoulder, "I caught, you boys can clean."

Gods, that female. Drives me crazy. When Garreth glanced back, he saw Damiāno was gazing after her as well. "Look at her again like that, Damiāno!" He stepped in front of the man. "Do it, and let's end this *now.*"

The man's eyes flashed to a glowing green.

In a low tone, Garreth said, "You're a goddamned shifter!"

"And you're an *escocês* dog."

That raised his hackles. "Scottish dog?" Revealing a good look of the beast within him, Garreth growled, "I've got your number, shifter. So stay out of my bluidy way."

In turn, Damiāno revealed a hint of his own beast—

a black jaguar with fangs as long as Garreth's fingers. "Don't get in mine, *escocês*."

No fear of me—interesting. "You better truly be here as a doc and for no other reason." Jaguar shifters were rumored to be exceptionally powerful. *Might actually be a worthy opponent.*

"I'm here to protect the Amazon. Don't ever forget that."

"I'm here to protect my mate. I'll do it to the death. Count yourself warned. In the meantime, you've got fish to clean, *gato*," Garreth said, turning away to look for Lucia.

What's new there?

She was hanging over the rickety rail, watching the pink dolphins that swam alongside the ship. Her short shorts rode up until he could almost glimpse the cleft of her generous arse. He gave a low growl at the sight. Then his gaze fell on the slender column of her neck. His mouth watered for her, his fangs aching to mark the tender flesh there.

Now I understand why my brother marked his mate so hard. When Garreth finally got to do it to Lucia . . . *I'll mark the living hell out of her.*

He was pleasuring her—hard and continually—but Garreth hadn't gained any ground with her, was no closer to claiming her. She'd made no request that he take her completely. At least not *out* of bed.

And the full moon was tonight. He'd hoped to have convinced her to forgo her vows before now. So he could take off the cuff and claim her.

Added to that, he couldn't shake the feeling of some

impending threat. Something more than the nearing apocalypse and the full moon. He felt as if he were running out of time on all fronts. . . .

A dolphin sprayed water from its blowhole, making Lucia laugh. She'd begun laughing more often. Whenever he let himself believe it was because of him, he stood a little taller.

The gift of a butterfly had been a stroke of genius. "You named it after me?" she'd asked, her expression growing soft, her eyes flickering silver.

That was what the wolf in him had been craving. Her approval, her delight. He'd soaked it up. Like a besotted fool, he tended that damned butterfly morning and night, feeding it with a sponge full of sugar water.

And the quiver he'd swiped from the fey? He inwardly grinned. That hadn't gone unappreciated either.

For nearly two weeks, Garreth had made Lucia his study, continuing to dig into her past. And every day he turned up something new and surprising.

She'd revealed more about the foe Nïx had dispatched her to kill, this Crom Cruach. "Those infected with his influence feel compelled to sacrifice whoever they love, in the most ghastly ways. The more they love something, the more they want to annihilate it. Cruach can control their minds, forcing his victims to see whatever he wills them to. Their eyes turn milky white—that's when you know they're lost."

"How does he do this?"

"His powers as a god. And he grows stronger with each sacrifice in his name. Whenever Cruach's human followers from the Cult of Death—the Cromites—

invoke him, they pray: *To him we sacrifice, for him our cherished.*" She'd said she couldn't imagine a worse apocalypse—because this one would sweep the world, perverting the purest love and turning it into evil and death.

Lucia was convinced that the dieumort had to be an arrow. Now he'd become convinced as well. If one could be infected by Cruach, then it made sense to strike at him from afar.

Garreth planned to. Alone. The more she told him of Cruach, the more Garreth resolved never to let her anywhere near him. But she'd yet to tell him *where* to find the god.

One night after much coaxing, Garreth had gotten her to admit she'd only been with one man. "If you've only had sex with one bloke in all this time," he'd said, "then you must've loved him verra much."

She'd turned away, her face paling. *So that's the way of it.* The man had hurt her.

"Or you hated sex so much you would join a celibate order and forgo it for over ten centuries."

She'd sighed, looking tired, with faint smudges under her eyes. Between her continuing nightmares and his attentions, she hadn't been enjoying much restful sleep. In fact, it was only toward dawn, once her nightmares had ebbed, that she'd fall into a deeper, nearly comatose slumber. "MacRieve, will you just let it go?"

He'd said he would drop it, but of course he hadn't. He needed to figure out exactly how bad it'd been for her. And who the male was. *So I can slaughter him—*

His phone rang then. It was Lachlain, no doubt calling to see what progress Garreth had made before the looming full moon. *In a word: none.* Still, the call was a welcome distraction.

Garreth answered with, "How goes it with you and the queen?"

"She took me to a mall yesterday." Lachlain sounded as if he'd just stifled a shudder. "And she pointed to a boy and said, 'I think I want one.' So naturally, I start thinking, *Where can I get a wee mortal?* But she meant . . . she meant a bairn—*our* bairn."

"You still fear getting a babe on your mate? Again, brother, how delicate can she be if she beheaded Demestriu?"

"Ach! No' you, too!"

Actually, Garreth couldn't talk. Before he'd found out the Valkyrie couldn't get pregnant unless they ate regular meals, he'd planned to take precautions.

"In any case, I dinna call to talk about me. How goes it with your Valkyrie?"

Garreth rubbed his palm over the back of his neck. "I'd been so busy chasing her down that I never stopped to see if I truly *liked* her, had never had the opportunity to discover if I could."

"And now that you've had the opportunity?"

Hesitation. Then he admitted in a low tone, "I *like* her." *Everything about her.* Each day, he fell deeper under her spell, his graceful, exquisite mate with her dark flashing eyes. "She's so clever." The speed with which she was learning Gaelic was uncanny. "And I like that she's proud." He'd never thought he would desire such a prideful woman, but now that he'd had a taste of Lucia, he could never settle for less. "And she's . . . passionate," he said in the ultimate understatement.

Lucia was the best bedmate he'd ever conceived of— and they hadn't even had sex. She brought him greater pleasure than he'd ever known, but released only the worst of the pressure—because she stoked his need beyond imagining.

"And does the Valkyrie return the sentiment?" Lachlain asked.

"I want her more than I've ever coveted anything— but I know she's no' mine. She holds herself away from me, keeps secrets. I fear she always will."

Garreth had told her, "We need to talk about what will happen once we complete this mission." She'd given him a cagey look and said, "Can't we just keep our focus on that for now?" He'd asked her to confide in him, asked her what her nightmares were about. She'd refused to tell him.

"You've got to give her a free rein," Lachlain said. "She's made up her own mind about things for over a millennium—she will no' take kindly to an overbearing male."

"Aye, I ken that." He exhaled. "If Lousha and I are fated, then why is this so difficult?"

"Everybody says the mate phenomenon makes the bonding easier. In my mind, it usually only brings grief, at least at first. Especially if a mate is *other*. Bowen and I could no' be more content with our mates, but we each went through hell to get her."

Hell. *I'm there right now.* Restlessness weighed on him. He wasn't running at night, wasn't providing for his mate, and could find no threat to protect her from.

"You're still no' bedding her?" Lachlain asked.

"Nay," he said, then added in a mutter, "Everything but." With each storm, he was taking her back to their cabin. But even when it hadn't been raining, he was tempted, barely stopping himself from it.

He'd grown so desperate he wouldn't have cared if Lucia's lightning struck all around them on a cloudless day.

And when they were in bed together, he was only just keeping his promise to her. Claw marks riddled the cabin wall from the times he'd struggled not to take her, when his shaft had prodded right at her tight core—and instead of fighting him, she'd moaned, *"Please . . ."*

Each time he somehow found the strength to deny her, he resented her vows more and more. "I'm trying to be patient," he told Lachlain now, "trying to respect her beliefs, but I doona know how much longer I can do this."

"What will happen tonight?"

"Unless I can get her to accept me, I'll be praying the cuff holds true . . ." His voice trailed off. Garreth scented her desire. And rain on the air. He turned to Lucia, found her gazing at him with expectation. "I've got to go!"

"Why, what's happening?"

Garreth said, "Ah, brother, a storm's coming!"

By midafternoon, once they were both spent, Garreth petted her hair, gently sifting his fingers through it, watching fascinated as the lamp light played off the strands.

"Your eyes turned completely blue," she said, her voice drowsy. "Is it because the full moon is tonight?"

When he nodded, she said, "The cuff will work?"

"Aye. It's working." Because already his reaction would've been much stronger.

"Tell me more about the beast inside you, about turning."

"It's like a possession. When we turn, we call the transformation *saorachadh ainmhidh bho a cliabhan—* letting the beast out of its cage. Think of it as four different levels of turning. Say I got into a heated dispute. I'd feel the beast stirring inside me—like it's waking. If I felt rage, it'd make my claws flare, my fangs sharpen. And lust to mark a mate?" He raked his gaze over her. "It'd take over my body. I'd still be there, still remembering all, comprehending everything, but the beast is definitely in control. To fight it would take a will that few are known to possess."

"What's the fourth level?"

"It's the worst—turning so much that you canna come back. If one of our kind canna handle some experience, something that's too hard to take, the beast rises too much, maddening its Lykae host forever. He'd never revert from his animal state."

"What happens then?"

"He'd have to be locked away in our dungeons," Garreth said. They should have known something was amiss with Bowen's first "mate"—since he'd still been able to carry on after he thought she'd died. . . . "That's why we doona change others into our kind—anyone newly made would have to learn to control the beast, a process that takes decades, if it works at all. We'd be forced to imprison them for all that time before we could even think of freeing them."

"Change others, like Rossiter."

"Exactly," Garreth said, not *un*moved by the mortal's plight. "He's no' out of the game yet. Maybe he'll find his orchid—or a pretty immortal who does no' follow Lore rules. . . ."

As the rain poured outside, they talked of other things, plotting what would happen tomorrow night when they arrived at Rio Labyrinto. With each stroke of her hair, her lids grew heavier, her expression soft and sleepy, until she finally drifted off.

Now he lay beside her with his head propped in his hand, lightly grazing his fingers up and down her sleek back. He exhaled, simply savoring the luxury of having her with him, in his bed, in his life.

But she didn't trust him. And that pained him.

When she whimpered, his brows drew together. Again, she suffered nightmares, her low cries building with the tempest brewing outside.

She was of a warrior race, and yet she was terrified, speaking in some old Norse tongue he didn't understand.

Who the hell had hurt his woman? Why did she refuse to tell him? His claws dug into his palms as he fought to control the beast within him, the beast that needed to punish any fuck who'd given her pain.

THIRTY-TWO

When Crom had asked Lucia to come with him and leave Valhalla, she'd eagerly agreed, though she'd known that once a Valkyrie left that plane, she could never return.

Lucia was sixteen and in love. Nothing, not her god-parents' warnings or Regin's pleading, could dissuade her. She'd wedded Crom with no reservations, despite his strange customs—they couldn't touch whatsoever until after they'd been married, and they had to wed in a bizarre stone temple with robed strangers all around.

At the altar, after they'd been joined forever, she'd turned to her beloved. And he'd vanished. In his place was one of the strangers with a raised club. He'd struck, knocking her unconscious.

Too late, Lucia had learned that Crom Cruach had never even been at the portal. Instead, he'd been trapped in a fetid lair in the earth, projecting the image of the fair-haired young man.

For as long as she'd been watching the sky, Cruach had been watching her. He'd needed a bride born of gods to beget heirs on, and like so many deities, he could project illusions for women he wanted to seduce.

When Lucia had awakened, she'd been trapped in

his prison with her fair-haired man standing over her. Only then had Cruach unveiled his true self to her. His beautiful face had fallen away, revealing the Broken Bloody One.

A cloven-footed monster, Cruach clad himself in scraps of metal strung together, taken from his slaughtered victims' proud shields or armor. On his massive head, stringy white hair hung sparsely around horns that jutted up like giant splayed fingers. His face was ghoulish, his eyes yellow, slitted with red and running with pus.

He *was* broken, his body misshapen, his bones having fractured and healed at odd angles. But even with his hunched form, he stood seven feet tall. He was bloody as well—his scaly snakelike skin seeped blood and was rotting away in places, exposing those fused bones beneath.

A line of drool had dripped from the corner of his gaping mouth when he'd smiled down at her.

Once she'd been able to scream no more, she'd learned the truth about *all* his lies. He had told her he'd make her mistress of his castle and shower her with gifts. His "castle" was a corpse-strewn tunnel in a seaside cliff, thick with maggots and stench.

The gifts? Dead bodies and parts of them—ragged limbs, heads with sightless eyes. He intended for her to . . . *eat* them.

The adoration he vowed? Each day, his Cromites had prepared her body with vile rituals, marking her skin with blood, drawing sinister marks from the black arts all over her.

There was no escaping him. Cromite swordsmen guarded the entrance to the lair and the tunnel ended in a cliff two hundred feet above the ocean.

Toward the end of her captivity, she'd been so starved, her stomach had cleaved to her spine. "You go hungry?" Cruach had said, waving at the pools of oily blood and gruesome limbs. "When I give you meat and wine, my love?"

Once she'd begun to sicken with fever, she'd heard someone calling her name from down at the base of the cliff and thought it a delirium.

But it was all too real. Young Regin—who'd sensed Cruach's deception and had begged Lucia not to leave— had followed her out of Valhalla. Never to return, cast out forever. Lucia had wept to hear her sister's plaintive cries for her.

"How do I reach you, Lucia? I don't . . . I don't know how to get up there!"

Never would she have let Regin enter that place— even before Lucia's eventual wedding night. . . .

As she weakly screamed, his followers laid her on his altar, holding her down. When he heaved himself above her, blood spilled from his mouth, from between gritted teeth, pouring over her face, into her eyes. His organ would rip her in two—she'd known he would kill her like this.

So long without food, with her heart racing with horror, she'd lost consciousness.

When she woke, he was roaring with fury, missing an eye. Beneath her claws were chunks of scaly skin. The Cromites had drawn their swords, leveling them at her.

With blood gushing down her thighs, she rolled off the altar into a pile of bodies. Flies erupted from the gore. She breathed them, hacking them from her lungs and mouth.

Somehow she made it to her feet, coughing, tears blinding her as she tried to stagger away through the line of Cromites. Knowing she was trapped, Cruach allowed her to go, snarling with rage at his pain, then laughing because he'd caused her more. "Do you think that was pain, wife? That was a mere hint! I'll teach you what misery is!"

She followed the tunnel to the very end. At the cliff's edge, she gazed out over the horizon, over the ocean. The first clean air she'd breathed in days.

Pure peace awaited her. . . . He couldn't pass this barrier, could never follow her down. When he yelled for her, she closed her eyes, and she leapt—

Hands snatched her shoulders, jerking her back.

No, no! That's not how it happened! She'd gotten free. Now he had her again!

She swiped out with her claws, desperate to jump . . . to die.

THIRTY-THREE

◆━◇◈◇━◆

"Lousha! Wake up!" Garreth reached to comfort her, grasping her shoulders. At the contact, electrical energy seared his fingertips just as her claws shot out, raking down his chest.

"What the hell?" He leapt back. *"Lousha?"*

When she opened her eyes, they were fully silver, glinting with tears.

"Shh, doona be afraid." He put his hands up as he neared her once more. "It's just me."

She collapsed back on the bed once more, staring blankly at the ceiling. When she closed her eyes, teardrops tracked down her face, making his chest ache.

He could never stand the sight of the lass's tears. "Your dreams are getting worse." She'd only been asleep for an hour, a brief afternoon nap, and yet it'd been enough to affect her like this.

"I . . . I'm fine. I'll be okay," she assured him, even as lightning still flared outside.

He sat at the foot of the bed. "You must tell me what you dream of."

"We've discussed this already," she said, running her arm over her face. "I don't want to talk about it."

"Is it . . . me?" When she frowned at him, he said,

"You have no' had nightmares like this over the last year, have you? But now, every day we're together, they get worse."

She rose up, drawing her knees to her chest. "No, you're making a big deal out of nothing."

"*Nothing*?" He pointed out the bloody tracks across his chest. "You attacked me!"

"I'm so sorry." She dropped her head in her hands. "I didn't realize it was you."

"I doona care about that! I just want them to end."

"So do I," she murmured. "They will. Soon, I'm sure."

He swooped up his jeans and yanked them on. "It seems the more pleasure we have, the worse they get."

She gazed up at him. "What are you talking about?"

"Just as I need to claim my mate, I need to make her happy. But now, you give me your body to pleasure, and then you suffer." He raked his fingers through his hair. "Maybe the dreams are getting worse because tonight's the full moon? And deep down you fear me?"

Gods, this male was fierce. Not only when protecting her, but when experiencing *anything*. MacRieve felt things so intensely. "I don't fear you." He was generous, protective, thoughtful. *All the things my husband isn't.*

"Then what do you fear? Give me an enemy to fight, Lousha!"

That was *exactly* what she couldn't do. "Lots of immortals have nightmares. The years build up—"

"Bullshite! Doona lie to me."

Lucia rose to dress, slipping on her underwear. "Just drop it, MacRieve."

"Damn you, Valkyrie, it just should no' be this complicated between us. You want me, and I want you. The end."

"Well, I'm not that easy—"

"*Nothing* about you is easy."

"My life is complicated, whether I want it to be or not." She hastily donned a halter top and shorts and began braiding her hair over her ears.

"So many secrets, Lousha. Will they keep you warm at night?"

She slowed her plaiting. "What does that mean?" *Is he breaking up with me?*

"It means you need to tell me what you dreamed."

She glanced away with a shrug. "I don't remember."

"Enough with the lies!" He grabbed her upper arms. "Why will you no' trust me?"

Lightning flashed as her own anger grew. "It's not in my nature to trust!" *Some secrets go to the grave. . . .* "Did you never think that the more I like you, the less I want to tell you my secrets? And how do you really know that you *want* to hear them, MacRieve?"

He drew his head back, wolflike, as though he'd been presented a trap he couldn't determine the mechanics of. "I doona understand you. That's no reason to hide things from me. Own your actions."

She flung herself away from him. "Gods, I hate it when you say that!" *Easy to say for someone who's never made a tragic choice in his long life!*

"One of these days, woman! You asked me if I'd ever thought about giving up on you. I had no' before, but now . . ."

"Now?"

"You have to meet me halfway, or I will stop chasing you. And when I do, you'll regret the loss."

I know this!

"Will you tell me?"

She thought he was in deadly earnest. *He's giving me a choice . . . and I don't want to lose him.*

Damn it, when had he gone from enemy, to necessary evil, to someone she didn't think she could live without? "MacRieve, I—" She swallowed, imagining how she'd tell him. *I have a husband. I married the devil. I'm his wife. Lucia av Cruach.* Shame made it nearly impossible to breathe, much less talk. She'd begun to care what he thought of her, and his knowing the truth wouldn't make a difference anyway! Her fate was woven—

"*We've got company!*" Schecter cried from above. "*Another ship.*"

At once, the engines slowed to idling. They could hear running on the deck above them.

"Oh, bluidy hell," MacRieve muttered.

"Why's everybody running? Couldn't it just be another research vessel?"

"This far out? No' a chance." He yanked on a T-shirt. "Pirates, mercenaries, or worse."

"Worse?"

Seizing her hand, he dragged her out of the cabin into the rain. Over his shoulder he said, "This is no' over, Lousha!"

When they reached the observation deck, four of the men were already there, scanning the river. Schecter stood under an umbrella, binoculars crammed against his glasses. Travis peered out with his weary gaze more alert and a shotgun in his hands. Rossiter was at the rail, unshaven, his light brown hair disheveled.

Charlie's hazel eyes were fierce as he stood by his captain, and a machete hung from a strap around the young man's wrist.

Yet there was nothing to see, nothing but a curtain of rain and the jungle closing in all around them.

MacRieve turned to Schecter. "What the hell, man?"

"Give it a second. There's a ship coming around the bend about a mile to the north. They've been trailing us."

Everyone fell silent as they waited. Then Charlie quietly said, "It's Captain Malaquí's ship."

Indeed, sailing up through the rain was ... the *Barão da Borracha*. The ship that potentially carried a vampire and supposedly sailed the other way.

The one Nïx warned me about.

When Malaquí decreased his speed just after that bend, Lucia said, "Why are they slowing?"

"Did they make a find?" Rossiter asked in an overly innocent tone.

MacRieve turned to Travis. "Does Malaquí ever go this route?"

The Texan looked like he had murder on his mind. Those two definitely had a history. "No, we never go the same way."

Like the *Contessa*, the *Barão* was a restored rubber boom ship. That was where the similarities ended. Malaquí's ship was spotless, meticulously trimmed. A shining smokestack jutted proudly, fresh with black paint. Even the lines were coiled at even lengths on the deck.

But no passengers were stirring in the dwindling rain. Only the captain could be seen, hanging out from the wheelhouse.

My first look at Malaquí. He was above average height with slick black hair and a glaring red tattoo covering his forearm. The right side of his face had been maimed—four deep scars sliced across his cheek, as if he'd been attacked by an animal.

He gave her chills. Here was a man who took passengers out, yet again and again they didn't return. What was he doing with—or to—them?

For all they knew, he could be feeding tourists to an insatiable jungle demon.

When Travis and Charlie hastened to the wheelhouse to get the *Contessa* going once more, MacRieve muttered to Lucia, "Malaquí's pure evil. Whatever we've suspected of him—he's more than capable of it."

"How do you know?"

"My Instinct's telling me."

The beast inside MacRieve was recognizing a prospective foe. In a low tone, she asked him, "Do you scent a vampire?" For some reason, she couldn't get past the idea that Lothaire was on that ship.

"They're downwind," MacRieve answered. "But aye, I think so. Whatever Nïx sent you to retrieve, someone aboard the *Barão* either wants it or wants to stop you from getting it."

"This makes sense, then. Nïx told me to beware of

two cryptic things—a guardian and a rubber baron. Confirmation on the second. And before you ask, I have no idea what a guardian is."

"The soothsayer warned you of the *Barão*? Then I'm going to take heed."

"Uh, how?"

"If they follow us for the rest of the day, then I'll disable their ship at the earliest opportunity."

"Disable?"

"Aye. When they anchor for the night, I'll scuttle her." At her questioning look, he said, "I'll swim over, dive underneath, and yank off the propeller. Simple enough."

"Get in the water—at *night*?"

THIRTY-FOUR

◆━━◆

Just before moonrise, Lucia and MacRieve stood on the platform in the drizzle. She plucked on her bowstring as he readied for his mission—by stripping off his shirt.

At sunset, the *Barão* had dropped anchor just upriver from the *Contessa*, within the very same bend—which, as far as MacRieve was concerned, was a declaration of war.

Nothing she could say would dissuade him from his plan.

She was beset with nerves, and for more than one reason. Tonight the moon was full, and though Lucia trusted the witches' power in the cuff, spells that went against the course of nature had a way of going awry. Like if Fate wanted her way, she'd figure out how to get it.

Plus, Lucia was uneasy about MacRieve being in the water at night. "Just take the skiff, werewolf."

He shook his head. "I have to get in anyway. And I doona want to be seen. If I stir the vampire I scented, he could attack you while I'm over there."

"It's too dangerous," she insisted.

"Well, I'm no' too keen on leaving you here with Damiāno, either."

Today MacRieve had told her that Damiāno was a jaguar shifter, one of a powerful species known for their strength, agility—and dirty fighting.

"If that *gato* comes near you, I want you to drill him between the eyes."

She had her new quiver at her thigh and her bow ready to shoot, but close quarters—like those on a ship—were an archer's most disadvantageous combat zone. "I'll do what I can."

He gazed at her anxious expression. "You're truly going to be worried about me?"

"Just because I don't want to tell all you my secrets doesn't mean I don't like you."

"Aye, we'll be talking about your secrets later."

After the *Barāo*'s sighting, they'd seemed to enjoy an unspoken truce for the last few hours. "You can't just let me have them?" *And keep your wolf's nose out of my business?*

"My Lykae curiosity demands answers. And now I've remembered how I can coax you to tell me anything." He reached out and cupped her breast.

"Wolf!" She slapped his hand away. "You're just trying to distract me from my worry."

"Aye, and I merely wanted to touch your bonny breasts."

"Can you be serious? I don't have a good feeling about this."

"Lousha, you've seen me almost completely

turned—do you no' think the things in the water should fear me?"

Good point. "Wait . . . *almost* completely turned?"

He chucked her under the chin. "Relax, this is a cakewalk. What's the worst that can happen?"

As if on cue, the skies opened up, pouring rain.

"Just be careful," she whispered as he slipped into the black water, beginning his silent swim to the *Barão*.

As she impatiently waited, she tried to analyze this worry. Nearly two weeks ago, she would've been over-joyed that he was leaving her behind. Now? She feared she was falling for him, her rough-and-tumble Scot. Which could only be a disaster.

MacRieve could never be satisfied without sex. Hell, *she* could never be. The last ten days had turned into bout after bout of sensual torment—

She heard something moving on the decks and tensed, her ears twitching. Seconds later, she let out a breath. Just Schecter, activating his lure. Every time he hauled it out of the water, her ears registered the frequencies anew. *Noise polluter.*

Though Lucia didn't know where Charlie or Damião was, she could hear Rossiter pacing as usual. And Izabel was with the captain in his cabin, discussing something with him in a low voice.

Lucia sighed. Those two had it so easy as a couple, with just two minor barriers between them: Izabel's twin brother was in love with the same man, and Travis was still in love with his late wife.

If so little stood in the way of Lucia and MacRieve, she'd have reeled him in and never let him go.

Try a marriage to the devil, a chastity-based power, and potentially the end of the world. . . .

Once Garreth reached the stern of the *Barão*, he drew a breath and dove beneath the ship. Barely able to see in the muddy water, he felt his way around until he could locate the propeller shaft.

After bending the metal out of shape, he surfaced for another breath. Just before he returned to mangle the rudder, he hesitated.

Blood. He smelled it, coming from within the *Barão*.

Ignore it, get the job done, and get back. But why was it so quiet inside? He didn't hear a single passenger. Not a soul was moving about.

And he still scented *vampire*.

His Lykae's curiosity got the best of him, and he leapt to the gangway, soundlessly landing.

Again he listened, hearing nothing but ship sounds, the eerie kind one hears only in the dead of night—the anchor chain scraping the windlass, wood settling, ropes tightening as a breeze picked up.

Dripping water, he stole into the main salon. The room was unsettling to Garreth, reminding him of a Victorian-era funeral parlor, overly gilded but somber.

He'd known the ship was a refurbished rubber boom trawler—the vessel's very name meant *the rubber baron*—but he hadn't suspected the *Barão* would be a time capsule from the rubber boom days.

And some of those days had been dark indeed.

As he moved farther within, he spotted a pair of reading glasses crushed on the plush floor rug. Atop a serving table, afternoon tea had been set out some time ago—now the cakes were crusted, the cream spoiled. When he spied a teacup with lipstick on the rim and a plate of half-eaten cake beside it, the hair on the back of his neck stood up.

Something had gotten these passengers—*unexpectedly.*

And a trail of crimson spatter led out of the room in the direction he'd detected the vampire's scent. Garreth followed the blood down a dimly-lit and narrow companionway, past one empty cabin after another. Wood creaked behind him, and he twisted around. *Just the ship settling once more.*

The trail ended at the door of the last cabin. *Locked.* Tensing for a fight, Garreth broke the polished brass knob. Inside, a coffin lay. An eerily simple casket—wood, no varnish or sets of pallbearer handles. Of course, the vampire wouldn't likely be carted around in it.

Garreth crouched beside the coffin. With fangs bared and flared claws raised to strike, he tore open the lid.

Empty.

But then another scent impression teased Garreth. He rose, exiting the vampire's room, tracking it farther into the boat until he stood before the freezer. Drawing a breath, knowing what he'd find, he opened the door.

All the passengers were inside. Dead. Their bodies had been butchered into pieces and stuffed within.

Among the limbs, he spied Captain Malaquí's glaring tattooed arm. When Garreth had seen the man just this afternoon, had Malaquí already known the others were dead? And that his time was nigh. . . ?

The vampire was missing, with a trail of blood leading to—or from—his cabin, and all the people aboard had perished. Should be easy to deduce what had happened. Yet these people had been *hacked* at.

What weapon could have done this? A sword, an ax?

His eyes narrowed. Charlie had had a machete this morning. *I knew something was off. . . .*

"Lousha!" Garreth twisted around, sprinting for the water.

"What the hell is MacRieve doing?" Through the pounding rain, Lucia had spotted him boarding the *Barão*! "Why would he go . . ." She trailed off.

The *Contessa* had just seemed to *ripple* beneath her feet before stilling once more. "That was weird." She'd no sooner spoken than the entire vessel shuddered, moving *sideways*, straining against the anchors. Wood groaned from the pressure. She hunched down, her eyes darting.

From his cabin, Travis barked, *"What the hell was—"*

Like a shot, the *Contessa* reared up, briefly tilting to the side, sending Lucia skidding to the opposite side of the deck. As she scrabbled for purchase, her mind tried to grasp what could do this—what would be *big* enough to do this.

And how much more could the *Contessa* take?

When the boat was hit again, rising up off its hull

before settling, Schecter shrieked from the port side of the boat.

Lucia's eyes narrowed as a suspicion arose, and she clambered around the pitching decks toward him. Once she'd reached the side, her jaw slackened at the scene.

Schecter. Hanging on for his life to a splintering railing. Directly beneath his dangling body, an immense caiman peered up, about to strike.

Her lips parted around a shocked breath. The creature was *colossal*, with red eyes the size of basketballs. And it wasn't alone. The water all around the boat churned with eddies.

MacRieve had told her that there were in fact giant caimans—but that they lived in Rio Labyrinto, not anywhere else!

Wait . . . the ship was only a few hours from there. Dear gods, was Schecter's lure actually working, drawing them here from the hidden tributary?

Lucia readied her bow, stringing two arrows. The creature's hide would be plated thick, so she aimed for the red eyes—big enough targets.

When she nailed the caiman in both sockets, it thrashed twice, sending up copious waves of water and mud that splattered the side of the boat. Then it disappeared.

Lucia strapped her bow across her body, then dove across the deck for Schecter, snagging his wrist. "What have you done?" she demanded. "What is this?"

He replied in hysterical gibberish—so she feinted like she was dropping him. "What was that, Schecter?"

"Lure. Worked!"

"Where is it?" She couldn't hear the contraption, which meant it was still underwater.

"I don't know! Got jostled, caught in the anchor line," he answered, looking so petrified that she believed him.

She'd just swung him back on solid footing when Travis and Izabel stumbled out onto the deck.

"What the hell's going on, doc?" Travis snapped. The big Texan was wielding his shotgun.

Izabel herself had a machete. "Wh-what could do this?" she cried over the rain.

"Ask Schecter!" Lucia turned, but he'd already disappeared.

Rossiter staggered out from the cabin area. "Somebody want to tell me what's happening?"

"Schecter's lure worked. We're surrounded by giant caimans," Lucia said, but no one believed her—they couldn't see in the dark.

When lightning flashed, illuminating the creatures swarming the boat, Rossiter's jaw slackened. "Schecter did . . . *this*?"

Travis's eyes went wide. "I'm going to kick his worthless ass."

"Can that wait?" Rossiter gazed around uneasily. "We need to get under way, stat!"

"Might help if I could find my fucking deckhand!" Travis said with a scowl. "We're taking on water—we've got to get the pumps going before I can crank the engines."

"I'm on the pumps!" Rossiter yelled, running at once for the engine room.

Gazing toward the bow, Lucia said, "The lure's still working. I'll try to find it, get rid of it."

"Wait, Lucia," Izabel said, "where's Mr. MacRieve—"

Another lurching hit to the ship sent Lucia tumbling across the deck, her claws like grappling hooks over the wood. From a distance she saw Travis and Izabel launched into the galley wall; Travis hit headfirst, the blow knocking him out cold. Looking dazed but unharmed, Izabel dropped her machete to tend to him.

The next rock of the boat loosed a weighty beam above the two. It plummeted toward the captain's motionless body, but little Izabel *caught it*, straining to hold it over her head.

Lucia dashed up to help, but before she could reach Izabel, the woman . . . *changed*.

Involuntarily backing up a step, Lucia gaped. She'd lived a long time. Never had she seen this. Giant caimans could be explained, but this . . .

Clearly, Izabel needed no help. Right before Lucia's eyes, she'd just morphed.

Into . . . *Charlie*. And . . . and *he* was managing the beam handily. *Can't think about this right now—*

"Lousha!" Dimly, she heard MacRieve yelling for her. She whirled around, hurrying to the platform to warn him away. He'd just run out onto the stern of the *Barão*.

"MacRieve, something's in the water!" she yelled as the boat rose up once more. "Stay there!"

"Fook that!" sounded back.

Then he dove in.

"Damn him!" She had to clear a way back for him. With the help of her new quiver, she shot repeatedly, aiming for the caimans' eyes, arrows flying as if she were flanked by a hundred archers.

She killed several of the creatures, but something was still rippling the water behind MacRieve. It was just below the surface but making a sizeable wake.

"Swim faster!" Had to be a caiman—but one as big as a freaking submarine. She couldn't see it through the muddy water and pouring rain. Though she shot it over and over, its rugged hide and the water buffer shielded it. She could do little to slow its advance.

And MacRieve kept pointing *at her*! Taking precious moments to yell.

"Just swim, Scot! There's something on your tail!" Why wasn't he swimming faster? The thing was right—

"Behind you!" he roared. Their eyes briefly met; his were filled with dread.

She whirled around just as lightning flashed. Damiāno had a machete raised above her head.

THIRTY-FIVE

◆━━◆◆◆━━◆

Garreth watched as Lucia ducked from Damiāno with uncanny speed, kicking out at the man's knee. She'd bought a heartbeat's time, scrambling away to another deck as Damiāno limped after her.

Knowing she was safe for a moment, Garreth dug in, swimming even harder. Yet he could eke out no lead on whatever was pursuing him. Had to be a caiman, but his mind struggled to wrap around the size of it.

He felt the motion of water behind him as it propelled itself forward, gaining. And without Lucia's arrows whizzing past him in the air, more of the caimans were circling.

Almost to the boat! *So close* . . . Just then, the caiman began rising, sending a sharp wave of water fanning out, briefly lifting Garreth. How big was the fucking thing? When it breached the surface, Garreth felt its foul breath spraying water over his head and nape like a sprinkler.

Doona look back . . . doona look back. He could hear its ancient bones grinding and clicking as its jaws opened wide.

Garreth dove, dropping like a stone. When he

reached the river bottom, he kicked against it with all his might and went hurtling to the surface, leaping for the boat. He landed on the platform, then sprang for the main deck just as teeth slammed down on the platform, biting out the middle.

With angry, almost *sentient* eyes, the caiman sank, disappearing into the black once more.

At once, Garreth lunged to his feet. "Lousha!" The storm boiled, lightning streaking the sky, thunder so loud it pained his ears.

"*MacRieve?*" She ran for him on the stern deck.

"Where's Damiãno?"

"I don't know—I lost him for a second." Twisting around, eyes wary, she strapped her bow across her body. "What is going on? And why did you get *in* the water?"

"Lousha, the *Barão*. It's a ghost ship."

"What?"

"Everyone on board has been killed. Hacked to pieces. I thought it was Charlie at first, until I saw Damiãno." Garreth grabbed her forearms. "I want you out of here!" The ship hurled up once more. "Goddamnit, why are those caimans attacking?"

"Schecter's lure. It worked! But I can't get to the front—"

"The creatures protect the Labyrinto," Damiãno intoned from where he'd crouched directly above them. "As will I."

The shifter leapt down with the machete, snagging Lucia by her neck, pressing the blade against her throat. "You're not to enter the Labyrinth."

Lucia dared a glance up at the male. His green eyes glowed with menace.

"*Let her go!*" MacRieve yelled. "Fight me!"

"You were never supposed to get this close. The tomb is forbidden to outsiders."

"You're the *guardião*?" Lucia demanded. The guardian Nïx had warned of.

Damiãno seemed unhearing. "You don't know what evil sleeps in the Labyrinth. The Gilded One will rise."

Her mind raced. The Gilded One? El Dorado *was* a man! An evil man?

"We're no' here to wake any evil!" MacRieve snapped.

Damiãno shook his head hard. "No one trespasses."

In as calm a tone as Lucia could manage, she said, "Listen, Damiãno, we're actually here to *stop* an evil from rising. Let's just talk about this. We're really on the same team."

Easing nearer, MacRieve added, "If we doona go to Rio Labyrinto, there's a god who'll take over the earth."

"There's no evil greater than the Gilded One!"

"Bullshite!"

Lucia made a sound of frustration. "You two are going to argue about this? My evil's bigger than your evil?"

"Damiãno, we're speakin' about a bluidy apocalypse!"

"As am I!" The male tightened his grip on her neck, pressing the blade into her skin.

MacRieve swallowed, still slipping closer. "Is that why you killed everyone on the other boat?"

Damiãno's gaze darted. "What are you saying?"

"They're all dead. All butchered. Likely *with a machete*."

The shifter stared down at the blade, muttering, "It's begun—"

Seizing the moment, Lucia went limp, dropping down, driving her elbow into his stomach. She ducked out of the way for MacRieve to strike.

The Scot did, tackling Damiāno. They crashed into a wall, cracking the wood supports, sending Damiāno's machete clattering across the deck into the water.

The shifter roared, heaving back, charging MacRieve.

She'd drawn her bow free and nocked an arrow but hesitated. Both battled for the upper hand, each grappling for a hold on the other. They were spinning so fast, it was a blur. If she shot MacRieve . . .

"Lousha, the lure. Cut it loose!"

MacRieve wanted her to leave him?

"Go, Valkyrie!"

The caimans were still circling. If Damiāno didn't get MacRieve, the caimans could get all of them. And Lucia believed the Scot could—and *wanted* to—defeat this foe.

So she forced herself away, dashing to the forward anchor. At the bow, she squinted down the length of the anchor chain, finally spotting the line for Schecter's lure—the line that was now tangled around the chain, pulled taut, and hanging five feet out of her reach. All around it, caimans clashed to reach a mad scientist's box of nothing.

Lying on her front, she hooked a foot around a railing post, suspending herself. Staring down into a tempest of snapping jaws, she stretched with her fingers splayed. Just out of reach. With a swallow, she relaxed her foot an inch . . . *Almost . . . got it!*

She hauled it up, shimmying her body back until she was safe on the deck. With no time to breathe a sigh of relief, she darted to her feet, swinging the line round and round like a bola, flinging it down the river. When the current began carrying it away, some of the smaller creatures turned to the signal. The big ones seemed to be committed, lurking—as if they *expected* a meal.

As she ran back to MacRieve, she passed Schecter huddled in a corner of the galley, babbling with a butcher knife in hand. His pants reeked of urine. Charlie must've taken the injured Travis back into his cabin. *Can't think about that . . .*

When she returned to the fight, Damiãno and MacRieve had both begun to turn, the beasts within them spurred to the fray. Their bodies grew, muscles expanding, rippling with power.

Damiãno's irises deepened to a fervent green. His fangs and claws elongated to wickedly sharp points. Patches of sleek black fur appeared.

MacRieve's own beast flickered over him, his eyes gone ice blue with rage, his onyx claws flaring, but he hadn't turned fully. *Why not?* This was no time for mercy!

Comprehension struck. Oh, Freya—MacRieve was prevented from turning by the cuff he wore!

With a chilling roar, Damiãno sank his canines into

MacRieve's arm. Blood spurted. MacRieve bellowed in pain, slashing his claws over Damiãno's face, cleaving skin to the bone.

Gushing blood from his wounds, Damiãno barreled into MacRieve's chest, crashing them into the side railing. They splintered the wood to pieces, then plunged into the murky river below.

They didn't surface. Thirty seconds passed, then a minute. The longest of her entire life—

The pair shot up in the water, still in a fight to the death. She took aim at Damiãno, but they were too fast, sloshing water up with each blow. *Might hit MacRieve.*

So she took up her vigil, shooting as many caimans as she could, but the big one was returning. She could see her earlier arrows jutting from its plated tail and back, yet it wouldn't rise for her to take its eyes.

Though she shot continuously, it never slowed. "MacRieve!" she screamed. "It's coming back!" She took another bead on Damiãno—

The stern of the ship reared up; she flipped back, crashing into the auxiliary boat. By the time she staggered back to her feet, she could only watch in horror as the giant caiman's tail whipped through the air, knocking both men into the depths.

THIRTY-SIX

Lucia's heart dropped to her stomach. *I can't lose him. I can't. . . .* She scanned the water but saw nothing.

MacRieve can't be gone, can't be dead.

She'd just strapped her bow over her body and tensed to dive in after him, when she heard from behind her, *"What the hell are you doing?"*

She whirled around. "MacRieve!" He was on the other side of the boat, swimming fast for what was left of the platform. "How'd you get over there?"

"Caiman tail, I think," he said as he climbed aboard. "A mite foggy on the details."

Eyes watering with relief, she clutched him. "Look! It's going away." The giant caiman was following in the direction of the trap, along with the other hold-outs as well.

"You were divin' in for me? Does *nothing* scare you?" MacRieve wrapped his arms around her, cupping her head to his heaving chest.

The downpour was still so loud, she had to scream over it. "What happened?"

"When the creature got Damião, he tried to drag me down with him. Till the thing swallowed him whole."

"The shifter's . . . dead?"

"Aye. And if he's no', he's wishing he is. Let's no' speak of this. We've got to secure this ship . . ." He trailed off, because she'd stiffened against him.

"MacRieve, wh-where's your cuff?"

Their eyes met, his widening. "Oh, bluidy hell." Before she could stop him, he dove back in.

"Nooo!" She knew there was no way he could find it. Again and again, he swam down. Finally, he hauled his body up once more, looking utterly defeated.

Side by side, they stood on the remnants of the platform, both of them staring at the water and pelted with rain. Now the cuff was gone, and Lucia was trapped on a boat with a werewolf about to go crazy. "What are we going to do?"

"I'm just fine, Lousha, doona fash yerself over me."

"But it's *gone!*"

"Oh, aye, and we canna break your vows. Nothing's more important than that. Even the fact that I could've been killed!"

"You couldn't have bought a backup cuff?" she demanded in a yell. "Had a spare in your bag?"

He bellowed back, "It never crossed my mind that I'd be battling a shape-shifter in the Amazon"—with an angry jab, he pointed out Damiāno's deep bite on his arm—"and then wrestling with him underwater. Or that a giant caiman would drag him down, and he'd be snatching at me to take down with him. I barely got back to you! Maybe you're wishing I dinna?"

"Don't be ridiculous!" No matter how incensed she was at him for putting her in this position, she didn't want him hurt. And fighting with him was changing nothing—their situation wasn't altering. *Think . . . think. This isn't happening tonight.*

Fate has a way of getting what she wants, no matter how we try to avoid it.

Ah, gods, unless she could get off this boat, it *would* be happening.

"Damn it, lass, I will try to be gentle." Garreth reached for her shoulder. "Maybe if we started now, I could get you accustomed. I could make sure you were crazed with needing, too. . . ."

But she flinched from him, clearly furious. *Rightly furious with him. I'd promised her that she had nothing to fear.* And Lucia had promised that she'd hate him forever if she broke her vows.

"It will no' be like your last time, Lousha."

"What do you know about my last time?"

"Does no' take a genius to realize you had a bad experience."

"Y-you have no idea." She shuddered, her wee ears peeking out from her soaked mane.

"The man hurt you?" *Wanting to kill some faceless male, needing to . . . Keep it together, Garreth.*

She nodded. And she hadn't had sex in a millennium because of it.

"I'm not ready, MacRieve. I'm just *not*. I don't want this." Her eyes were bleak.

Over the last ten days, Garreth hadn't eased her mind about sex. Or *changed* it. Either because of her vows or because she'd been scarred from the last time,

Lucia wasn't ready for this night—couldn't endure a moon-crazed Lykae taking her untried body.

Without mercy.

"Listen, we can fix this."

"H-how? Nothing will stop you. No cage can hold you."

"You can put me out of commission, make it so I canna chase you," he said.

"And how exactly am I supposed to do that?"

Garreth answered, "Shoot me between the eyes."

"I-I can't do that!" Lucia cried.

"Then you'll do to me as my kinsmen did."

"What?"

"They beat me within an inch of my life, then tied me up in a dungeon," MacRieve said. "Broke a leg or two. Worked like a charm those times. We doona have a dungeon, but if you—"

"No, no, you had other women. I found condoms in your bag!"

He frowned. "I bought those for you, so I would no' get a babe on you too soon. Had no' found out your diet, or lack of one, would work just as well."

She was still shaking her head in disbelief.

"Lousha, I have no' been with another since I met you."

At that, the worst of her anger sieved from her, and she whispered, "You had them beat you?" Her heart seemed to twist in her chest. *I'm falling for him.*

Lucia had thought she'd been in love all those centuries ago with the fair-haired suitor from her dreams.

She still remembered so vividly how it'd felt. *Nice.* Rainbows-and-kittens nice.

What she felt for MacRieve was raw and hurting, and she knew she'd never be the same.

"Dinna want to scare you off," he said, then added in a gruff tone, "Though it bluidy happened anyway."

Falling for you, MacRieve. "I can't . . . I can't hurt you."

"We doona have a choice."

She was shaking her head when the clouds briefly broke, circling the full moon. Like a spotlight upon them, silvery light shone down. To reveal what he was inside.

His eyes turned fully blue, the image of the beast wavering over him.

"Ah, gods, you're already turning!"

"Then you've got to hurry."

"No, damn it! I'll leave, try to get downriver. Help me put the skiff in the water."

"No' a chance. The caimans—"

"Are heading in the other direction. And they were only interested in the lure."

"And what about the vampire? There was a coffin aboard the *Barão.* I canna let you do this!"

"Listen to me, Scot. You and I both know that until the moon sets, you're more of a threat to me than a vampire."

"Nay, Lousha. I would never hurt you."

"I'm not *asking* you about this. I wouldn't be in this position if you'd let me go in the first place. You got us into this mess—now trust me to get myself out of it."

Whatever he saw in her expression made him hesitate. "It's only a few hours till sunrise. We'll find each other then."

"Lass, if anything happened to you . . ."

"You have to let me go, MacRieve."

After long moments, he exhaled a deep breath. "I'm giving you a free rein, then." He hastened to the motorboat, slashing the lines that secured it to the *Contessa*. He lifted the skiff as if it were a feather and dumped it in the water. "I'll try to get as far as I can in the other direction."

THIRTY-SEVEN

W hile he got the little engine started, she grabbed her bow, quiver, and pack, then jumped into the boat.

"You know how to drive this?" he asked, brows drawn with worry.

"I live in bayou country, werewolf."

"You stay in the boat, doona make land." His eyes were growing bluer. "Lousha, go. *Now.*"

"Be careful," she whispered, leaping up and daring a kiss good-bye before she put the boat in gear. The engine sputtered, then dug in.

Glancing over her shoulder, she peered back at MacRieve—who was clenching the railing, looking as though it took everything in him not to follow her. Just before she turned a bend, driving out of his sight, she saw him crush the railing with his grip.

How far could she possibly get before he succumbed to the moon's pull?

With each mile gained, the renewed downpour stymied her retreat, filling the boat with more rainwater. She bailed as she steered, blinking against the stinging drops as she maneuvered around debris in her way.

An hour passed like this, then two . . . And all the

while, she began encountering more and more vegetation. The Victoria water lilies were everywhere, their pads bouncing off the bow of the boat, their lengthy stems trailing behind them. They usually lined the banks. So what were they doing out this far in the middle of the river?

She tried to steer around them but there were so many. Each time she ran over one, she held her breath as the engine sputtered. If enough stems tangled in the propeller, the motor could overheat—

With a series of smoking coughs, the engine quit.

She hauled it up, frantically tearing the knotted clumps from the propeller, then lowered it back into the water. Again and again, she yanked on the pull-start.

Nothing.

After several more futile tries, Lucia dropped down into the seat, releasing a stunned breath. Helpless to do anything but drift with the current, she raised her face to the sky. *I'm doomed.*

She knew MacRieve would find her. That's what his kind did. He would have to cross the river, then make up all the distance she'd gained by boat, but she had no doubt he could do it.

Part of her thought, *If he does this, then it will be over.* The responsibility, the pressure, the fear of pain from a missed shot—all finished.

The last tie to Skathi.

This chore of killing Cruach would fall to another, a stronger immortal. One who wasn't as tired as Lucia. Part of her wanted that so badly—

Something bumped the skiff. Then again. Gazing

down with dread, she saw more of the caimans. They weren't as giant as those from before, but they streamed out of the jungle, following a swath cut through the riverside lily pads. Probably lured by the siren call of that bait trap.

All Schecter's fault. She could see where the larger creatures had torn out of some concealed tributary, ripping that new pathway through the vegetation, slashing free all the lilies that had eventually fouled Lucia's motor.

Congratulations, Schecter, you're a freaking genius. Can't hold your bladder worth a damn, but—

Then she frowned. The exodus of caimans came *out of seemingly nowhere.*

Her eyes widened. The swath through green led to . . . nothing. She couldn't see a tributary.

"Oh, Freya!" It was Rio Labyrinto!

But she was drifting past it! With a swallow, she peered at the water again. She was going to have to put her arm in and paddle.

She knew what would happen if a caiman got her. The same as had to Marcos Damião, who'd been eaten whole by one. She'd read about that species—the caimans had some of the strongest stomach acid of any creature on earth. Would it be enough to kill an immortal like Damião?

If the shifter woke trapped in the belly of some primordial monster, would he pray for death? Immortality could be a curse, if one wanted—or needed—to die.

Yes, Lucia knew what she risked. *But I'm so close! If I can just reach the river.* Before she'd been despairing, ready to give up. Now she wanted to fight. Damn it, she would *win*. She would kill Cruach. Once and for all.

I'm here, aren't I? She'd found Rio Labyrinto, which meant El Dorado had to be close. *I can do this.*

Skathi had said, *You'll be my instrument.*

Lucia was ready to be. *My responsibility, my kill. Now I need my weapon.* With that thought in mind, she gritted her teeth and dipped her arm in, paddling for a patch of shore just downriver from the portal entrance.

Once she was about five feet from land, she leapt into thigh-high water, grabbing the front rope. Trudging her way to the shore, she dragged the boat behind her, tying it to a limb.

After gearing up with her backpack and bow, strapping both on, she started into the jungle, following Rio Labyrinto. Yet soon she discovered it was aptly named—there wasn't a winding river but a maze of streams, intersecting and diverging.

Slogging through waist-high water. Onto solid ground. Vaulting fallen trees. Back in the water. . . .

Her ears twitched. Things were moving all around her, creeping in the water. Were they the *matora*, giant anacondas? *"Even an immortal could no' fight one off if it wrapped around the arms,"* MacRieve had told her.

And she'd read that once one coiled around its prey, the snake would constrict with each of the victim's exhalations, until the lungs were flattened.

Ignore them. Nothing was worse than Cruach, and damn it, a weapon to destroy him was within her reach! *So close . . .*

Then she froze when she heard a more chilling sound

not far in the distance—an agonized roar. *MacRieve's here.* Already tracking her. She took off at a sprint. The rain had lightened to the merest drizzle. *The better to scent me.*

I am going to have to shoot him. Yes, to take an arrow from the quiver he'd gifted her with, then shoot him between the eyes. Earlier she hadn't been able to even consider it—yet that was before she'd gotten this close to her salvation . . . to the world's salvation!

Shooting MacRieve would buy her enough time until sunrise, possibly enough time to find the dieumort.

But then she'd be leaving him defenseless here. Just as the creatures of this place had left, they would return. Anything could attack him.

Despite her speed, MacRieve was gaining. She heard him crashing through the jungle, raking his claws on trees, and ran as if for her life.

Lucia *was* running for her life, for her future! *You can always appease Cruach.* The hell she would!

Faster, faster . . . As she scaled a rise, the brush thinned somewhat, allowing her to increase her already manic pace. When she heard him roar again, she dared a glance over her shoulder; her front foot landed on . . . air.

She pitched forward into nothing, her body plummeting to the ground.

THIRTY-EIGHT

"**N**ot here," Garreth muttered as he ran. "*She dinna come here.*" Not to this treacherous place.

His mate had somehow found . . . the labyrinth.

Stalking headlong after her, he tore through the jungle, limbs abrading till blood ran. But he felt no pain.

If she could get to the necropolis, she'd be safe. The *matora* didn't come off the towering levee walls. Otherwise . . .

Can't even think of what they do to their victims. He somehow charged faster, hurdling rivulets and downed trees. And all the while he was turning more, the beast taking over.

Even if she hadn't been in danger, he couldn't have stopped chasing her, no matter how hard he fought it. Her scent was irresistible to him, like air. He needed to reach her as much as he needed to breathe.

Must be gentle with her. If he hurt her, he'd never forgive himself. *Accept me, Lousha, surrender to me. . . .*

The terrain steepened. He knew this marked the beginning of the levees—a place he'd hoped never to see again. Capped with debris and growing brush, the walls teemed with anacondas.

As he ascended the rise, he peered around him. The

jungle had fallen silent. Night insects, nocturnal birds, and the normally boisterous howler monkeys grew quiet. Because of a predator?

Or because they fear me?

He scented the air for Lucia again, realized he was almost upon her. Because she'd . . . *stopped*?

No! *"Just get into the city, Lousha. Just hang on. . . ."*

Lucia snatched at vines as she fell. Hands flailing, grasping . . .

Caught one! Just above the ground, she jerked to a stop.

Dizzy, breathless, she lowered herself to her feet, then backed up several steps. "What have I found?" All around her, stone walls soared, shaped like a giant wishing well. The levees! They had to be eighty feet high and thirty feet across, all draped in those liana vines.

MacRieve had told her that the engineering was inconceivable, and he was right. Every rock in these walls had been cut and pounded into the next, flawlessly arranged. No mortar necessary—a blade wouldn't have fit between them.

To her right was a sizeable accumulation of discarded rocks piled against the walls, thick at the bottom, then tapering all the way to the top. *My way out of here.*

The necropolis had to be near. Lucia set off, pushing on for the interior. When she found a clearing, she sucked in a breath, awed, turning in a slow circle.

All around a central expanse, boulders were strewn, monoliths crawling with vegetation and vines. Lining a cobble drive were imposing twenty-foot-high statues of gods or royals, gazing down with watchful eyes. Stone structures of two or so stories dotted the grounds. They were open-aired like small temples. *So where's the tomb?*

Great ceiba trees grew in profusion, producing a roof of unbroken canopy, woven so densely it kept out most of the rain—until the wind blew and the leaves turned, splattering hard drops.

Then her jaw slackened. In the distance was a circular, domed structure—a *panteón*.

A *tomb*. Though it was nearly shrouded in those vines, she could tell it was massive in size.

She hastened over but found no visible entrance. In a rare patch of stone still uncovered by foliage, she spied a carving depicting a triangle of gold gleaming in a woman's uplifted palms. Lucia cleared more vines. Another glyph showed a half-man/half-jaguar being drinking from a shining chalice.

Everything in Lucia said this was the tomb of El Dorado. *To be this close.* To finally have the means to kill Cruach—

She heard something tearing down that stockpile of rocks and jerked her head up. MacRieve was near. She faced the sound and raised her bow.

Moments later, MacRieve burst into the clearing, sagging as if with relief to find her safe. As he raked his gaze over her, her raised bow warranted barely a glance.

He was barefooted and shirtless, the shifter's bite on his arm red and swollen, lacerations crisscrossing his chest. His massive shoulders rose and fell with his heaving exhalations.

The beast flickered strongly over him, just like the night at Val Hall. "Do it . . . shoot me, Lousha." His voice had already started to change.

I have to. If I don't, then I'll never shoot again. This bow would never be in her hands. Her life as she knew it would be over. *Shoot him, Lucia!*

Instead, she backed up a step, then another, until she came up against a vine-covered rock. Nowhere left to run. *Attack or submit.* With a swallow, she pulled the string tighter.

Yet then she gazed at his face, at his brows drawn as he awaited the shot. He expected it.

It had always felt wrong to hurt MacRieve. Even *before* she'd fallen for him. *Ah, Freya, I can't do this.* She eased the tension on her bowstring. "I-I can't." *I'm in love with him.* From the first moment she'd seen him . . . this had been *inevitable.*

"Do it!" He lunged at her, trying to provoke her. "Lousha, shoot your arrow . . . only way this will end without me claiming you."

The wind gusted and moonlight pierced through the canopy. A spear of silver hit him, and he shuddered. "The moon . . . is *pulling* me. You canna know . . . the strength. Can you no' choose me over your vows this night? For once, damn you!"

She slowly shook her head. "It can't happen."

"Then bluidy shoot me!" He stabbed his fingers through his hair, looking desperate, feral. "Goddamnit, I doona know what to do!"

This was the first time he'd ever shown doubt, ever shown a moment's hesitation in front of her. Even now, when the moon demanded, he was resisting its call for her. For over nine hundred years he'd awaited this night—and he would rather have an arrow bored into his brain than take her like this.

Fate has a way. . . . He hung his head for long moments. When he raised his face, his eyes were pale blue, his fangs and claws grown long. The skin of his broad chest was damp with sweat and rain and sheened in the moonlight. He was erect, his shaft straining against his jeans.

The beast was clear to her; MacRieve would lose all control soon. And with that realization, she was amazed to feel something she never thought she'd experience at a moment like this—*lust.*

Deep, wet, undeniable lust. Her claws curled and lightning struck nearby, searing through limbs above, letting more moonlight blaze in.

She lost her focus for the merest instant. With unfathomable speed, he lunged for her, knocking her arrow away. Before she could even react, he'd taken her into his arms, squeezing her to him, his hands and mouth seemingly everywhere, stoking her need. When he snared her bow and quiver, tossing them away, she cried, "MacRieve, no! You have to fight this!"

With his harsh, beastlike voice, he rasped, "Woman, you are everything to me!" He wrapped her hair around his fist, forcing her to meet his frenzied gaze. "Why can I no' be that for you? Let me claim you for my own. Choose *me* this night. . . ."

His scent, his need. The wildness in her—that darkness she'd tried to hide, to extinguish—flared with a vengeance to meet his. As if she'd waited her entire life for this, just as he had.

Every cell in my body is telling me to do this . . . is answering him.

Against her neck, he grated, *"How I've ached for you."*

She couldn't catch her breath. Panting, trying to recall consequences, she struggled to remember exactly why this was so wrong, but her mind was shutting down.

Until all she could do was feel. *I ache for you, too.*

He cupped her breast, thumbed her throbbing nipple. That one burning touch sent her house of cards tumbling down. When she cried out with pleasure, another bolt of lightning struck. Then another. And another.

With a whimper, she grabbed the back of his head and yanked him in for a kiss.

THIRTY-NINE

Growling against her lips, Garreth met her tongue for a deep kiss. She's surrendering. She needs me, too . . . He wanted to roar with satisfaction.

Before she could change her mind, he snatched off her pack, tossing it away, then slashed through her clothes with his claws. As soon as he'd uncovered her creamy breasts, his mouth latched onto one of her nipples. She gave a cry when he suckled her hard, groaning against her.

By the time he'd ripped off her panties, she was shivering—but not from cold. He'd trained her body to respond to his, had learned how to pet her, how to make her melt.

As he moved to her other nipple and his hand skimmed down her belly, she rolled her hips up for his touch. Before he obliged, he remembered to bite his claws off the fingers of one hand. Then he delved between her legs, finding her slick and ready. With another growl, he collected her moisture and spread it over her swollen little clitoris, rubbing her there in slow circles.

His gaze held hers as he rasped, "Goin' tae press . . . my finger into you." He began easing it between her folds. At first, she tensed, but as he went deeper, inch by inch, her lids grew heavy.

He gave a sharp groan. "First time I've felt you inside." So tight. So *hot*. He stirred that finger, building more wetness. Then he withdrew, but only to return with two fingers, stretching her sheath as her head fell back and she helplessly moaned.

"*You like that, mate.*" He began thrusting them inside her.

"Yes!"

He clutched her body to his own, and with each plunge of his fingers, he ground his shaft against her hip.

"Don't stop, MacRieve. . . ."

He feared he'd come like this, ejaculating against her. And though everything inside him was screaming to pleasure her, he didn't want her to come either, sensed he needed her crazed like this or she'd change her mind. When she cried out that she was so close, he released her, slipping his fingers free of her sex.

"Wh-what are you doing?" she asked, sounding dazed. "Why did you stop?"

"Turn around," he commanded, positioning her body toward the vine-covered rock. With his palm flat across her back, he bent her over it, pressing her face against the leaves.

Movement behind her. The sound of MacRieve's clothes torn off.

Once Lucia knew he was naked, her body tensed in anticipation even as her flesh quivered for the orgasm he'd denied her. "Please . . ." *Panting, wanting, aching.*

He answered by running the head of his penis up and down her sex.

"Ah, yes!"

Kicking her legs wide, he lifted one of her knees up to the rock, spreading her. She was as open for him as she could be, vulnerable, and he was about to shove that shaft into her. . . .

She had a moment of sanity. Her desire-drenched mind again tried to call up—

His big palm squeezed her ass, giving her a loud slap as he grunted with approval. In turn, she moaned, arching her back down, opening herself even more to him.

Then she felt . . . *his mouth*. He'd knelt and was madly licking between her thighs.

"MacRieve!" she gasped, her eyes sliding closed with pleasure as he tongued her flesh. When he eased those fingers back into her sheath at the same time, she moaned to be filled, still so unused to the feeling. For so long, she'd craved this, had begged him for it.

With one hand, his fingers thrust, and with his other, he parted her for his feasting mouth. "MacRieve, ah, gods!" There was no fighting this—she grew closer and closer, tension building.

Right when she was at the razor's edge, when she'd drawn a breath to scream, he . . . stopped, drawing away.

"Nooo! I can't take much more of this." She gazed back as he stood. He was losing control, more completely turned than she'd ever seen him, and gripping his engorged shaft to take her. So why did she have the urge to raise her hips, rolling them to signal her need?

Yet he seemed to change his mind, positioning

her again. He lifted her, turning her to face him, then pressed her back onto the rock. She realized why and felt a pang—he didn't want to take her from behind their first time. For herself, she was still desperate for any touch. He'd made her frantic to come.

After lifting her bodily in place, he climbed up for her. *He's rising over me.* She swallowed, fighting her burgeoning disquiet. Just before he lowered his hips between her thighs, his erection hung down, huge, angry. He could hurt her—rip her in two. *Blood streaming down my thighs . . .*

She tensed with fear, but MacRieve began praising her in Gaelic, with adoration in his pale eyes. He lovingly suckled her nipples, his palms sweeping over her as if he were worshipping her. Against all odds, he kept her desires simmering.

Too soon, she felt him feeding his shaft into her, the broad crown demanding entrance. Lightning sheared the night above the canopy. *This will hurt . . . this will—*

He reached between them and began circling his thumb over her clitoris.

"MacRieve!" She bit her bottom lip and moaned. *So far, no pain.* It felt . . . *good.* His erection was hot and unyielding in her wetness. Felt *right.*

He slowly flexed his hips, forcing his penis deeper. Tightness, pressure, but still bearable. As long as he kept *rubbing.* Her eyes closed with bliss. *This is why women adore sex.* She absently whispered, "I never knew before."

When he wedged it deeper inside her, he threw back

his head and roared so hard she could feel the vibrations from his chest.

She'd barely taken a gasping breath when he somehow plunged even farther. Now there was pain. "No!"

He stilled. *"No?"*

"Just . . . just go easier."

He let her adjust, seeming to shudder from the effort, his neck and chest muscles corded with strain and slick with sweat. Though his eyes were frenzied, he somehow held his shaft still within her, even as his claws raked down the stone on each side of her body, slicing the vines.

When the leaves fell away, she saw symbols carved on the face of the stone. Symbols? The rock was long, flat, waist high. . . .

Not just a rock. *An altar.* Lightning exploded.

"No, no!" Tears filled her eyes, then tracked down her cheeks. "I can't. . . ." She struggled, shoving against him. *We're on an altar.*

Still inside her, MacRieve cupped her face. In that beastly voice, he rasped, "Whatever you fear . . . whatever you've known . . . this is different."

She couldn't imagine what this effort was costing him—to defy the Instinct screaming inside him, to patiently speak to her when the beast was ravening within.

"Lousha, we're different together . . . come back . . . tae me."

"No, you don't understand!"

He pulled her up to his chest, clutching her against him. "Wanted you for months . . . been obsessed with you . . . but now . . ."

"N-now what?"

At her ear, the beast rumbled, "Now you've taken . . . the heart from my chest."

At that, she gave a little sob. "MacRieve," she whispered.

He'd brought her back to the present, but she still trembled in his arms—it tore at him, even as he had to clench his jaw, grappling with the drives inside him. He had to ignore how her soft breasts rubbed his chest, her dusky pink nipples rigid and damp against him. Her sheath squeezed like a fist, taunting his throbbing cock to thrust. Gods, he needed to plunge hard into his mate!

But her fear . . . he could scent it.

"Ride me."

"Wh-what?" She frowned when he gripped the curves of her arse, holding himself within her as he turned to his back.

Once she straddled him, her hands flew to his shoulders, her wee claws digging in, her dark eyes wide with surprise. But when he rubbed the pad of his finger over her clitoris again, her sex clenched around him and she murmured, "That feels so *good.*"

"Need you tae . . . ride me."

After a hesitation, she gave a shaky nod. "Sh-show me?"

He clasped her hips to guide her, easing her body forward until her breasts bobbed just above his hungry mouth. Then he worked her back down. Forward and back . . .

When she took over, he knew she was his. *This will happen. At last, I'm claiming my mate. My Lousha.*

Each time she rocked over him, one of her nipples dragged across his waiting tongue. The fear in her disappeared—her eyes grew silvery and wicked as she rode him for her pleasure.

Lightning struck as her long hair lashed over her breasts and face. Rain misted her skin as she panted.

So beautiful. Mine. And he needed *more.* "Harder," he bit out. *Need to mark her neck . . . claim her forever.* "Ride me harder!"

She arched backward, hands behind her on his thighs, her hair sweeping over his legs. Breasts jutting to the sky, she frantically ground on his cock.

"Lousha! Canna last." As she continued to whip her hips in his lap, he rose up to meet her gaze.

With her eyes half-lidded and her voice a sultry purr, she asked, "Are you going to mark me?"

"The ever livin' hell out o' you," he growled. "Right as you're about tae come on me." Seizing her arse with both hands, he shoved her down on his cock just as he bucked upward.

"Ah, gods! MacRieve!" Her breasts bounced against him. "You're making me . . ."

She was already there? Gritting his teeth to keep his seed, he thrust up again, harder. The stone beneath him began to fracture.

"I'm . . . I'm . . ."

Eyes fixed on her neck, he leaned in, licking her, lulling . . . As he shoved up into her slick heat, he bit her flesh in a frenzy.

Claiming her . . . marking her . . . His eyes rolled back in his head as she cried, *"Coming!"*

Desperate to feel it, he snarled into the bite, plunging her up and down. *Harder . . . harder.* As the stone cracked, she screamed with pleasure, her sheath contracting, milking him, demanding.

He followed her, ejaculating inside her with a broken yell against her skin, mindlessly pumping wave after searing wave.

She sagged against him, gasping, "It's so *hot*. . . ."

After-shudders. Arms wrapped around each other. Hearts thundering.

He reluctantly released his bite, but he remained aching and stiff inside her, still needing to drive into her. So he dragged her to the ground with him.

Just before he took her on her hands and knees, she gazed back at the rock they'd broken with a fierce look.

Cupping her waist and gripping her long hair, he bucked into her, roaring with pleasure as she moaned his name.

Then they both gave themselves up to the beast within him.

FORTY

What have I done?
  When Lucia woke, her eyes opened wide—
with realization. She was lying in MacRieve's arms, her
back tucked into his chest, both of them naked.

Ah, gods, he was still . . . *inside* her.

He roused then and gave a self-satisfied exhalation.
The sound was so utterly masculine, and grated on her
like nails on slate.

*Job well done, conquest is complete, I came, I saw,
I conquered her.*

His mark on her neck burned. . . .

When he began hardening again, she stifled a cry
and shrugged out of his grasp, disentangling her body
from his. *Can't handle this. Aching everywhere.*

Without a word, she rose, unsteadily sifting through
the clothes she'd worn last night. All ruined when he'd
ripped them from her.

Once she found her pack, she dug for underwear,
shorts, and a T-shirt. As she quickly dressed, she kept
recalling that satisfied sound he'd made. *The conquest.* He'd gotten everything he'd wanted with her.
From her.

I've gotten nothing *I wanted.* She couldn't be here,

had to get away from him, away from the bow that had been a part of her for centuries.

She was no longer an Archer. *Do I feel different? Dazed? Crazed?*

I feel . . . wrong.

"Lousha?" MacRieve leapt up, snagging his jeans and stabbing his legs in them.

After shouldering her backpack, she staggered toward the levees. The statues along the cobble walk glared down.

MacRieve hurried after her, shoving the bow in front of her face. "You left this and your quiver, lass."

She wouldn't look at it. At him. She couldn't. He'd done this to her. Ruined her ability. Now with no means to finally destroy Cruach, Lucia would be expected to sacrifice herself, to appease that monster.

Going back in that foul lair? Without an arrow trained on his heart? At the idea, Lucia couldn't catch her breath. *I can't do that! Even now that I have nothing else to offer . . .*

Her neck burned, the pain seething, a constant reminder of her sins. *Can't catch my breath . . .*

"Uh, I'll hold the bow for now." He slung it over his shoulder. "Love, talk to me. Did I hurt you?" He scowled at himself. "O' course I hurt you. But how badly?"

She didn't answer.

"Where are you going?"

"H-home."

He jogged in front of her. "What about the dieumort?" he asked, turning to walk backward. "Saving the world and all that? We're so close."

They'd never been farther away! "Nïx sent me down here for an arrow. Because I'm . . . I *was*"—her breath hitched—"an archer. All that's different now." Lucia couldn't even stop Cruach from rising with one of Skathi's arrows. "I have another job to do." *And I'll grow to hate you for it.* "This is where we part ways, MacRieve. *You* go retrieve the dieumort." Hell, maybe that was why Nïx had sent him down here. Maybe *he* was the one on the quest.

"Lousha, it's no' over yet."

"You have no idea what the repercussions from last night will be. No idea what will be expected of me now!"

"Nay, because you will no' bluidy tell me!" He gripped her forearms in his fists. "Talk to me!"

She gave herself up to her outrage, to her need to blame, both preferable to this wretched fear. Imitating his accent and low voice, she said, "Lousha, o' course the cuff will work. That's why I got it from those bluidy witches. I would never hurt ye!" Flinging herself away from him, she screamed, "You shouldn't have come for me! You should've let me do what I needed to."

She can't even look at me.

Maybe this was one female who shouldn't have given up her career for her man. There was nothing in her eyes but . . . bitterness? It was as if a piece of her had died.

And he'd helped kill it.

She was no longer a Skathian. Thousand-year-old vows had been broken last night, and as she'd clearly told him, she hadn't been ready for it. She'd also warned him that she would *hate* him forever if he pressured her to go against her beliefs.

When he reached for her again, she backed away. "In the beginning, I asked for one year, and you ignored my wishes, dismissed them so easily."

"I know I fucked up." He scrubbed his palm over his face. "Gods know this is all my fault. But would it be so bad to be with me? You've seen what we can have together—"

"You vowed to me that you wouldn't hurt me, but you have! Permanently. I hope last night was worth it!"

His eyes widened. *Permanently?* "What did I do?"

"My archery, my ability, was based on the vows I took, you brute. Now I'm nothing!"

"What are you talking about?"

"I can't shoot!" she cried. "My talent is gone—forever. I kept my power only as long as I kept my legs closed. And now, because of you, I will never shoot again. It's *gone.*"

His own anger flared as the truth hit him. "I knew this was about more than just your 'religion'!" Finally, he was putting the puzzle together. When some male—some soon-to-be dead male—had hurt her, she'd sought asylum with Skathi. In exchange for Lucia's vows, the goddess had given her the ability to shoot as no other.

Practice hadn't made Lucia this good. *A deal with a devil . . .*

He narrowed his eyes. "You dinna give a damn about your beliefs. This was about ego, about being *The Archer*, best in all the world."

"Didn't give a damn? I lived nearly my entire life in service until you came along. Now I'm shrugging off an apocalypse and giving in to my basest needs! I'd aspired before, was selfless. Now I've committed my most selfish act in a thousand years."

"You should've told me what was at stake!" He couldn't remember the last time he'd been this infuriated.

"When should I have? Maybe when you were going on about women sacrificing their careers for their men? I knew you'd react just as you are now, unable to comprehend why I would choose archery over sex with you."

"*Why* did you no' tell me? Why lie about this?"

"Oh, like the truth would have made *any difference*? Like last night wouldn't have happened *if only I'd come clean*? As soon as you stepped on that boat, this was as good as done, events set into motion. You caused this! I asked you for time, and you wouldn't give it to me."

He hadn't. She was absolutely right. But if she'd just told him why she couldn't have sex . . . Garreth exhaled. He still would've done the same thing, still would've trusted the cuff.

"You forced me into last night!"

"Wait just a goddamned minute. You grabbed *me* for a kiss."

"Because it was the best option in an impossible situation."

"Doona forget, Valkyrie, that you screamed my name all night. You canna tell me you dinna want me."

"I did—*then*! That doesn't mean I can't be sorry for my actions *now*. It doesn't mean I'm not filled with regret," she snapped, her tone laced with resentment.

Best night of my life, and she's taking it back. When he'd awakened, he'd been so relieved, believing she was finally his. *What a bluidy fool you are. . . .*

For the last year, he'd thought about her every second, from the moment he woke to the second he drifted to sleep. Even then he wasn't free. Any night that he'd slept, he'd dreamed of her, dreamed of the life they could have—traveling the world, hunting together, eventually raising a braw pack of bairns. "Filled with regret, then?"

What he'd considered a culmination—and a *revelation*—she believed was a mistake.

Realization hit him. If she wasn't going to be won from their night together—the most incredible one of his entire existence—then she *never* would. He'd spend the next nine hundred years of his life chasing her.

"You don't know what I've lost, MacRieve. For the first time, I have no way to protect myself, no means to—"

"*I* will protect you."

Her fists clenched; lightning struck. "I knew you'd say that!" she screamed. "I knew you wouldn't understand why that would be like a dagger to the chest."

His own fury ignited. "You knew I'd say I'd protect you? And that vexes you? Should I have said that you're shite out of luck and all on your own, but thanks for the hot fuck!"

She narrowed her eyes, gazing at him with absolute disgust. *She's never looked at me like this.*

He raked his fingers through his hair. "By the gods, you're the most maddening female I've ever known! If you've lost your archery, then we'll figure something out. We'll comb the ends of the earth to get it back. But we'll do it *together*."

"We won't have *time* to figure it out. I've got no way to stop an apocalypse." She turned to go.

"No, Lousha, doona turn your back on me." He moved in front of her. "I will no' follow you!"

When she sidestepped him, he blocked her way. Between gritted teeth, she hissed, "Let me pass."

His crossed his arms over his chest. "Nay, Valkyrie, I think you'll be stayin' right—"

A slap cracked across his cheek.

"Bluidy hell, woman! Have it your way! You'd rather bemoan what you've lost than seize what we could have together? Then to hell with you! I've chased you over the world, protected you, offered everything I am to you. No longer. *I've reached my end*." He threw the bow and quiver at her feet. "For once, you're going to watch my back as I leave you behind."

Stalking away from her, he headed toward the levee. And she said nothing. He hadn't expected her to beg for him to return. But he'd hoped. . . .

Five minutes passed, then ten, and still she didn't run after him. She truly was going to let this end. *Just like that.*

Crazed, cursing to himself, Garreth slashed his claws along tree trunks.

I'll leave her arse in the goddamned jungle! I'm done!

He would return to Kinevane, spend some real time with his brother and sister-in-law. Help Lachlain acquire a mortal child for Emma.

Garreth could go back to his clan, see his kinsmen

for the first time in a year. He could play a bluidy game of rugby and shag nymphs without cease.

He reached the pile of rocks against one of the levee walls, began climbing. As he ascended, his mind was a riot of conflicting thoughts.

How easy it would be if his feelings could turn to hate—as hers obviously had. Hate would have to be less painful than this obsession with her. To *not* feel this gnawing lack each minute of the day. . . .

Yet then he frowned. Lucia might be acting as if she despised him now. But before, she'd shown she cared for him again and again. He recalled her worry as he'd been preparing to swim to the *Barão* or when she'd been about to dive into the water after him. Even her own words: "*. . . the more I like you, the less I want you to know my secrets.*"

At the top of the levee wall, unable to help himself, he glanced back down. In the far distance, he spied Lucia on her knees crying. Exhaling a breath, he rubbed his aching chest. He never could stand the sight of her tears.

Damn that female! It seemed that when he'd told her he was done, he'd just been talking a big game. Because the truth was . . .

"She's my lass," he muttered.

For better or worse. I could never leave her.

His heart heavy with regret, he began making his way back to her—not seeing the movement in the brush until it was too late.

FORTY-ONE

⟶◈⟵

Still in shock, unable to stop shuddering, Lucia stared at her bow as if she were staring at her severed arm, knowing it would *never* grow back.

Sorrow suffused her, despair ripping at her. *I'm nothing. I have nothing to offer the world. Nothing that makes me different.* Earlier, Lucia had feared that she'd go from being the Archer to the Lykae's Mate. Now she wasn't even that!

When MacRieve had left her, she'd sunk to the ground, putting her head in her hands to cry. Twelve months ago, she'd predicted he would be the key to her ruin. She'd been right.

Is he really leaving me? Yes, he'd meant it. They'd just had incredible, mind-blowing sex, and then she'd started attacking him.

But she'd never been so furious, had never felt so used. Because of him, she was altered forever, yet she couldn't say the same about him. He'd claimed her—had fulfilled at least that primal Lykae need—so it was possible that he could content himself with others now. And since his brother had reclaimed the throne, Garreth could go back to being the Dark Prince, a womanizing brawler.

For Lucia, there was no going back to her life before MacRieve.

And now I've lost him. He'd warned her that one day he'd hit his limit. Today, he had. Reasonable, rational Lucia cried harder.

What was worse? Knowing that she'd lost him? Or that she might miss him more than her archery...?

Suddenly her ears twitched. She heard a curt yell, jerked her face up. It sounded like MacRieve.

But it had also sounded like he'd been *cut off.*

Darting to her feet, Lucia ran her arm over her face and peered around. Sunlight pricked the canopy above, casting strange shadows from the tomb and the lofty statues.

She gazed up, far off in the distance, and saw movement. Yes, up on the levee, perhaps a mile away.

Wait ... At first, Lucia didn't believe what she was seeing. Tears made her vision blurry, and the sight was so distant. But her mind vaguely comprehended that the biggest snake she had ever imagined had its rippling green coils wrapped around MacRieve, its face bobbing mere inches from his own.

On its meaty body, black spots looked melted on, like scorched wax dripped over daubs of yellow. Boned ridges flared from its nose, past its slitted eyes, back over its skull.

Anaconda.

Panic jolted through her. MacRieve was in the grip of one of those *things.* It'd pinned his arms at his sides, squeezing the life from him. Every time he exhaled ...

No way for Lucia to climb the rocky rise to the levee in time. Not before the anaconda began . . . *feeding*.

Without thought, she dove for her bow and quiver. Nocking two arrows, she aimed—*a mile away, into the breeze, have to pierce its eyes or it won't make a dent in a creature that large.*

If she missed, she might hit MacRieve, putting him out, taking away any hope he had of fighting.

She swallowed, pulled the string, and tried to slow her heart. Concentrate. . . . *But this is MacRieve!* She blinked through tears.

I'm so in love with him.

His head slumped forward. Oh, gods, he wasn't conscious. *Release the string, release it!*

When the snake began distending its lower jaw—to swallow its prey whole—her fingers relaxed; the bowstring sang. She exhaled in a rush, going weak with fear—

The snake reared up, two arrows jutting from its eye sockets. Then the head collapsed to the ground.

Lucia had . . . nailed it.

Disbelief. No time to succumb to her shock. With a cry, she sprinted for MacRieve, climbing up the terrain. As she ran, she inwardly chanted, *How, how, how? How did I do that?*

Once she reached him, she saw the dead creature was still squeezing! Heart racing with panic for MacRieve, she dropped her bow, trying to lift the snake away, but she couldn't budge it. Tractor trailers with Regin were one thing—lifting a snake's dead weight by herself was another.

"MacRieve, wake up!" she cried. Nothing. Peeling off

her backpack, she rushed to a young tree, then kicked it at the base, snapping it to the ground. Returning to the snake with it, she jabbed the wood in between its hefty coils, using it as a lever.

She gritted her teeth with effort, hanging bodily from the tree. Again and again, she jabbed and levered. Finally, she heaved the last coil away with a *thunk*.

After dragging MacRieve far away from the creature, she sank down beside him, cradling his head in her lap. He was unconscious, rattling his breaths, a fine bloody mist spraying from his lips with each exhalation.

"Please, wake up!" His torso was mottled with blood under his skin. *Internal injuries*. She lifted one of his eyelids. His eye was filled with burst vessels, as red as a vampire's.

But her Scot was an immortal. He'd live through this—he just needed to regenerate. She gingerly eased out from under him, making a pillow of leaves for him.

Once he was resting more comfortably, she started a fire to keep other creatures away, gazing around warily. She was on edge. Yes, she had her bow to protect them— but she scarcely trusted her abilities. Maybe they were gradually *fading*?

"I've got to know," she muttered. She collected her pack, drawing out her sat-phone. Surprised it was still working, she dialed Nïx.

The soothsayer answered right away. "Lucia! How's your vacay?"

"Eventful. Nïx, you know how you told me I'd have

to restrain myself? I . . . didn't. MacRieve and I—"

"You tagged him? You marked his teeth with your neck?"

"Uh, yeah. But here's the thing. I think I can still shoot."

Nïx said, "*Of course* you can. Are you fishing for compliments? Fine." As if reciting, she said, "Lucia the Archer, you are the best. You are unmatched in skill, peerless in all of the world—"

"Nïx! I had sex. Skathi vowed she'd revoke my powers."

The soothsayer made a dismissive sound. "Oh, that? She took them back weeks ago."

"What are you talking about?"

"Didn't I tell you? Yes, it seems Skathi wasn't on board with your mission to unearth the god killer."

"You mean I've had . . . no ability *this entire time*?"

"No mystical ability."

"That can't be right. For the last two weeks, I've made incredible shots. Now I can still shoot as well as I ever could."

"Well, naturally." Nïx sounded puzzled. "You practiced for over a millennium."

"Practice wouldn't make me *peerless in all the world*! Look how hard Tera the Fey trains, and I still outshoot her."

"Maybe you got the talent genetically? Your mom could've been Robina Hood for all we know, you impish wittle mutt."

"*Robina Hood?*"

"Or it could be—hey, here's an idea—the fact that

your other two parents are gods. Hello? You're a *Val-kyrie*, the daughter of Freya and Wóden. The last I checked, we don't suck at anything."

"This ability is all mine?"

"It wasn't in the beginning. But it is now. The pain Skathi 'gifted' you with to make you remember was actually *teaching* you. Teaching you *all* of her tricks."

Just as everyone had always assumed. "I can't believe this. Are you sure?"

"Skathi didn't teach you to track or give you that ability, yet you're an expert at that as well."

I am. I learned to be. "And Skathi couldn't have told me this would happen?" Lucia felt as if she'd been slapped.

"Oh, she didn't know what an apt pupil you'd be. Had no idea you could grow to be as good as she is."

"No idea?" Yes, slapped—bitchslapped by the goddess of the hunt. "Then she believed I was going on a quest with no defense?"

"What a whore!" Nïx agreed. "She's one of the gods who thought you should offer yourself up to Cruach to appease him, rather than uncover the dieumort."

Appease Cruach. Despite the fact that Skathi had witnessed how Lucia had suffered at his hands. "I'm going to kill her."

"Now, Lucia, you can't go offing gods willy-nilly. Unless you find some more dieumorts!" she cried. "Regrettably each one only has a single shot before the power is extinguished."

"Skathi had to know I would never abuse the weapon, would never harm anyone but Cruach with it."

"Yes, but to find the dieumort, you have to open a tomb, and there's an evil deep inside it."

Exactly what Damiãno had said. "I think I've already found the tomb."

"Within it is a being so powerful that if loosed, it would change the world forever. Even the gods fear its awakening."

"What evil being?"

"The Gilded One," Nïx breathed.

El Dorado. "Can I get the dieumort without waking the evil?"

"There're house rules at the tomb door. You break them, and you'll have to leave the party."

"Damn it, what do you mean? This is no time to withhold . . . Wait! *You* couldn't have told me all this earlier, Nïx?" she asked, her aggravation spiking. "You advised me to *restrain myself* for nothing!"

"I'd totally forgotten about this until I found a Post-it note to myself stuck to the underside of Annika's bed."

"What were you doing under her— Never mind, I don't want to know." Yet her irritation with Nïx soon dwindled when Lucia comprehended all that had happened.

Lucia was no longer a Skathian, a slave to the goddess's whims. No longer a celibate in plainclothes.

No longer a victim. *I broke an altar with my werewolf lover.* How fitting, how utterly empowering.

Broke that bitch!

Lucia swallowed as a sudden thought struck her. She could even have . . . *children.*

She cast a smile down at MacRieve, but it quickly faded. He was leaving her! Had made up his mind.

One of these days, Lucia . . .

When Garreth coughed, waking, Lucia was right beside him, gazing down, her eyes swollen from tears. "Nice nap?" she asked.

"What . . . what happened?" His body was a mass of aches, his head and wounds throbbing.

"Big snake got peckish?"

"You killed it?" When she nodded, he frowned, recalling more with each second, his ire toward her returning. "You told me you couldn't shoot anymore."

"I believed that. But clearly I was mistaken."

"Aye, clearly. You must've shot it from down below." He tried to rise, then coughed, flinching as pain radiated through every inch of him. All his goddamned ribs were cracked.

"Is the pain bad?" she asked.

"What do you bluidy think?"

Her eyes narrowed. "I think that'll teach you to leave me!"

"I was coming back."

Her expression unreadable, she asked, "For me?" Before he could answer, she added, "Probably to convince me to continue on the mission."

"I was coming back *for you*! Though you dinna deserve me to, stubborn Valkyrie."

She didn't deny that. "Why? I thought you were done."

"I'll *never* be done!" he snapped, wincing again as his

ribs screamed in protest. "You're my woman, Lousha. Damn you, I'll never want another!"

At that, she leaned down and pressed a tender kiss to his forehead. "Good."

"What?" Was this an olive branch—from her? Just when he'd thought she couldn't confuse him more, she put them into completely unfamiliar territory. "I thought you hated me."

"I hated the consequences of what we'd done—or at least what I'd thought they were. I took out all my anger and fear on you. I'm sorry."

"Ah, bluidy hell, lass." Never would he have thought an apology from her would be as sweet to hear as her laughter. "For what it's worth, I am sorry to have lost the cuff. I bollixed that up."

She stroked his hair from his forehead. "Things are going to be different, MacRieve. With me. If you want them to be. Once we save the world, that is."

He could tell things were *already* different. Garreth had claimed her, yet she could still shoot—and she looked more at peace than he'd ever seen her. "What happened to you while I was out?"

"I have no more ties to Skathi. *None.* Any talent I possess is my own."

"Will you finally confide in me, then?"

"I . . . can't. Not yet. I'm asking you for time." At his scowl, she said, "Look, I wasn't ready for two things: sex and sharing secrets. Now, we both know how the first of those turned out. Can't you accept one out of two for now?"

He scowled deeper. "Sex or secrets?"

Lucia jutted her chin. "If that's how you want to look at it."

She'd played the sex card—as in the promise of *more of it*. More of what they'd shared the night before. And o' course, he'd do just about anything for that. "You keep your secrets *for now*. As for the other, I *have* been getting my way with you. Tis true. And I'll be getting it again as soon as I'm able."

FORTY-TWO

❖

"So we're no' to wake a big evil," MacRieve said as they gradually made their way back to the necropolis. Though she could tell he was still in a great deal of pain, he'd insisted that they gear up and set out by noon.

On the way down, she'd filled him in on everything Nïx had said and they'd speculated on everything she *hadn't* said. For instance, though the soothsayer had never actually *confirmed* the panteón was the tomb in question, they'd still grown convinced that the dieu-mort was there. It had to be in the tomb Damiāno had been talking about—the one that had hieroglyphs of gold.

"Who do you think Damiāno worked for?" Lucia asked. "If he was the guardian of this place, then who hired him?"

"Doona know. Maybe he's a descendant of the people who lived here."

"Do you really think he hacked up those passengers?" She kept recalling the look on his face when Mac-Rieve had accused him. Had there been a brief flicker of surprise?

"If no' him, then who? He wanted to prevent anyone

from getting close to this place, and the *Barão* was right behind us."

"That's true," she said, seeing MacRieve's reasoning. So why was she unconvinced. . . ?

Just as they reached the central expanse and started on the cobblestone walk, a new text message arrived.

RegRad: BTW, that "darkness" Skathi went on about w/ U = UR being a Valkyrie, DUMBASS!

"Regin is *texting* you?" MacRieve shook his head. "Now?"

"She doesn't know this is a . . . momentous time."

He sputtered, "Aye, but why're you texting her back?"

"Have to. This has been a long time coming." Lucia replied: *I'm about 2 go play Tomb Raider . . . but it's REAL. Bet U wish U were here. HOOKER!*

She finished with a satisfied grin—that lasted until Regin responded. *RegRad: Why're U being so mean? I wanna play TR, too.*

Lucia sighed, deciding then to make all this up to her sister. When she returned to New Orleans, she'd buy Regin something nice. Maybe a gaming chair, or a new sword.

MacRieve said, "My brother told me that to win you, I'd have to . . . deal with Regin."

Win me? Lucia had thought it impossible for so long that she was taken aback now. He *could* win her. But Lachlain was right—Regin was a part of her life and always would be. "Well, she and I had planned to live out our immortality in adjacent mansions on some seashore. Since we were kids. But I'm sure anyone would think she's a fine neighbor."

"Neighbor, then?" He *almost* stifled his grimace.

Yes, there was bad blood between him and her sister. But Lucia now knew that MacRieve could be remarkably forgiving. . . .

Once they reached the tomb, he hacked at the cloaking vines with his claws, tearing them away until they found what appeared to be an entranceway—a slab of unbroken stone, probably eight feet square.

A smoothed knob of rock jutted out beside it. "Check that out," she said. "It looks like a dial." Carved all around it were more hieroglyphs, expanding out in a circular pattern.

"So which way do we turn it?" MacRieve asked. "Seems to me this could go really bad. Go the wrong way . . ."

"I saw a movie once where someone's hand got trapped around a knob, then sliced off. How attached are you to your paws?"

He gave her ass a quick squeeze. "No' as much as you were last night."

"Werewolf! Wait, I've got an idea." She took out her phone, scrolling through her address book.

"Who are you calling?"

"Language specialist."

He stepped back, gazing at the scene. "Doona think this is Mayan or Incan."

"I know someone who's omnilingual."

"Omni?"

"She knows every language in the world and adjoining planes."

He raised his brows as if he were impressed, until she added, "A female called Tera the Fey." When he glowered, she said, "What is it?"

"Nothing. How do you know her?"

"We were competitors in the immortal tournaments of old."

Lucia's half sister Atalanta would compete in the foot races, Kaderin the Coldhearted at swords, and Lucia at the bow. They'd dominated.

And Lucia had smack-talked Tera unmercifully.

Still, with nothing to lose, she rang the number.

"Valkyrie," Tera said in a cool greeting.

"Tera, I need a favor. I need you to translate something."

"Indeed. And why should I help you?"

Lucia said, "To stop an apocalypse." Then she explained where she and MacRieve were and the highlights of the threat.

Once she'd finished, Tera sighed. "Can you take a picture of the symbols and e-mail them?"

"What's your e-mail addy?" Lucia asked.

"Hmm. Thegreatestarcherever at gmail dot com."

"Surely the greatest archer ever had already taken that one?"

Tera said tightly, "Terafey at thenoblefey dot com."

"Pics are on their way." After she'd hung up, Lucia used her phone to snap photographs of the hieroglyphs, then e-mailed them.

Tera wrote back directly. *I'll call shortly. P.S.: Tell werewolf I want my quiver back.*

Lucia faced MacRieve with raised brows. "Tera says she wants her quiver back."

He cast her an innocent expression. "Huh? What? Bluidy daft fey . . ."

The phone rang within five minutes. Lucia turned on the speaker feature.

"Congratulations. You've discovered a previously unidentified language," Tera said. "It's logosyllabic, combining about three hundred syllabograms, which represent syllables, and eight hundred logograms— whole words."

"Right, whatever. What does it *say*?"

"There are three warnings. First, you're not to get any kind of moisture upon the watchers' . . . husks. Second, do not disturb the Gilded One's rest. And third, no gold leaves the confines of the tomb. Basically, be dry, don't take any gold, and hands-off the important dead person inside."

The Gilded One *was* within!

"Or what?" MacReive asked. "How are these enforced?"

"Or tragedy awaits," Tera said. "We're likely talking ancient loss-prevention technology—booby traps. So essentially, the fate of the world rests in the hands of a sticky-fingered Lykae and an avaricious Valkyrie about to enter a tomb of off-limits gold. I believe I'll be going out tonight—"

"Just tell us how to get in," he interrupted.

"Turn the dial to the right, then immediately left, then back to the right."

"How sure are you?" he asked.

"As certain as I am that Lucia's wearing my quiver strapped to her leg right now."

With raised brows, MacRieve followed her instructions. At once, the stone slab rumbled, inching to the side, revealing a downward-sloping tunnel. Air released, as though the ruins had gasped.

He narrowed his eyes. "This place was airtight."

"They meant what they said about moisture," Lucia observed. Then she told Tera, "Hey, we're in. Thanks for your help—"

"What about my quiver?"

Lucia gazed at MacRieve who'd raised his stubborn chin, as if to say *stolen fair and square*. To Tera, she said, "I guarantee *nothing*."

After she hung up, Lucia and MacRieve prepared to head inside. She shrugged from her pack and took her bow in hand, while his dark claws flared in readiness.

"Let me go first." He took her free hand. "I can scent traps—or enemies."

As they began journeying down the dim tunnel, she could feel his excitement, sharing it in spades. Yet then he paused to say, "Probably should've addressed this before, but Valkyrie are notoriously . . . *acquisitive*, and I'm taking one directly to what might be El Dorado. Are you going to be able to handle this?"

"I'm not as bad as some of my sisters." *And I want something far more precious than treasure.* "I can handle it."

Slanting her an undecided look, he finally gave a halfhearted nod, then continued on, farther down the passageway. From the ceiling, spiderwebs dangled. A warm draft blew, whisking the dust on the floor and fluttering the webs.

Though the tunnel had to be subterranean by now, all the walls were dry, the temperature stifling.

"I can barely imagine what this arrow will be like," she said in a hushed voice. Skathi's had been a sight to behold, but this dieumort . . . "I bet it's beautiful. And solid gold, only more perfectly weighted and aerodynamic than any I've ever seen."

"Whatever it is, let's be cautious about this." When the webs grew increasingly thick, he used his claws to slice through them. "I doona relish facing *loss-prevention technology*."

"Agreed." Five minutes later: "MacRieve," she murmured urgently. "Do you see something glimmering ahead?"

"Aye, we're coming upon a chamber."

When they entered it, Lucia breathed, "My gods, it's El Dorado."

The "chamber" was the size of a warehouse, and its floor, ceiling, and walls were each tiled with solid gold. All along the perimeter, treasures were stacked high—gold bricks, chalices, and jewelry.

"How are we doing, lass?"

"Wowed." She released his hand to turn in a circle. "But not tempted." *Yet.*

As they neared the center of the chamber, she spied a mammoth gold sarcophagus atop a stone pediment.

Exhilaration surging within her, she said, "MacRieve, look! The resting place of the Gilded One. It has to be."

Desiccated bodies lay around it, *husks* of some kind of humanlike creature. *Must be the watchers.* There was something familiar about their long, withered faces. Just as she remembered what it was, MacRieve muttered, "Wendigos?"

Wendigos were flesh eaters like zombies, but *fast*. They had elongated faces and dripping fangs. "But I thought they're only found in the northern forests."

"I'd believed so as well. No' anymore."

The Wendigos were spread around the pediment like a pack of animals at their master's feet, as if they'd fallen asleep like this and had never woken.

"How did they dry up like this?" Lucia asked.

"I doona know—" Suddenly, he lunged forward with his hand outstretched, palm up above one of the bodies. "Careful, woman!" He'd caught a bead of sweat that had dripped from her chin.

"Sorry," she whispered, briefly turning away to wipe her face on her sleeve.

Cautiously stepping around the creatures, they made their way to the sarcophagus. The top was uncovered, as if for a wake viewing. After wiping her face again, she leaned forward, heart in her throat.

Under the cover of the finest gold netting lay *a mummy.* . . . The body was decorated with elaborate jewels, a gold breastplate and crown, and rings on every finger. *Stunning.*

◆ ◆ ◆

Lucia peered over the sarcophagus, her eyes widening with awe.

Though he was keen only on finding the dieumort, Garreth's curiosity got the better of him, and he briefly glanced down at the jewel-covered mummy. "No' tempted to swipe a gem or two?"

"I'm not staring at them. Look at the mummy."

"It should no' be so preserved," he said absently, his attention back to locating the weapon.

"No kidding," Lucia said.

"What does the paleopathologist in you think?" he asked, scanning the room.

"That something else isn't right."

He glanced down again. "Yeah, El Dorado has breasts. *Big* ones."

Lucia cast him a glare. "Try to be serious."

"So El Dorado is no' a man."

In a soft tone, Lucia said, "She's La Dorada, the Gilded *Woman*. History had it wrong. Really wrong."

"Makes sense."

"What do you mean?"

"Say you were a conquistador, hunting for the Gilded One's gold, yet the native was clever enough to keep a tomb full of it hidden. A native—a *woman* native— somehow outwits you?" He shook his head. "Back in the day, I met a few gold-hungry conquistadors, and let's put it this way—the fragility of conquistador ego canna be overstated."

"She was smart and kept her gold." Lucia gazed down almost *fondly*. "How evil could she be?"

"Does no' matter. Let's get what we came for."

With that, they began scouring every inch of the chamber, passing by more riches than he could ever have imagined. But they found no weapons.

Finally, in a shadowy corner, he spied an archery quiver, coated with dust. Inside was a single arrow. Not gold. Not beautiful. But something about it drew him. He sensed . . . *power*. "Come, Lousha. I think I've found your dieumort." He collected the battered quiver, brushing away the accumulated layers of dust.

With a look of breathless excitement, she hurried to his side. Then her face fell. "No, this can't be right. *Wood?* No way!"

"Maybe you're to fight an old evil with an old arrow?"

When he drew it out, she said, "MacRieve, the arrowhead is *bone*! Look at those old-fashioned flights— were those feathers plucked from a dodo bird?"

"Come, then, hold it."

She reluctantly accepted it from him. And her dark eyes widened.

"You feel something with it, no? Some power?"

"I do," she admitted. "But wood and bone?"

"Trusted stand-bys for euphemisms *and* arrows."

"MacRieve! It'd be like Serena Williams going to Wimbledon with a flyswatter."

"Aye, but if she were as good as you are at shooting, she'd still win."

At that, Lucia gave him a coaxed smile. "You're right, werewolf. Schwag-looking arrow or not, I'll take it." She slipped it into her thigh quiver.

In a solemn tone, he said, "You chose wisely." Then he added, "I'm relieved it is no' gold. I dinna want to alarm you, but my Instinct was screaming warnings about this. Now, we can take it without waking an ancient evil. So, as far as afternoons-after go, this is looking up."

She chuckled, leaping into his arms, kissing him soundly on the lips. "We did it!"

He grunted. "Easy, lass, go easy on the ribs."

"Oh, sorry!"

She slid down, and just that was enough to make even his battered body stir. With a steadying breath, he set her away. "Let's get you out of here." On their way to the entrance, he thought he heard something and turned back to the sarcophagus. "Did you hear that?"

But she was already jogging ahead, chattering happily.

"Wait, Lousha!" He would've been right behind her . . . but he could have sworn he'd heard something *moving*.

FORTY-THREE

—◆◆◆—

Lucia couldn't stop a grin as she exited the tomb. The arrow might be unremarkable *looking*—hardly the golden one of her dreams—but she'd sensed its latent power.

In fact, Lucia had never felt the like.

Last night in the skiff, she'd thought she was finished. This morning she'd lost all hope; now she was back in the game and in a better position than she'd ever been. *I'm going to destroy my nightmare.* How many beings had that opportunity? To rid herself—and the world—of an abomination.

At the thought, her aggression, her darkness, surfaced, filling Lucia with the need for raw violence. She *wanted* to kill Cruach, to hurt him.

Her path was clear: journey to the Northlands where Cruach's lair was located, meet up with Regin, then execute a god. All she had to do was lose MacRieve in Iquitos—

A vampire appeared out of thin air, not twenty feet from her.

Lothaire. Just there, standing in the canopy's shade. She'd been right—he *had* been aboard the *Barão.* Though his face was expressionless, she sensed his menace. She had her bow up and her arrow shot so fast it was a blur, but he traced out of the way with incredible speed.

The arrow whizzed off into the distance.

I . . . missed. Preparing for the crippling pain, she shut her eyes and awaited it. . . . *Still waiting.* She cracked open her eyes. Nothing.

Because Skathi has no hold on me—

Suddenly, Lothaire did. He'd traced behind her, grabbing her around the neck in a tight choke hold.

Getting sick of males grabbing my neck!

In his thick Russian accent, he commanded, "Drop the bow, Valkyrie. Or I'll trace you from this place."

In the blink of an eye, he could teleport her to the Horde dungeons. She unwillingly tossed her bow beside her pack. "I knew it was you aboard the *Barão.*"

MacRieve exited the tomb just then. *"Let her go."* His beast flickered, his fangs lengthening. Pale blue eyes evaluated, spying for any weakness in Lothaire.

"Come closer, and I'll punish her," the vampire said, so coolly. To Lucia, he asked, "You're hunting for a dieumort?"

"Aye, take it," MacRieve bit out. "Just doona hurt her."

"I'm not here for that, but for something much more interesting. Back inside, Archer."

She resisted. "Lothaire, we're here to stop an apocalypse, a real end-of-the-world scenario."

As if she hadn't spoken, he said, "Take me to the Gilded One. *Now.*"

She hesitated until MacRieve gave her a quick nod. "Do it."

Lucia saw no choice but to comply. With the vampire's arm a constant pressure around her neck, she headed back inside to the chamber.

MacRieve followed, a continual low growl in his throat.

"Don't you care that we're averting an apocalypse?" she asked Lothaire. "Don't you have anyone on this earth you'd prefer, oh, I don't know, *not* to die?"

The pressure on her neck increased. At her ear, the vampire grated, "You don't know me, Valkyrie." His voice was low, ominous. "You don't know what I care about." *So chilling.*

"We're not supposed to take any treasure or disturb the Gilded One," she heedlessly continued. "Or else we'll wake an ancient evil." As soon as she spoke the words, she cringed. Like he would care—he *was* an ancient evil. He'd probably think, *The more the merrier.*

When they returned to the chamber, of all the treasures inside, Lothaire's attention grew riveted to a plain golden ring—on La Dorada's thumb. The one *on her person.*

"You can't take that, vampire!" Lucia said. "If you remove anything from her body, we'll all be doomed."

"Will *we*?" Amusement. Never relinquishing his hold on Lucia, he reached down, snapping La Dorada's thumb clean from her body.

Lucia gasped.

"Why *that* ring, Lothaire?" MacRieve demanded. "Of all these riches?"

"There's no accounting for taste." He shoved the finger and gold band into his pants pocket.

"Bastard! You can't take that from here," Lucia cried, still in his grip. "You don't understand—it will set off traps. We'll *all* be killed."

She felt Lothaire shrug behind her. "Then it's fortunate that I can trace."

"Not if I can help it." She grabbed his arms, sinking her claws into them. "You're not taking that ring, vampire!"

"Lousha, *no*! Doona fight him!" As MacRieve charged for them, Lothaire's hands flew up. Lucia felt pressure, then heard an uncanny crack.

Then came darkness.

As Garreth ran for her, he saw it all as if in slow motion.

With no hint of expression, the vampire calmly gripped her chin and the back of her head and snapped her neck. The pop of bone was deafening.

Lucia's limp body dropped. With a roar, MacRieve tackled thin air; Lothaire had traced twenty feet down the corridor.

"I told you not to come closer," the vampire said. "She's been punished."

Garreth bellowed in fury, but the vampire was already gone. At once, he heard whirring gears. *The traps . . .*

"Lousha, wake up, baby." She couldn't be killed like this. She couldn't—but who knew in the Lore? He'd also never thought his cousin would marry a witch or that the Lykae queen would be a vampire!

From outside came the deep crackling sound of rocks breaking. The tomb began shaking, gold tiles raining from the ceiling. Garreth clutched Lucia's limp body, cupping her lolling head, and tore down the corridor.

Once he reached the tomb entrance, he could barely see—stone dust filled the air. The levees were self-destructing! Walls were collapsing, water shooting through. With no mortar, they'd crumble like a sand castle.

The city was about to be wiped out. About to be bombarded with water, boulders, and four-ton anacondas.

Which left him with two choices: hole up in one of the temples, trying to shelter her body from the impact, or run for it with her, leaving her completely unprotected. . . .

FORTY-FOUR

——◇◈◇——

*H*owler monkeys screeching. Boulders knocking together. The very ground quaking.

In and out of consciousness, Lucia dimly perceived
that MacRieve had her in a fireman's hold, spread over
his shoulder, hanging upside down. He'd yelled, "Oh,
fook this!" snatched up her gear, and then he'd taken
off running.

With his every step, pain spiked through one spot in
her neck. The rest of her body was numb.

As he sprinted down the cobbled path, the totems
flanking it began to topple, giant dominoes collapsing.
MacRieve ducked and sidestepped while they crashed
all around them.

Then came a minefield of those huge ceiba trees
exploding up from the rupturing ground, their roots
shooting out like grasping arms.

Lucia could do nothing to help him.

When MacRieve leapt once, then directly again, she
gaped down. Beneath them, crevasses in the earth fis-
sured, opening and closing like gills. . . .

At last, against all odds, MacRieve made it to the levees. He scrabbled up, scaling the rock wall even as it
crumbled. Vines snapped, whipping as though alive.

Every time she thought he'd gotten his footing, stones would disappear, plummeting below. On each side of them, unimaginable water pressure shot rocks like they were cannonballs. Directly above them, water jetted with a bullet's velocity.

"Just hold on, lass," he told her. "I'll get us out of this." He added in a mutter, "*Somehow.*"

With that, she blacked out once more.

The next time she woke, he was laying her flat in the bottom of the skiff. Then she dimly heard him trying to start the engine, again and again. "Come on, fire, you little bugger!"

It roared to life—they'd be saved!

"Can you hear me, Lousha?" he asked as he got them under way.

She blinked open her eyes, squinting against the afternoon sun streaming in through branches. With a frown, she lifted her head—

Pain radiated through her neck, then down her back. "Ow!"

"Damn it, stay put!"

She couldn't move her head without pain, could only look straight up. Probing her neck, she cried, "That hurts!"

"Then stop *doing* it. Just lie still for a bit."

"Are we safe yet?"

"Uh, no, no' as such."

She could hear the propeller churning, could smell the engine smoking, and yet the branches overhead weren't moving. The boat was staying in place? Ah, gods, the river was equalizing, and they were caught in the current. "We're about to be sucked back into the necropolis, aren't we?"

"Oh, aye."

Come on, come on! Garreth inwardly commanded. But how much more could this engine take?

She'd been quiet for long moments. "*Now* are we safe?"

Just as he'd muttered, "No' yet," the current released them at last. The boat shot forward, freed. He briefly closed his eyes in relief.

"MacRieve, you're going to have to narrate. I can only look up."

"We're out of danger for now—and on our way back to the *Contessa*." *If the ship's even there.*

"How did you get us out of that back there?" she asked.

Sheer luck. "Great skill. How's your neck?" Though it was such a devastating injury, the actual break would be small and quick to regenerate. "If it's hurting, then it's healing."

"Then I'm definitely on the mend. I think I can sit up soon," she said. "I can't believe Lothaire gave me the neck adjustment from hell. Strike that—I can totally believe it, but I'm shocked he was right there at the tomb. Makes one wonder how long he'd been watching us."

Doubtless the leech watched me claiming her. Bluidy vampires!

"When did Lothaire get so freaking *strong*?" Lucia asked.

"He's an ancient, the Enemy of Old." And immortals grew stronger with every year.

"What do you think he wants with that ring?"

"Doona know. It was the simplest piece of gold in all of the chamber. It must have some powers that we doona know of."

"Do you think he'll be back?"

"I think he's long gone from this place." *Like we should be.*

"What are we going to do about the great evil getting her finger broken off? Also, I'm going to go out on a limb and say we probably got water in there on the *watchers.* Three out of three house rules broken."

And I'd already heard something moving within. "I doona know that anything could have survived that impact. The city was razed and then submerged." *But if they did survive* . . . Wendigos were rapacious killers. And then La Dorada—who knew what she was capable of? A warrior as strong as Damiāno had feared her.

Lucia grew quiet for a moment, then asked, "What do we do if the *Contessa* left us? Or, um, sank?"

"Paddle this boat for double the amount of days it took for the *Contessa* to motor here. Or attempt to fix the *Barāo.*" A ghost ship. Filled to the brim with hacked-up bodies. "Let's just hope they dinna."

She stretched her hand out to him. "Help me up."

"Lousha, it's too soon."

"I won't move my head." When he grudgingly tugged her upright, she looked stiff and hurting, but not too bad. "See."

"Aye, then. So tell me, what's the last you saw of the passengers and crew?"

"Travis was injured. He head-butted the wheelhouse and was knocked out cold. Schecter was urinating on himself in fear, Rossiter was in the engine room, manning the pumps."

"What about Izabel and Charlie?"

"You mean Chizabel?" At his frown, Lucia explained what she'd seen. How Izabel's body had morphed—much like a shifter's would—from female to male.

"You *saw* Izabel change into Charlie?" Garreth asked.

"Right before my eyes."

"No shite?" Then his brows drew together. "You dinna change your swimsuit in front of Izabel, did you?"

"Only a couple of times."

"Bluidy hell. Charlie's seen my woman naked," he said in a surly tone. "I almost liked him better when I thought he was a machete murderer." He steered around a log. "You need to find out what his—and her—story is. Sate my Lykae's curiosity for me."

"So what are we going to tell everyone when we get back?"

"Partly the truth. We tell them that Damião attacked with a machete last night. So we got in the skiff heading for the *Barão*. But he'd already killed all the passengers there. Then we say the motor got fouled up and we drifted until I could get it working again."

"Sounds good to me," she said, with a shrug, then winced at her aching neck.

"Easy, lass. You have to give that time. Coinciden-
tally, we have some to burn. . . ."

For hours, they traveled upriver, praying that the
Contessa would still be there. Toward late afternoon, he
said, "It should be just around the bend." Then he pro-
ceeded to hold his breath. . . .

"They waited for us!" Lucia gave a relieved sigh when
they saw the ship, still anchored. "And they're afloat!
I don't know whose decision it was to wait, but they're
my new best friend. I need a dry bed and a shower."

"Aye, and coffee and food for me. Seems like our luck
is turning."

The *Contessa* appeared to have taken on some water, but she wasn't listing—a good sign. The old girl had
more in her than Garreth had ever imagined. Her gen-
erator was still working, the water pumps humming.

Of course, the ship *looked* like shite. Most of the railings were gone, and the windows were shattered. The
sole air-conditioning unit dangled precariously from a
sagging window frame.

All over the decks, river vegetation dried, and
twenty-foot arcs of mud sprayed over the ship's sides,
most likely from caiman tails digging down as the creatures attacked.

"I bet the ship can make it back to port in half the
time." He motored on. "We'll be running with the current, and with all the rains, the water's moving," he said,
adding silently, *And once I have you tucked somewhere
safe, I'll go take care of this Cruach business. Alone.*

"Oh, gods, look at that," Lucia said, pointing out a
dead giant caiman hung up on a nearby log. Her arrows

still jutted from its eyes. Flies swarmed the bloated carcass from above—piranhas from below. The fish were fighting over it, tearing at it so viciously, the caiman's limbs and tail jerked as if it were still alive.

"Rain forest garbage disposal," Garreth said. "It'll be picked clean in seconds." Giving the piranhas a wide berth, he steered them to what was left of the *Contessa's* platform. Once he'd tied the skiff to the ship, he carried Lucia aboard, setting her on her feet so gingerly.

"Stop treating me like crystal, MacRieve. I'm all healed up."

He wrapped an arm around her waist. "As am I. So we can be all healed up in the shower together."

"It's a date, but first thing's first. Let's find everyone."

Garreth called out, *"Travis?"*

No answer.

"I think Travis will probably be out of commission," Lucia said. "That hit he took would stagger even an immortal."

"Anybody here?" Garreth yelled, sniffing the air. No vampires, no Damiāno, no Loreans . . . so why was he uneasy? When he heard sounds coming from the salon, they headed up.

Izabel and Schecter stood within the room, their faces pale.

Lucia asked, "What's going on?"

Only when Garreth and Lucia had entered did they see three robed men behind them in the salon, covered in dried blood, with guns drawn.

FORTY-FIVE

❦

"Cromites," Lucia sneered. That was why the *Contessa* hadn't left them. These bastards had been lying in wait with hostages.

All three had eyes glazed with fanaticism and blood-stained robes. Though they brandished guns, their customary weapons were holstered at their hips—swords with Cruach's horned symbol on the hilts, and more blood smeared on the blades.

"You're the ones who killed the *Barão*'s passengers," Lucia said. *Not* Damião.

The eldest Cromite, clearly the leader of the trio, answered, "All were sacrificed in his name."

The shifter had merely picked up the machete that Izabel had dropped. Of course, then he'd been quick to shove it against Lucia's neck.

"And you brought guns?" MacRieve scoffed. "Did you come here to tickle me?"

"Give us the dieumort," the leader said. "Or we'll kill these two."

MacRieve shrugged. "So be it."

Schecter gave a cry, seeming to go weak in the knees, grasping Izabel's arm. The girl flung him away.

"Are you crazy?" Schecter said. "Just give them whatever they came for."

"You canna comprehend the shite day I've had." MacRieve's expression was thunderous. "I will no' be giving anything to anybody!"

The leader said, "I'll shoot *you*."

"At your bluidy leisure." MacRieve's beast was already stirring. "Let's do this—"

"We don't actually care about retrieving the dieumort. We only want it destroyed." The leader motioned to the youngest-looking one, and the man opened his robe, displaying a belt laden with explosives. He raised his shaking fist, his thumb just above a red button on a detonator.

MacRieve muttered, "You've got my attention."

"Don't give it to them!" Lucia said. "They're going to try to kill us all anyway. They'd love to sacrifice themselves."

MacRieve shook his head. In a low tone, he told her, "This could actually kill you." His eyes flickered pale blue as he gazed at her face. "I canna risk it—"

Suddenly, a deafening boom sounded. The bomb man's head burst, blood splattering the wall map behind him.

Lucia jerked around. Travis sagged against the wall just outside the salon doorway, with his shotgun smoking and his head bandaged. "Run, Izabel!" he yelled. "Go!" She and Schecter were already darting through the doorway.

The remaining two Cromites turned to their dead comrade. And aimed their pistols.

"MacRieve!" Lucia screamed. "They'll shoot the bomb!"

He was already diving in front of the fallen man, intercepting the bullets, his pale blue eyes locked on the ones shooting.

Knowing the carnage to come, Lucia shoved the door shut in Travis's ashen face, slamming the bar lock in place.

Under a hail of fire but still shielding the bombs, MacRieve lunged for the two Cromites, slashing out at their throats with his claws. The two crumpled to the floor, one nearly decapitated, the other futilely clamping his hands over his severed jugular.

Dashing to MacRieve's side, she cried, "Ah, gods, look at your chest!" It was riddled with bullets.

"Reminds me . . . of our first date."

"You crazy Lykae." She pressed her lips to his forehead.

"He wants you, Lucia," the last living Cromite gurgled, making her entire body tense.

She leapt up, reaching the mortal, then gripped his bloody head. *Broken neck day, paying it forward.*

"Wants Lucia av—"

She twisted, gazing at the ceiling as satisfaction rushed through her. Every time she slew one of these followers, she imagined the Broken Bloody One *felt* the pain.

And that was just a hint, husband. I'm about to teach you what misery is. . . .

With effort, MacRieve turned to her. "We could've used him for information."

"My temper got the best of me. Sorry," she said, returning to his side. She hated lying to MacRieve, but she was so close to keeping her secret buried forever. And somehow her motives for secrecy had shifted from concealing her shame to protecting her Scot.

"Lousha . . . think one o' these bullets is inching to my heart. Might pass out for a bit. You stay out o' trou—" He went unconscious.

Banging sounded on the door, and Travis yelled, "I'm about to blow this fucker down!"

"You'll hit us," Lucia called. "Just give us a second. We're fine."

Yes, fine, yet with gored bodies to get rid of. *Can't get discovered now!* She was already in enough trouble. *How to get rid . . . how to get rid . . . ?*

Her gaze fell to one of the busted windows. Rain forest garbage disposal. She hastened to the lead Cromite's body, maneuvering it to the opening. Then she tossed it over the side.

Floating, floating.

Travis began assailing the barricaded door with what sounded like the butt of his shotgun. He'd break through soon.

Come on, fish!

She exhaled in relief when the piranhas boiled up in a feeding frenzy to consume the man. Two more Cromites to go. She made fast work of them, carefully extracting the bomb belt from the last one before dumping him to the fish.

"*Clever girl,*" MacRieve rasped, opening one eye.

She whispered, "So what do I do with the bomb?"

"Sink it . . . weigh it down."

She peered around for something heavy to tie it to, coming up with nothing . . . Then she narrowed her eyes on the second busted window, on the air-conditioning unit drooping from it.

Lucia hauled it back into the salon, then punched the center out. Digging out the guts of the machine, she cautiously buried the bomb inside. Then she lobbed the whole contraption into the river, watching it sink with satisfaction.

By the time Travis broke down the door shortly after, Lucia was kneeling beside a semi-conscious MacRieve, having just tied the embroidered coffee-station tablecloth around his chest to conceal the worst of his wounds.

As the captain's weary gaze took in the scene, Lucia glanced around, trying to see it from his eyes. His late wife's embroidery now served as a bandage. Air conditioner parts littered the floor. Copious amounts of blood had spurted from the Cromites' jugulars when MacRieve had attacked. Yet there were no robed men to be found.

"I think I need a drink," Travis drawled, sinking down on his stool. "Every damned trip gets weirder than the last."

Oh, if he only knew *half* the weirdness aboard his ship.

"Where the hell did those men go?"

"They escaped," she lied baldly. "Darn them!"

Nodding slowly, he said, "The one without his head—did he make tracks too?"

"They took him with them. Madcap fanatics!"

"What did they want?"

"An artifact we own. It had a religious meaning to them. End of the world, doomsday type of stuff."

"I saw MacRieve catch at least two bullets before you shoved me out," Travis said, "but he looks like he's just taking a nap."

"Scottish men are . . . *hardy*?"

The captain rubbed his hand over his face. "See, what I think happened is this—"

"Travis," she interrupted in a steely tone. "You've got a head wound, you're a drinker, and if no one ever hears about what you think happened, then I'll pay for all the repairs to the boat. A lump sum."

After a hesitation, he narrowed his eyes, "Quadruple it, and you'll see my memory go real fast."

"Done."

"One question though. Damião wasn't with you?"

She shook her head, giving him the story she and MacRieve had agreed on, amending the identity of the *Barão*'s killers to the robed fanatics.

When he heard the fate of those passengers, Travis's pale visage grew leached of even more color. "Are you sure it was those three that did it? It could've been Malaquí."

"Malaquí was killed, too." She thought she detected disappointment in him. Which couldn't be right.

Izabel ran in then, her eyes going wide at the sight of MacRieve. "*Deus do céu!* Is he going to be all right?"

Lucia said, "It's just a flesh wound."

She nodded dumbly. "And where'd those creepy men go?"

"Escaped," Travis answered. "Long gone."

When MacRieve roused once more, Lucia said, "Here, help me get him back to the cabin."

With Travis and Lucia's help, MacRieve was able to make it to his feet. But when he lurched, Travis ducked under his arm, laying it over his shoulders to help him walk. "Big bastard," he said with a grunt.

Once they'd navigated MacRieve back to cabin seven and heaved him into the bed, Travis said, "We've gotta get underway right now, get him to a hospital."

Lucia gazed at the fresh blood seeping from the captain's head wound. *MacRieve's not the one who needs to get to a hospital.*

The captain raised his face and called, "Chuck!" He frowned when no reply came, then asked Izabel, "You've seen him since last night, right?" Travis seemed genuinely worried.

Izabel said, "He's fine."

Travis's concern shifted to ire. "Then where the hell is he?"

"Charlie's . . . he's . . ." Izabel trailed off, looking at Lucia with pleading eyes.

I can't believe I'm doing this. "Charlie was patching a hole when we came in. Looked pretty bad."

Izabel quickly added, "*Capitão*, your head's bleeding again. I'll put you back in bed, then go help Charlie. We'll get the *Contessa* under way in no time."

Lucia waited for Travis to bark that no one could improve anything. Instead, he gazed down at Izabel and muttered, "What would I do without you two?"

Izabel, in turn, looked crestfallen. And now Lucia

understood why. *Okay, perhaps they do have a decent-sized barrier between them.*

Just then, Schecter came running into the cabin. One of the lenses in his glasses was cracked, and his cowlick had finally deflated. "Uh, there's a beam wedged against the engine room hatch."

"So?" Travis snapped, looking like he wanted to murder the professor.

"So . . . I think Rossiter's in there."

At once, the captain and Izabel charged out. When MacRieve cracked open an eye and muttered to Lucia, "Go. Like that mortal," she ran after them, hurrying to the engine room.

She found the captain straining to move the beam, his head bandage already saturated with red. Schecter was worthless. Izabel was gone, no doubt "looking" for Charlie.

"Here, let me help!" Lucia said. Acting as if she struggled, she wrenched the beam away, then dashed forward to open the hatch. When steaming fumes gusted out from within, she coughed, waving her hand in front of her face.

Once the miasma cleared, she saw Rossiter on his hands and knees clawing his way up the steps. He was shirtless, covered in grease and sweat, and up to his waist in water. He also looked drunk from fumes, his eyes bloodshot.

As Lucia rushed down to help him up, she spied a line of oil residue high on the wall from where the water had risen. "The water got that high?" If so, then the ship had been sinking.

Rossiter rasped, "I was singularly motivated . . . to keep the pumps running."

She couldn't imagine how terrifying that would have been for him—a mortal trapped with little light, the water rising, knowing he was about to drown.

Travis said, "If not for you, we'd have gone down." Over his shoulder, he added, "All because of the giant fucking *caimans*!"

Everyone on board hated Schecter, but Rossiter had the most reason to. Aside from his harrowing night, the doctor's mission was now finished—with no hope for finding his orchid. Schecter might just have killed him.

Once they got Rossiter back on the deck, his wild-eyed gaze landed on Schecter. With a maddened bellow, the doctor attacked.

FORTY-SIX

<hr/>

"I haven't seen a punch like that in ages," Lucia said as she entered the wheelhouse. Chizabel was piloting the boat into a dramatic orange sunset.

The already cracked windshield had been no match for caiman attacks, and now as the wind streamed in, her long black hair flowed behind her. Izabel was so feminine; you'd never know she was half-man.

"And then when Doc Rossiter kept beating Schecter?" Izabel said. "I never knew the expression *beating the piss out of someone* was literal."

"I meant to step in and break it up sooner. Really I did," Lucia said. "So where's Travis?"

"*Capitão*'s sleeping in his cabin. Rossiter shot him up with some morphine."

The doctor had wanted to examine MacRieve as well, but Lucia had insisted his wounds were superficial, assuring Rossiter, *You'll see him up and running in no time.*

"Is MacRieve still alive?"

"He's resting, too." The Scot had been passed out again but was regenerating nicely. "Prognosis is good."

Izabel raised her brows at that. All the humans had thought he was surely at death's door.

Lucia guessed she and Izabel would dance around the subject of her being part man a little longer. So she stared at the sun over the water. As distraught as she'd been just this morning, Lucia was now filled with hope.

In her possession was a dieumort, which moved her one step closer to freeing herself from Cruach. And one step closer to a future with MacRieve, the Lykae who'd somehow gone from enemy to lover to love of her life.

But she wasn't prepared for MacRieve just yet. Earlier, on the ride back to the *Contessa*, Lucia had feared he would ask her to marry him. Though it wasn't necessarily the Lykae way, he'd told her she'd be his wife one day. And if he'd proposed, what could she have said? *Rain check? Let me get back to you when I'm a widow.*

Now, in a matter of days, she could return to the Scot—free at last. Free of Skathi *and* Cruach. "How much longer until we get back?" Lucia asked.

"Four days. Max."

"You know the way?"

Izabel glared. "Better than anybody on this river," she answered. "So *Capitão* told me about your night. Damião really attacked you? I knew he was *louco!*"

"In a big way."

"Travis said the robed men were religious fanatics after some relic you and MacRieve found."

"That's it exactly. I'm just glad we made it out alive." Lucia pulled up another stool. "So, last night was revealing in a lot of ways." Rossiter was a hero, Schecter a criminally irresponsible scientist, Izabel part . . . guy. "You want to tell me what's going on? Are you human?"

Izabel gazed around as if she were being pranked. "Uh, yes. I am. Is there another option?"

Lucia answered with a question: "So do you know why you're . . . like you are?"

"I was cursed by what I can only figure was an evil woman. Voodoo, Santeria, who knows?" She frowned. "How come you're not freaking out?"

"I was rattled at first. But I've always believed in the supernatural, so I got over it soon enough," Lucia answered. "So when did Izabel Carlotta became Isabel and Charlie?"

Izabel sighed. "Two years ago, I'd just gotten dumped by my first love, and I was drinking and wished with all my heart that I knew why men thought the way they did. This strange, mesmerizing woman told me she could answer my question. The next morning I woke up hungover. Oh, and a man."

Evil sorceress, had to be.

"I came to the Amazon, hoping to find a cure or an explanation."

A cure wasn't likely. Sorceress spells tended to stick, unless lifted by another one of equal or greater power. Lucia knew a witch—Mariketa the Awaited, a party-hearty mercenary of the Wiccae—who could possibly nullify it, but she'd had her hellacious powers bound for fifty years, until she could better handle them. Izabel was doubtless stuck like this for the duration.

"Can you switch back and forth at will?" When Izabel nodded, Lucia asked, "Are you going to tell Travis? It's only a matter of time before he figures it out."

Izabel's eyes watered. "He'll never understand. I'm leaving as soon as I get him to the hospital."

Poor girl. Before she would've been thrilled that Izabel was leaving Travis. Now Lucia resented the fact that the girl felt she had to.

What's with all the sympathy I'm feeling for humans? Maybe Lucia should open up a stray shelter for mortals. Feed them kibble. "Iz, you need to give him a chance. He might surprise you."

"It's not that easy. You see, 'Charlie' needs love, too. And Travis . . . there's just no way."

"If you can change back and forth, then just stay in your female form."

"It makes me sick when I don't change into Charlie enough and vice versa."

"That's why Charlie was often pale." Now that Lucia thought back, she recalled both twins had dressed in the same plain T-shirts and cargo pants. Iz had worn baggy clothes in case she'd had to transform into him without notice. "Can you change into Charlie right now?"

"Yes, but I don't take requests," she quipped, wiping her nose on her sleeve. "You won't tell *Capitão*, will you?" She looked utterly distraught at the idea of him knowing.

Lucia raised her brows. "You really think he'd believe me?"

"No, not in *um milhão de anos*, a million years," she answered. "So are we still . . . friends?"

"Yes, we're still friends, Chiz. Though I'm not going to change in front of you anymore or anything."

Izabel gasped. "Oh, like Charlie would have your skinny ass, skank!"

"No, because Chuck digs the drunk dudes like his low-hanging-fruit sister."

Izabel choked out a laugh, her expression startled. "First time I've ever been able to laugh about this!"

Then my work here is done. "Listen, if you're ever in New Orleans, I want you to look me up. There's some crazy stuff in that town, maybe we could find someone who knows what happened to you."

Her eyes went wide. "Do you mean that?"

"Yeah. I'll get you my number before we make port. . . ."

As she exited down the companionway steps, Lucia met up with Rossiter. He'd showered and dressed—and still hadn't slept.

"I was just looking for you," he said. "Are you sure you don't want me to see to your husband?"

"*What?*"

"I could examine him."

"Oh. MacRieve. He's fine. It truly was only a graze. But thanks for the offer. And thank you again for keeping the ship afloat."

He gave a rueful grin. "There was an element of self preservation at work."

If he'd ever needed to rest, it'd be after that hellish night he'd just spent. But for him, there would be no succor in sleep, no oblivion. Again, sympathy rose in her. "Look, I'm sorry this expedition didn't work out for you."

With a shrug, he said, "Hey, I'll live." Then he almost stifled a grimace.

No, he wouldn't. *I don't like humans, I don't like humans.* . . . As much as she inwardly chanted that to herself, she still had the mad urge to help this one.

Before she did something she'd later regret—like telling him *Psst, you wanna become a myth like us?*— Lucia said, "Um, got to go make a call." Then she brushed past him.

As she headed for the stern deck, she dialed Nïx— and actually got her. She found the soothsayer lucid. Mostly.

"Nïx, I have some good news and some really shitty news," Lucia said. Then she explained everything that had happened, finishing with, "So, uh, a jot of water might've gotten in the tomb."

"Now *who* did you wake up?" Nïx asked in a confounded tone.

"The great evil. Gilded One. Ringing a bell?"

"We'll worry about that later," Nïx said. "For now, let's stop at least one apocalypse. Aren't you on the books for an attempted assassination soon? Where *is* that Post-it . . . ?"

"Yes, Nïx, I'll be back to port in four days. I need transportation, warmer clothes, jeans, and boots."

"I'll have a helicopter standing by in Iquitos, then a jet to the Northlands fueled and waiting with clothes and gear for you. Assuming I remember any of this."

"Nïx!"

"Oh, oh, I do remember this one bit. You have to get the dieumort and get away from MacRieve."

"I was already planning on ditching him, but why do you say so?"

"Because he's intending to do just that to you. To go face Cruach—without you."

"No, he wouldn't!" He didn't even know of her involvement. She'd thought if she could keep it hidden, she'd prevent something like this.

"Oh, but he would."

Probably for some stupid noble reason like keeping her safe! Bastard! Besides the fact that this was *her* fight—and she'd waited a *long* time to destroy the Broken Bloody One—Cruach could infect MacRieve.

A plan arose for how to deal with the Scot. In fact, he'd been the one who'd given her the idea. *I just have to break into Schecter's cabin in the next four days. . . .*

"Nïx, put Regin at the ready," Lucia said. As per usual, it would be Regin with the assist and Lucia shooting for the goal.

Not some werewolf with high-minded ideals. When all this was over, Lucia would come back to him and explain . . . *something*.

"Sadly, Regin's going to have to rain-check the god killing and after party," Nïx said. "Seems she's just been abducted."

"*What?*" Lucia stumbled. "Who would—who *could*—take her?"

"The details are unclear, but I've narrowed it down to about fifteen suspects, among them: aliens, a boy band, the CIA, and a berserker."

As the rain poured outside the *Contessa*, Garreth dragged Lucia across his chest, her body relaxed from hours of sex. "It's hard to believe we're nearly to Iquitos," he murmured. He'd gotten all his strength back—just in time. They'd arrive in port at first light.

"I'm almost sad to leave this ship, even after all we've been through." She lazily traced her fingers over his mended chest. "And I already miss my butterfly."

Though he'd assured her he could figure out a way to keep it, she'd gotten a strange look on her face. *"I think Lucia Incantata needs her freedom."*

"I'm partial to this ship, too, lass," he said. "I've spent some of the best nights of my life on this boat. And in this bed."

She nodded against him. "Most definitely in this bed."

He sifted his fingers through her hair, so wrapped up in her that he almost forgot his plan. Garreth intended to take her so long and hard this night that she'd pass out toward dawn, slipping deep into that near comatose state. Then he'd go to take care of business. "But you've been pensive for the last four days." And the nightmares had been as bad as ever. He needed to help her and couldn't.

She shrugged. "Probably just nerves over the upcoming battle. Plus, I'll rest easier once we use the dieumort. I worry that more will come after it."

In their hands was an archaic secret—kept hidden for millennia in a previously impenetrable site, guarded by creatures of legend—and now they'd brought it forth out into the world.

Each Lore faction had its own seers to direct them to a weapon like this, not to mention the assassins sent by the gods.

Garreth was more than ready to use it, too. This afternoon, he'd called Lachlain to make sure Bowen's witch could scry for this god. Lachlain had been thrilled that Garreth had finally claimed his mate after so long, and had found the dieumort as well. Lachlain had been less thrilled that his younger brother had nearly been eaten by a snake.

"Oh, for fuck's sake, Garreth!" he'd bellowed. "I'm goin' with you on this mission. Bowen, as well."

"No' a chance." After all the two of them had been through in the last year, Garreth refused to lay more trouble on their doorsteps. "Can the witch find my target, or no'?"

"Aye, she can still do many of the easier magicks. But you doona plan to deprive Bowen and me of a fight?"

Garreth had answered, "So as to no' piss off a vampire queen and the most powerful witch ever to live? Oh, aye."

"What are you planning?"

"Steal the arrow from Lousha, sneak off, shoot the god. Then I'll come back with a present and an apology, promising she can shoot the next god." Garreth had sounded far more confident than he actually was. He couldn't predict if she'd forgive him—or if she'd disappear again.

But he didn't feel like he had much of a choice. He could never risk her. Just having the weapon in their possession was a danger. He had to go, and he had to hope. Maybe if he could get some kind of commitment out of her. . . .

"Things will change when we return, Lousha," he said now. "But I trust no' too much." Cupping her face, he pressed kisses to her forehead, her eyelids, the tips of her ears. "I know you Valkyrie fancy marriages and such. So if you wanted to be my wife . . ." When she stiffened against him, he added in a surly tone, "Or no', then. Only asked because my brother wed his mate."

"Can we table this for now? And talk about it as soon as this killing is done—"

A man's scream ripped through the air.

Lucia said, "I recognize that scream."

Schecter. "He must've found another lizard in his cabin," Garreth said. "He's terrified of anything cold-blooded now. Almost as much as he's afraid of Rossiter."

The mortal Rossiter had seemed stoically resolved to his fate until Garreth had mentioned that another crew would likely go right back out to salvage the rich *Barão* and retrieve the bodies. If the doctor could hitch a ride, he'd only lose a month total. *Only.* For a mortal, a month was a long span. For a dying mortal, it was eternity.

Lucia sighed. "Okay, so maybe there are some things I won't miss about the *Contessa*." She leaned forward and kissed Garreth's chin. "But I meant what I said, Scot. I want to talk with you about the future, just not yet."

Hell, that was more than he'd expected. He relaxed once more, drawing her over his body. "I can wait. *For now*," he said, talking a big game; Lucia was worth *any* wait.

She felt him hard against her and gasped. "Again?"

"Again." *The things I do for the sake of the world.* "As many times as you'll have me. I canna get enough of you, love."

"MacRieve?" she murmured.

"Aye?"

Her hand shot forward, an oversized syringe in her fist.

Before he could react, he felt the sting in his neck as she injected him. "Lousha! Why?"

As he fought to keep his eyes open, she whispered, *"I'm choosing you."*

FORTY-SEVEN

"**B**luidy hell," Garreth muttered. "No' again."

Moments before, he'd awakened, barely, and found Lucia was gone. Memories from last night flooded him. She'd *tranqued* him—likely with Schecter's stash. She'd been plotting against him the whole time Garreth had been making love to her—as part of his plot against her.

He sniffed the air. This ship was in port. But she was long gone, departed maybe two hours ago. He snatched up his phone, calling Bowen. "Need a favor from your witch."

"Good to talk to you, too, Dark Prince. Hold on."

As he waited for Mariketa to get on the line, Garreth dressed and loaded his pack, intending to set out at once.

"Yello?"

"I need you to scry for Lousha," he said. "You told me once that you could."

"Yeah, I can get you in her vicinity."

Garreth had taken Lucia's scent into him and could find her from miles away. "That'll work." Witches could come in handy, he supposed.

"But I don't do gratis."

Garreth bluidy hated witches! "Charge me what you will! Just give me the fucking coordinates."

In the background, he heard Bowen say, "Mari, never let it be said that I doona support your extortion—"

"Entrepreneurial-ness," she corrected.

"But a family discount, love, would no' be amiss."

"The *whole* family? Fine," she said. "I'm scrying." While Garreth waited, she groused about how extended the "MacRieve pack" was.

Suddenly she sucked in a breath. "Garreth, I don't know why Lucia's going to this particular place, but it's a confluence of evil. Great evil."

"Aye, I ken that," he snapped, then added impatiently, "Home of an evil god I'm off to murder. So be quick with the details, witch!"

A woman's severed leg.

It'd been left at the entrance to Cruach's lair—as if in greeting.

Yet when Lucia had arrived at twilight two hours ago, she'd found no Cromites there to battle, and everything about the situation had screamed, "Trap!"

Now as she awaited Cruach's rising, pacing in front of the cave with her bow strapped over her shoulder, her mind raced, flitting from memory to memory: the look on MacRieve's face just before the tranquilizer took hold, her mad dash out of Iquitos, the interminable plane ride to these cold Northlands.

All of that had culminated in her hike through these barren woods to Cruach's lair. The forest here was a fitting precursor to his cave. Filled with shadows and petrified trees, it was separated forever from the cleansing ocean by Cruach's foul mountain.

She'd never had difficulties finding this place even after so much time had passed. Nothing ever grew around the yawning opening, and old, bleached bones were perpetually strewn before it.

Pacing, thoughts flitting . . . Lucia was beset with worry about Regin, who was still missing after five days. After unsuccessfully calling Nïx again and again, Lucia had begun harassing Annika.

Annika had already warped past aneurismal straight into action, dispatching search parties and hiring witches to scry. Neither had turned up a trace of Regin.

Who'd abducted her? Surely it was the berserker, Aidan the Fierce, reincarnated once more. But Aidan had never *taken* Regin before.

Well, at least not without witnesses.

Lucia needed to get this killing over with and return to locate her sister. She *yearned* for this to end. And yet she knew how risky it would be to do anything before Cruach made his move. . . .

In the past, the longest they'd had to wait for him to emerge was two days—Lucia's nightmares had proved chillingly accurate. So as bad as they'd been the last few nights, why was he not coming forth?

Trap.

From her thigh quiver, she drew the dieumort out once more, gazing at the wooden shaft and ancient feathers. It was so unlike Skathi's perfect golden arrows, and yet Lucia was more confident in her weapon than she'd ever been. On the plane ride here, she'd no-

ticed the finest inscriptions near the arrowhead and
had again sensed the latent power.

She'd begun to suspect the arrow had been carved
from an enchanted world tree, *a tree of life.* There were
fewer than a dozen in number scattered all over the
earth, but one was rumored to grow in the Amazon.

What better way to defeat a being that reveled in carnage and death?

And what better way to get myself killed? she thought
as she replaced the dieumort amid her regular arrows.
She was uneasy safeguarding such a weapon—one of
the most powerful ever to exist. It was only a matter of
time before some enemy came after her, and after this
prize. She wanted to use the arrow as soon as possible,
to extinguish it—and Cruach—forever.

A chill wind blew, and she pulled her jacket closer,
wishing she was back in the sultry warmth of the Amazon with MacRieve. Instead of waiting at the gates of
hell. Which was no exaggeration.

She couldn't imagine a more gruesome place. Decorated with piles of rotting bodies and infested with
vermin, the cavern was a fitting hovel for the monster
within. She remembered how Cruach would drink
from a goblet and blood would dribble down his chin
and out from his rotting cheeks. She remembered how
he would *feed.*

But the smell was the worst. Right now, the stench
oozing out from the lair was so thick, it seemed visible,
diffusing into the cleaner air outside.

Damn it, how much longer could she wait? Eventually, MacRieve would find her, somehow; that was what

his kind did. Regin needed to be located and then rescued from her obsessed berserker. And with each hour Lucia remained, she risked Cromites returning, or enemies seeking the dieumort.

If she faced Cruach, he'd be no match for her speed, not with his hunched and broken body. She had a weapon in her quiver that would exterminate him. The sooner she completed this kill, the sooner she could return to MacRieve.

I want to start our life together. She could ask the Scot to help her find Regin—

Cruach's voice rang out then, echoing through the tunnel. *"Come to me, fair Lucia. For I was soon to come to you."*

Her fists clenched. *Fair Lucia.* More memories bombarded her. The gristle-covered altar, the lecherous robed ones, the . . . *pain.* Her rage toward him had always been seething, buried deep within her. Now it welled like a font; she needed raw violence, wanted to mete out her wrath.

After a thousand years, she *craved* destroying the Broken Bloody One.

The huntress would slay the bear—in his cave.

Taking a deep breath, she readied her bow, prepared to pull either the dieumort for Cruach or a regular arrow for one of his guards, then started into the passageway. As she went deeper within, the ground grew soggier, making a sucking sound with each step. It was a pulp of decomposing flesh and blood. Dotting the walls were torch lights made from the bones and clothing of his victims.

She hadn't been back inside here since the first time. And it was so much worse than she remembered. *How could I have been fooled by this fiend?* Thank the gods that MacRieve would never find out she'd wed this monster—

"Imagine running into you here," a voice said behind her.

Lucia whirled around, gasping. "What are you doing? H-how did you find this place?"

"I have ways," he answered with a choked cough. "Gods, the *smell*."

"Mariketa scried, didn't she?"

"Oh, aye." The witch had gotten him in the vicinity, but still Garreth could scarcely believe he'd found this tunnel. The stench coming from within had made scenting Lucia difficult—and paining. "For a price, witches can be accommodating."

Yet he feared there'd be a downside to asking the witch for this. Bowen and Lachlain might meet up and follow Garreth here.

"How are you still standing?" he asked. "The smell nearly felled me coming in. Next time, get Nïx to find you a less revolting god to off." He wiped his sleeve over his face. "I mean, have you ever smelled anything this bluidy awful before?"

At that, Lucia's face seemed to pale even more. "You have to leave!" She kept glancing over her shoulder.

"I'm no' leaving you—as you did me. Why did you take off again?"

"This is too dangerous. You d-don't understand."

She looked like she was about to hyperventilate, the closest to panic that he'd ever seen her.

"If it's so dangerous, do you think I'm just going to let you go in there?"

She shook her head hard. "You can become infected!"

"No more than you could be."

"MacRieve, I will never ask you for another thing as long as we live. But right now, I'm *beseeching* you to leave this place."

"In what universe would you think I'd be leaving without you?"

"I've told you—Cruach can make you see things that aren't so, can make you feel things. He will take over your mind! The longer you're in here, the greater your chance of infection."

Garreth curled his finger under her chin. "Lousha, do you think there's any power on earth that can make me harm you?"

"You're not strong enough to fight it." She shrugged from him, backing up a step. "No one is!"

"That right? Then worry more about your own reaction—"

"MacRieve, I'm . . . immune to him."

"How? Why?"

Her eyes darted, tears wetting them. "P-please, you have to leave!"

Was he *finally* going to learn her secrets? "Why are you immune, Lousha?"

Seeming to bite back a sob, she whispered, "Because . . . because I'm his wife."

FORTY-EIGHT

———◆◇◆———

How will he react? MacRieve's expression was inscrutable. She'd put the truth out there, a shameful secret she'd dreaded his learning.

"This is what it's all been about with you," he said in an even tone. "All the fear, all the running. The nightmares." When she nodded, he said, "You called him the devil."

"He is." *What are you thinking, Scot?*

"But you . . . married him?"

MacRieve's disgusted with me. "Basically? Yes."

"Ceremony and everything?"

She swallowed. "He tricked me into it. I-I was only sixteen."

A muscle ticked in his cheek and his irises grew pale. "Then know this . . ."

She stopped breathing.

"Lass, I'm about to make you a widow—"

The sound of swords against scabbards rang out in the distance. She and MacRieve twisted around, found an army of robed Cromites approaching, eyes feverish with fanaticism.

"More of those fucks?"

There had to be over a hundred of them. "Please,

MacRieve, let's both leave before they attack. Take me from here!"

He appeared torn. At length, he said, "I'll take you away—but I'll come back for him."

Yet more marched from the other direction, blocking them in.

"Looks like we fight, love!" Without warning, MacRieve charged them, slashing with his claws.

With her customary arrows, Lucia fired into the skirmish, dropping her mortal foes swiftly, careful not to hit MacRieve.

But they were in such close confines, and he seemed to be *everywhere*. . . .

With his mind still reeling from her revelations, Garreth tore into the fray, stamping out one Cromite after another. Yet every time he eliminated one, another appeared—even with Lucia's arrows continually whizzing past him, plugging their enemies between the eyes.

"Why dinna you tell me you were married?" *To some revolting god.*

"I didn't want you to know—I didn't want anyone to know!"

This fuck tricked my Lousha into this hellhole? He was as good as dead!

"What are you thinking, MacRieve?" she cried, shooting three arrows at a time.

As he slashed, he figured he should be reflecting on the fact that his mate was married and that things were much more complicated than he'd ever realized. Instead, his thoughts were simple, *primal.*

Get past these pricks, shoot the god, and Lousha is mine, *forever.* Rage mingled with clarity—at least now he had an enemy to fight.

"MacRieve?"

"You should have told me." He ducked under an arc of arterial blood, kicking a headless body out from under his feet.

"I was trying to prevent exactly this!"

"And all the times I asked about your nightmares?"

"The dreams are portents. They tell me when he's about to rise." Another three arrows in rapid succession. "I couldn't reveal that to you because I knew you would come here. But this is *my* responsibility. It has been for over a millennium."

Bodies piled up, blood spraying, Cromites screaming. *Good headway.*

"What are you trying to prove?" Lucia demanded.

Between strikes, he bellowed, "That you should no' have left me!"

"You were going to do it to me—don't bother denying it!" When he didn't, she said, "Then why are you different?" Another volley of arrows. "What gives *you* the right to risk yourself?"

He snapped, "Because you could move on if something happened to me." Then he charged for the last Cromite.

◆   ◆   ◆

That's where you're wrong, she thought as she watched MacRieve finish off their foes.

As Lucia fought to catch her breath in the dank tunnel, he stood over his last kill, his chest heaving as well. He'd warred like a madman, slaying so many.

And now that they could leave, they needed to at once! "Scot, again, you have to listen to me—you can't confront Cruach! You'll get infected."

"Lousha," he rasped. "I want you to know something."

"Can you not tell me outside?"

He shook his head. "I need you to know this. I'm in love with you."

"And you're declaring this now . . . ?" She trailed off when he faced her once more.

His eyes were milky white.

"No, no, no." Her heart seemed to stop; she couldn't get enough air. He was already infected with Cruach's influence, would need to harm whoever he *loved.*

Ah, gods, he loves me. "MacRieve, you have to fight this!" She strapped her bow back on, holding out both of her hands to him. "Come with me—let's leave this place together."

"I love you so damned much, it pains me." His words were rough. "Wanted to tell you before."

MacRieve was . . . lost.

Cruach's laughter sounded, echoing along the walls of dank earth, then he ordered, "Bring my wife to me, Lykae."

When MacRieve obeyed, lunging forward to grab her arms, she cried, "No, don't do this to me!" She struck out at him to free herself, but he was far too strong. "MacRieve, you have to resist this!"

He was unhearing, forcing her past the fallen Cromites toward Cruach's chambers.

Just like before. When she'd been a terrified girl. Now she was a terrified woman, reliving the dread, the dawning realization of how doomed she was.

He dragged her into the ghastly main chamber of Cruach's jail, a larger space with higher ceilings—and bodies strewn all around. Wiggling maggots dotted the corpses stacked high against the seeping walls. Women, children, no one had been spared. The concentrated stench made her gag, her eyes watering.

First, she spied four Cromite altar keepers who'd remained with their god. Then her gaze fell on the altar itself, still moist from his last sacrifice. Her heart thundering, she pleaded, "MacRieve, take me from here! Please . . ."

Then she saw *him.* Nothing had changed—Cruach was still the same nightmare that had haunted every day of her long life. The horns, the misshapen body, the hideous yellow eyes. His scaly skin was decomposing, rotted through in places, down to his bloodstained, broken bones.

"Ah, wife, I've been dreaming of when you would return to me." He motioned for her to come to him.

"No! No!" When she shook her head, digging in her heels, MacRieve forced her closer. "Let me go!"

"If this is how you wish to proceed, Lucia, then so be it," Cruach said. To MacRieve, he ordered, "Chain her down."

MacRieve snatched her into his arms, crushing her in his brutal grip. Already, the god was driving him to harm what he loved.

Though she struggled against him, MacRieve slammed her down upon the altar with so much force that her head cracked against the stone. Her vision wavered and her breath hitched. The bow at her back gouged into her skin. Still, she fought when the robed men seized one of her wrists. MacRieve easily closed a manacle around her other.

"Please don't do this! Garreth!"

No reaction.

As she flailed and clawed, they chained her to the altar she'd prayed she'd never touch again.

She lay prone, defenseless, as Cruach limped over to her. "What do we have here?" With a lustful gaze, he groped his gnarled hand from her knee upward.

She shuddered, bile rising in her throat.

But he stopped at her thigh quiver. "Was the huntress planning to make me her prey once again?" he asked, his meaty fingers wrapping around the arrow she'd brought to kill him. Leisurely drawing it out, he said, "Ah, a dieumort. My bride came to make herself a *widow*."

He raised the arrow over her, but no matter how strong she was, nor how frantic, she couldn't break the manacles. "Garreth! Help me!"

Yet instead of stabbing her with it, Cruach snapped it in two, dropping it on the ground. Crushing it beneath his feet, he pulverized it to dust. "What will you do now, Archer? Try to shoot me with that."

"No, no . . ." Not the arrow. There wasn't even a fragment left to drive into his heart. All the work, all the sacrifice in the Amazon.

Now two evils could be loosed on the earth.

"Fair Lucia, all's not lost. You've pleased me with your offering," he said with a wave at MacRieve, who stood motionless, staring straight ahead. "Luring into my jail such a fine slave as this one. Especially since my followers were so worthless, so mortal. It was good to be rid of them." He grinned at Lucia, exposing blistered gums and rotting fangs. "And I bet their meat is tender."

Cruach could force MacRieve to serve him forever. To stay in this hell with Lucia. Panic surged through her until she felt like choking on it. "You have me. Let him go! He means nothing to you!"

"Nothing?" Cruach's repulsive countenance suddenly changed to an expression of utter rage. Bloody saliva dangled from his bottom lip as he yelled, "He cuckolded me! He despoiled *my* bride." His voice pained her ears, echoing off the walls. "For so long you'd kept yourself pure for me, but now I smell him all over you. I want no wife such as you!"

She screamed back, "Then what do you want?"

Seeming to calm himself once more, Cruach said, "I want the sacrifice of a powerful huntress—offered up by someone who loves her. A sacrifice like that, committed in my name, will make me strong enough to break free, to become incorporeal and invincible forever." He motioned for MacRieve, who joined his side without hesitation. To Lucia, he said, "I want the one who sullied you . . . to punish you. And free me for eternity."

MacRieve was unseeing, his eyes blinded to reality. When Cruach handed him a Cromite sword, he accepted it.

The robed men began chanting, *"To him we sacrifice, for him our cherished . . . to him we sacrifice . . ."*

"Take her head, Lykae," Cruach intoned. "To me you sacrifice, for me your cherished."

"No, MacRieve!" She strained against the bonds, ignoring the pain as the rusted metal cleaved into her skin. "Fight this! I'm Lucia—you don't want to hurt me!"

With a chilling smile, Cruach added, "I bet we'll find your meat is tender."

Blood began streaming from her wrists. She could almost . . . almost squeeze one hand out of a manacle.

MacRieve crossed over to the altar, standing at her shoulders. Positioned there, because he was going to cut off her head.

"Don't do it, MacRieve—you can't do this to me!"

"Do it, MacRieve—you must do this for me!" Lucia was gazing up at Garreth, pleading for him to end her.

Trying to reassure her, he told her again, "I'm in love with you, Lousha."

Her eyes were filled with dread, tears spilling over. "If you love me, then why won't you end my suffering?" She feared he wouldn't? "End *me*."

"Aye. I will." Crom Cruach was bestowing power on him, filling him with the strength to do what needed to be done.

"Do it, Garreth!" she said more urgently, nearly screaming.

He raised the proud sword over his head. It would land directly across her delicate neck. And her suffering would end. "I do this for you."

She was writhing with anticipation, eyes wide, screaming, "Now, MacRieve! Yes, please!"

"Love you." The sword came down, slicing clean.

FORTY-NINE

"MacRieve!" she screamed, watching helplessly as he drove the sword into his side—the sword that had been aimed so fixedly for her neck. In midair, he'd changed his grip, shoving it into himself instead of her.

He staggered back, dropping to his knees, the blade still planted inside him. With his body visibly shuddering, he yanked the sword free, throwing it across the cavern. Then with his hands squeezing his head so hard she thought he'd crack his skull, he roared in agony.

"Garreth, no!"

"That was ... fascinating," Cruach said, staring at MacRieve. "I could control *him*, but not the beast inside him—the one that would rather die than harm its mate. Still, the damage is done. I'd already implanted in his mind the memory of your execution. The memory of his killing you." The fiend laughed. "Right now he believes he's rocking your headless body, feeling your skin cooling against his as your blood drains away."

"Lousha, doona leave me," Garreth rasped, his breaths ragged. He reverted to Gaelic, uttering anguished words. *So sorry ... love you ... joining you.*

His voice wretched, he pleaded for her to come back to him. *"I'm beggin' you, lass."*

Tears ran from her eyes as she choked out the words, "Garreth, it's not real. *Not real.*"

He was unhearing, beginning to dig his claws into the dirt around him.

"Oh, now your Lykae's turning," Cruach said. "The beast is rising, roiling in horror and confusion, gathering the . . . *pieces* of you to his body. How touching."

"Cruach, I will kill you for this!" Lucia lifted up against the chains. "You'll never leave this place! You belong here." When Cruach closed in on her, she screamed, "You're not a god—you're a worm in the earth, a parasite!" She spat at his face.

His long tongue darted out and collected the spittle from his chin. Ignoring her words, he murmured, "What to do with you? I could reclaim you or dine on your flesh." He leered down at her with those yellow, slitted eyes. "I know. I will do *both*. At the same time. Take from you as I give." He stepped back, signaling the four robed Cromites to approach the altar. "And since you've become such a slattern, you won't mind if I share."

The Cromites neared, their eyes covetous, as depraved as their god—

Suddenly, black claws appeared, projecting from the *front* of Cruach's throat, then slashing to the side. Cruach yelled, gurgling, trying to hold his head to his neck. As she gaped in bewilderment, his blood spewed over her, into her eyes.

MacRieve had stabbed through Cruach's neck from

behind? Cruach's slitted eyes were dilated with shock as he stumbled toward the altar.

The remaining Cromites wailed, then drew their swords to attack MacRieve. Cruach lurched ever closer. He was gravely injured, but the wound wouldn't be enough to kill him.

If she could just free her hands, she could try to get MacRieve out of here. Her gaze darted for something, some tool to help her—

Wait, what the . . . ? Struggling for comprehension, she blinked at her quiver.

Inside it was an arrow just like the dieumort, with old-fashioned flights. She swallowed. *Another* dieumort? How . . . why . . . ?

Oh, Freya, the never-emptying quiver! Was it giving her another chance, providing one more shot at Cruach? The arrow had been replicated. But would the Banemen's awesome power follow?

How to reach it? *An idea. . . .* The skin on her wrist was now serrated all the way around. So she took a fortifying breath—then yanked her arm back with all the power she possessed. She screamed in agony as she skinned her hand, peeling it clean to her fingers like a glove.

But she'd freed that arm.

As MacRieve faced off against the Cromites, she gritted her teeth and forced her ruined fingers to close around the new dieumort. Once she'd drawn it free, the same power as from the first surged through her.

When Cruach fell to his knees before her at the altar, her arm shot out, planting the tip right into his black heart.

He stared down at his chest in disbelief. Extending out from the arrow, ash began to replace his scaly skin, spreading like a poison through his monstrous form.

Crom Cruach was dying . . . truly *dying*.

As she beheld the end of her nightmare, she sneered, "Do you feel it, husband?"

He faced her. With his last breaths, he grated, "The beast . . . saved him from me"—blood bubbled at his lips—"and will forever keep him . . . *from you*."

Just as MacRieve finished the last of the Cromites, Cruach collapsed, his eyes as lifeless as the corpses' all around them.

His hulking body disintegrated, becoming a layer of ash atop the blood pooled on the floor. *The Broken Bloody One is no more.*

With his death, MacRieve's infection would eventually burn off. He could be saved—from this. But could Cruach have been right about the beast?

"Garreth, I'm right here!" she cried, yanking on her other hand. "Scot, come back to me!"

MacRieve had told her, *The beast rises too much, maddening its Lykae host forever.* Now his eyes flashed from that white to the palest blue and back. And he never saw her.

Was it already too late?

"MacRieve, I'm alive! You have to come back to me!" Her voice broke on a sob as she cried, "Garreth, I *need* you."

He gazed back at where he thought her headless body was. As a tear tracked down his blood-splattered face, he dug his claws into his chest, ripping through his own skin.

Though she screamed for him, he ran from this place, yelling from deep within his lungs, a deafening roar of misery.

When Lachlain and Bowen finally spied Garreth in these bleak woods, he was raging, clawing himself. As they closed in on him, Lachlain stared at his brother in shock.

Blood covered him and his tattered clothes. The flesh of his chest was maimed. His eyes were an opaque white and wet. With tears?

"Grab his arms!" Lachlain told Bowen. "Garreth, stop this! What has happened?"

In a harsh beastly voice, Garreth muttered, "Begged me . . . to leave . . . said I wasn't strong enough . . . her *head*." He bellowed with pain, thrashing from their grip.

"Where is your mate?"

He roared, *"Dead!"*

Bowen hissed in a breath. "Oh, Christ. I know this well. We have to get him out of here."

"No, this canna be right," Lachlain said. "He's been maddened. Look at his eyes. Garreth, why do you think she's dead?"

Garreth choked out, "Slammed the blade . . . through her neck. Ah, gods, *her head*!"

"Who did this to her?" Lachlain's own beast was stirring to avenge his brother's mate.

Bowen's eyes were turning as well. "Tell us who!"

"Me! I cut off her fucking head!"

"Ah, Garreth, no!" Fear for his brother gripped Lachlain, like a hand wrapped round his throat. "You could no' hurt her."

"I killed . . . my Lousha." With a yell, he flung himself free from their grip, clawing at his chest again.

"Damn you, Garreth, stop this!" But he wouldn't.

The beast wanted to rip out its aching heart.

As they grappled with him, Lachlain saw the milky white of Garreth's eyes turn to the palest blue.

It's taking over. "Fight it, Garreth! You have tae fight this."

He gazed up at Lachlain. Just before Garreth turned irreversibly, before the beast claimed him for good, he rasped, "Brother . . . *I'm lost.*"

FIFTY

━━◆━━

Into the desolate woods Lucia had run with her bow, her hands still flayed and dripping blood from escaping those bonds.

She'd left behind that lair forever, running from a forsaken past into her future—with MacRieve. *If I can find him . . . and bring him back.*

For two days, she'd searched this forest, tracking him. He'd run in a frenzy, with no rhyme or reason. She might have lost his trail if it hadn't been for his claw marks on trees.

Lucia couldn't fathom the pain and loss he was feeling, the confusion. At repeated intervals, her eyes would tear up, and then she'd berate herself for being weak. He *needed* her, needed her to be strong.

Now, at last, a break—his footprints in the muddy ground! And beside them, the prints of two shoed men, two *big* men, as towering as Garreth was.

In her mind flashed the memory of Lachlain standing tall next to Garreth in that cell.

The tracks changed. The shoed men had dragged him away.

Garreth had once told her, *My brother used to get*

me out of scrape after scrape. If the witch Mariketa had given Bowen and Lachlain the coordinates to this place, they could have found him. . . .

Her eyes narrowed. The Lykae had taken Garreth.

They'd taken him home.

Kinevane Castle, Scotland

Lachlain and Emma gaped at the security feed of the mystically-protected front gates of Kinevane. Realization had just dawned on both of them that the rain-drenched female who'd been frantically banging on the impervious gates was—

"It's Aunt Luce!" Emma cried. "I told you she was alive! We would've felt it if she'd died."

"That is the *reasonable* one?" It *was* Garreth's mate. If nothing else, Lachlain recognized the bow slung over her shoulder.

"Let me the hell in!"—two rapid kicks—*"I know he's in there!"* With a boxer's jab, she punched the proud Lykae seal in the center.

Lachlain let out a stunned breath. "She *lives.*"

Emma hit the intercom button. "Two seconds, Aunt Luce!"

"Aye, it's freezing outside, so let's get her the hell in—"

Emma had already disappeared; Lachlain hated it when she traced without him.

Exactly two seconds later, Emma had returned with her sodden aunt.

Lucia wasted no time. "Where is he?" There was a wild glint in her eyes, a dangerous one, and Lachlain felt the tiniest spark of hope for his brother.

Though I know better. There was no record in their clan's thousands of years of annals of a Lykae ever coming back from this state. And Lachlain had already had Bowen bring Mariketa, the most powerful witch in existence, to Kinevane. She'd tried to help, but with her magicks bound, she could achieve nothing.

For two days, the only thing Lachlain had been able to do was watch as Garreth continued to regress further and further. "We have him here," Lachlain told Lucia. "He's safe. But he's . . . *gone.*"

Emma added, "Aunt Luce, it's bad." A maid rushed up with a towel, handing it to Lucia, then bustled away, likely afraid of the wild-eyed Valkyrie.

Dropping the towel without interest, Lucia said, "Explain to me what happened."

Lachlain related how they'd found him in the woods. "He was maddened. For some reason, he was certain that you'd died. He thought he'd killed you."

"In his mind he did," Lucia said. "An evil god made him believe that—made him *see* it."

Lachlain's beast stirred, and he asked slowly, "What god did this to my brother?"

"A dead one. Now take me to Garreth."

As he and Emma walked with her down to the dungeon, Lachlain said, "He will no' likely understand how you're here. Just seeing you will no' bring him back. Our kind . . . we doona return once gone this far."

How would Lucia react when she saw Garreth?

When she saw the claw marks up and down his body from where he'd torn at himself? They'd drugged him, but for some reason, he readily shook off the effects.

The three hadn't even reached the dungeon's outer door when Garreth scented his mate and roared.

The sound of his pain made Lucia's façade of strength waver, tears threatening again. Lachlain gave a low growl in answer, so clearly desperate to help his brother.

Inhaling a steadying breath, she followed them in front of the cell. Inside, a cot lay mangled. A pallet was tucked into a corner of the floor. Darkness shrouded most of the spacious area.

From the shadows, Garreth's eyes blazed, just as they had the first time she'd met him. But now, they glowed the palest blue. She could see his muscles were bulging, his fangs glinting, his black claws so long. The beastly image that usually flickered over him was so strong it concealed the man beneath. He wore only jeans, and they were in tatters. He'd dug his claws into himself and all the brick walls around him.

The pale gaze that had been locked on her face now turned away. He refused to look at her and kept to the back wall of the cell, as far away from her as he could be.

Emma whispered, "He doesn't think you're real."

She couldn't imagine his misery, was wishing she could bear it for him. "Then I'll have to convince him."

Lachlain said, "It's no' just the turning at this point— the beast is so entrenched it's like a madness."

Lucia was only half listening.

"The drugs have worn off again. I need to dose him."

She shook her head. "No, I need him awake. Just let me in."

"Verra well, then." Lachlain exhaled. "You must stay behind me—"

"I need to be alone with him." Lucia would do *whatever* it took to get Garreth back.

Could get ugly. Just look away, Lachlain, this doesn't concern you. . . .

"Damn it, Valkyrie, I canna guarantee your safety. And Garreth would expect me to protect you if he could no'."

Lucia could tell he didn't dare hope that she could save his brother. He was tempted to let her try but torn by his sense of responsibility.

I'll make it simple for him. Drawing her bow free, she said, "Where do you want it this time, Lykae?"

"Aunt Luce!"

"You doona ken how strong he is in this condition!" Lachlain snapped. "I'd be sending you into the lion's den. He could hurt you in his confusion, could think you're a spirit sent to torment him. And considering he's a male in his prime with his mate, he'll likely . . ."

"Understand me, Lachlain. I came here for my man, and I'm not leaving without him. If I have to live in there with Garreth, I will."

"You might just. There's no' a single record in our history of a Lykae returning from this state."

"And there was no record of anyone fighting the evil he just fought. Garreth won't hurt me now."

Emma softly asked, "Aunt Luce, would you bet your life on that?"

"He *is* my life now."

Emma and Lachlain gazed at each other, until finally, he nodded. As he opened the cell door, Lachlain cleared his throat and said, "He'll respond best to, uh, physical checks from you."

Physical checks? At her nonplussed expression, he said, "He truly is like a wolf now. Just use whatever you know about wolves."

"Got it," she said, placing her bow on the ground near the cell. Lucia would growl, scratch, and bite if she had to. "Lock up behind me and leave. Please."

When Lachlain hesitated, Emma told him, "Let's go. She knows what she's doing."

"Verra well," he muttered. He laid his hand on Lucia's shoulder. "Bring my brother back to us."

"I intend to. Oh, one thing." She unstrapped her quiver and handed it to Emma. "You trace this directly to Annika. And bring your big husband with you."

Emma frowned, accepting it. "What's this?"

"Potentially the most powerful weapon in existence. Something *lots* of people and gods would kill for." *But for me—it was an afterthought compared to Garreth.*

With a swallow, Emma nodded. "I'll do it. Good luck, Aunt Luce."

Once Lachlain had locked her within and escorted Emma from the dungeon, Lucia eased closer to Garreth in the back of the cell. "Shhh, Garreth." She reached for him so slowly. He still wouldn't look at her, as if it would hurt him to. When she gingerly touched his chest, he flinched, not because of his wounds, but because *she* pained him.

She leaned up close to his ear and whispered, "I'm

here, Garreth." He stiffened when she gave a stroke down his tense back. "I'm going to take care of you."

He openly scented her, probably no more than he ever had before, just more obviously. Not that he'd tried to hide it when he'd buried his face in her hair, inhaling deep.

"It's me. Lucia," she said softly. "I need you back."

Finally he faced her, but he still refused to meet her eyes. She wanted him to look directly at her, to *recognize* her. If he met her gaze, he might comprehend that this wasn't a dream.

Instead he was eyeing her like a wolf with its paw in a trap, warily, *angrily*. She sensed that any second he'd attack.

He doesn't think I'm real. Maybe he did think her his punishment.

With tentative movements, she gradually eased her arms around him, her hands meeting at his nape. She sighed with pleasure, merely from feeling him warm against her. "I missed you. So much. I don't want to part from you again."

The love she felt for this male overwhelmed her. Once, so long ago, Lucia had dreamed of a hearth, a husband, and children. Now it struck her that she'd always been waiting on this Lykae to help her realize those dreams.

"There," she murmured. "This isn't so bad, now is it?" His body was tense, thrumming. "Let's just calmly—"

Like a shot, his huge hands wrapped around her waist, and he tossed her down to the pallet on the floor.

As he loomed over her, an animal intent burned in his blue eyes.

When he reached for her to claw her jeans from her body, she cried, "Scot, wait!" But she knew he wouldn't. The beast was in control, its image so pervasive, overlaying Garreth's face. The sight unnerved her, but if she loved Garreth, then she had to accept this facet of him.

So she didn't resist as he sliced her shirt and bra from her, nor when he bit away her panties in a frenzy. Her reflex was to close her legs, but he overpowered her, shoving her thighs open. He gazed at her naked sex for long moments, until she was squirming in his grip, surprised at how aroused she'd grown.

He slowly licked his lips, making her whimper. Then his hot mouth descended to her flesh. *Licking, suckling . . . hungry.* The beast was ravenous for its mate.

Her exhaustion, her worry for him, and the constant dread she'd been battling all were no match for his mouth's furious taking. Her legs fell wide, and she dug her fingers into his hair, gripping him tight.

When the pleasure hit her, she screamed, "Ah, Garreth, yes!" As he growled and licked, she rocked to his wicked tongue again and again until her orgasm finally subsided.

Once he tore his mouth from her, he ripped his own jeans away. Naked and crazed, he knelt before her. His swollen shaft strained toward her, pulsing, the broad head moist as it prepared to enter her.

He gripped her waist once more, positioning her on her hands and knees. She twisted around to lie on her back, but he shoved her right back the way he wanted her. Spreading her sex with his thumbs, he mounted her from behind with one swift thrust, bellowing with pleasure. After her orgasm, she was more than ready for him.

Clapping his palms under her shoulders, he drove into her with all his strength, seating himself so deep.

"Garreth!" She gave herself up to him. *For now . . .*

FIFTY-ONE

Long hours of frantic sex had passed, sweating bouts of animalistic pleasure as MacRieve had taken her from behind repeatedly. But now at last, by dint of her coaxing—and biting—Lucia had gotten him positioned above her, with his hips wedged between her thighs.

Finally, they faced each other. Yet even as he moved over her, languidly rocking inside her, he still hadn't met her gaze. "Look at me, Garreth."

Without ever increasing his savoring pace, he thrust deeper, growling as he kneaded her breasts.

She bit her lip, fighting to keep her eyes open. "Please come back to me." The act was not as crazed—measured strokes instead of writhing bodies—but it was just as intense. Already she was on the edge. "I'm here, and I need you." When she tried to kiss him, he buried his face against her neck, licking her heated skin.

His sweat-slicked chest slid across her nipples, his rigid shaft plunging relentlessly. Her claws dug into the taut muscles of his ass as he worked to pleasure her. Tension stole through her, coiling tight. Head thrashing, she undulated beneath him—

"Garreth!" she screamed, coming around him, bucking wildly.

At once, he yelled out, the sound reverberating off the walls around them. She could feel his spurting seed, his shaft pulsing with each forceful wave. Rising up on straightened arms, he arched his back sharply, grinding his hips between her spread legs, groaning as he poured hotly inside her. . . .

When he collapsed atop her, his heart thundered over hers.

Still panting, she grasped his face, tugging him to look at her. "Garreth, I'm here." He'd made love to her. Surely he'd return now! "Come back to me. . . ."

Instead, he averted his eyes and pulled out from her. Settling on the pallet to sleep, he dragged her to him, tucking her back against his front. Though fatigued from her earlier trials, and now exhausted by his merciless attentions, she lay tense under the weight of his arm.

While he slumbered, she strove not to cry. *I've failed.* She couldn't bring him back. He would've been better off if he had never found her.

When she carefully slid out from under his arm, he gave a chuffing growl in sleep, but he didn't wake. Sitting with her back against the cool stone, she gazed up at the ceiling, eyes watering. Her efforts not to cry— and not to give up—continued, but she waged a losing battle.

She'd just been so certain that Garreth would recognize her, had been so sure that the reason no Lykae came back from this beastly state was that they'd never had a new reason to. Mourned mates never came back from the brink—but she had.

Yet Garreth lay unaware. *I couldn't save him.*

She drew him closer, cradling his head in her lap. When he emitted another soft growl, she gazed down at him. His brows were drawn, his eyes darting behind his lids, his muscles jerking in sleep.

Was he remembering killing her? Would he relive it over and over again?

She loved him so much. But it hadn't been enough to bring him back. Lightning struck outside as a tear fell, followed by another and another. She couldn't stem them, stopped trying to. "I w-want you b-back, Scot," she murmured as she wept. "I *need* you so much. And I c-couldn't save you." Soon she cried too hard to speak, sobbing with her mouth open, lips parted around stammering breaths. Rocking him, her teardrops fell—

"Lousha?" he rasped.

She stilled, every muscle in her body going tense. "G-Garreth?" She stared down at him; her tears had been spilling onto his face, wetting his cheek.

Now he frowned. *"Canna have you cryin',"* he vacantly muttered.

"Just stay with me," she pleaded, swiping the back of her hand over her face.

"Want you, Lousha. So much."

"I'm h-here!"

Turning his head, he gazed up, finally meeting her eyes. His irises flickered from blue to gold and back. "My Lousha. Dreamin' you?"

"No, y-you're not dreaming me!"

He stiffened against her. "What is this?" He sat upright, separating his body from hers, leaving her feeling cold, bereft. "You're . . . dead," he bit out, his eyes tormented.

"I'm not! I'm safe here with you." She sidled up to him on the end of the pallet.

"You're no' real." He ripped at his chest again. "You *died*."

She clutched his arm. "Please stop hurting yourself! I'm real, Garreth. I'm here."

He reached out to touch her face, yet then he closed his hand in a fist. "Nay, I hurt you . . . with that sword. I-I . . . *killed* you."

"You did no such thing!" She caressed his wet cheek. "You could never hurt me. Cruach infected you—made you see things. He made you believe you'd harmed me, but you *couldn't*. The Instinct wouldn't let you."

"How do I know I'm no' seeing things now?" He shook his head hard. "How do I know I'm no' still there?"

She could tell he so desperately wanted to believe. But he would have to doubt his own mind, his own memories. "You're not there. What you thought happened was nothing more than the trick of an evil god." She grasped his face. "You're here with me in Kinevane. Believe this, believe in us."

He heard her words as if from a distance, had dreamed that for hours they'd spent their lust together. Harried, aggressive sex over and over. Until this last time, when he'd made love to her.

And then had come her tears, each drop like a slap, waking him from some murky twilight.

Now Garreth couldn't distinguish what was real or illusion. For days, he'd slipped deeper into the abyss, convinced he'd murdered the only woman he'd ever loved—as she'd begged him to spare her life.

Now he was supposed to believe that Lucia was in his arms, warm and safe. She expected him to accept that the woman he wanted more than life had come here *for him* and was in this dark cell right now.

He yearned for it with everything in his being, wanted it so much he was probably deluding himself. "I saw your . . . body. How can I no' believe that was real?"

"Choose *me*, Garreth. Right now, choose me and believe this." She wrapped her arms around him, pressing her cheek against his neck. He buried his face in her soft hair.

Choose her? Could he be imagining how warm she was? Imagining the exquisite scent of her hair or how she trembled against him?

If this is a dream, then I never want it to end. . . .

He clasped her shoulders, holding her before him. "Lousha, I'll always choose you."

"G-Garreth, your eyes . . . they're turning golden." She gave him a watery smile. "You're really back?"

"Ah, gods, I thought I killed you." He hugged her tight to him again. "I thought I'd lost you forever." He held her for long moments, shuddering against her, rocking her in his arms. "I have to have you—canna live without you."

"I've got you back now, Scot." He felt her shuddering, too. "And Cruach's dead. He's gone forever."

Garreth barely remembered the god, had only brief flashes of memory. That was more than enough. "How? The dieumort . . . he destroyed it?"

She pulled back to face him. "The quiver you gave me came in handy. Of course, now we have a slight problem." When he frowned, she explained, "It's replicating the dieumort. Now I understand why the gods were so resistant to this. Annika will have to decide what to do with it."

"You should have told me about Cruach."

She curled her knees to her chest, sitting against the cold cell wall. "I was . . . ashamed. You saw him—he's a monster. Only Regin and Nïx knew."

He moved beside her, rubbing her arm. "How did it happen?"

"He disguised himself, becoming everything I thought I'd ever wanted. I was so young, and I believed I was in love."

A spike of jealousy burned in Garreth's gut—*I want her love. She should love* me!

"I wouldn't see reason. I left Valhalla with what I thought was a young man named Crom."

"Why would your parents no' help you? They're gods, right?"

"They forbade me to wed him and forced me to make a covenant that I would never see him again. Once I'd broken the covenant, they were forever unable to help me." Her eyes were stark. "Even after I was trapped with Cruach in that lair."

That had been the vilest place Garreth could ever have imagined. And for her to be a mere girl, captive to that monster? How terrified she must have been. "How did you escape him?"

"At the back of that cavern is a high cliff overlooking the ocean. I . . . jumped. I hit the water, mostly, but was tossed upon the r-rocks."

Jumped. Which meant she'd been driven to kill herself.

Lucia was studying his reaction. Could she tell how his rage was building? Or how badly he yearned to punish that fuck for ever laying a finger on her? Garreth's claws flared—to slash through his neck once more. Slowly. . . .

"Garreth, your eyes are turning blue."

"Go on, Lousha."

"But—"

"Tell me!"

After a hesitation, she said, "Regin had followed me out of Valhalla—at twelve years old, she'd given up everything to go after me, because she'd sensed Cruach was evil. She rescued me from the ocean, refusing to let me die."

"She saved you?"

Lucia nodded. "For days, she dragged me across dimensions. Then she basically dropped me on Skathi's altar and commanded the goddess, 'Fix her.' Though Skathi knew she'd bestow her archery skill with the life force necessary to save me, she ultimately agreed to heal me. In return for those gifts, I had to make concessions. Just like the rest of her followers, I was to be as untouched as she was. And I was to become Cruach's jailer."

"What did he do to make you jump? You had to believe you were going to die. Lousha, what did he do to you?"

I'm losing him again, Lucia realized with dread, *and just when I've gotten him back.* Everything in her rebelled against burdening him with this tale. And she knew in this critical time, the pain she'd impart might drive him directly back to the solace of the beast.

"I have to know, Lousha. You canna keep secrets from me any longer!"

"I'm not saying I'll never tell you, but right now, with all that's happened—"

"I must know. Everything!"

After a hesitation, she gave him a firm nod. "Then I'll tell you everything, Scot. It was bad. I've never been more frightened. I jumped, Regin saved me, Skathi healed me. And I lived a very long time until I met this Lykae, who was everything I should fear, and yet I wanted him more than I'd ever wanted anything. Though I still had to run from him, I secretly thrilled every time he chased me." Lucia knelt before him on the pallet. "Together he and I found a weapon to kill my nightmare. And together we did just that, freeing me forever and saving the world. Yet now, when all my trials are done at last, and I can finally look forward, he wants to look back."

MacRieve moved to kneel before her as well, cupping her face in his palms. "Because he feels if you were strong enough to face those trials, he should be strong enough to hear of them."

"But he doesn't know that I plan to spend eternity with him." She leaned up to kiss his stubborn chin. "He'll have plenty of time to learn everything about me, and eventually I will tell him everything. At this moment, I just want to start my life with him."

"Life with me," he rasped, his voice breaking low. "You said for eternity?"

"Absolutely, Garreth." She laid her palm against his stubbled cheek. "I'm in love with you. And I can't lose you again."

His eyes were warming to that intense gold once more. "This is like the deal you offered in the jungle— the sex or secrets deal," he said. "Except now it's eternity or secrets?"

"Basically, yes. I *need* some happiness. I need *you* to help me find it."

"You will tell me everything? Every secret you hold?"

"I will, in time."

Yet he dropped his hands, sitting back against the wall. "You canna know how much I've wanted to hear you tellin' me you love me." He stared at the ground, looking lost. "And I want to make you happy, *crave* to. But now that I've gone under like this, it's possible I will again. If you were ever endangered . . . I've got to be more susceptible to reverting."

She clutched his shoulder. "Then I won't let you." He was still shaking his head when she said, "Garreth Mac-Rieve, you've gotten your way with me again and again. Now it's my turn! I want you to be my man—you and no other. Are you going to deny me?"

After long moments, he exhaled and faced her once

more. "Nay, I canna. I love you too bluidy much." He gazed at her with so much yearning in his eyes it staggered her—as if now he would no longer hide it. "Tell me you love me again," he said, pulling her into his lap, holding her against his chest.

"I love you, Garreth. With all my heart."

"Then I'll take your eternity. You're tae marry me in the morn."

She gave a wry grin. "I thought you'd never . . . dogmatically order it." Then her smile faded. *To wed him without Regin there for the assist?* "Wait, I-I can't. Not yet."

"Why the hell no'?"

"Garreth, my sister's missing." She bit her bottom lip. "Regin's been gone for days—it's not like her to disappear. And I can't get married without her there with me."

"If she's missing, then we'll find her." He tipped her face up, gazing down at her "Especially if you will no' wed me till then. Love, we'll get her back, I swear it." He gently brushed his lips against hers. "But first things first. Do you have a key to our cell?"

FIFTY-TWO

"What's happened here, lass?" Garreth asked the next morning when he returned to their suite after a half-hour-long absence. Earlier, Lucia had been in high spirits, optimistic about finding Regin. She'd wanted to fit in a quick visit with Emma—and a Valkyrie raid on the queen's notoriously extensive wardrobe—so Garreth had fled to share a farewell scotch with Lachlain:

"You're off again?"

"Aye, afraid so, brother."

"Garreth, one thing before you go . . . you marked her hard, no?"

Now, Garreth found Lucia pensive. "What's got you upset, love? Is it because you've seen how pitiably Lachlain spoils Emma? Know that I've planned the same for you," he said, studying her face.

The faint smudges under her eyes had vanished, erased after a single stretch of dreamless sleep. Last night, as soon as Lucia and Garreth had been released from their cell by a delighted Lachlain and Emma, they'd begun recuperating in Garreth's old rooms—talking about the future, soaking in a bath together, talking some more—then she'd slumbered in his arms.

With no nightmares. . . .

"There's been news," Lucia said, beginning to pace. "I just talked to Annika." Also not one of Garreth's favorite Valkyrie. "She told me Regin's not the only one missing."

"What do you mean? I thought some berserker had her." Garreth and Lucia had planned to head out for New Orleans, interrogate Nïx for leads, and find the berserker. Then Garreth would teach the male how ill-advised his actions had been.

"All morning news has been flying in from every corner of the Lore," Lucia said. "Creatures from across all factions have been taken. Which means it's not Aidan the Fierce who'd abducted her."

"Who else got grabbed, then?"

"Who hasn't? So far there've been confirmed reports of a siren, one of the fey, an arch fury—"

"Arch? You doona mean . . ."

"Yes, the ones with wings. They don't often rise from their nests, but when they do . . ." She gave a mock shudder. "A witch called Carrow Graie, also known as Carrow the Incarcerated, was taken around the same time as Regin. Carrow's best friend to Mariketa the Awaited—and Mari is *displeased*. The entire House of Witches is up in arms, yet they can't locate Carrow or Regin through scrying."

"So it's some contingent taking out the Valkyrie and their allies?" Which now meant the Lykae as well. Over the past year, Lachlain had made sure that all Loreans understood his clan was a steadfast ally to the Valkyrie—whether the Valkyrie wanted them to be or not. All the Lykae were in full support of this, especially since their queen and princess were from that faction.

Lucia shook her head. "That's just it. *We* were accused of taking out players from the other side. A couple of Sorceri, some fire demons, a centaur viceroy, even one of the Invidia are all missing, too."

The Invidia were female embodiments of discord, purely evil. The centaurs and fire demons had warred against the Valkyrie in Accessions past. The Sorceri were unknown entities who could slide either way on the evil scale.

Lucia added, "There are rumors that even Lothaire has gone missing."

"Now, that vampire could've been tagged by La Dorada, looking for payback—and a thumb," he pointed out. "Does Nïx have any ideas?"

"She hasn't been lucid. Annika told me she'd screamed like a banshee right after I spoke with her last. She's been muttering gibberish for days."

"Doona worry. We'll unravel all this," Garreth said. "And we'll find your sister."

She bit her bottom lip. "We've just finished one mission, and now we have to go searching again." She crossed to the balcony that overlooked the gardens.

Garreth followed—he would always follow her, as any wolf would his mate. He joined her at the marble railing, savoring the scene. A light Highland fog was rolling in, carrying the tang of the nearby sea.

"You were right all along, Scot. I *am* high-maintenance." She sounded remorseful, which wouldn't do.

"Aye, but you're high-output as well." He gave her arse a possessive squeeze.

"Werewolf!" she cried, but her lips had briefly curled.

He took her in his arms. "The truth is that I'd rather march into hell with you than bask in heaven without you." He curled his forefinger under her chin. "And lass, going to help Regin will be a little like hell for me."

She knuckle-punched his arm. "You didn't just say that!"

"I'm kidding," he said, then added in all seriousness, "It happens that I owe Regin one. You said you wanted to live out your immortality with her next door? Well, as much as it grieves me to say this, we will no' rest until the glowing one's our neighbor on some seashore." *And until you're my wife. . . .*

Her dark eyes widened. "You promise?"

"Aye, but that does no' mean I canna tease."

She gazed away. "Still, I'm taking you from this. Look at this place." She waved over the misty grounds. "Deep down, you've got to be disappointed that my life is so complicated. I bet you wish things with me were easier."

He clutched her to him, hugging her tight to his chest before he finally eased his grip. If only she knew the depth of his feelings for her. But then, she'd given him her eternity, so he planned to show her. "Lou-sha, you're my lass. And I'm lovin' you dearly." When she gazed up at him with her silvery eyes glinting, he cupped her nape and brought her to him for a soft kiss. Against her lips he murmured, "Besides, nothing good ever came easy."

EPILOGUE

—◆—

One week earlier . . .

Volga Uplands, Russia
Target: the Vampire

On a windswept and craggy plain, a lone cabin endured, buffeted by a gale. Inside, Lothaire the Enemy of Old stood before a broken hanging mirror, staring at his fragmented reflection. Through cracks in the grimy windows, chill drafts sieved in, welcome after the heat of the jungle.

Retrieving the finger and ring from his pocket, he slipped the gold band free, tossing the mummified thumb to the ground. With utter awe, he gazed at the band, knowing what it meant, knowing the power he'd just seized.

Unspeakable power.

"With this," he grated, "I will be invincible." The winds howled, the cabin walls groaning. "I will be *unstoppable*." He raised his shaking hand, lowering the ring to his own finger, nearly groaning with expectation—

The cabin door exploded open; electricity surged in,

hitting him in the back, shooting him forward. The ring clattered to the ground as his head crashed through one of the windows. A jutting shard raked down his forehead, deep across the surface of his eye.

Sightless in that eye, blood obscured his vision in the other. *Trace. Leave this place.*

Not without his ring. . . .

His fangs sharpened, rage burning inside him. *What enemy is this?* Another bolt of electricity hit him, then another, each one draining him. He began blindly tracing throughout the cabin to evade them.

Through the red haze, he listened for his prey, sensing movement, striking. Appearing and vanishing, he plucked one heart from a male's chest, biting the throat of another. The floor grew slick with blood.

Get to the ring . . . get *closer.* Another flash shot toward him; he traced to dodge it, reappearing—

A short sword plunged into his side. Behind him, a tall shadowy form wielded the blade, twisting it deep within Lothaire's body. A mortal wound for a human.

An incapacitating one for an immortal. *Whatever is here . . . doesn't want me dead.*

Lothaire attempted to trace a retreat, but he'd grown too weak—as his foe obviously intended.

Holding him fast, the blademan twisted the sword again. "Bag him." Once the male drew the weapon free, Lothaire dropped to his knees in his own pool of blood.

Others besieged him, quelling his weak resistance, cuffing his wrists in unbreakable bindings. When he roared, they slapped duct tape over his mouth.

He'd just cleared his vision in his one good eye when more men approached with a black sack.

To put over his head.

He bellowed behind the tape, thrashing in the blood. But they shoved the cloth over his head, cinching it tight.

Lothaire heard the gold ring scraped over the floor as another collected his treasure. Seething wrath burned to a fury. *When I get free, I will unleash hell.* . . .

Back streets of New Orleans
Target: the Valkyrie

"*That all you got, muthafuckas?*" Regin the Radiant cried after her third dose of electricity. "I *like* electricity, you dumbasses! Hit me with another."

Apparently not taking her at her word, they did. She sucked it in, and her skin glowed brighter in the night. The street lamps nearby flared from her radiant energy.

A smile of utter bliss lit her face.

"Know what else? I'm a freaking conduit." She caught a jolt in one hand and with her other, she funneled it back, hitting her attackers, blowing them into the air. "You want some of this?" She shot again. "How 'bout you?" And again.

They were feeding her—and it felt *glorious*! She glowed brighter, brighter, illuminating one city block, then two . . .

But within that blaze of light, a shadow moved behind

her, a towering male with superhuman speed. Before she could defend herself, he struck with a sword, planting it into her side, twisting. Lightning speared close by, and she gasped at the pain, choking as blood bubbled at her lips.

Her light dimmed. When the man withdrew the blade, she collapsed. Curled up on the street, bleeding out, Regin gazed up at him. "*You*," she bit out. "You'll *pay.*"

The male ordered, "Bag her."

Too late, she drew a breath to scream—duct tape slapped over her mouth. Eyes wide, shaking her head wildly, she watched as they neared with a black sack.

Orleans Parish Booking and Receiving Facility
Target: the witch

"Miss Carrow, what are you doing in here again?" Martin, her favorite guard, asked her. He was the youngest of the guards, cute, with a ruinous crush on Carrow. "When will you learn better?"

"Oh, I've learned better," she said, strutting to the bars. He swallowed to see how short her black leather skirt was. "I just choose not to use what I've learned in real world applications."

"Huh?" Martin scratched his head. "What'd you do this time?"

"Beat up a cop, stole his horse, and rode it into Pat O's." Before he could ask, she answered, "I needed an accessory."

At that, her repeat roommates, sex workers from the Quarter, cheered, *whoop whoop whoop!*

She curtsied for them, then turned back to Martin. Through the cell bars, she tickled him under his chin with her print-stained fingertips, sending him in raptures. "So, did you bring me and the girls some chow?" He often brought Popeye's to Carrow and the roommates. In a throaty voice, she asked, "Maybe some *diiiirty* rice?"

He swallowed hard. "N-no, ma'am. Came to tell you that you made bail."

"Really? No way!" She held out her flat palm behind her and someone gave her a low five in celebration. The sun had just set—Carrow would have the entire night for mayhem! "Who divvied the cash?"

"Dunno, ma'am," Martin said, sliding open the cell door.

She frowned. The House of Witches had vowed never to bail her out again. And Carrow hadn't even called Mariketa, not wanting to bother her best friend again. Twice in one week was too much for even the most committed bail buddy.

Carrow had actually been considering using her powers to liberate herself. Which was a big, freaking, honking *no-no*.

With a shrug, she turned to say farewell. "See ya, Moll, Candy Cane, Lexxxie, Chastity. And Exstacey, chin up, your ex is not going to bother you any more. I promise." Carrow made a mental note to cast a spell on that asshole, making him fall in love with clumping cat litter. *Used* clumping litter.

Once Carrow had collected her belongings, she donned her jewelry and light jacket, then strung her numerous plastic beads around her neck. Few outside the Big Easy could grasp what a hard-earned and valuable currency those beads were.

Martin gazed on longingly. "You want me to look up who posted you?"

"Hey, I'm not one to look a gift horse in the mouth. Night, Martin." She winked and blew him a kiss. "See you soon."

But as she sauntered to the front doors, she thought about that ole gift-horse saying. She'd lied to Martin— Carrow was *exactly* the kind of person who would look in its mouth.

She grew cautious, building energy in her palms to shoot an enemy if she had to. Mariketa had been teaching her tons of new spells and funneling power to her— since she was on the bench for five decades. Carrow was quite the badass, when she could concentrate.

Stepping outside onto the street, she gazed around warily. No one was out here.

Ah, but the city was just waking for another night. With sirens and food scents and throbbing music, it roused like a beast from slumber. She could sense all the emotions, the excitement suffusing her. Like a vampire, she wanted to drink from it. Wanted to be amidst the chaos, *provoking* it—

A frying surge of electricity hit her in the face, blasting her through the air. She shrieked until she landed on her back a block away. Her beads had melted all over her, sizzling plastic searing her skin, smoking.

Dazed, nearly sightless from the assault and the smoke, she drew energy in her palms once more. What the hell happened? Males nearing? *Can't see . . . can't see to fire on them.* They looked like shadows. She shot from her palm, might have hit one. *Can't see . . .*

She tried to rise, to blindly run, but only made it to her knees. No choice but to gasp out the reaper spell, hoping no bystanders were near: *"Ooth sbell nooth latoret—"*

"Gag her!" a deep voice interrupted.

"Ooth sbell—"

The shadowy hands seized her, shoving duct tape over her mouth. Though she resisted with all the strength in her body, they bound her wrists behind her. She flailed, defenseless, more terrified than she'd ever been.

Carrow's sight was just returning when she heard that same voice order, "Bag her."

"No, no!" she screamed behind the tape. They stalked closer with a black sack, rolling it up like hose to force over her head.

And her world went dark once more. . . .